Francis Goldie

The Life of the blessed John Berchmans

Second Edition

Francis Goldie

The Life of the blessed John Berchmans
Second Edition

ISBN/EAN: 9783337054007

Printed in Europe, USA, Canada, Australia, Japan

Cover: Foto ©Raphael Reischuk / pixelio.de

More available books at **www.hansebooks.com**

Quarterly Series.

SEVENTH VOLUME.

---

*THE LIFE OF THE
BLESSED JOHN BERCHMANS.*

THE
LIFE OF THE BLESSED JOHN BERCHMANS.

BY

FRANCIS GOLDIE,

OF THE SOCIETY OF JESUS.

SECOND EDITION.

LONDON:

BURNS AND OATES, PORTMAN STREET
AND PATERNOSTER ROW.
1877.

✝

CUM · ADHUC · JUNIOR · ESSEM · PRIUSQUAM · OBERRAREM
QUÆSIVI · SAPIENTIAM · PALAM · IN · ORATIONE · MEA
ANTE · TEMPLUM · POSTULABAM · PRO · ILLA
ET · USQUE · IN · NOVISSIMIS · INQUIRAM · EAM
ET · EFFLORUIT · TANQUAM · PRÆCOX · UVA
LÆTATUM · EST · COR · MEUM · IN · EA
AMBULAVIT · PES · MEUS · ITER · RECTUM
A · JUVENTUTE · MEA · INVESTIGABAM · EAM
INCLINAVI · MODICE · AUREM · MEAM
ET · EXCEPI · ILLAM
MULTAM · INVENI · IN · MEIPSO · SAPIENTIAM
ET · MULTUM · PROFECI · IN · EA
COLLUCTATA · EST · ANIMA · MEA · IN · ILLA
ET · IN · FACIENDO · EAM · CONFIRMATUS · SUM
ANIMAM · MEAM · DIREXI · AD · ILLAM
ET · IN · AGNITIONE · INVENI · EAM
POSSEDI · CUM · IPSA · COR · AB · INITIO
PROPTER · HOC · NON · DERELINQUAR
VIDETE · OCULIS · VESTRIS · QUIA · MODICUM · LABORAVI
ET · INVENI · MIHI · MULTAM · REQUIEM

(*Ecclus.* li.)

✝

PREFACE.

"Wʜᴀᴛ I here offer to my readers is neither a
completely new Life, nor is it a mere translation. It
has followed the old biography too closely to have
claim to the title of an original work. But a completely
new form has been given to so many portions of it,
that it cannot be called a translation. However, it
matters little under which head it is classed, if you
will please to accept what I have undertaken for the
benefit of devout persons, and especially for my brethren
in religion, and if this slight effort of my pen turns to
the good of souls."[1]

This modest notice, which **Father Frizon**, S.J., put
at the head of his Life of Blessed Berchmans, is much
more applicable to the present volume. The labours
of Father Vanderspeeten have left nothing to be done
in the way of original research. The perusal of his
Life of Blessed John[2] gives no idea of the profound
and wide-spreading study which he brought to bear on
his labour of love. It would be difficult to express

[1] *La Vie de J. Berchmans, C. de J.* Par le P. N. F. MDCCII.
Translated for the Oratory Series. Vol. xv. Richardson, 1849.
[2] *Vie du B. Jean Berchmans, de la C. de J.* Par H. P. Vanderspeeten, de la même Compagnie. Louvain, 1865.

the amount of help that learned author has given to the writer. The difference of treatment of sacred biographies, owing to national tastes, has suggested certain additions, especially of biographical notices, not to be found in the original work. These details are due to the kind cooperation of so many, that it is almost invidious to single out any name from the number, but mention must be made of Father Waldack, Father Boero, Father van Lommel, Father Ryan, and Father Morris, while to the Rev. Dr. van Cauwenberge is due the translation from the original Flemish of the letters of the saint.

The whole Life is founded on Father Virgilius Cepari's exquisite memoir, and the original Italian has been all through closely followed, the only natural additions to the text being the insertion of the proper names, partly by the help of Father Vanderspeeten, partly from the *Acta et Decreta* of the process of beatification. The list of students at the English College, Rome, during the time of Berchmans' stay in that city is owing to the kindness of the Rev. Joseph Stevenson, M.A.

F. G.

Oxford, Feast of our Lady of Ransom, 1873.

CONTENTS.

Contents.   xiii

CHAPTER VIII.

John's practice of virtue, attachment to his vocation, obedience, and love of poverty.

CHAPTER IX.

John's humility and charity.

CHAPTER X.

Berchmans' spirit of piety.

CHAPTER I.

Childhood and Boyhood.

ON the main line from Antwerp to Maëstricht is the
ancient town of Diest. Fortifications of modern date
have changed its outside look ; but when they are passed
the road brings us into a broad opening—the market-
place, with a fine church of dark brown stone on the
left, and old-fashioned houses round about. The place
gradually narrows to the width of an ordinary road, and
just before it crosses Kettle Street, a house of three
storeys high is on the left. Its front is modern and
modest ; but in a niche in its midst is a statue of a
young man in a religious habit, holding up in his clasped
hands, a book, a rosary, and a crucifix, while underneath
is an inscription—'The house of Blessed Berchmans.'
A broad flight of stairs, incasing the steps of the old
building, leads up to the room wherein, on the 13th of
March, in the year of the Lord, 1599, the saint was born
whose life and virtues are recorded in these pages. The
wainscoting or plaster is gone, as also the tiles from
the chimney corner. The brick walls, with the rough
oaken frame they inclose, the rude rooftree and
rafters alone are left. This, then, is all that remains of
the old house, or rather of the two houses run into one,
where lived, at the close of the sixteenth century, at the
sign of 'The Great and the Little Moon,' a worthy cord-
wainer, named John Charles Berchmans. His sterling

B

honesty and his love of all that was just won him the esteem and confidence of his townsmen, who voted him chairman of the Town Council, while he was made churchwarden of his parish of St. Sulpice ; and his sovereign, the Archduke, made him échevin, one of ten, a magistrate of the peace.

Unlike their Spanish masters, Flemings of gentle birth did not consider themselves lowered by trade. The Berchmans were one of the best families in the once thriving town. John Charles' father was échevin several times ; so too were his eldest and youngest brothers, and burgomasters as well. His wife, Elizabeth vanden Hove, though probably of no better family, was far his superior in worldly position and wealth. Her sister married William von Enckevort, captain of cuirassiers in the Imperial Army, whose son Adrian, first cousin to our saint, rose to be field-marshal in the same service. One of his ancestors had been raised to the purple by Pope Adrian VI. The son of another of John's cousins, Godfrey vanden Straeten, became colonel of an infantry regiment.

No sign of cordiality is recorded between the two families. This looks as if the marriage had not found favour. Peregrine von Hamel, the husband of another sister, Catharine vanden Hove, lived next door to her sister-in-law, in the corner house at the sign of the 'Sun ;' yet —if we except the fact that he was named guardian of his nephews and nieces—no trace occurs of any help being given by him to John's parents in their difficulties. The 'Great and Little Moon' was the property of Elizabeth Berchman's mother, and though reputed to be very wealthy, she claimed her rent from the suffering tenants as though they had been strangers.[1]

---

[1] The family vanden Hove has survived to this day. One of them, a religious of the Society of Jesus, was present at the solemn beatification of John Berchmans in the Vatican Basilica.

Charles John Berchmans and Elizabeth his wife bore a high name for their virtue and piety. Their **holiness seems to** have been rewarded by the birth of **a son** whose sanctity was to make their name familiar to the household of **God's Church. The day on which he first saw the light was** a Saturday. The very next day he was baptized in **St. Sulpice, the** parish church, which though shattered by the **storms of** war, still **stands, as** we have **seen, in the** principal place of the town. **The child received his** father's second name, John. The **font is gone; but** the frailer record may still be seen in the pages of the old baptismal register.[2]

A sketch of the times in **which he was** born may prove useful. The struggle between **Spain** and its subjects in the Netherlands, which had **lasted for** some forty years with little or no cessation, **was now** drawing to a close. **The** ultra-Spanish rule **of** Philip **II.,** while giving a plea for revolt to the Reformers, **had** leagued against him Catholic and Protestant; for he showed signs of attempting to stamp out with equal rigour the rising heresies and those old liberties which had been **to** Flanders and the Low Countries the legacies of ages, the source of their power and splendour. Don John of Austria, **and** still more Alexander Farnese, saw the greatness of the error, and by protecting their ancient franchises, and coming forward **as** the champions of their faith, so roughly trodden down by the German, English, and Dutch Protestants who fought in the name of liberty, rallied around them, and recalled to their allegiance, **first**

---

[2] **The godfather** was brother-in-law **to** Elizabeth Berchman's mother; **the godmother, the** widowed sister of John's paternal grandmother, Gertrude **van de** Kerchove, though registered in her maiden name. ' Martius, **1599, 14. *Parentes,* Jan** Bergmans, Jans soon en **Leyskeezyn** hvysvrau. *Filius Bapt.* **Joannes.** *Patrini* Adriaen Claes en Geertruyt van Steyvoirt.'

the Walloons, and then, by degrees, the other people of what is now called **Belgium**. This, however, was only achieved after a long and desperate struggle, which the rapacity of the illpaid soldiery of Spain on the one hand, and on the other the constant connivance and support of Elizabeth of England and Henry IV. of France, lengthened out into a dreary chronicle of horrors. But the exchequer of Spain, exhausted by the gigantic effort of the Armada, and the constant wars sustained by Philip II., could no longer bear the strain. A decisive victory at Turnhout had shown the power of the revolted provinces. This, together with the death of the sovereign, and the peace concluded between Spain and the King of France in 1598, made the new Governors of the Netherlands, Archduke Albert and Isabella, all the more anxious for peace. Clement VIII., Aldobrandini, was Pope; Philip III. had just succeeded to the crown of Spain; Henry of Navarre was ruling as a Catholic Prince. The days of Elizabeth's reign were numbered; her evil days of treacherous intervention were nearly over. The Catholic reaction had fairly set in. Parties were better defined. The real reform effected by the Council of Trent was beginning to show its fruits. The new errors had but slightly tainted the faithful Brabant; they were known to its people chiefly by the outrages on the churches and the other memorials of the faith of their fathers—outrages wrought by the hands of those who had professed to defend them against the foreigner. So, in a word, the war was not done, but nearly so; the terrible reverse of Nieuport, where Archduke Albert was entirely defeated, had its counterbalance in the stubbornly contested and hard won taking of Ostend in 1605 by the great captain Spinola, and a peace was talked of. Elizabeth died in 1603, and James I., her successor, did not share her views of foreign policy; so at last, in

1604, a truce of twelve years between Holland—the new Republic, and the crown of Spain, was concluded. With each success of the Catholic arms, the faith revived over the land ; while even in the revolted provinces religion grew and prospered. Spite, then, of the nearness of his home to the terrible scenes of war, we scarcely catch a trace of them in the quiet life of our saint ; but we do see clearly that a powerful breath of life was passing over the face of Europe, quickening and invigorating it after the shortlived triumph of its enemies ; a triumph which owed half its success to the blunders of Philip II.

When the friends of the newborn babe bore him to his christening, the venerable Church of St. Sulpice still bore the marks of its fierce wrecking by the victorious Gueux, who held the town from 1580 to 1582. The graceful Gothic sacrament-house had been shattered to pieces, the statues torn down, the altars desecrated, and only by paying a heavy ransom had the burghers headed by some of John's relations, saved the building from utter destruction. Though Diest was retaken by Alexander Farnese, it needed many years to repair the ruin done by those whom Veuillot has so truly called the Communists of their day. The aspect of the place was undergoing a change, and on the ruins of a flourishing mediæval town, more modern buildings, much as they are now, began to rise, yet leaving many ancient features unaltered.

In after years people loved to recall how, when as yet only a child, John Berchmans showed that God had blessed him with a natural sweetness of temper, which grace was hereafter to perfect. And this helped him so to control the fire of his ardent temperament, that a more patient, more gladsome child, had never been known ; none of the little troubles of daily life ever put him out.

He bore without a tear or complaint a painful eruption, which made his little face an object of compassion to all who saw him. If, when on his return from school, where he went from a very early age, he got no answer to his knock at the house door, he would go off to St. Sulpice, the nearest church, and there, on his knees before a statue of our Lady, say five or six rosaries in succession. Once, when another boy abused and made a jest of him, our holy child bore all without a word, not even complaining of this shameful treatment to any one. His grandmother was pained to see a child of seven years up before break of day, and asked him why he was out of bed so early. 'Oh, my dear mamma, I must serve my two or three Masses before schooltime. What better place could there be to win knowledge quickly and surely ! '

He was only just nine when his mother was first stricken with that terrible illness which kept her to her bed for some eight long years. The affectionate child was constantly at her side, and his words were so sweet, so apt, so consoling, so full of piety and affection, that the bystanders could scarcely believe their ears. But his very presence was a consolation to his suffering mother, such was the charm of his smiling, modest face, the very picture of trustful loving innocence. Yet though so engaging a child, he shunned society ; he never left his home save to go to church or school, and his master attests—' Nowhere did he see him so often as in the church, nowhere so seldom as in the streets.'[3] When he was eleven he was committed to the care of one Wouter van Stiphout, who held his class in the ancient Halles, or mediæval cloth market, which to this day serves for the public school of the town. Stiphout never lost the

---

[3] Nusquam sæpius quam in templo, nusquam rarius quam in plateis (Summ p. 46, sec. 85).

deep regard he gained for his pupil. John's love of work was only equalled by his quickness of parts; he surpassed all his comrades in both. He seems to have shone in Latin versification, which he was just beginning to learn. His progress, and quick and retentive memory, first attracted the esteem of his master, but the more he knew of him the greater became his admiration and his affection for him. 'I looked upon him as a sort of natural wonder; I praised him before my scholars, and proposed him to them as a model for their emulation. One day, when his father asked me how he was getting on, I recollect saying—"How blessed you are in such a son: he will be your consolation, and my honour and glory."'

John Berchmans had but one ambition. His innocent heart aspired to the priesthood, and the flattering character that Stiphout gave him, made his father consent to his putting on the clerical dress, and determined him to place the boy with Father Peter Emmerick, a Premonstratensian monk. This religious was then the parish priest of the Church of our Lady in Diest. He had exchanged the quiet of the great abbey of Tongerloo for pastoral work, as the rule of St. Norbert allows. And in the presbytery he had gathered round him a number of boys destined for the priesthood, so that it had become a sort of little seminary. The portrait of the good monk hangs, with those of other parish priests, his predecessors and successors, in the sacristy of the solemn Gothic church — 'Rev. Petrus Emmerichus, Pastor **XXIII.**' There is a look of great resolution in his dark eyes, his sharply cut face, and firmly set mouth; and yet withal a sweetness of expression that might be a reflection from the joyful face of his sainted scholar.

Hard times were beginning for John's father, his means were already seriously crippled; but the good shoemaker feared for the innocence of his children if they were allowed to mix with the workmen and apprentice boys of his shop. So, at no small expense, he sent them all from home. God blessed his pious care. Charles, the fourth son, the special favourite of our saint, followed him into the Society four years after John's death, on October 25, 1625. Like him, too, he made some of his studies, as well as his novitiate, in the Jesuit College of Mechlin. Twelve years later Charles was ordained priest, on the Holy Saturday of 1637. The next year we find him engaged in the dangerous work of the naval mission, an apostolate the Jesuits undertook in behalf of the sailors and soldiers of the Spanish fleets. He took his last vows in 1642. And after many years of great privation and peril spent in keeping alive the faith in the distant province of Friesland, Father Berchmans died at a ripe old age, sixty-one years old, at the College of Oudenarde. He is described as being of a calm and tranquil character, and an eminent master of spiritual life.

Adrian, the second child, took to the ecclesiastical state, and received the tonsure on March 11, 1618, the day after that on which his father, as we shall see, dedicated himself finally to God by being ordained subdeacon. The Augustinian Fathers succeeded Master van Stiphout in the charge of the communal schools the same year that John went to Mechlin, and opened a house in the town.[4] Adrian, who no doubt attended their schools, received the grace of divine vocation to their illustrious order, and made his religious profession in their house at Mechlin on November 10, 1621. He took for his religious name that of his blessed brother,

---

[4] Prince Maurice of Orange, the lord of Diest, so well known in the history of the time, offered, though a Protestant, to build a house and church for the Fathers. The present church, not far off John's house, was not began before 1656.

who had died .but a few months before. **Nine years** afterwards, when the **sons of St.** Francis, of St. Dominic, and St. Augustine were thronging in with the children **of** St. Ignatius to gain a certain **crown of martyrdom in the** Japanese **persecution,** then at **its** height, Father John was sailing on **this errand** with a devoted band of religious, in the **Spanish fleet, from** the Philippine Islands to Japan. But **another crown awaited him.** The plague broke out **on board.** Fifteen of his brethren had fallen victims **to the** scourge, and he had attended them, and given them **the** last sacraments with the greatest charity. Then his turn came, and his end was most saintlike.

The other two children—to complete the **story—did** not fare so well. The youngest, Bartholomew, **was born** in 1606; and all that is known for certain about **him is,** that he became a soldier, took a wife **in** Germany, **and** that his two daughters became nuns at St. Agatha **of** Liége, the convent having been founded by Helena Enckevort, sister to Feld-Marschal d'Enckevort, and therefore first cousin to Berchmans. In 1637, a Bartholomew **Berchmans was assassinated** by the soldiery **in** the streets of **Diest.** But as there **was** another of the same name then living in that town, it is not certain that the murdered man **was** Berchmans' brother. In any **case, the murder** probably had its cause in the passions aroused by the rekindling of the religious war, thanks to the ambitious plans of Richelieu.

The only sister of our saint, the third child, seems to **have** gone with her brothers to Mechlin, where, **when** twenty-three, she married Henry Roeck, a lawyer **attached to the** Parliament of that city. After his death, she **was left with** six children, **in** such embarrassed circumstances, **that** she **is** said **to have** been cast for debt into the **common** prison of Antwerp. **One of her** daughters, Jane, became a Béguine at Mechlin.

John Berchmans' **new home at** the presbytery of the Nôtre Dame grew so **dear to** him, that he rarely visited his father's house, though so near to the school, which he still frequented. Every morning he was delighted **to** serve Mass, which **he** did with the greatest exactness, pronouncing clearly and devoutly **every word of the** answers. There was **an** old Middle Age custom in **those days at Diest,** that on Holy Innocents a child **clad in** miniature vestments acted the part of the priest **in** the church at the office. **We** can hardly be surprised that Father Emmerick should choose for this function **his** favourite pupil, and the good Father records that he sprinkled the holy water, incensed, and sung the collect at Lauds with such gravity, that **the good people of** Diest marvelled greatly. **From that** day a reverence, which the part he had played **seems** to have first developed in him, and which **ever went on** increasing, filled his little heart and mind towards the dignity of the priesthood. He never forgot **that his** master deserved the respect to be paid to God's anointed; **nor** would he ever keep on his cap **in his presence. Even in** the sharp cold of a Belgian winter, it needed **a** positive order to make him break **through this** rule. **The same** feeling prompted **him to** love the ecclesiastical dress; and that he might resemble a priest, he would never turn down the **collar of** his cloak as the other scholars did. **But he set little store on these** outward signs in **comparison** with the desire he had to wear ecclesiastical **virtues in his** heart. He loved to **hear the Word of God, and would sit** on the floor **of the church** drinking it in with profound attention, as grave **and** thoughtful **as an old** man. He was very sparing of **his words,** only speaking when spoken to, and then weighing carefully what he said. Though very merry, Emmerick declared he could not remember that **John** ever gave way **to a** fit of laughter.

He was always ready to obey and to oblige. His turn came the oftenest to read at table ; he coveted that duty most when the reading was from the Book of Proverbs, or the Lives of the Saints, or Meditations on the Passion, his favourite subjects, and he would carry these books off to his room to read and read them again. He pushed his desire to be useful so far, that he used to do a good deal of the servants' work, and would sit down with his books near the door bell, to answer its first call. One cannot be surprised that so hard a student grew accustomed to its sounds, and required often to be roused up from his brown study after the bell had been rung more than once. So little of a boy's love of eating had he, that he never seemed to give his meals a moment's consideration ; never a word of complaint was heard from him about his food, nor indeed about anything else in the house. He eat but little, and seemed so wrapt in thought, that people used to joke him that his mind was away on its travels when he was at table.

But John was ever the best of companions, for the equable sweetness of his temper endeared him to all. He was never known to quarrel, and if his companions fell out, and he could not succeed in pacifying them, he would go off and play at ball by himself in some quiet corner of the house. So much did he love to be alone, so much was he respected when with others, that it was rare that any one attacked him ; and then he met all angry words as quietly as if said to some one else.

Van Stiphout explains his shrinking from society by the exquisite delicacy of his conscience. 'John was ever so simple and so innocent, that he did not even know by name vices to which boyhood has too often so great an inclination. And this was why he was kept away so much from his companions.' At playtime he used to stay in his room, studying or praying, till his master, fearing his application was too close, made him join the other boys. And though he obeyed, and thoroughly too, he never allowed himseif to be carried away by the game ; for as soon as ever all the rest were fairly in the spirit of it, he went quietly off to the most out of the way parts of the house, to pour forth his soul in prayer. One day they found him in a box which was just big enough to hold him. He had been hidden there for two hours ; and all felt sure it was not the first time he had betaken himself to that strange cell. After night prayers, and when the blessing of the good Father had been given, Berchmans would kneel for some time by his bedside. It happened more than once he was found to have lain down with his clothes on ; and when asked the reason he would answer sweetly, ' I fell asleep '—wearied, no doubt, in his prayerful vigil. John was about eleven or twelve, when the day of his first communion arrived. He begged his Superior to hear his general confession, and Father Emmerick, touched at this mark of confidence, was still more moved when he saw disclosed before him the exquisite beauty of the boy's soul, and he could not refrain from weeping, as he tells us, ' over the angel who was at my feet, all bathed with tears, as with the deepest contrition he accused himself of faults which were but the lightest.' Such was, in fact, the simplicity and innocence of his penitent, that Emmerick hesitated some time whether or not he had sufficient matter for absolution.

His confession over, John gave himself up to prepare for his great Guest ; his prayers were made with redoubled fervour, his beads were multiplied, and desires went up fast and burning for the speedy coming of his Lord and Love. The great day came, and in the solemn Gothic church of Nôtre Dame, from Emmerick's hands, he received his God. The Father was thus enabled to record the superhuman look of the holy child at that sacred moment, when, with profound reverence and downcast eyes, a sort of shining forth of his holy desires lit up his face. This was an epoch in his life. His love of God grew quickly beneath the warmth of the Divine Presence. The Holy Name—the first word he had learned in his mother's arms—filled him with holy transports. His master tells us: 'When he began to make progress in Latin versification, I gave him leave to choose a subject for a theme in verse. He brought me an elegy on the Name of Jesus, so full of feeling, tenderness, and unction, that it was easy to surmise, even then, that one day he would enter the Society of Jesus.' A copy of this still exists. The original passed into the hands of Father Otho Zylius after the death of John. This first poetic flight of a boy of thirteen is certainly an extraordinary production for one so young; and taking into account the rampant classicism of the time, it is a pleasing and graceful proof of feelings which would have spoken still clearer if not fettered with unaccustomed members and incongruous comparisons. 'Not—though Calliope gave me a thousand tongues; not—though she gave them to drink at the fountain of Philetas; though the leader of the Castalian chorus should dictate my song—should I be able to tell the sweetness of His Name. Honied Name of names—laden with the sweets of spring, sweet to the heavens, to the earth, to the salt sea. Full of good promise to men—sweeter than any nectar that Hybla nurtures in its reedy cells, breathing perfumes of lilies and violets, of deep red flowers, of roses from Elysian fields; above all the glories of the field, more glorious than their scarlet or ethereal hues. Hail to Thee, Son of God, old beyond all ages. Hail, All-Excelling! Never was word more grateful to our ears; never was name thought of like to Thine. Happiness of man, every way blessed—the one hope of salvation for all mankind.'

So for some forty verses does he labour to express, as in a strange tongue, the love of his young heart. The royal library of Brussels, where the copy of the poem is preserved, has in its archives one of his Latin and Greek themes rendered almost unintelligible by the carelessness of the transcriber and its torn condition.

There is also a Latin elegy on the old subject, 'Tempus fugit: cœlestia quære!' and labelled as composed at Diest; but its greater perfection of composition rather points to a later period, when John was at Mechlin.

Every week he went to confession: and twice a month, and on the greater feasts, he went to holy communion. The preceding evening he used to come with graceful humility, and frankly ask his Superior's pardon for any faults he might have committed.

After Jesus, Mary had the next place in his heart. We have already seen how he loved her from his childhood, and there is not a single witness to his virtues before the various tribunals in the cause of his beatification that has not attested to his singular devotion to our Lady. And this she seems to have rewarded, for every event in his life happened on some feast day or other dedicated to her honour. No one could mention her name in his presence without his face lighting up with a smile; and when he spoke of her, there was an expression in his eye, a sound in his voice, all telling of his love. He never passed a statue of her, so common in Catholic towns and Catholic homes, without saluting it with a prayer to her whom he held as his Mother. He made a rule never to leave a church before he had knelt at her altar. He used his pen, when a boy, in her honour; and one of his companions kept in after life, as a relic, his translation into Latin hexameters of the *Salve Regina*. One day his master took him with him to Bois-le-Duc, to pay a visit to Arnold Hesius, the bishop's secretary. As soon as he arrived, he cared for nothing better than to go round the different sanctuaries of the town to pay his homage to his Blessed Lord and to His holy Mother.[5]

Oftentimes he went with Father Emmerick on pilgrimage to our Lady of Montaigu. This, the great sanctuary of Belgium, is but a league from Diest, and the road[6] leads along the crest of the range of hills, on the highest of which there stands the stately domed church which was rising at the time when John first visited it, but which he did not live to see completed. Known to the piety of the neighbouring town of Sichem, there had been on the crown of the hill a little picture of our Lady in the trunk of an old oak tree. The story ran, and some of the oldest burghers were prepared to attest to the tradition on oath, that a shepherd had wished to convey the Madonna to his home, and had been found rooted to the ground, and only able to move when the image was restored to its original place. There it stayed till 1580. Then came the troubles. Sichem, with its parish church, and a convent of Augustinian Nuns, was six times taken and retaken, suffering from friends and foes alike, till from a flourishing town of sixteen thousand inhabitants, it had dwindled down to a few mud cabins that sheltered some three hundred, all ruined and poor. From 1578 till 1586, when the genius of Alexander Farnese gave victory to the Catholic arms, the whole country side was harried by the Iconoclasts, Dutch, German, English, Huguenot, who, under the compre-

---

[5] At the taking of Bois-le-Duc by the Dutch in 1629, the Catholics were allowed to leave the town. They did so, with their bishop, Op-hovius, at their head, and bearing with them the church plate and sacred vessels, and as their most precious treasure, a miraculous statue of our Lady, which the archduchess placed in St. Géry, at Brussels.

[6] The old road of John's time still exists ; it leaves the present highroad by a little chapel at the Aerschot Gate, where tradition says John used to begin his pilgrimages, and curving much to the right, falls into the highway not far off Montaigu.

hensive name of 'Gueux,' fought for the supremacy of Protestantism. The independence of the Netherlands was to them a secondary consideration. Their all-absorbing aim was to drown Catholicism in blood. When comparative security was restored, a councillor of Sichem placed a fresh picture—the gift of a widow of Diest—upon the old oak. There, among many from far and near, came often, in 1598, the soldiers of Sir William Stanley's Irish regiment, then in the service of the Catholic King, and in garrison at Sichem.[7] Indeed, the old chronicler[8] tells us—'Many of them were wont to use no other physik or remedy for their diseases, but their prayers at the aforesaid place of Mountague, amongst whom very many were healed, in such sorte that Father Walter Talbot, an Irish priest, one of the Societie of Iesus (who at that tyme was their preacher and ghostlie father), was moved to go thither sometymes

[7] Motley is very hard upon Stanley for his desertion from the Protestant standard of Queen Elizabeth, and the betrayal of Deventer. But we cannot doubt the illegal character of the contest, and we may fairly credit the colonel with having followed the dictates of his conscience and those of his men when he took a step which in other circumstances and at other times would deserve the most severe blame. A William Standel (Stanley?) appears in the registers of Nôtre Dame of Antwerp as godfather to a brother of Father Thomas Worsley, S.J., the fellow novice of John (*vide* p. 50). Sir William ended his days as a Carthusian at Gravelines.

[8] 'Miracles lately wrought by the intercession of the glorious Virgin Marie at Mont-aigu. Translated out of the French copie into English by M. Robert Chambers, confessor of the English Religious Dames in the citie of Bruxelles. Dedicated to King James I. 1606.' The original was written by a Jesuit, perhaps Nicholas Boonart.

Father Sailly was canon of Arras, when, struck by the patience of the Jesuit Fathers during their expulsion from Douay, he threw up his living, and though past forty, entered the Society at Rome. Father Possevin took him as his companion on his remarkable embassy to the Czar. Father Sailly was completely prostrated by the weary journeys on foot with that apostolic man. The great work of his life was the Missio Castrensis—mission to the Catholic soldiers—by which he endeared himself to the great captains Alexander Farnese and Spinola, and did inestimable good to the wild mercenaries that followed their standards.

devoutly in procession, accompanied with the said Irish and townesmen of Sichem. Whereof he wrote to Father Thomas Salius (Sailly), who was Superior of the Fathers of the Societie which attended upon the Catholic King's army in the Low Countries.'

Pilgrims multiplied every year, and the outbreak of the plague added to their number, till in 1603 the Governors of the Low Countries, Albert and Isabella, in fulfilment of a vow made on the occasion of raising the siege of Bois-le-Duc by the arms of the great Spinola, came in solemn state to the sanctuary. Besides making the princely offerings of vestments which still remain there, they gave orders for the building of the church, which, with its vast, star-spangled dome, and lofty sacristy tower, serving for a place of safety for the treasures, now crowns the height. The 13th of June the following year, 1604, the Archbishop of Mechlin[9] transferred the image to a stone chapel, and cut down the oak, the wood of which was distributed as relics. On the eve of the 8th of September, when many pilgrims were gathered there, a troop of some eight hundred to one thousand Protestant cavalry from Breda made a dash at the sanctuary, but not before the image and the more precious offerings had been carried away to a place of safety. They wreaked their vengeance on all they could find, smashing pictures, benches, confessionals, and then, piling up the fragments, they tried in vain to set fire to the chapel.[10] Five years later, when peace, or

[9] Matthew vanden Hove, of the same name as John's mother.

[10] Father Cornelius a Lapide nearly gained, on that occasion, the crown of martyrdom he had been praying for every day since his entry into the Society. He was engaged in preaching and hearing confessions in the chapel. His retreat was cut off, when at the first alarm he had rushed to the tabernacle, to save from sacrilegious outrage its sacred Guest. But our Lord, Whom he carried, and our Lady, to whom he made a solemn vow, brought him out of the danger in a way that all looked on as miraculous.

C

rather, a truce, was at last arranged with the Dutch, Albert and Isabella, in magnificent pomp, on the feast of the Visitation, laid the first stone of the great church, which it took eighteen years to complete. At its solemn opening, the widowed Isabella and her brave captain, Spinola, were present; but the good Archduke Albert had gone to his rest. Thus the works were going on during the several visits of John. The fortifications and the town, all laid out symmetrically around the great central object, were taking the place of the ruins of the first village.

The frequency of our saint's pilgrimages adds a special interest to the sanctuary, which the pen of Justus Lipsius has made famous. Thither, then, he used to go in silence, saying his rosary, or making his meditation on the road, Père Frizon tells us, on our Blessed Lady. Nor was this his only offering to Mary; he had even then begun to deprive himself of a part of his meals in her honour, and some of his breakfast used to be found at times hidden away in an out-of-the-way corner. Such devotion bore its fruit in the marvellous and angelic purity of Mary's favourite. Innocent of the very name of vice, a sort of holy instinct warned him of the most distant danger against that exquisite virtue; he would never allow any one even to touch him. The slightest lightness in words or carriage of a companion made Berchmans for ever after shun his acquaintance or company. The boys knew this so well, that if anything was being said that was not as it should be, the appearance of John sufficed to change the subject. 'Once,' says Father Emmerick, 'he had to take the part of Daniel in some college theatricals. The young Berchmans acted admirably, and was warmly applauded by a numerous audience. You would have said that he was in earnest, and not merely acting a part, with such feeling and energy did he upbraid the wicked desires and guilty revenge of the two elders.' Father Cepari assures us that he had already taken a vow of chastity when yet a child.

Meanwhile, the difficulties to which allusion has already been made, had not decreased for the father of Berchmans. The long sickness of his wife had no doubt entailed heavy expenses, while a household without its mistress would add to the expenses of his crippled fortune. He had nothing to support him but what he could gain, for his parents and those of his wife were still living, and little willing to assist him. His other children were growing up, and their education must be seen to. John was past thirteen, showing already great talents; he could gain something for his own support, or at all events assist his father in his trade. He was sent for from school, and by the bedside of his mother the hard news was broken to him. 'You see, my child,' said his father, 'it is impossible for me any longer to bear the expenses of your schooling. Up to this I have made great sacrifices, but I feel it impossible to continue them. It seems to me you must learn a good trade. You will by this means be able to be of great use to us; and instead of being a burden to your family, be a real assistance.' These words were a crushing blow to the boy. For a moment he was silent; then he cast himself sobbing and weeping at his father's feet, and stretching out his hands in an agony of supplication, first to his father, then to his mother, begged them with eyes streaming with tears to continue their former kindness for a few years longer, and so enable him to reap the fruit of the past. 'You know, father, God calls me to the Church. A little longer, and I shall be able to follow that holy vocation. In heaven's name, do not hinder my happiness. As to the expenses, you shall have no reason to be alarmed on that score; I will be

content with so little, you shall not suffer. I can live on
bread and water. But pray do not refuse me permission
to finish my studies.' The father was moved to tears,
and fearing the touching scene would affect the poor
mother too seriously, he raised his son up from his knees,
and promised to talk over some plan by which his wishes
could be met.

In the Béguinage of Diest lived two of his aunts,
Catharine and Mary Berchmans, who had a great affection for their nephew. Through them, no doubt, Dean
Aimon Timmermans, their parish priest, offered to take
John into his house, and continue his education free of
charge. This good priest stood high in the estimation of
his prelate, Matthew vanden Hove, or Hovius, as we
generally see him called. The Archbishop knew of the
boy's merits, and hoped one day to see him amongst the
number of his clergy. Such, too, was then the sole ambition of John. Meanwhile, his father was on the look-out
for a place where his boy, in return for domestic work,
should receive his keep and his schooling. This seems
to have been a common arrangement in days when
Seminaries were few; and some of the religious orders,
as, for example, the Society of Jesus, owed to it some
valuable subjects. John had been but a short time with
the dean, when a situation such as was desired was
heard of in the house of a canon of Mechlin. God's
finger was in the change. To live under the shadow of
the cathedral seemed only a step to the archiepiscopal
Seminary; but the journey to Mechlin led to another end.

The news of his leaving Diest raised a storm among
John's acquaintances, for to know him was to love him.
Timmermans, with whom he had lived, some say but for
a few days, was so taken by his innocent face and manner,
that he told all he met, 'The boy is an angel.' There
was some difficulty in persuading him to part with his

charge. Van Stiphout, his old master, thus records his chagrin at his leaving Diest—'While I was congratulating myself on having such a pupil, and was enjoying in peace this favour from heaven, when my townsmen, with one voice, gave him the title of the flower of the school and the pride of its scholars, some persons who envied my good fortune, tried to get his father to send him to Mechlin. They unfortunately persuaded him.' He never got over the loss. Soon after he threw up his post as master at Diest, and went, it seems, to open a school at Turnhout. When, many years after, he was called as a witness in the cause of Beatification, he declared, 'Life has been very bitter to me since I lost that holy child.' We may be sure the parting from his parents and friends must have been felt deeply by John's affectionate heart ; but he tore himself away from those who wished to detain him. He begged his father and mother's blessing, and with his scanty outfit, set off to Mechlin in the early part of 1614.

Raised to the dignity of the primatial city of Belgium, after having enjoyed for some time the proud position of the seat of Government under Margaret of Austria, Mechlin, had, like its sister towns, suffered cruelly in the civil wars. The lofty tower of her cathedral was left unfinished, her palaces untenanted, her manufactories almost all closed, and the interior of her churches showed the marks of the pillage and devastation they had suffered when, in 1580, Colonel Norris, serving by Queen Elizabeth's order under the colours of the rebels, took the city and gave it up to the tender mercies of his fanatical followers. A succession of worthy prelates, backed by the liberality and wisdom of Albert and Isabella, had done much to repair the evils of those bad days.

John Berchmans could hardly have found a better master than was the Canon John Froymont, grand precentor of the cathedral chapter, and all his life his regard and affection for him was unchanged and profound. The canon kept a sort of boarding school for the sons of people of good family.[11] As, even in Emmerick's house, Berchmans had gladly put himself to the most humiliating work, so now that he considered himself bound to pay for his situation by his services, he, without requiring an order, began in earnest to undertake the most disagreeable duties, and every day to sweep out the yard of the house —a duty not very pleasant in Continental towns—and, had not the precentor interfered, would have washed up the dishes and plates in the scullery. It did not need long for Froymont to see what a treasure he had in John, and he soon learnt to look upon him more in the light of an adopted child than of his servant, and to reverence him as one whose holiness would not fail to bring a blessing on his roof. To free him from menial work, and yet to satisfy the delicate sense of justice which made him wish to give his equivalent for the shelter and home afforded him, the canon intrusted to his entire care some of his little pupils, three brothers of a family, De Roone, or De Boone, by name. He threw himself thoroughly into his new occupation, and became their earthly angel guardian. Each morning he called his little charges, and helped them to dress; then he knelt down with them, and made them repeat with him some short and simple prayers which he had taught them, and which were perfectly suited to their tender years. Each day he

---

[11] In the Rue de Befort a house is pointed out as that in which the precentor lived. Its stepped gable, and the crane in its topmost story, its many windows, and the lazy canal that runs close by, are features common in the Belgian towns. But its date—told by the iron stays on the front—1556, reminds us that it was built the year of St. Ignatius Loyola's death, and of Philip II.'s accession to the throne. A wide fireplace is in a back room, and an antique cork-screw stair of oak leads to the upper rooms.

went with them to holy Mass, instructed them in their catechism, and gave them what little learning they were able to take in. Then came their daily walk; and at night before putting them to bed, he would say prayers again for them. Froymont was delighted with his attentive care. He too was fond of Berchmans' company, and several times took him with him when going to call on his friends, who were always pleased to see the modest and engaging youth; in fact, young men of the best position in the town were pleased to make the acquaintance of the servant boy. He never seemed to notice their attentions, and far from allowing himself to grow conceited, always kept the reserve which his position demanded of him. There was for all the same amiability, the same smile, the same modest glance of recognition, and then his eyes remained cast down without constraint or affectation. Although constantly coming across people of a higher station of life, he never was ashamed of his poor clothes. So long as they were clean, he thought they were always what a servant should wear, and he never dreamt of asking for new clothes, or getting any, except when positively ordered to do so by his master. He took the greatest care of those he had, and even, when they required it, mended them himself, ever trying to spare expense to his benefactor. Once he was sent all the way to Louvain, a distance of some fourteen miles, and though the canon had given him money, he did not spend a penny on his journey, but having executed his commission, came back on foot the very same day.

Piety is sometimes stiff and repulsive; it certainly was not so with our saint, holy as he was. No one could be more winning, no one more obliging, or more truly courteous. A witness tells us, 'No dinner, however little out of the common run, came off at any of the canons', but Berchmans was asked for to wait at table. I could appeal to every member of the chapter,' he goes on, with perhaps a little tinge of humorous roguery, ' but it is enough to mention Canon d'Ittre and Dean vander Lane, who certes will not gainsay me.' Every Friday Berchmans went with his master to the chapter meeting which assembled on that day ; but instead of amusing himself by talking and playing with the servants of the other canons in the vestibule, he withdrew modestly to the church, which was close by, and spent his time saying his beads before our Lady's altar. God was so truly the centre of his life, that every place was to him a place of prayer ; everything naturally turned his thoughts heaven-wards. The canon had a dog, which he was training for shooting on the marsh land by the Dyle. Berchmans used to delight in seeing how it watched the least sign of its master, and how for a little bit of bread it would go and come, take to the water again and again, however tired it might be. 'See,' he would say, 'how complete should be our obedience to God, Who promises us an everlasting crown, when this poor animal makes such efforts to gain so small a reward.' Every day his delight was to snatch some moments from his employments to spend the time before the altar. Every Sunday was almost entirely devoted to God, and on his knees, with clasped hands, he would, without changing his position, hear two, or even three Masses, one after another ; nor did he ever fail to be at vespers and the sermon.

We learn these details from two of his fellow students, Henry Nobelaer, or Nobeleir, who succeeded him at the canon's and then in the Novitiate of the Society of Jesus, and Francis Boels, whose life deserves a passing notice. His father was a native of Mechlin, and a painter by profession ; but being a Calvinist, he had gone to Holland, and Francis was born at Amsterdam. Francis paid a visit to his relatives at Mechlin when but sixteen years old.

Providence threw him across Canon Froymont, for the severity of the winter obliged him to protract his stay. The good priest was grieved to see one so young brought up in error. He endeavoured to persuade him to come and board with his pupils. Francis was taken by the canon's attention, and accepted his offer. He went to school, and was not long before he learned the higher wisdom of Catholic truth. Not long after, on January 28, 1613, he abjured heresy, and the canon stood godfather to him at the font. Boels freely avowed that it was the attractive virtue of John that had led him, under God, to know and embrace the truth. When his mother heard of his conversion, she came privately to Mechlin, and did everything to make him abandon his religion, not sparing the most shameful and outrageous violence to gain her end. She vainly endeavoured to remove him by force; and failing this, laid an appeal before the States-General of Holland. The Government formally demanded him of the Belgian authorities, the mother having declared that her son was kept as a common servant by the precentor, and employed by him to carry his cloak. The Archduke ordered an inquiry to be made, which proved conclusively that the young man, then nineteen years old, was in possession of an entire liberty. September 24, 1618, he entered the Society, just at the close of John's second probation, in which he lived and died a fervent religious. In the report of the Commission of Inquiry, it is stated that Francis sat every day at the canon's table, waited upon by a certain John Berchmans, the servant man.

CHAPTER II.

Call to Religious Life.

JOHN BERCHMANS had so far been following the classes
at the archiepiscopal Seminary. The buildings it occupied were formerly a College founded by John Standonck,
a celebrated doctor of the Sorbonne, in 1490, and which
for nearly a century had been under the direction of the
Brothers of Common Life. The flood of invasion had
left it tenantless for about sixteen years, when Archbishop vanden Hove, in 1596, turned it into his
Seminary. The historians of the Society of Jesus are
pleased to connect their beginnings in Flanders with the
hospitality which St. Ignatius received in Antwerp in the
great house, near St. James', when he went there to beg
from the Spanish merchants during the interval of his
studies at Paris. That very house was opened to the
earliest of his followers, who were sent by Father Laynez
in 1563. But for the crime of Henry VIII., the like
good fortune might have befallen the Spanish merchants
on the banks of the Thames, who, too, had a visit from
the Saint. Some few Fathers of the Society had already
established themselves in Louvain, where they opened
a College in 1560. But the new order had won
the hatred of the Reformers. The Gueux held them
in special abhorrence, as of Spanish origin, and as
unflinching and uncompromising defenders of the faith.
Their infant foundations were rudely crushed, and the

victory of the Confederates in any town, like that of the
Revolution of to-day, was generally the signal for their
instant expulsion. But Alexander Farnese covered them
with his protection, and in 1584 they were legally established in Belgium. Attached to the Spanish troops as
military chaplains, they shared with them the fortunes of
war, and three of them met with a glorious death, being
killed in hatred of their name, while ministering to the
dead and dying on the battlefield of Nieuport, that most
disastrous episode of the great siege of Ostend. With
the peace, the various towns of Belgium, anxious to
repair the wounds inflicted on the national faith by the
religious war, called in the Fathers of the Society.

Their blood had flowed in England and in France; and
in the other extremity of the world, the great persecution
was beginning in Japan—the first victims had been
offered up, the holocaust was soon to follow. Germany
was full of the name of a Netherlander, d'Hondt, or
as we know him, Blessed Peter Canisius; Spain boasted
of its Xavier and Borgia. The names of Bellarmine
and Acquaviva were then household words in Europe,
and Italy was proud of her sons.

In was in these circumstances that Father Charles
Scribani, the provincial of the Society of Jesus, consented, at the request of the magistrates of the town,
to open a public College in Mechlin. The remains of
the palace of Margaret of Austria, so long the brilliant
residence of Charles V., were bought for this purpose.
The old building is still standing in a broad, grassgrown
street, its neighbour the over-ornamented façade of the
ancient church of the Jesuits, contrasting with its mediæval outline, and the quaint octagonal turret that runs
up one side. In after years the College increased, until
at last, with the Novitiate at its side, it covered the
whole space now occupied by the city hospital. Father

de Greeff was sent from Antwerp to be one of the masters. He has left us a long letter, interesting, as well on account of the details he is able to give as professor of Greek and confessor of John Berchmans, as of the circumstances under which he wrote it, while labouring, in 1630, in the midst of dangers, on the Dutch mission at Nimeguen, the birthplace of Canisius. The name of 'provincial,' concealed under the military phrase, 'chiliarch,' and other like devices, to prevent risk of discovery, remind us of the perils which they ran when war had again broken out between the Republic and Spain.[1] We cannot do better than quote this letter here, adding only such details as can be derived from other sources. 'When, by order of Father Charles Scribani, in the August of 1615, I came to Mechlin from Antwerp with Father Antony Sucquet, where I had been repeating my theology, John Berchmans passed from the archbishop's Seminary to our College, not without a good deal of feeling on the part of his former master and rector, on account of which between them and us "there was fixed a great chaos."'

Father Bauters, speaking of the change, says, 'That it seems the work of God's hand, as all who were concerned made every resistance to the step.' As we find that other of Froymont's pupils attended the new College, and that he himself steadily backed up John's vocation, it seems impossible, taking into consideration the relations of the young man to his master, that the change should have been made without the wish and desire of the precentor, even though, as Père Frizon states, it was at the entreaties of John in the first instance.

---

[1] It was owing to such disguises in a correspondence which fell into the hands of the Dutch, that the libel, famous in its day, *On the secret Traffic of the Jesuits*, owed its origin.

Berchmans was found fit to enter 'rhetoric,' the highest class in classical studies, where he had for master, besides Father de Greeff, Father Paschasius vanden Straeten, as professor of Latin. He now redoubled his zeal for study. He never lost a minute of the day. Whatever his occupation, on whatever errand he might be sent, he always had a book with him, and every spare moment he read it with the most fixed attention. Oftentimes, seated on his bed, he would study the whole night long, always taking the precaution that the light from his lamp should not prevent his companions' sleep. Sometimes it was prayer that robbed his rest, and, though no doubt his hours were early, he was found kneeling on the bare floor past midnight, or fallen asleep on the ground at the foot of his bed. He soon rose to the top of the class, and carried off the first prize at the end of the year, and his masters looked upon him as fully capable of teaching others. This success, and still more his genuine goodness, gained him the respectful affection of both superiors and equals. There was one of the scholars who, whether through jealousy or a naturally bad disposition, took pleasure in tormenting John for months together. Berchmans needed only to have made it known to have found protectors on every side, but he never said a word about it to any one. And though the persecution only seemed to grow worse for his patience, in after times the memory of that silent heroism came back, and brought the former tyrant to attest the virtue of his victim.

Although only a day scholar, he most scrupulously followed every order of his masters, and even their smallest advice. He never would join any game of which they disapproved, and on this account he never would bathe in public with his companions. The delicate modesty with which he sheltered the marvellous purity

of his soul, no doubt, was an additional reason for this.
He seems to have been naturally chosen to take the
part of the heroes of chastity in the sacred drama, so
much the fashion of those days. As he had acted Daniel
at Diest, so at Mechlin he acted St. Natalia, and he
another time took the part of St. Henry of Germany. He
had already learnt by heart more than four hundred
verses when the part was taken from him, for fear that
his delicate chest should suffer from the exertion, and
that his weak voice should prevent his being heard,
speaking, as he would have had to have done, before a
large audience in the open air. Though he made no
complaint, it was easy to see, from the flush that rose
to his face, that he felt not being able to make a public
declaration of his love for holy purity, as in his part he
would have had to utter the solemn vow of the virgin
Emperor. His very company seemed to breathe forth
the perfume of that angelic virtue.

At Mechlin, as wherever the Society of Jesus has a
College, the Congregation, or Sodality, of the Blessed
Virgin Mary had taken root among the frequenters of its
schools. This idea, so fruitful in good, owed its origin
to Leo, a Belgian of the Roman College, in the year
1563, while engaged in the care of the young students;
and Gregory XIII. set the seal of his approval upon it
some twenty years later. Still nearer the time of which
we are writing, his successor, Sixtus V., had twice confirmed this approval, and Clement VIII. had published a
brief in its favour. So much encouragement from the
Holy See, so many aids which it offered to piety, the title
it bore of his Blessed Mother Mary, all made Berchmans
anxious to be a candidate, while we may be sure that
the sodalists were only too glad to have so worthy an
addition to their numbers. We know, at all events, that
when once admitted, he had nothing more at heart than

to get others to enter their name on the rolls ; and the very fact of his being a member was of itself a sufficient inducement. He became a model to all. Every day he recited, prostrate on the ground, the Office of the Blessed Virgin, or, as others assert, the Psalter of St. Bonaventure. Every Saturday, and on the eve of the greater feasts, he fasted in honour of our Lady, and to join humiliation to his penance, always insisted on scrubbing the kitchen pans and cooking apparatus.

Whenever he went to holy communion, he spent two or three hours in thanksgiving. On Good Friday[2] he stole out of doors at nightfall, and went through the Stations of the Cross barefoot. The better to hide his penance, he had on shoes without soles, and stockings without feet, as St. Gertrude used to walk of old. The fervour of his daily life could not escape the precentor, who, as he knew him more and more, came more and more to reverence him as a saint. This belief in his holiness no doubt gave a supernatural colouring to the following incident, to which he solemnly deposed after the death of John. One Whitsuntide, Froymont went with his young charge on the well loved pilgrimage to Montaigu. They wished to return by Aerschot, and not knowing the road, they hired two guides in succession, each of whom, after securing their pay, had gone and left them. They had got into a wood which bore an ill name for robberies and murders committed there ; and, to add to their misfortunes, a terrible storm burst overhead. The poor canon thought his last hour was

---

[2] Father Cepari says, 'Every Friday,' thus rendering the *feriis Christo patienti sacris* in Father Bauter's evidence (the novice master of John), but it is much more likely that the real meaning is what we have given, as Father Francis Boels, from whom this detail was no doubt learned, says simply, *nocte Passionis.*

come. For more than an hour they wandered up and down, the storm continuing with pitiless fury, till at last they got into a path which grew so narrow that the canon's horse could hardly go forward. In his distress, he determined to trust to the protection of John. He got down, and making the holy youth mount, he followed on foot, praying with intense earnestness to the angel guardian of Berchmans to rescue them from danger. That instant a clap of thunder burst immediately above them, with a noise as if the sky was rent in two. Half dead with fear, Froymont, on looking round, saw a peasant woman fling herself down from the top of a hill close by, change in an instant into a gigantic cat, which with foaming jaws and glaring eyes began to roll at the foot of the horse; and then, after strange contortions, the frightful animal, with hideous sounds, fled into the thicket. At that moment the storm ceased, and they saw the towers of Aerschot glistening through the leaves.

The people of the town found a ready explanation of what Froymont described, in the fact that a woman who bore the reputation of a witch lived near the wood. Though we may not readily admit the testimony of the scared canon, or the belief of the gossips of Aerschot, there is no superstition in supposing that the powers of darkness had a hand in conjuring up this storm, as no doubt they could, with God's permission. For it seems likely that this pilgrimage had a special end, and that at the shrine of our Lady, Berchmans had just bound himself to enter the Society of Jesus. We know, however, for certain, that it was about this time that he began to feel himself drawn so strongly to that order, that he could not but recognize in that impulse an expression of God's will. He had not always had this inclination. 'I recollect very well,' says Father Henry de Vriese, a fellow student of Berchmans at Mechlin, and afterwards his brother in religion, 'having **heard him say that at** the beginning **he had** had great difficulty to **make** up his mind **for the** Society, **and that perhaps he never would have done so, but for the kind** encouragement he met with from one **of our Fathers.** But once convinced **of the** design **of Providence in his** regard, he burned **with an incredible desire to** consummate, as soon **as** possible, **the sacrifice he was to** make ; and nothing, neither **caresses nor** threats, **nor** even the promises held **out to** him by the archbishop and by other persons of influence, could make him hesitate for a moment.'[3] We **must let** Father de Greeff tell the inner story of the vocation. 'John Berchmans, who was my pupil and penitent **at the** time he was attending **our College, opened his** mind **to** me about entering the Society ; and **for the** same end, by my advice, **he used** to go to communion every Sunday and holiday, and later on, every Thursday, **even when** there was no **feast day ; and** on those days, for **a year or more, he frequently came to me to have a private conversation on** the subject. Whatever bad behaviour there might be in class, he was ever the same, modest, attentive, hardworking, never **a shadow on his** brow, and his **face always** wreathed **in** sweetness ; he was always goodnatured, and to all. One would have said he was an **angel in the flesh.** In conversation he was constantly trying to **find out, when he** had to do or **to** say something, **what would be the** most perfect. Indeed, once or twice, **by the ardour of his conversation, he lit up in my** cold heart **some** flames, though feeble, **of divine love ; and** the **very thought of them to this**

---

[3] John, **in after life, was fond of giving to** St. Jerome's letters the credit of having **in a marked way developed his** leaning to a religious state, while **the** *Life of St. Aloysius,* **which had** but lately been published in Belgium, **decided him in favour of the** Society of Jesus.

day fills me with confusion when I recall several practices which I suggested to him, and which I have read
of in his life.' The resolution was not come to without
much prayer and much consideration. In addition to
his communions, he began to hear a second Mass every
day; he divided the money he possessed, some twenty-
five florins, into three parts. One share he gave to the
poor, with another he got Masses said at Montaigu, with
the remainder he paid a similar tribute to our Lady
the *Sedes Sapientiæ*, in St. Peter's Church at Louvain.
To a Belgian student this venerable image, recalling by
the severity of its type what we call the Norman period,
was specially an object of devotion. Before it, for four
centuries, have the doctors of the old University and the
new pledged their oath of fealty to God and His Church
after receiving their degree. How many illustrious
men have knelt at its feet, how many prayers for
light and petitions for success have gone up at that
side chapel from students from every part of the
Christian world !

When once his decision was taken, or rather, when
once he saw clearly in that vocation the will and wish of
God, he bound himself by vow, as we have already
mentioned, to enter the Society at the earliest opportunity.[4] His confessor recommended him to inform his
parents of his intentions. The Royal Library at Brussels
has, amongst its other treasures, a copy in the original
Flemish, and a Latin translation of the letter, which will

---

[4] Charles Scribani was the Provincial. His memory is ever present in
the history of the Society in Belgium. His father had come from
Piacenza, an honoured friend of his Prince, Alexander Farnese.
Father Charles entered religion in Trèves, but he lived all his life in
Belgium, up till its last four years, which he spent in preparing for
death, ever working for his Divine Master as a professor, an author, or
governing his order. He accepted John at Father de Greeff's recommendation.

best speak for itself.   Its date, which is not affixed, must be somewhere in 1616—

' My honoured father and dearest mother,—

' It is now near three or four months that our Lord has in a most marked way been knocking at my door, and that I, so to say, have kept it shut.   But when I saw that whether I played, walked, or whatever I did, one thing always was present to my mind—the choice of a fixed state of life—I have come to the conclusion, yes, I am determined to serve our dear Lord, with His grace, in religious life; and this after many a communion, and many other good works.   For who is there who, seeing all the miseries, dangers, and fearful sins in every state of life, is not filled with horror? And, again, when one sees those perfections, humility, &c., and lastly, that burning love of God and our neighbour, how can one not betake himself to it?   It is very true it is some way hard for parents and for relations to give up their children, but what would they do if our dear Lord— may He long spare them!—should call them to Himself? Again, when sometimes I am thinking in my heart that if I saw here before me on the one side father, mother, sister, &c., and on the other God the Lord with His, and, as I trust, *my* Blessed Mother, and those (*sic*) on one side should say—" My dear son, I beg you, by the trouble and labour I have endured for you, follow me;" and on the other side Christ Jesus should cry—" I have for you been born, scourged, crowned with thorns, and at last died on a Cross : see here My five holy wounds ! And have I not endured these for you?   And do you not know that up to this time I have nourished your soul with My sacred Body, and slaked its thirst with My sacred Blood?   And will you be now so ungrateful?" When I think of this, my dearest parents, my heart so sets me on fire that, were it possible, I should this very hour fly into religion; and my heart, my soul, will not be at rest till they have found their best loved Master. But you will say: "It is as yet too soon, wait till you have taken your degrees." I ask you, if a poor man were to come to your door to ask an alms, and you were wanting to give it to him, would you not take him for a fool and a madman, were he to say, "I will come for it in a year or two?" It is doubtful whether you would be willing to give it to him. Are we not all beggarmen before the face of Almighty God? It pleases Him now, after much prayer, through His goodness, to give me one of His best alms, that of a vocation to religion, and in particular to the Society of Jesus, the hammer of all heresies, the vessel of virtue and perfections; and shall I spurn this grace away with my foot, and despise it? It is doubtful whether our Lord would allow it to last on me for two years; and then I might have to hear—and what a misfortune that would be—"I know you not." So now, from my whole heart, I offer myself to Jesus Christ, willing even to fight under His colours (company). I hope that you will not be so unreasonable as to oppose yourself to Christ; but that, like the people of Egypt (who, as I have read in history, offered their children to their false god, the crocodile, to be devoured by it, and while they were being devoured, made great rejoicings), so, I hope, you too will rejoice, like them, and give God our Lord praise and thanks that your son should be found so worthy, not to be *given* to God, for he does not belong to you, but to be *restored* to Him. I commend myself to your good prayers, that our dear Lord may give me perseverance to the end of my life, and may grant you with me, hereafter, eternal life.

'JOHN BERCHMANS.'

It does not require much penetration to understand what a blow this letter gave to those dreams of love and hope which centred in such a child of promise. His father hastened over to Mechlin; but finding that words were wasted on his son, he addressed himself to Father de Greeff. 'He urged,' against this vocation, we again quote his confessor's letter, 'that he had educated John, at a cost far exceeding his means, to be the support of his numerous family, and accused me of putting the idea into the boy's head. This last statement I absolutely and positively denied, asserting, as was the fact, that his son was the first, of his own accord, and by God's guidance, to speak of his vocation, and to consult me as to how he could put it into execution. I pleaded that I was bound to give him that assistance by introducing him to Father Scribani' (the then Provincial), 'a service which I myself would have wished for under similar circumstances. I told him that I too had met with just such opposition from my father, who like himself was a shoemaker (for John's father was of that trade before he became a priest), for I was not merely his eldest, but his only son; and though he had exactly the same ideas about me as Charles Berchmans had about John, I had brought him round by strong reasons; that the temporal consolations parents look for from their children are little worth and uncertain, especially when, not understanding the greatness of the heavenly gift, and without good reason or necessity, they endeavour to turn them from the path of perfection; I was sure that, as far as spiritual assistance went, John would be able to give much greater help to his parents and relations in religion, than by remaining in the world and taking some living or rich benefice, though he should by so doing seem to bring some relief to his friends in a worldly point of view. I recollect urging many similar things, and with a good deal of trouble, on John's father, who, though not without many tears, at last seemed to give into my arguments.'

But the old man was not completely persuaded, or if he admitted the reasons alleged, he gladly sought some way to escape from the bitter sacrifice. He ordered his son to lay the whole matter before the Capuchin Fathers, who counted among their number a relative of his wife. She had made them promise beforehand to do all they legitimately could in her behalf. John obeyed, confident that religious would never give a verdict against so manifest a vocation. Nor was he disappointed. They put before him the sacrifices he would be called on to make, the difficulties of the life he was about to embrace, the responsibility of the apostolic ministry ; but his answers were so full of common sense, so thoroughly to the purpose, that the community were convinced of the reality of his call to the Society, and even encouraged him to persevere. His relative, however, did not give in to the general opinion, and paid several visits to the precentor's house, to persuade Berchmans to abandon his vocation. For some time John bore patiently these painful ordeals, and answered frankly but respectfully to all that his cousin could urge. But when he saw that it was no longer question of determining whether his vocation was true or false, but an absolute and direct assault upon his firmness, he thought it high time to put a stop to what was simply a temptation. The Capuchin called again, and reopened the attack. Berchmans calmly, but with Flemish bluntness, got up, took his visitor by the arm, and led him to the door—'If you are determined to speak about this subject, there is the door ; you may go back whence you came.' Such a determined proceeding on the part of one always so quiet and mild, had the desired effect. He met with no further opposition from that quarter.

The summer of 1616 had been passed in these struggles between love of his father and mother and the love of his Lord and Master. As a last effort, his parents wrote to urge him to delay his resolution for a few months. John's answer is still extant, and no words can paint better than his own the picture of his thoughts and feelings at this time. It was written probably about September, 1616.

' Ever honoured father and dearest mother,—

' I am very happy to learn that you are in good health, and I hope and heartily pray our Lord God that He will always spare you all in the same. Still I am greatly surprised that you, in place of loving and thanking God for the great favour that He has willed to do not only myself, but yourselves also, in calling me to holy religion, and to such an order, where men lead the lives of angels, that you, I say, should counsel me not to listen to our dear Lord, and to put off my vocation for five or six months. It is not right, as you well know, that in order to obey you I should be disobedient to God. Our dear Lord, when He called a young man to follow Him, would not let him go to bury his father, who was just dead, though this was a good work, and one which needed but a short time. And when He called another, He forbade him to say good-bye to his friends, saying—" No one putting his hand to the plough, and afterwards looking backwards, is fit for the kingdom of God." Why do you think He did this, if it was not to show us that we must follow our vocation then and there, without delay? So then, my ever honoured parents, that I may obey God our Lord, that I may make my salvation sure, and, in fine, that I may avoid that fearful sentence,

Vocavi et remisisti. Ego quoque in interitu tuo ridebo—" I
called and you refused.   I also will laugh in your
destruction," [5] I mean, with God's grace, in a fortnight
hence, to share the joy of my brothers in religion.   And
I trust, through God our Lord, through the prayers of
my brethren, and through yours also, and my own poor
petitions, to obtain that He Who has given the good will
may grant me perseverance to the end.

'John Berchmans,

' Your obedient son.'

We must ask the reader to listen to the last letter
written before John left the world, only a few days after
the one we have just given.   It is in answer to the request
to come over for a visit to Diest.   Canon Froymont had
watched the long and painful struggle of his young pupil.
He thought enough had been done to prove the sound-
ness of his vocation.   He positively refused to expose
him to fresh assaults and to fresh sorrow.

The date is somewhere about the 18th of September,
and, like the other, is kept, in copy, in the Brussels
Library.   It was addressed—'To his honoured father,
Jan Berchmans, residing at the Golden Moon, Diest.
Cito, cito, cito.   Favoured by friends.'

' Honoured father and dearest mother,—

' I am very glad, and rejoice greatly
at your good health, in which may our dear Lord long
spare you.   I wish to let you know by this post, that my
master does not judge it well that I should go to Diest,
as you desire, and that for many reasons.   I pray you
then humbly, honoured father and dearest mother, by the
parental affection you have towards me, and by the love
I have of you as your son, to be so good as to come

[5] Prov. i. 24, 26.

here by Wednesday evening at the latest, either by the Mechlin coach from Montaigu, or by Stephen's conveyance, that so I may say, "Welcome, and good-bye" to you, and you to me, when you give me, your son, back to God our Lord, Who has given me to you.

'One thing, though, I should like very much from you, dear parents, for I cannot do it myself, and each hour of delay seems to me like a day; and it is that you, with my aunts, the two Béguines, and my brother, and any other good friends who are willing to do so much for me, and for my soul's salvation, should go to receive our dear Lord at our Lady of Montaigu, and that you would offer me to her ever Blessed Son and to herself with the same joy of heart with which our Lady offered her Son Jesus Christ to God the Father. Should this act of devotion delay your journey here, I had rather you would defer it till your return. I recommend to you heartily this good friend (the bearer of the letter?), who, for my master's sake and for me, does me so great a kindness. Treat him well; I pray you also to get him a lodging at grandmother's, or in our own house.

'Remember me most kindly to my grandfather, my grandmothers, and above all, to my special and best of benefactors, the reverend precentor, Van Groenendonck,[6] that he may be good enough sometimes to think of me in his prayers, and to Uncle Pellen and Auntie Kathleen.[7] I have still some little souvenirs which I hope you will take away with you. Pray for me, all of you, very heartily, that our dear Lord may give me perseverance to the end of my life. This recommendation I ask you to make to all my friends. I send it them as my adieu.'

---

[6] A canon of St. Sulpice, Diest ; a relative or connection of John's family.

[7] Peregrine Hamel and his wife Catharine, sister to the saint's mother.

Canon Froymont added a postscript—'Mynheer President John Berkemans, do not fail to come the very first opportunity this week.'

John's prayers to heaven, his unalterable fidelity to the call of God, at last prevailed over all difficulties. The long wished for permission to enter the Society was obtained; but we can be sure many a secret struggle has remained unrecorded, many a victory untold. One of these, however, has been preserved to us. His father was deploring his so called obstinacy, and with a strange threat refused to bear any further expenses which might be necessary to enable him to carry out his intentions. Berchmans took a lesson from the great Patriarch of Assisi. 'See here, father, if I thought the clothes I have on my back would stay me a single moment, I would strip myself of them this very instant to follow my Jesus nailed to the Cross.' And this was no sudden burst of enthusiasm. The eve of his leaving the world, he was bidding good-bye to Henry de Vriese, one of his most intimate friends, who congratulated him on his having overcome at last the stubborn opposition of his family. John answered at once, looking up with a face, all lit with deep feeling towards heaven—'What! should I leave God to follow man—that God Who is calling me to Him, and Who has shed for me torrents of blood?' Then his expression resumed its wonted calm, and he said, with a sweet smile—'No, no, if these clothes of mine had been an obstacle to me, I would have cast them down at my father's feet, and naked I would have followed my Lord, Who was nailed naked to a shameful gibbet.'

CHAPTER III.

The Noviceship.

On Saturday, September 24, 1616, John Berchmans presented himself at the door of the Belgian Novitiate, then in Mechlin. He had just entered on his eighteenth year, and his face, always beautiful and winning, was taking the form and shape of manhood. His costume was simple, and even poor, as we gather from the record of the wardrobe keeper at the Novitiate, whose entry of the secular clothes John brought with him is still preserved. He wore a black cloth doublet, and breeches of the same, a grey cloak fell from his shoulders, and a stiff white collar, without frill or plaits, supported by a black stock, ran round his neck. Henry de Vriese accompanied him to the gate. On entering, he found another young man who had arrived the very same day, Theodore vander Meer, a student of the College of Bois-le-Duc, eight months our saint's junior. He made friends at once. 'Come, brother,' said he, 'let us rejoice that we are in the house of the Lord. We must not be found unworthy of so great a favour. May both of us always live in this holy Society of Jesus, where God's service calls us; and may we meet in heaven after long and hard work, never to be separated again.' And noticing a lay-brother digging in the garden—'There,' said he' 'we can begin at once; there is no better opening for religious life than humility and charity;' and throwing off his cloak, and taking his newly-made acquaintance with him, he went to help the good brother, to the no small astonishment of those who witnessed the scene. One of the first to welcome the new comer was Father de Greeff, who was delighted to fold to his breast his spiritual child, now his brother in religion. 'And at night,' so he tells us, in the letter quoted above, 'as is the custom in the Society, I washed his feet, and he in turn performed the like act of charity for me, though so unworthy.'[1] When seated at the recreation, and treated as one of themselves by those who were sent to be his companions, Berchmans, realizing that at last he had gained his end, was so full of delight, that he could not stay his tears, and he kept on weeping tears of joy through that day, and gave vent to all the deep feelings of his heart in words full of love and gratitude.

He had often told his director that he aimed at nothing less in entering religion than the most scrupulous fulfilment of the least of the rules of the institute. 'I want to be a saint; yes, and a great saint, too. Is it possible to conceive that one should not attain an eminent sanctity with all the powerful means of sanctification the Society has at its disposal?'

And these were the ideas which he began at once to carry out in every detail of his new life. He knew 'that perfection does not consist in doing great things,' as he loved to repeat, 'but in doing well what obedience orders or advises;' or, as he tersely puts it in one of his writings, *Maximi facere minima*—'Set great store on little

---

[1] 'The following year, being summoned from Friesland by the visitor, Father Henry Scheren, I passed through Mechlin, and I returned to my old post enriched by great spiritual alms, which John begged for me of the novices for my mission. The next year when hoping, but vainly, again to see him, I learnt that his Superiors had sent him to Rome. I sent a letter to him there, asking for prayers, but as no answer came back, I never could learn whether mine had reached him' (Father Greeff's letter, A.D. 1630. *Vide supra*, p. 28).

things.' And that this was more than a mere saying, we find elsewhere—' Do great penance for small faults. Be a miser and a merchant in spiritual things.'

Before we tell the story of his novice life, it may be interesting to glance round at those who were his companions.

During a period stretching over two years there was, of course, a succession of arrivals and departures ; some who left on taking their vows, some, unfortunately, who left before. Their total number was, during John's stay, one hundred and seventy-four, a large one, when we consider the Flemish Novitiate had only begun in 1611, when Archduke Albert obtained the division of the old Belgian province of the Society into the Gallo-Belgian and Flandro-Belgian provinces. Of these novices two died during their probation, some twenty-three gave up. One of these last was the Flemish poet and historian, Oliver de Wree, or Latinized, Vredius ; if, as is probable, he was not gone before John arrived. Among the others, we do not find names like those the biographer could record as the fellow novices of St. Stanislaus. Still, there were some who are not unknown beyond the home annals of the Society of Jesus. Sidronius de Hossche ranks as one of the first Latin poets of his country, and a statue has been raised to him in his native village of Merchem, near Dixmude, in West Flanders. His health was so delicate at Mechlin, that his Superiors had decided to dismiss him, but he pleaded so hard to stay, even as a lay-brother, that he was allowed to remain.

James van de Walle ranks very near to Hoschius as a Latinist. Theodore Mouretourf was great grandson of Plantijn, the founder of the Plantinian press ; his mother, Henrietta Plantijn, and her sister, married two brothers Mouretourf, or Moretus, and Theodore's first cousin was the princely Balthazar Moretus, the great printer of

Antwerp, and generous benefactor to the Jesuit College
in that city.   Young Father Moretus was one of a band
of nineteen who were sent by the General of the Society,
in 1625, to the post of danger in the new province of
Bohemia, which Father Mutius Vitelleschi had just
detached from Austria.   Of these others three were
fellow novices of John's, and all four became men of
mark, as professors, authors, and heads of houses in
their adopted country.   Perhaps the most distinguished
of the four was Moretus himself, whose excellence in
natural science placed him for fourteen years in the
Chair of Mathematics at the Universities of Prague, and
afterwards of Breslau.   The chronicles of their province
tell us of their zeal, humility, religious life, and holy
deaths.

Six or more others served in the still more perilous
mission of Holland, of whom was Henry van Suercq,
one of seven sons, all of whom entered the Society.
His brother and fellow novice, Iodocus, left Louvain in
1627, to join his elder brother Justus in Paraguay.   A
fourth brother, Jerome, was also missioner at Horn, in
Holland.

When the plague swept across the Low Countries,
it gave the crown of martyrs of charity to twelve
out of Berchmans' former companions, not counting
some three lay-brothers, who probably made their
novitiate with him, and died in the service of the
sick.   Another lay-brother novice won a place in
Tanner's Martyrology of the Society.   Philip Notijns, a
shoemaker's apprentice, entered the Novitiate seven
months before John took his vows.   A hardworking
imitator of Martha, after serving as tailor, porter, baker,
and brewer, he was appointed to a place of trust as
socius, or secretary, to the procurator, or bursar.   In
1632 he was sent to Utrecht; there he put down his

name as a volunteer to serve the plague-stricken. It was volunteering to die, and God accepted the sacrifice, though in another way. The town had fallen into the hands of the Dutch. Its governor was Tour de l'Auvergne, Duc de Bouillon, whose brother was the famous Turenne. Like so many other illustrious houses, the Tour de l'Auvergnes had deserted the Church, and the duke's mother, daughter of William the Silent, had brought her sons up with all the political and religious hatred of her family against the faith.

The duke, when he came in contact with the zealous Fathers who still remained at their post of danger in Utrecht, saw the falseness of Protestantism, and consequently, as did Turenne after him, embraced the faith. This exposed him to the suspicions of the Dutch. He withdrew for a time to Sedan, and the deputy governor, in 1638, wreaked his revenge on the authors of the conversion by arresting the rector and another Father, with Brother Philip, on a charge of conspiring to render up the town to the Spaniards. A craven adventurer, who turned King's evidence to save his life, swore against them, and they were subjected to the most revolting tortures to extort a confession. The nature and reality of their sufferings are attested by documents still existing,[2] the reports of the surgeons who dressed their wounds. For ten hours the poor brother had to pass through the ordeal through which the two Fathers had gone. Stripped, and seated on a triangle, his head was kept erect by a collar armed inside with a triple row of spikes, which was supported by chains attached to the corners of the torture chamber. His hands were bound back to his feet; and then a ring of coals was lighted

---

[2] These are printed at length, from the originals in the State Paper Office of Brussels, by the learned Father Waldack, S.J., in his *Historia Provinciæ Flandro-Belgicæ S.J.*, an. 1638.

round him, and as the blisters rose, they were cut, and
gunpowder and salt rubbed in. The blood ran down in
streams from the neck, and great gaping wounds were
opened all over his body, half roasted by the blazing
fire. When, maimed and mangled, he was at last brought
out to the block, he roundly denied each count of the
accusations, and pushing away the ministers who pressed
around him, proudly confessed that his faith was the
only reason of his death.

As may be supposed, the bulk of the novices were
Flemish or Dutchmen, but there were also five Irishmen,
and one who may fairly be called an Englishman. Of
the five, the best known is Father William Stanihurst,
son of Robert Stanihurst of Dublin,[3] and first cousin to
the martyr Father Southwell, who for years was a
brilliant preacher in the Belgian capital. Numbers were
converted to a virtuous life and to the faith by his
sermons. He coveted the more brilliant crown of martyr
of charity in the time of the plague ; but though he
caught the disease in the discharge of his work of
mercy, he was instantaneously cured by St. Ignatius—
it being in the octave of his feast. He lived to a ripe
old age. His elder brother, Peter, who entered some
months before him, had a much shorter career. He had
only just been ordained priest when, in 1527, he was
lost in the Bay of Biscay, with Father de Vriese, the
friend of John, and another Flemish, Father Brouwer.

Of the other three, one was George Comerford, who
was back in Ireland in 1626, when Charles I.'s accession
gave a short space of breathing time to the faithful and
afflicted Irish.   Then there was Peter Carthy, probably
from the south of Ireland, who was on the Dutch
mission in 1628 ; and Thomas O'Meagher (Macarius),

---

[3] Father Morris, *Troubles of our Catholic Forefathers,* First Series,
pp. 249. 289.

who worked hard in his native country, and at last, after some years, **died of fever and** fatigue while serving as chaplain to Strafford's army, which was **composed almost** entirely of Catholics.   In 1626 he was still **in Belgium,** and the year before his death, Father Nugent, his Superior, wrote to Rome asking **leave to publish** a work of Father **Meagher's,** *Volumen Inscriptionum de Heroibus utriusque Testamenti.*   He speaks with great **praise** of his subject's talents, **and declares that he** was fitted to teach classics in any University—' as, indeed, he has done in Flandro-Belgium.'

A notice of Thomas Worsley must close our long list. As the details have never been got together before, there is some excuse if we dwell **for a page or two on** his life.   Sir Nicholas Hervey, whose **father was the** ancestor of the present **Lord Bristol, was ambassador** from Henry VIII. to the **Emperor** Charles V. at Ghent ; his son, **Sir** Thomas, **knight marshal to Queen Mary,** went over with her royal **husband into the Low Countries just before her death.**   He never **dared to return to England,**[4] though some three years **later exile and** poverty doubtless combined **made him sue for leave to** return **from Cecil.**   The cunning **Throgmorton** was civil to him **when he passed through Paris, on** his way back from Spain.   **Then he was accused of plotting** Queen Elizabeth's death **with Cardinal Granvelle, and** he no doubt gave up all hope of returning **home.**   He married a **lady,** Holland by name,[5] and had **by her two** daughters, **one** of whom, Leonora, married **Mr.** John Worsley, a **young** English exile of the **great house** of **that** name.

---

[4] Another Hervey died in exile for the faith and loyalty, in 1700, in Antwerp, Elizabeth, daughter of Baron Hervey, and wife to the gallant Cavalier John Hervey, who was boon friend of Charles II., and treasurer to his Queen, Catharine of Braganza.

[5] Collins says, 'Sir Thomas married d. of —— Holland.' Vide *Collins' Peerage*, ' Bristol.'

E

His story is an illustration how in those days families were split up by the fatal sword of heresy and schism. His grandfather was Sir James, who, through his wife, had come into the rich domain of the old church lands of Appuldurcombe in the Isle of Wight. Sir James had two sons, Richard, the favourite of Henry VIII., and John, the father of Leonora Hervey's husband. From him are descended the present Earls of Yarborough. Richard's wife, after his death, married Sir Francis Walsingham, and when Sir Richard's children were on the same day blown to pieces by gunpowder in the gatehouse of their princely mansion, Sir Francis seems to have seized the property spite the protests of their Uncle John. Strangely enough, he seems also to have got possession of John's son, Thomas Worsley, the heir to the property, and to have brought him up. How his brother John managed to preserve his faith, or when he regained it, we do not know. Another Worsley,[6] some time before this, had gone to Spain with Philip II., and had married at his Court a Spanish lady of noble blood, though poor. His two daughters joined the Spanish Teresians at Antwerp, in the old convent founded by Mother Anne of Bartholomew, the companion of St. Teresa, which yet remains in the hands of her children. The name of the eldest of these two, Sister Anne of the Ascension, is held dear by English Carmelites as the first of a long and glorious list. John Worsley had five children: William, born at Antwerp, whose godfather was Sir William Stanley; Thomas and John, born at Louvain; and Andrew and Margaret born at Antwerp.

Thomas entered the Mechlin Novitiate nearly two years before John Berchmans, and so could have spent but a short time with him. In 1632 he was made Rector

---

[6] Perhaps one of the Worsleys of Birkenhead—like all the other branches, descended from the Worsleys of Worsley, near Manchester.

of the College at St. Omers, and at the term of his office went on the English mission, in the middle of Charles I.'s reign. He bore his mother's maiden name as an alias, and under that name of Hervey, was accused by an informer of having plotted with him the firing of London. His great work was among the numbers of poor wretches that used to lie in Newgate under sentence of death, and he is said to have made as many as sixty converts to the faith every year. The magistrates, furious at his success, would have wished to have seized him and had him whipped at the cart's tail from Newgate to Tyburn. He continued, however, a long time to evade their watch. Once, however, he was imprisoned in Newgate, and while there we find him signing the declaration of the Franciscan martyr, Father Heath, as he went to the gallows. Through the interest of the Spanish Ambassador he was released. Perhaps he had not been recognized as the apostle of the condemned. Perhaps he only took to the apostolate after his release. He contrived to be one of the many Fathers who assisted the martyr, Father Wright. The execution took place in the third year of the Commonwealth, and Father Thomas Worsley mounted on the top of a covered cart, so as to be able to be near the martyr, and give him the last blessing. He had the additional consolation of receiving into the Church a gentleman, whose wife was converted by the sight of Father Wright's heroism. When broken with old age, Father Worsley returned to Belgium, and was the confessor and spiritual director to the English College of the Society of Jesus at Liége. He had the happiness of receiving, by delegation from his provincial, Father John Clarke, the solemn vows of Sir John Warner, known in religion as Father Clare; and he assisted, by command of the Bishop of St. Omers, and in his place, at Lady Warner's profession as a Poor

E 2

Clare at Gravelines. We are tempted to make an extract from the Life of that pious woman.

In an hour of grievous spiritual tribulation, 'being able to receive no assistance on earth, because Father Thomas Worsley (the only person from whom she used to receive comfort, or at least direction how to bear her afflictions) was absent at Watten,[7] she, kneeling down in her cell in this desolate condition, chanced in a chink of the wall to perceive a little paper rolled up sticking between the bricks (their cells being then only separated with bricks, without any plastering), which she taking out and unfolding, found these words written in it; "Be at rest, and afflict yourself no more; all is well between God and you." This filled her sad heart with joy, she looking upon it as a seal from heaven, because she had never before received any such paper from Father Worsley, whose hand she found it to be; and when she showed it him, he owned it was so, though he never remembered to have writ it, and doubted not but that God (for a reward of her fidelity) had permitted her good angel this way to play the part of a comforter in his absence, hereby to increase her confidence in His all-powerful assistance, even in the greatest desolation.' Father Worsley found great consolation in his last sickness in being near to the relics of Father Wright, which had been brought over to Liége and laid in the chapel of the College infirmary. He died at the advanced age of seventy-four, February 8, 1671.

We are singularly rich in notes written by Berchmans when we consider the shortness of his religious life, and how young he was at the time of his death; and they reveal, better than other words can do, the hidden thoughts that struck him either in time of prayer, or during the course of a day given up, as it is during

<hr>

[7] The Novitiate of the English Province of the Society.

the Jesuit novitiate, almost exclusively to religious duties. These have been all published under the title of *Spicilegium* **Asceticum** *Beati Joannis Berchmans*, by his indefatigable client, Father Vanderspeeten.

We have his *Monita Generalia*—‘ General Instructions,’ containing the minutest details of what may be called the outer life of a novice. One can trace in them, amid much that is common to all the Houses of Probation in the Society of Jesus, many allusions to national habits which make them very interesting. The peasant youth of a Flemish farm, judged by St. Francis Xavier the best rough material for a missioner to Japan, was to learn in religion not only spiritual wisdom, but good breeding, and manners fitted for the confessor of Courts and the companionship of men of the first families of Europe. Most of these John probably noted down carefully, according to his resolution, as they fell from the lips of his novice masters. Berchmans’ special office—of which we shall speak hereafter—made him the official means of communicating the Superior’s wishes to his brothers in religion ; and accordingly these regulations have numerous additions in Father Bauter’s own handwriting.

Then follow a number of spiritual notes, including an order of the day which he wrote in Belgium, and another when at the Roman College: ‘The Good Scholastic of the Society of Jesus,’ the model of what a young religious who is engaged in study ought to be, an unintended but life-like sketch of his own perfection ; a scheme of a little ‘ academia ’ of our Blessed Lady he used to hold in holiday time at Rome ; with other devotions in her honour. All these are kept, in copy, at the Brussels Library. In the Jesuit College of Louvain there is the original manuscript of a collection made by John of pious stories about our Blessed Lady and the Blessed Sacrament, which he made use of to flavour, as we shall see, the daily hours of recreation, and others about persons and things of the Society, which he had met with in books, or heard in conversation. They are not written for cold critics, but are the expressions of a love which must needs be shared by those who read, if they are to pass a fair judgment on them. We shall return to these again in another portion of this work. The rest of the volume, all of which has its intrinsic value as a relic of the saint, is occupied with an analysis of Father Rodriguez's well known treatise on Religious Perfection. Its great interest lies in the proof it affords us of John's diligence, for he used to note down whatever he heard read in the refectory, where, as is the custom in all religious houses, the mind, as St. Ignatius has it, gets its food as well as the body. The work in question had then only lately been published—in 1614, at Seville—and was being read at table during Berchman's stay at the Roman College. No doubt its novelty and the fewness of the copies then to be had was an additional reason for his undertaking the task. He used to write it as soon as he had said his beads in the tribune of St. Ignatius, which he did at the close of afternoon recreation. These pages have the simple and familiar heading, *Ex Patre Alphonso*—' From Father Alphonsus ;' a testimony, if one was wanting to the high esteem in which the author was held ; for he had been dead for some few years, and his Christian name was surely no uncommon one among an order in which Spaniards and Italians chiefly prevailed. Three or four of his former companions at the Roman College speak in terms of great admiration of this work, and it deserves it. The ink is beginning to corrode the paper, and the writing is not of the best ; but so faithfully does it follow the text, that a reference to the work itself fills up any lacuna in the analysis. Another manuscript contains the Meditations and Examens of

Conscience used by John Berchmans in his noviceship. They are no doubt the work of the novice master, who used each evening, either to propose by word of mouth the subject for the mental prayer of the following day, or make the 'porter' distribute written copies to the novices. One of Berchmans' orders was not to allow them to be taken away for private use.[8]

So much diligence soon bore very evident fruit, and the novices who had been the longest in the house could not but feel that in his very first month he had made more way than they had in twenty-four. He went through his duties so naturally, yet with such fervour that all his companions looked on him as sent by God to be a model son of the Society. He was regarded as something angelic, and one of them said one day, pointing to the new comer, 'Just at the very time when our Lady began to work miracles at Montaigu, she wrought a still more extraordinary wonder at Diest, by making an angel come down in the flesh.' We constantly meet similar expressions in the many witnesses summoned after John's death, to speak to his virtues. Those who had known him in the world, his fellow novices, the few strangers who caught a glimpse of him in religion, all give him the name of 'Angel' as just expressing that supernatural beauty which shone in his face, and that marvellous holiness of which it was the outcoming. His unchanging good nature and cheerfulness gained him the additional title of St. Hilarius, or St. Lætus. 'The mere sight of him,' says one witness, 'used to give a sort of spiritual gladness to one who,

---

[8] It is remarkable that in the sixty-eighth meditation, On the Blessed Sacrament, there is given as a composition of place, ' Consider Christ our Lord as if He were appearing visibly with His Angels, and offering *His Heart* to each one as a sign of His love.' This must have been written at least twenty years before the birth of Blessed Margaret Mary

either naturally, or owing to any circumstance, was sad and gloomy.' 'His looks were enough to recreate me when I was a postulant,' says a Father Matthias. Another tells us he heard a new comer ask who was that modest humble angel, so full of kindness. Father **Hossche** speaks of his ever present smile and the attraction his sweetness of manner exercised on all. 'I lived two years with him in the Novitiate. Well, I am ready to declare on oath I never noticed in him the smallest movement of impatience or anger.'

With all this gaiety, there was no shirking the severity with which all the saints have treated themselves—'A mother to others, a judge to myself.' Obedience was the only limit to his self-inflicted humiliations and penances. His Superiors, indeed, gave him little latitude. At his age it was no small cross to follow with such minute fidelity as he did, the routine of community life. 'My penance, above all others, is common life. May I die rather than violate deliberately the smallest order or rule; I would rather lose my health altogether than not keep a rule in order to preserve it,' or, as he puts it still more emphatically, 'Rather die than, for health's sake, break a single rule.' But his desire to follow still closer to his crucified Lord made him importunate for more, and his director found it impossible to refuse him, what seems to our self-indulgent notions, far beyond the endurance of his delicate frame. Father Frizon tells us that in his time there was kept at the Novitiate of Mechlin part of a rough and prickly hair-shirt, which he usually wore, and cloths with which he had staunched the blood his scourgings made to flow. During the keen frosts of a Flemish winter, he hardly ever went near a fire, though his hands and ears were cruelly chapped by the cold.

He ambitioned and obtained the office St. Aloysius

had loved, of trimming the lamps for the use of the house, no pleasant task in so numerous a community; but he did it with all the care and pains that one would have given to the most important duties. Father Nicolas Gregorii tells us—'I remember a few days after entering the Society, I had the happiness of helping him in that office. The saint was on his knees, when, on a sudden, with his eyes lifted up to heaven, he said to me, "O brother! would that we could do this humble work in public, for the greater glory of God."' With a holy consistency, or rather, because he knew the all-importance of the great central virtue of humility, he sought humiliations in every detail of his life. He loved its livery; and gladly wore the oldest, most worn out clothes, and asked for them when not given to him. He sought with avidity reproofs and corrections, and gladly accepted them from whatever source they came. Not content with the usual admonitor charged to correct any faults that might be remarked in him, he asked to have at least four fellow novices to watch and reprove him. It fell out one day that Berchmans, in the midst of an employment that completely engrossed his mind, forgot some duty or other, and one of his mentors at once reproved him for it. Though the omission bore its own excuse, and the censor could not but feel that there was really no fault, the correction was received as a most welcome gift. Berchmans looked upon its donor as his best friend, and promised to say for him the chaplet three times, and to pay the same price for every future reproof. The novice valued the prayers of his holy brother so highly that he set to work with a new zeal to win a new reward; but he was forced to own that he never again got the chance. Father Bauters confirms what otherwise would seem too strange to be true. 'After repeated requests on the part of this excellent young man to have his faults publicly made known, as is the custom in the noviceship, I could not any longer refuse him this satisfaction ; so I told all the novices, then more than one hundred in number, to jot down and give me in writing any defects they had noticed in Berchmans' conduct. I got these notes, and on opening them, found that not one had been able to observe the smallest defect in him. This seemed to be a thing unheard of among so large a body of young men whose exceedingly delicate consciences—to say nothing of a very praiseworthy rivalry and a vivacity suiting their years—were well fitted to spy out the very least faults in any of their companions, especially, too, when he was the mark of more than ordinary proofs of respect and esteem. The result of this meeting caused much greater confusion to our humble novice than if he had been convicted of the gravest faults. We could not help pitying the sorrow which crushed him, and we tried to console him as though he had fallen into some terrible disgrace. All present, in one word, were delighted and edified by his innocence and humility.'

The Fathers who lived in the same house were so struck by Berchmans' holiness, that some of the oldest and most respected among them used to notice him with great care, and were delighted to see that there were no virtues a novice could practise in which he did not excel in a very high degree.

The first year of John's noviceship was not ended, when Father Sucquet, his first novice master, made him ' porter,' an office which, as has been noticed, invested him with a species of authority over his brothers in religion. Its chief duties were to see to the observance of the various regulations, to ring the bell for the different duties, and to announce the order of the day as fixed by the Superior. He had the command of all the novices, and was assisted in his duties by two of them, one of whom was John de Buijre. He enjoyed also the privilege of a room to himself, where the meditation papers were stored. He was guest master, too, and as such received any strangers who visited the Novitiate.

His post, though one of confidence and honour, like worldly dignities, had its thorns. One can easily imagine that among so many, most of whom are fresh from the world, unaccustomed to the details of religious life, and still less to the self-command it teaches, there would often occur trials which would put to a severe test all the patience of one who, after all, was but a novice himself. But such was his lowliness and meekness of heart, so delicate and unselfish his forethought and attention to others' wants, that he only grew more and more in the affection and esteem of all. He was fully persuaded that he had only been lifted up in order that his faults might be the better detected, by having all eyes turned upon them, and that his want of virtue might be a means to exercise that of others. He looked on himself as the scapegoat for their faults, and if ever his novice master bade him in his name to give a penance to one of his brothers, he would throw himself on his knees at his Superior's feet, and beg to be allowed to do the penance himself. If he got his request, God alone knew of the sacrifice; if it was refused, he executed his painful commission with such kindness and tact that no one ever felt hurt by the infliction.

He never allowed his feelings to prevent his fulfilling his distasteful duty of reporting a fault, if he thought it necessary to do so. But lest he should be too hasty, he always first sought counsel of our Blessed Lord in the tabernacle, praying for a long time before Him, as was his wont in all difficulties that might occur. If he still deemed it his duty, he laid the case frankly and openly before the Superior; but then, with all the earnestness of his soul, he conjured the Father to let him bear whatever punishment might be adjudged.   One day some of the novices who were gathered round Berchmans' door had got into hot dispute.   What it was about we are not told; but to tyros in self-restraint, difference of age, and education, and country, and of social rank, not to speak of the ordinary sources of human frailty, give plenty of occasion in the intimate intercourse of daily life for trials to the temper, and it requires more than a few months to be able thoroughly to subdue the risings of nature.   The good porter tried his best to calm the storm.   But in vain; his advice was drowned in the clamour of angry words.   In an instant he threw himself on his knees in their midst, and with a touching voice, he said, 'If I am in fault, forgive me, but I beg you, do not let there be a dispute among brothers.'   Peace was made at once, and Berchmans, delighted at so speedy and happy an ending, promised to take the discipline that night for their intention, and we may be sure he was not alone in his self-inflicted penance.   Can we be surprised that before such charity all bowed respectfully, and though there were many his seniors in age and in religion, and one or more already in priest's orders, they cheerfully awarded him the highest place, as, without compare, he was the highest in sanctity? For long years in that house his name was as a proverb and when they wished to praise a ' porter,' he was called a second Berchmans.

The Superior himself often proposed him as a model to his companions, and used to say he felt unworthy to have the charge of one so upright and perfect.

The secrets of that soul were all open before him, all its efforts, all its difficulties, all its successes; and though his director was dazzled with the sight of its marvellous beauty, he took care not to let John know the profound veneration he had for him, but rather tried to hide it from himself. He encouraged in every way the ardent desire he had to lower himself in the eyes of God and man, and to learn more and more the lesson of interior and profound humility by the knowledge of his own nothingness. It was this virtue, which John practised so perfectly, that prepared his soul for that close union with God, the cause of all his perfection. Few minutes in the day were allowed to pass without his thoughts going naturally to Him Who was their centre ; every action was for His Blessed Lord. We learn his plan from his order of the day. Once every hour he recollected himself, saying, *Ave crux, spes unica !* then a 'Hail Mary,' and ' O good Jesus, Thou wast scourged for my sake, what have I done for Thee in return for such great sufferings.' Then he considered whether his actions had been done with a pure intention, and how he stood with the subject of his particular examen. ' Pardon me, O Lord, and aid me to keep the coming hour in a better manner.' And then he made resolves to amend whatever he thought to have been faulty. When in his room, which he shared with other novices, he never omitted this practice. If any one happened to be engaged with him when the clock struck, he begged to be excused for awhile, and without affectation or human respect, knelt down at his *priedieu* for the space of a *Miserere*, and then resumed, with a smile, the conversation.

As we have seen, his visits to the Blessed Sacrament were very frequent ; every day at least seven times he went before the tabernacle, and when his duties made him tear himself away, he prayed the Blessed Aloysius and St. Stanislaus to take his place, and keep up a perpetual adoration of his Lord and love. It was to

John the Society owes the pious custom which prevails in many of its houses, of going to make a last visit just before retiring to rest. He noticed one day that thirty of the novices had followed his example in this holy practice; he could not help expressing his delight to one of them. 'O brother, what joy I feel at seeing the hidden God of our altars so honoured.' He used to say that he had remarked that the modern saints were remarkable for two things, great devotion to the Blessed Sacrament and to our Blessed Lady.

Holy Communion was the crown of his happiness; his daily life was one long preparation, and on the eve it often happened that, unable to contain his feelings, he exclaimed, 'Brothers, to-morrow, to-morrow, we shall go to the wedding feast of the Lamb;' and then went on to speak with such enthusiasm that the coldest hearts grew warm before the fire of his words. We may easily guess how close must have been his union in prayer with God. Whether in church or in his own room, the moment he began to pray his whole exterior spoke of recollection and reverence; his eyes were slightly closed, or gazing upward fixedly towards heaven, his hands were joined on his breast; he remained motionless on his knees, never moving except when overcome with weakness he stood up for a brief space. The smile which played habitually about his lips became specially bright, and his whole face was often lit up by a glow which told of the secret fire that was burning in his heart. His companions used to seek to be near him, as if to catch some of his fervour. He, on his part, thought his prayers little worth except when joined to those of the community, and for that reason he never would ask to rise at a later hour, though both his delicate health seemed to require it, and it would have needed but a word to his Superior to obtain the necessary permission. 'I prefer,' he would say, 'to lie down again, if necessary, after meditation, rather than lose the benefit of praying with others.' This conviction led no doubt, to a triple convention entered into between John and two other Flemish novices, Josse (Jodocus) van Suercq[9] and John vander Vloet. They bound themselves to ask each day at holy Mass for one another three graces—the constant prayers at all times of our saint—an angelic purity, faithful constancy to their vocation, and grace to become fit instruments for the work of the Society. They were, besides, to offer up the first communion of every month for these intentions. When one of them died, the survivors were to say twelve Masses for his soul, or if they were not then priests, twelve rosaries. The departed, on his side, was, as soon as he should be admitted into the presence of God, to obtain for those he had left on earth, the triple grace which they had so often asked for in common. And certainly, as regards himself, this prayer was most fully heard. Of his love of the angelic virtue and its perfection in him much has already been said. But all his freedom from assaults did not dispense him from guarding with the most jealous care the exquisite but delicate beauty of the heavenly lily. He kept the strictest watch over his senses. Brother Jenin, a lay-brother, an old soldier and son of a captain in the Spanish service, deposed that one of the scholastic novices, Giles de la Rue, never would read the Life of Blessed Aloysius, because, as he said, he had it always before him. In fact, the Marquis of Castiglione seemed born again, as they often used to remark, in the shoemaker's son of Diest. His eyes were ever cast down, save when he raised them slightly on beginning a conversation. But there was no constraint in this, either for himself or for others, and he assured Brother William

---

[9] *Vide* p. 46.

Stanihurst that it cost him more to raise his eyes than to keep them lowered.

There were rare occasions when even his meekness seemed to give way in favour of the claims of this his favourite virtue. They were, however, very rare in an atmosphere so free from all that could shock the conscience or offend the most delicate ears. Once in recreation, however, John happened to be in a circle when the conversation turned on the history of their respective calls to religion. One of them was narrating how he had been forced to give up an engagement which he had ardently desired, and which was on the point of being finally concluded. Berchmans broke in upon his story in a way most unusual for him. 'Have done, brother, with these particulars; they are quite right, I am willing to believe, but surely they are little in harmony with the sort of life we have embraced.' Perhaps he had read in his favourite, St. Bernard, that certain styles of conversation are blasphemies in the mouth of a religious. However strict he was on these points with others, we might be tempted to think he carried his strictness to an excess with regard to himself. Careful to a nicety in all that the most perfect modesty requires, he was, as was said of him, a living transcript of St Ignatius' celebrated rules. At night he assigned to his guardian angel and to his patron saints their places around his bed—a practice which is so well known by the old nursery rhyme in many an English home where otherwise the love and invocation of the saints is utterly gone by. At his head he planted his crucifix as his standard, to sleep in peace under its folds, and to be able as soon as he awoke to press the sacred image to his lips. He lay the whole night with his arms crossed upon his breast, and neither in the heat of summer or the cold of winter did he change his position. True, he once owned that he knew not what sleeplessness meant, for he laughingly told his fellow novices, he never heard the clock strike nine, though he could only get into bed some few moments before that hour. As he undressed, he remembered our Blessed Lord stripped of His clothes before the crucifixion. His bed reminded him of his last resting-place ; and so with many a devout prayer he lay down, and, with his mind engaged in thoughts in harmony with the subject of his next day's meditation, fell tranquilly asleep. John was so well aware of that axiom in spiritual writers, that purity can hardly be preserved unless we mortify ourselves even in lawful indulgences, that he seems to have carried it out with too severe a rigour. Spite of the watchfulness of his Superior, his extreme abstemiousness passed constantly into a real fast which taxed severely his young and delicate frame. His searching self-examination never discovered to him any fault of sensuality in eating or drinking. In fact so mortified was he that he never gave his meals a thought till the bell summoned him to the refectory, which he entered with a look so recollected, and said his grace with such devotion that it was evident his thoughts were elsewhere. When he was seated, before unfolding his napkin or touching anything, he remained for the space of an Our Father renewing his intention and offering his repast to God ; then he divided his food, giving the best share to Christ, Whom he imagined as at table with him, leaving the daintiest morsel for his Lord ; and as soon as a fresh course came round he put aside the unfinished plate. Brother Jenin, however, records that one day he happened to be seated next him, and he tells us—' I noticed he kept on eating to the end, and because of the idea I had that he was thoroughly devoted to mortification, I was astonished ; and though I was arguing with myself that he did it through obedience,

F

I resolved to know the truth, and in fact I asked him. He told me that formerly he used to mortify himself by leaving a good deal of what was given him ; but that Father Provincial had ordered him to eat all that was put before him, and so to obey him he kept on eating quietly till the end ; and then, if he had eaten everything he had done what he was told, if he had not, he stopped, and the second obedience delivered him from the first.'

He had a saying that with practice and in time man could acquire temperance by degrees. Accordingly, with a view of leaving the morning freer for his spiritual duties he began gradually to diminish his breakfast, till at last he could go without it altogether. He suffered for some time from an inclination to sleep, but he got the better of it by biting his lips till they bled, and pinching his arms till they were black and blue. And he taught this severe remedy to those who complained of the same drowsiness. In a word, he knew that other maxim of perfection, that there is no chance of self-deceit when we choose what is most counter to our tastes and likings.[10]

His tender love of our Blessed Lady was at once a cause and an effect of his marvellous purity, and, deep as it always had been, it naturally grew in a religious order which glories in being all for Jesus through Mary. For love of her he had vowed his virginity to God ; for love of her he thirsted for a more irrevocable offering, and when his first year's noviceship was over he earnestly begged and obtained the happy privilege of making the three vows of devotion. Every day he recited the

[10] There was a case of conscience started among the novices whether if one had permission to take the discipline twice a week, and had got special leave for an extra penance, he were bound in conscience to give up one of those ordinarily permitted. Berchmans, with a smile, settled the case, no very difficult one, in favour of austerity, on the ground that no privilege can deprive one of an acquired right, but rather protects and augments it.

psalter called St. Bonaventure's, the rosary, and the act of consecration used by the sodalists of the various congregations of Mary; not to speak of other prayers and frequent aspirations in her honour. He kept up his old practice of fasting on Saturdays and the eves of her feasts. He sought every means to spread devotion to her, and constantly spoke in recreation of her dignity and goodness. A conversation without something in her honour seemed to him stale and insipid. His office as porter enabled him to spread the pious practice of talking about his Queen and Mother amongst all the novices. He had to arrange the 'companies' into which they divided at time of recreation. Having found some of his brothers to whom he had communicated his zeal for her glory, he got them all to agree never to let a recreation pass without some words about our Lady. Then he took care to place one of this band in each of the little circles, who might be as good seed cast on good soil and bringing forth fruit of increased devotion to Mary in good season. John felt he never could repay his debt to Mary, for as he told Father Bauters, to her he owed his education, his success in his studies, and his thrice blessed vocation; it was through her he hoped to win his salvation, of which without her he would, so to speak, despair.

After love of Mary was his love to her spotless spouse. The devotion to St. Joseph was but little known at that time, but as John used to say, 'What God has joined together, let no man put asunder.' Josse van Suerck, one of the three confederates alluded to above, tells us, 'Once when we were walking together, he began to talk to me about the prerogatives of the foster-father of Jesus. At his request I agreed to spread among the rest as much as possible the devotion to so great a saint. We bound ourselves in particular to speak of his dignity

F 2

whenever we had the chance, and never, if possible, to say the Litany of our Lady without adding at its close the collect of St. Joseph.'   Our saint must feel a special joy at seeing his pious practice become the universal custom of the Society, that prayer being said at the end of the litanies which are recited every day in its communities.

It was natural that John should be drawn to the great panegyrist of our Lady, and that St. Bernard, who spread so wide her devotion, should have a special place in the heart of one who was full of desire to do the same.   It needed only to mention his name to transport his young imitator.   One day he was sent on a walk to the Cistercian Abbey of St. Bernard near Berchem on the Scheldt.[11] So anxious was he to reach a spot sacred to his beloved saint, that his companions found it impossible to keep up with his rapid pace.

The second subject of the united prayer, was perseverance in the Society of Jesus.   We have already seen plenty of the traces of his love for the order to which God had deigned to call him, and it grew as he came to know it better.   He had but one fear, to lose the great grace bestowed upon him.   No doubt the failure of some vocations stimulated his zeal, and, as his letters prove, he prayed and asked others to pray that no such a misfortune should ever happen to himself.   External difficulties had not been altogether removed by his entry into religion.   His father, who had only consented to that step on account of his avowed hope that a few months would bring a change of purpose, returned again to the charge, and endeavoured to persuade him to

---

[11] This vast abbey had been burned down in 1582 during the religious wars.   The Bishop of Antwerp, who had been made commendatory abbot, began to rebuild it in 1611, and brought thirteen monks to re-open it.   Like so many other religious houses, what remains of this sacred monastery now serves for a Government prison.

complete his studies at Louvain University. 'Thus,' he urged, 'you may both render your name famous **and** add to your brothers' means.' Good Charles Berchmans could have little understood his son's mind. 'No, no, father,' **he answered;** '**there is** something else **to do** besides heaping up riches, of which no one can guarantee the possession. **If you** really have at heart the prosperity of your family and the well being of your children, it is in the service of Jesus Christ you must seek these favours.'

And so strongly did he put forth the high thoughts which filled his soul, that he not only convinced his father, but made him seriously think, **in** view of the death of his wife, of seeking admission into an order capable of calling forth such affection in its subjects. Though **God** willed it otherwise, we shall **see the** precious words bore their fruit. We may be sure **that** Berchman's love of the Society found its special **expression** in a great devotion to those firstfruits of the order who had already been ennobled by the solemn decree of Beatification, the Patriarch and Father Blessed Ignatius, the Apostle of the Indies, and the two angel-saints Blessed Aloysius and Stanislaus. To honour them, he, who **was** one day to share their honours, invented **a special** devotion, which he named the 'Rosary of **our Beati.**' It consisted of a prayer—'Blessed Ignatius, pray for us sinners now and at the hour of our death. Amen'—to be repeated **a** certain number of times, and then in succession the same **formula** addressed to Blessed Francis Xavier, Aloysius, **and** Stanislaus.

The third object of the united prayer was to become a fit instrument for the work of the Society. One of the attractions **which he had felt** before entering had been the vast good that it was then doing for God's Church—one of its wings battling in India and the far off Japan, and pushing forward steadily into China, the other fighting to the death in Peru, Florida, Brazil, and Canada, while its centre, from Madagascar and Abyssinia in the south to Sweden in the north, was in hand to hand combat with the enemies of God's Church, and in the van of her defenders. Father Ogilby had shed his blood in 1615 on the scaffold at Glasgow, and the memory of those who had fallen in England, France, and the low countries, were household names to John. He had been but a few months in the Novitiate when a circular letter from the new General, Father Mutius Vitelleschi, arrived, and was read in public. It was his opening address, and at its close occurred the following passage— ' I recommend to the prayers of all, the flourishing state of Japan and the Indies, conjuring the Lord to light up in the souls of many members of the Society the most burning desires to go thither, that they may water with their sweat, and even with their very blood, that thirsting waste.' The flame was already burning in the heart of our saint, and the thought that he might yet be an apostle, and even a martyr, filled him with joy, and brought tears of consolation to his eyes. China seemed especially to captivate his mind — he longed to hear news from that mighty empire, and loved to retail it to his companions. Brother John Baptist Callant, who died in 1625, a martyr of charity at Antwerp, tells us that his sainted fellow novice actually asked his Superior to be sent on that mission. His good sense and spiritual knowledge saved him from the not uncommon error of forgetting the present in the fancied achievements of the future. He knew if he was to do anything hereafter for God it could only be by using well the time of preparation, and laying that deep foundation on which alone could be built up a virtue able to hold up against the temptations, the difficulties, and dangerous distractions of missionary life. At the same time he never let slip any opportunity which occurred for exercising zeal for souls, or for preparing himself more directly for his wished for career. He gave the greatest attention to the acquisition of French, and took every pains to see that the regulation which in the Flemish Novitiate ordered the use of that language, should be thoroughly carried out. He did not know a word of it on his entry, but such was his application that he was able after some time both to write and preach in French with success. Unfortunately none of these his first essays in the pulpit have been preserved. Father Cepari relates that one day his theme was the virtues of Blessed Aloysius, and he spoke with such feeling and fervour that his Superior noticing how moved he was, had fears lest he should injure his health by his exertions.

The very time of relaxation, the hour of recreation ordered by the Institute after dinner and after supper, was turned into a time of spiritual profit. To a heart so full of God, so opposed to the world, so empty of himself, to speak of spiritual things was no difficulty, but a simple delight; and so attractive was his conversation, that all sought and enjoyed it. His resolution, as we find it written by him under the heading, 'Recreation,' was '(1) pure intention, (2) resolve to speak on pious subjects in the presence of God.' And this, faithfully carried out, made him confess that—'For my part, the after dinner recreation gives me strength for the rest of the day; and the evening recreation is a capital preparation for the meditation and communion on the morrow.' We see clearly in this the teaching of his novice master, Father Sucquet. It is recorded of him—'He had one joy, to think of God, to speak of God; besides God, he had no joy whatever. Would you please him, did you wish him to like you? You

must talk about God. Did you wish to displease him?
Throw in jokes on worldly matters. God alone was
in his heart, on his lips and pen. He knew nothing
else. You would not have thought him himself when
God was named. He could not talk about other matters.'
His well-known *Via Vitæ Æternæ*, with its quaint illus-
trations, confirms all this. If any subject was brought
forward more or less wide of his mark, John tried
skilfully to bring the conversation back to his favourite
topic ; and if the presence of a priest or of a Superior
prevented his intervention, he remained perfectly silent,
as though he were deaf to all besides God. During
his novitiate, he never spoke in recreation of the lights
he received in prayer, because he noticed that if he
did so, all the fruit of his meditation seemed to dis-
appear. Perhaps God wished to hide from notice His
great gifts, to keep the holy novice in profound humility.
Certain it is that after taking his vows this reserve
ceased, and the way in which he revealed the secrets
of his heart has afforded us many a marvellous lesson,
as it ever served in his lifetime to be a source of good
to all who had the happiness to talk with him. There
had been some proposal, in one of the general meetings
of the Society, both on account of some abuses which
had crept in, and in order to give more time for religious
exercises, to shorten the recreation, and to devote the
time so gained partly to narration of incidents from the
lives of saints, and partly to prayer and recitation of
the rosary in private. The proposal was overruled, and
the ancient custom reasserted. ' How well,' said he, ' the
Fathers of the Congregation were counselled to oppose
that partial suppression of time allowed for conversation !
They acted, I am sure, on an inspiration from God.'

He had another field for his youthful zeal outside the
walls of the religious house. Every Sunday and holiday,

accompanied by a lay-brother, he went round the villages near Mechlin to teach the catechism to the country people. Such was his success, that the peasants would rather listen to him than to a practised preacher. The children followed him in crowds as he left the church, and often accompanied him back to the door of the Novitiate, where he distributed among them some little objects of piety, and sent them home rejoicing. He did not confine his efforts and his zeal to those who came to hear, but would go into the cottages, consoling the poor and afflicted, and inducing them to attend the catechism in the church. It seems, from Father Frizon, that the novices used to give, besides these instructions, missions on a small scale to these simple-hearted people.

It chanced one day, that walking home with a number of the children, John gave to each of them a rosary, and taught them how to say their beads in honour of our Lady. A few hours afterwards he had to pass by the same road, and along the way he noticed his little scholars diligently engaged in the practice of their new devotion, kneeling in the open air, half concealed by the bushes and underwood. Even in his ordinary walks, if he saw a child in the fields, he would go with his companions, and begin to talk to it about *le bon Dieu* and His holy Mother, and then try to explain to it some mystery of our holy faith. And if, as we may be sure often happened, the poor child, alarmed at the black-robed strangers, took to flight, he would follow it to where it sought the protection of its mother's apron, and gain a double fruit, for he not only would make friends with the little fugitive, but would leave the memory of his holy and well-timed words as a blessing to its poor parents.

Brother Jenin has left us an anecdote which shows how well John knew how to temper his zeal with equal prudence. 'When he had finished his instruction, he only heard part of the Mass which was being said, telling me once that he would willingly have heard it all, but he was frightened of scandalizing the peasants, because those who used to give the catechism before him used to do the same, and had he done otherwise, people would have thought the others had not heard Mass elsewhere, and would have thus taken occasion to judge them rashly, and be scandalized.'

His charity towards his brothers in religion was of a still deeper character. He felt for all their troubles, and sympathized with their misfortunes. The troubled looks of one of them told him plainly that there was something seriously wrong, and gaining his confidence, he learned that a violent temptation to leave the Noviceship had nearly mastered him. Seeing that soothing words were vain to one in so excited a state, he threw himself at his feet, and with tears in his eyes, conjured him not to act hastily, and at least to put off his design. The poor novice could not refuse to promise to wait a few days longer. John made good use of the delay, and by his own prayers and those of others, obtained from our Lady the grace of a complete victory for the young man, who remained steadfast in his vocation.

Another time, one of his brethren died just as the community were going to bed. Berchmans reproached himself with not having prayed sufficiently for him during his lifetime, and extorted from the novice master leave to say three chaplets for him that very night.

He was always at the service of the others. 'You must not spare the little ass,' he would say; 'it is good to shake him up from time to time.' Save when there was question of rule, he was always most ready to do whatever he was asked. He was sent once on his favourite pilgrimage to Montaigu. His Superior had given him permission to go on to Diest to visit his friends, but John declined, and stated his reasons in such a way, that he was told to do as he thought fit. They had not gone far, before his companions, finding that he did not intend to profit by the permission, brought every argument to make him change his mind. 'We omitted nothing,' says his intimate friend, Van Suerck, 'to persuade him, first of all, that it was evidently the intention of the Superior that he should go to see his father, although he had not quite given a positive order to that effect. Again, that such a visit might be for the greater glory of God. He, on his side, gave very good reasons against it; but after a few moments' discussion, which had been sustained with the best intentions on both sides, seeing that we held firm, "Listen," said he, "examine the thing seriously, and tell me what seems best to you in the Lord; I engage to give in to your decision." We made a short prayer to our Lady, and then decided he ought to visit his father. He gave in without another word.'

He knew too well that a perfect obedience was the best preparation for after life, and delighted to hear and read about that virtue, so essential to a Jesuit. The letter written by St. Ignatius, in 1553, to the Fathers and Brothers of Portugal—a perfect treatise on the nature, the degrees of obedience, and the manner of acquiring it—was his special study. 'Nothing is hard to the humble.' And certainly his profound humility rendered its acquisition so easy as to seem natural to him. He thought and acted on the belief that he had been admitted into the Society out of pure compassion, and ever held himself the least and lowest among its members. One of his brothers asked him if he was ever by chance tempted to vanity? 'No,' he replied, 'I do not fear that beast.' As much as to say, 'What can I find to be proud of?' His familiar maxims were—'Obey even in the smallest **things**; obedience **in** these is a preparation for what will **be required** in important affairs hereafter; nothing proves **the** respect we have for our Superiors **so** much **as our** fidelity in executing their orders on the most trivial occasions.'

' If **Blessed** Aloysius and Stanislaus were obedient to the very letter, it **was** not for fear of being guilty of a fault by acting otherwise, but out of pure love of virtue.' This was precisely the spirit of Berchmans' obedience. His **love** of God made him **seek in** all things, both as **to will and** judgment, **to be** perfectly conformed to the first and chiefest rule of every good will and judgment, **the** Eternal Goodness and Wisdom itself. **He** ever saw in his Superiors and in his rule the image **of** Him Whom He so ardently loved, and 'Fear is **not in** charity, but perfect **charity** casteth **out** fear, because fear hath pain.'

He did not **seek,** under the pretence of prudence or common **sense, to** take off the corners of obedience when painful **to flesh** and blood ; but rather preferred to incur **the reproval of** folly than grieve his Lord and Master **by** the least failing in docility to His commands. Such conduct, when consistently carried out, never, **even** to the imperfect, shows like imprudence. The brother **who** distributed the manual **work to the novices, set John** to sweep **out** the strangers' room. The next day, **when** allotting the work, he scolded **him for** having sprinkled too much water **about while sweeping,** and ordered him to fetch up from **the well to the** room—a **very** considerable distance—the **water** he needed, **a** cupful at a time. John owned afterwards, he never had such **joy** as when he was carrying out in all its harshness, the imprudent order.

John never lost sight of the principle of his obedience, and, accordingly, never failed in **its** practice. He **was** sent one day to the door, by his Superior, to see a stranger who had come to call upon him. A second visitor arrived while engaged with the first ; but he begged him to be so good as to wait, till he had gone and asked permission to talk to him. He always acted in the same way, but with such grace, that no one ever thought of being annoyed at it. His very silence, in such cases, had a politeness about it which gave a flavour to his strictness. His plan was, in his own words—' I salute heartily any one I meet ; if they require anything of me, I do it as quickly as possible ; if any one asks me a question, I answer them in a few words, taking care not to say any more than are necessary.' John de Buijre, who was assistant porter, was talking with him about some arrangements to be made. Our saint smiled and said—' Let us be short, or we shall break our rule of silence.' What made it a pleasure to all to meet him, was a pious practice he had of saluting the angel guardians of the passers-by with a modest smile, making way for them, out of respect for their invisible companions.

Not to allow the troubles of the outer world to cloud the bright sky of novice life, all direct account of the family of John has been avoided. Now when the history of the inner world is done, before passing on, the story must be told of the changes that had taken place in his former home. Shortly after the last effort made by his father to shake the resolution of Berchmans, the state of his mother became every day more critical. Her son was informed of her approaching death, and the letter he wrote to her whom he loved so tenderly shows how thoroughly faith had mastered in him all lower views, and how, in the loss of the dearest and the nearest to him on earth, he could see only the entrance of her soul into its reward, and the exchange of a life of sorrow for one of eternal joy.

'My dearest mother in the Lord,—

'The peace of Christ be with you, and with all. I rejoice and am delighted at seeing the great blessing which the unending goodness of God—praise be to Him—has up to this time bestowed on all our household, in, first, calling me, unworthy as I am, to the fellowship of His only Son Jesus here upon this earth, and now also, by inviting you, my dearest mother, to His bridals in heaven. Now, for seven or eight years, you have proved the miseries of human nature, and have tasted, with Christ Jesus, of the chalice of His bitter Passion. See Him now, standing there at your bedside, with outstretched arms ready to embrace you. "Come, My bride, My friend; up to this thou hast been nailed with Me to the Cross, so henceforth you shall rejoice for all eternity." See the holy Mother of God, Mary! See St. Elisabeth! See your holy angel, and cry out with me, "O Lord Jesus! behold here Your poor handmaiden, standing with Your all-holy Mother, Mary, ready for whatever You wish. O Jesus, Son of David, have mercy on me! O Mary, behold my children, whom I with so many tears have nurtured in the fear of God; I offer them up to you to be your sons, your children; be thou, O Mary, their Mother." I, too, pray thee, with all my heart, to adopt me as thy son, and my brothers and my sister. Well, then, ever dear mother, fight bravely. Think of the crown that is being made ready for you. I hope we shall not lose you, but that in heaven you will cherish us with greater love and affection. I pray you with all my heart not to refuse me a mother's blessing. Here we are all praying for you, that God may give you what is best for you. I hope you, in return, will not forget me. Fight bravely, dearest mother.

'Your loving and obedient son,

'JOANNES BERCHMANS.'

On the 1st of December, 1816, after little more than two months of John's novitiate had gone by, his mother passed from her cross to her crown. Another tie to earth was sundered. Of those that yet remained, his father and one of his brothers were to be joined more closely to God. We cannot doubt that the words and the letters of his holy child had great influence upon John Berchmans' father. He bore the loss of his wife with Christian resignation, finding his support in prayer. A short time after, he went to the Jesuit College at Louvain, to seek there in the Exercises of St. Ignatius a decisive answer as to his future life. The Society of Jesus seems to have been his desire. He could not forget his last visit to Mechlin ; and the impression made upon him by his son's affection and esteem for his newly adopted life. But, no doubt, prudent counsel showed him that his young children had the first claims on his care ; and his advanced age was of itself a barrier to admission into religious life. His heart, however, was set on high things, and in a year's time he received the tonsure, on January 24, 1618. On the 9th of March, the same year, he received the four minor orders, and the next day bound himself irrevocably to God by the subdeaconate. Twenty days after he was ordained deacon, and at last, but a few months before his son's first vows, on the 14th of April, the sacred unction flowed upon his hands, and John rejoiced to know his father was at last a priest. His high reputation, and the respect in which his townsmen held him, no doubt merited for him the benefice he received—a canon's stall in St. Sulpice, a church whose name has been so often met with in these pages. His second son, Adrian, received the tonsure shortly after his father, on the 11th of March—a step towards his higher vocation to the Order of St. Augustine.

CHAPTER IV.

The first Vows.

THE death of his mother, the ordination of his father, the vocation of Adrian—all cleared away human obstacles to the completion of Berchmans' sacrifice. Two full years of such a noviceship as he had spent had still more perfectly removed any supernatural hindrance. Bound though he was before God by his vows of devotion, which he had been permitted to take on the 27th of September, 1617, he longed for the day when these promises would be ratified by a public acceptation on the part of the Society he loved so well. We have still the copy of his declaration—four times required of him —that he still adhered, with the full knowledge of what it involved, to his first wish to be admitted into the Society. One more formality was required. The novice master had to ask the advice of his official advisers as to the admission of the young novice to his vows. There was but one answer—one almost of surprise at any doubt being raised. And then the good news was formally announced to the saintly youth. Fortunately the letter has been preserved in which he pours out, without reserve, the delight of his heart into the willing ears of the new canon of St. Sulpice. He knew his father now would share his joy.

'Most honoured father in Christ,—
'Pax Christi.

'Worldly parents, who are filled with a false ambition, are greatly pleased when their children get married to the princes and great ones of this world, and especially when these bring to them a larger fortune than their own. Yet this joy is often empty, and even foolish; would that such parents were not forced now and again to bewail and abhor for all eternity the lot of their children which once had so delighted them! To you, dearest father, this letter of mine offers a far other joy, pure and without dregs. Rejoice, rejoice! here is a cup of gladness, not empty but real. What is it? Thy son, on the 25th of September, so he hopes, will die. Will die? Yes; but he will die to the world—by the death of the just. O sweet death! O death! no death, but sweetest life! May my soul die the death of the just! Where, and by what torture? On the Cross of Jesus, with Jesus, pierced with the three nails of poverty, chastity, and perpetual obedience, he will die with Jesus. Oh, how sweet it is to die in the Society of Jesus, in the arms of Jesus! Rejoice, my worthy father; in this death your son will live, and will live happily. What can be happier, what more delightful, than this life, passed with such a Spouse? Oh, that my soul were clad with a garment of virtues fit for the presence of its Beloved! Oh, that it could spread the rich banquet of its vows for the most Holy Trinity, the Blessed Virgin, and all the angels with a fitting love and dignity! I will try hard on my part to do this during the days on which I am just going to enter. But as it is not within my unaided power, again and again I beg of you to ask the help and protection of the Blessed Virgin—by three Masses of the Holy Ghost at Montaigu; I hope, too,

G

that grandfather and grandmother, my uncles and aunts, and other friends will not let me miss their prayers. For the rest, with all my heart I commend myself to your Reverence's Holy Sacrifices.

'Your Reverence's most humble obedient son in Christ,

'JOHN BERCHMANS.

'*Mechlin. The Novitiate of the Society of Jesus.*
1618, *September* 2.

'Please send me by his reverence the Precentor eleven ells of cloth, six ells of flannels, three ells of linen, two calfskins, to make my clothes.'

In the close of his letter there is an evident allusion to the eight days' retreat, the usual prelude to the vows, and he asks specially for prayers that this last touch which is to be given may add the crowning perfection to his offering to God. He was, however, to have another and a bitterer preparation. His Superior, out of a conviction no doubt of his perfect fitness, did not wish that he should make the retreat. It was a sharp cross, but he saw the hand, the will of God, and the first joys returned to his soul. Not in the privacy which old laws of persecution enforce in England, nor yet with the external pomp and ceremony with which other religious orders vow themselves to God, were the sacred nuptials celebrated ; but simply and in presence of the community gathered together, as on a festival day. The receiving of the first vows of the Society in the Church of Montmartre seems to have been the model of a ceremony, which while solemnly binding to religion, yet did not, as in the other monastic professions, bind the order reciprocally to its new subject. And as the external elements of habit, inclosure, or public choir, were to be wanting to a religious life which was in its outside to differ little from that of the secular clergy, so simplicity rules the rites by which St. Ignatius receives his children into his order. His novice master, to whom John was now bound by so lasting and so affectionate a tie, celebrated the Holy Sacrifice ; and when the moment of Holy Communion was come he turned round with the Blessed Sacrament to John who was kneeling at his feet. With the Sacred Host uplifted before him, our saint read the formula of his vows ; and then his Lord and Master sealed with His Sacred Presence the engagement those lips had so fervently pronounced.

A new life now opened out to the young religious. The two years of recollection and prayer were at an end. He must begin at once the long course of study which was to fit him for the exercise of all that he had learned to desire. Accordingly, but a few days after, he received orders to go to Antwerp to begin there his course of philosophy.

Before leaving, he gave to Father Bauters as a souvenir a little engraving with the inscription—' From the unworthy son of such a Father,' and to Father Sucquet, his old novice master, and present rector, he wrote in Latin the following lines—

' It is a pleasure to me, Father, to be allowed to have recourse to your Reverence as to my heavenly Father, for you hold His place. So, confidently, and spite of my unworthiness, I come to you to beg one only favour with my whole mind and heart, as a son would do from his father—that as my Father, you, who for nearly three whole years have had me under your charge, would be so good as to let me know my faults. For these are what close heaven against me, and put a hindrance to grace. So, Father, as you love my soul, stamped as it is with the image of God, pray tell me them ; as a father

let me know them. I have good reason to ask this one
favour as a last gift **from your** Reverence ; for **if I** go
away without this knowledge, who I pray **can give it me?**
Who is there that knows my faults better than you?
Again, **I** have never acknowledged all the pains **you**
have taken about me, all the favours you have done **me.**
But what **can I do in** return? How can I repay you?
I confess, I **confess,** Father, how exceedingly I **am**
 ndebted to your **Reverence.** I am yours, I am yours
entirely ; I never can be other than entirely devoted to
you. **Pray make use of me as often** as you wish and for
whatever **you** wish. You know my feelings and attachment towards you, and I know yours towards me. And
so, as without fail from the first day **of my** noviceship,
I have to the best of my power ever been mindful of
your Reverence in my poor prayers; so, as long as I live,
whithersoever I go, I will ever cherish your memory
affectionately **and** inviolably.

'Your Reverence's servant in Christ,

'JOHN BERCHMANS.'

Bidding good-bye to his Superiors and companions he
set out on foot with some other scholastics to his new
destination. **Once the house of** the English merchants,
then for more than one hundred and fifty years the
College of the Society, and now the military hospital,
the old building still exists which was for two months
the home of our saint. Time has left **on** one wall of
its inner court the Jesuit escutcheon—I.H.S. On
reaching the College he asked on his knees the blessing
of the rector, Father Clerici (De Clercq), and took the
first opportunity to make to him a full manifestation of
his conscience. Before a week was out, he had 'told
his fault' publicly in the refectory ; the first to **do so**
among the new comers. Anxious to test the virtue of

John by his own experience, the rector fully satisfied the thirst the young religious ever had for reproaches and corrections ; and, as nothing worthy of blame could be found in his subject, he had to pretend to rebuke what was in reality no fault. Berchmans was overjoyed to be under so severe a Superior; but his gratitude and delight was so manifest that the rector could not continue these trials of his virtue, and not only then and there proclaimed his high esteem of our saint, but was the very first to make a formal declaration in his favour when his cause was solemnly begun in 1623 before the ecclesiastical judges at Antwerp. His stay at that College did not last more than a few weeks, but he left so profound an impression of his holiness that three or four years later Father James le Thiry, or, as we best know him, the commentator Tirinus, declared at Rome on oath in 1622, 'that he, then Præpositus [1] of the Professed House of Antwerp, as well as many others, having only known Berchmans during those few days, regarded him as a fervent Jesuit, a perfect servant of God, a real saint.'

It seems certain that for some time John had been aware of the intention of his Superior to send him out of Belgium to pursue his studies. What was his delight when on Thursday the 18th of October he learned from the Provincial, Father Scribani, that Rome was to be his destination ; and that he was to make his philosophical and theological studies in the capital of the Catholic world. He was allowed the delay of a few days, till the following Monday, to bid good-bye to his relatives.

---

[1] Præpositus is the title of the Superior in the regularly constituted Professed Houses of the Society, in distinction to the Colleges, which are governed by a rector. The Professed House and its church, now called St. Charles, are well known to visitors to Antwerp.

In answer to the congratulations he received from his companions, he could not help exclaiming—'Really and truly, I do not know what can have merited for me this favour. When I look round me, and see others so full of talents and piety, qualities entirely wanting to me, I cannot at all understand the preference shown me.'

John wrote at once to his father, informing him of his Superior's determination, and asking him to come over to Mechlin, where he would be on Saturday the 20th. Accordingly, he went there on the day fixed, but a cruel blow awaited him on his arrival. There he met an old companion, Otho Esquens, who was soon to enter the Society, and from him he learned that his father was no more. And what made the news far more bitter was, that more than a week had elapsed since his death, and not a word had been written by any of his relatives to inform him of the sad event. Coming, as it did, on the eve of his departure, burdening him with the responsibility of his orphan brothers and sisters, without the consolation of asking the last blessing of his father, or even of kneeling at his grave, all this would have broken down ordinary virtue. But he had a saint's view of God's doings, a saint's view of death. He looked for it as the ship that was to bear him to port, and the angel who was to lead him to his home. The tailor was taking his measure at Antwerp for a new habit, before his journey to Rome, and he asked John if he was not pleased to get new clothes? 'I should be far better pleased if you were taking the measure of my coffin.' This was from no gloomy weariness of life, for his heart, as his face betokened, was always full of joy. And so, when he learnt this sad news, he lifted his eyes towards heaven, and with a feeling no words can render, exclaimed with St. Francis of Assisi, 'Then I can henceforth really say, "Our Father Who art in Heaven."'

But with all his resignation, the thought of the orphans at Diest came strongly before his mind, and he hastened back to Antwerp to ask the advice of his Superiors. They at once delayed his departure a few days, to give him the opportunity to do all he could for his brothers and sisters. With this object he wrote two letters, one rather reserved and cold to his relatives, the other to Canon Froymont, full of feeling, as to one whom he knew would fully sympathize with his anxieties.

'I.H.S.

'A friendly greeting be this letter to you all—grandfather, grandmother, aunties, uncles, and to all my friends. The reason of my writing is this. I received an order on Thursday last—to wit, the 18th of the month—from my Superiors, that I should get ready immediately to start on the coming Monday. And when I came to Mechlin to recommend myself to my father's prayers, and those of all of you, I learnt that my father died long ago. I was very much astonished and ill-pleased that you had not let me know this. However, I consoled myself with the thought that I have every day of my life fulfilled the office of a good son towards his father; with this difference, that I had prayed for him every day as if he were alive, while in reality he was dead. I pray all of you, my dear friends, with all my heart, that you will take care of my two brothers—to wit, Bartholomew and Charles—that they may be brought up in the fear of God, and in good manners, remembering that so doing you will be very pleasing to Almighty God. I hope that Mary, my sister, and Adrian, my brother, will behave themselves well, and that Adrian, for the years that I shall be at Rome, will give his brothers a good example, and sometimes even good advice. I should wish our guardians to consult the

precentors of Diest and Mechlin to see where these two
children might best be placed. **I** should have come to
see and bid good-bye to you, but as the time is so short,
I am obliged to recommend **myself to** you by this letter,
begging earnestly **of you to recommend** me and **my
journey to** our Lady of Montaigu, that I may complete
it without accident, **and** with good health. You will
learn shortly how it all fared. Will you let all my friends
read the first part of my letter?

'My **dear** aunties, **Mary and** Catharine Berchmans,
and Margaret Berchmans, Catharine van Hove, and
Anne van Olmen, I beg you, by your friendship towards
your nephew, John Berchmans, that each of **you** would
get two Masses said at Montaigu, **to help** me on
my way, that I may accomplish this journey to Rome
with the good of my soul. And have a little care of my
brothers and sisters, and principally of our Charles,
whom I should never like to see taken from his studies,
for I expect great things from him. I hope that our
dear Lord will soon provide for them, and I will do my
best for this ; and in all the holy places in Rome, I trust
I **shall** think of you.

'Yours devotedly,

' JOANNES BERCHMANS.'　

'I.H.S.

'Very Reverend Precentor,—

'On the 23th **of this** month, I was sent by
my Superiors to Mechlin to say good-bye, perhaps for
ever, to my relatives, to the Rev. Father Rector, to my
earthly father, and your Reverence ; and to commend to
you all my journey to Rome. I was to start for that city
on the 23rd, or at latest on the 24th ; my first stage
being from Antwerp **to** Ghent. At Mechlin **I** was

informed that my father had died some days back, and that his funeral had taken place. Though this gave me **no anxiety as far as I am** concerned, I am in no small anxiety about my youngest brothers, Charles and Bartholomew. Still, supported by Divine Providence, which so far has governed our family and myself, and trusting in the goodness of your Reverence and my other friends, I hope they will be thoroughly brought up in virtue and learning, and above all, in the fear of the Lord. I have commended my brothers to their guardians, and I would write also to the precentor of Diest, the greatest friend **of** our family, if I imagined—what **it** would be wrong to think—that they would fail in their duty. **I beg** your Reverence not to refuse to lend your aid **to** these wards and orphans, a work so blessed by God. **I say lend,** because God has promised to pay it with a most plentiful reward. I, on my part, will ever try to obtain for you a reward for your constant favours and your faithful care of these orphans, praying for your Reverence, through the **intercession** of so many saints, in all the great sanctuaries **I shall visit.** Good-bye. **Do not forget your** servant, or should I say, your son, in your memento at Holy Mass.

'Your Reverence's servant in Christ,

'**JOHN** BERCHMANS.'

'Say everything kind from me to my Adrian, Bartholomew, and Charles, whom perhaps I am never to see more ; and the keepsake I leave them is this— "Increase in holiness and the fear of the Lord and in learning." Good-bye to all.'

There seems a **presentiment of the end. Three more** years were **to run ;** but it was **only** that Rome might lay his sacred relics side by side with those of St. Aloysius, **not** far from the shrines of St. Ignatius and **St.** Stanislaus, and so add another to those bodies of the just from every land, which of themselves would give it full right to the title of the holy city.

Before we follow John Berchmans on his long and wearisome journey, there is a witness who must be cited to give a last touch to the picture already drawn of his holiness during his life in Belgium. Father Cepari, the biographer and confessor of St. Mary Magdalene of Pazzi and St. Aloysius, was to have the privilege of the closest intimacy with John, as rector of the Roman College, and the Life which he wrote of his brother religious is one of those which may fairly be placed with St. Bonaventure's *Life of St. Francis.* When he had composed the first portion of the Life, he sent it to the Superior of Belgium, requesting him to lay it before those Fathers who had known the saint, that they might pass their judgment on the correctness of the portrait. Father Bauters was thought the one best able to speak to its truthfulness, and we quote at length his letter, written with all the freedom of a friendly correspondence—

'The Reverend Father Provincial has sent me, some days back, the first part of the Life of our blessed brother, John Berchmans, of holy memory, written with great diligence by your Reverence. It has been to me the most delightful reading, and I do not know if anything ever pleased me so much, for I seemed to see once more that holy young man, living like an angel amongst a hundred and more scholastics at the Novitiate of Mechlin, and there came to my mind the virtuous memories of his life in religion, and all he did, which delighted me so when I had him before me; and now, when I hear all this narrated by your Reverence, it has moved me and those under my charge to seek with a fresh zeal to imitate him and to praise God in His servant. To tell the truth, Father, although by the will of my Superiors I had for some time the charge of him, and he looked up to me, yet from the time I came to know his soul, and even now, I beg the good Jesus each day to grant me grace, if not to equal him in virtue, at least to be able in some way to imitate him. Indeed, I am ashamed, whenever, as I often do each day, I reverence a little engraving he gave me on leaving for Rome,[2] on which he has written of me as his Father and of himself as my unworthy son. I cannot read those words without sorrow and deep shame, for they make me feel the vast gulf that separates me from the perfection he acquired in so short a time. I fear greatly that God will one day bring it forth against me to reproach me for my sloth and ingratitude. Often, too, do I accuse myself of having left undone so many good actions I saw him perform, of having left unsaid so many words I have heard him make use of for God's glory, his neighbour's instruction, and to renew amongst us the exact observance of the rules of spiritual fervour.'

'I have sent you (in a former letter) a number of details which have occurred to myself and others who knew him intimately; and yet all those are but few in comparison with the variety and frequency of good actions he performed every day, without ever getting tired or weary. In the exercise of his vocation, this young man knew not remissness nor sloth. Xavier's phrase of " Enough, O Lord," he never could have used,

---

[2] Father de Greeff in the letter already quoted, says—'I frankly own that ever since his portrait was sent to me, after his death, I have it always before me ; its very sight inflames me with a very great desire of chastity and perfection. May the Divine Goodness grant that, now he is reigning in heaven, I may sit at the feet of him who so often knelt at mine, and that the perfectly taught scholar may make his sorry master learn, as he has learnt, the one great lesson of the one Master, Christ— that of true humility.'

for the generosity of his heart urged him forward, ever
forward, with the spur of an eagerness for progress never
to be satisfied. Many more examples of virtue has he
given us, and far more still was he wont **frankly to make**
known to me of his **very** innermost feelings. **For he
was not** content to do so every fortnight, like the other
novices, **but he wished** to manifest them much **more**
frequently. And this way, I have always had a fixed
judgment that **he** was forestalled by the blessings of
sweetness, and elected by **the Lord** from childhood **as
a special and very pure** dwelling-place of the Holy
Ghost, and that he persevered in this grace, to which
he had **opened his heart from the dawn, and** to which
he **had** cooperated with extraordinary promptness and
courage.

'During the whole time **he** lived in the Society in
Belgium, he was a striking, and, as far as nature allows,
a perfect model of religious observance, a mirror of
regularity. **Still** more, from what he himself has told
me, and **from what I** have been able to notice myself, **I**
have always **had the** impression, and I have it still, that
he **unfailingly** corresponded to the grace of his vocation,
and that he led amongst us a most holy life, without any
laxity **or** falling off **in his virtue.** All of us **who** have
had the happiness to live with him and to know him,
have been but of **one opinion on that subject. He** led
in our midst a truly angelic life, **by the great** innocence
of his heart, **the** modesty of **his behaviour, his** wondrous
courtesy and gentlemanly manners, his peaceful way of
acting, **his perseverance in all good he** undertook, **his**
perfect **and prompt** obedience, **his rare** prudence on
every subject, the fervour displayed in **all** he did, without
ever losing sight for a single moment of **the** presence of
God, like **the** angelic spirits who walk ever in **His sight.**
I shall **say it** all in **one** word if I quote the **passage of**

the Canticle—"The blessing of the Lord is upon his head."[3] "He chose him out of all flesh. He gave him commandments, and a law of life and instruction; He girded him with a girdle"[4] of justice, guiding him in the exact observance of the religious life. He has made him a saint; He has crowned him with a crown of glory. This high opinion, which the admirable qualities I have noticed in our worthy brother have made me form of him, is still more confirmed by the love borne towards him throughout Belgium, by the veneration it shows him, and the confidence it puts in his prayers. This is a thing that will, I am sure, astonish you, as it astonishes me every time it comes to my mind; nor am I aware that the same fact can be alleged about any other saint. Certainly it is a clear proof of the esteem in which he is held, and of the wish God manifests to exalt him. Though he died in Rome, and but few of his countrymen knew him by sight, ten[5] of our best engravers have already published his portrait. At least twenty-four thousand copies have been struck off. This calculation I base on my knowledge of similar portraits. I do not count among these the works of inferior artists, either Belgians or foreigners. Nor do I include numbers of paintings of him our artists have produced. From all this I conclude that this young religious is not less honoured by men than by God; and that your Reverence will do a good service by continuing your Life, which will be, for those who did not know him, a subject of edification, and for all a spur to gain the glory of God by imitating his virtues.'

[3] Prov. x. 6.

[4] Ecclus. xiv.

[5] The name of Wierox, who was then living, is only one of the many whose etchings added to the artistic glories of Belgium.

CHAPTER V.

Journey to Rome, and studies there

THE day at last came for John Berchmans' departure. On the 24th of October, 1618, with another Fleming, Bartholomew Penneman, a young Jesuit scholastic of his own age, as his companion, he began the long journey to Rome. It is difficult to realize now-a-days what such a journey means, when made, as our travellers were to make it, on foot. Winter, too, was fast approaching, and though they were going southward, it would have fairly set in before they reached Italy. The many ranges of mountains to be crossed would be deep in snow. The Thirty Years' War was then raging, and there was no security for two young Jesuits through Germany. In France, under the protection of Louis XIII., the Society prospered, spite of its many enemies. These circumstances, no doubt, made their Superiors decide on the route by Ghent, Paris, and Lyons. We have but few details of their journey; but we know that, although the travellers rarely stayed more than a night in the houses of the order along the road, they left an impression never effaced of their modesty and bright cheerfulness. Father Bauters, who made the same journey the following year, met on every side with congratulations on having had the good fortune to be novice master to so saintly a young man, and many were the inquiries about John. Letters from various houses, expressing their admiration at his virtue, reached

Rome before his arrival, and made his coming anxiously awaited.[1] A venerable old Father, of the Province of Champagne, who had filled some of the most important posts in his order, recalled with delight, to his dying day, the memory of the travellers, whose piety had so charmed him. One would like to think that Père Lallemant, then master of novices at Paris, had embraced his saintly brother on his journey. Or perhaps Berchmans stayed at the house of third probation, where Père Gaudier was master of tertians, and that great spiritual writer showed this model of young religious to his charge. It was on the feast of the Immaculate Conception, that very year, while John was on the road to Rome, that another saint of the Society, St. Francis Regis, finished his novitiate and took his first vows at Thoulouse. St. Vincent of Paul could not have seen him, as he then was at Chatillon, but he may, from the report of others more fortunate, have gained that opinion of him which he expressed to his Sisters of Charity—'It is very much to be desired, my children, that both you, and I, and all of us, should ever have thoughts and feelings like John Berchmans; for I regard him as a great saint.'[2] The Bishop of Geneva, St. Francis of Sales, however, was then in the French capital, in the train of Cardinal Maurice of Savoy, waiting the arrival of St. Jane Frances de Chantal, on affairs of her recently founded order.

It was a constant source of astonishment to John, that he should have had the good fortune to be chosen to make his studies in Rome, and in the Roman College, so fertile in great men. The fatigues of his journey were forgotten, as Father Cepari tells us, in his delight at the thought that he should see the Vicar of Christ, the General of the Society, and so

---

[1] Father Philip Aleyante, *Proc. Ord. Rom.*
[2] Maynard, *Vie du S. Vincent de Paul*, p. 239.

many holy places; that he would be allowed to venerate so many sacred **relics,** the tombs of **St.** Peter and
St. Paul, and **the shrines of** the beatified saints of the
Society.   And then he hoped that **being at** head-
quarters, he might obtain more easily his heart's grand
wish, **to** be sent, if not to China, at least to some of **the**
foreign missions.   **He** did not foresee that neither he
nor his companion were long for this earth.   Penneman,
who was sent to the German College, probably to help
as a 'repetitore,' **or private tutor** to the young semi-
narists, while continuing **his own** studies, was attacked
by a violent spitting of blood, and died shortly after at
Naples, where **he** had been sent **by** medical advice.
And John did not long survive **him.**   **The** splendour of
the Italian cities, then in all **their richness, and** contrasting with **the** simplicity of more **northern** towns,
interested but little the young religious, whose heart was
set on higher things.   On passing through Milan, **he**
was taken, with several others, strangers passing through,
like himself, **to see** the **ducal** palace; but he confessed
afterwards, to one of his companions at Rome, that **he**
had **not allowed** himself **a sight of any** of its treasures.
Probably the College of **the** Brera, where **St. Aloysius**
had **stayed in** 1590, had **more** attractions for our **saint;**
and the shrine of St. Charles, **and the venerable Arch-**
bishop Frederic **Borromeo, who kept fresh** in his holy
life the memory **of his sainted uncle.   On** Christmas
Eve, the travellers saw **the 'Santa Casa' of Loreto.** What
a day to spend in **the sanctuary of the** Incarnation !
The pilgrims made **their first visit to the Holy** House that
very evening, and **then** returned **to the** Jesuit College.
Then John had **a** conversation **with the** Father Minister
about the virtues of the Blessed Aloysius, whom **the**
Father very probably had known, either at **Rome, or
on one of** the **saint's journeys.**   John Berchmans

expressed how he longed for the day when he should kneel before his tomb; and the Father made him a present of a small relic of the saint as a parting gift. He received it with the greatest reverence, thanking the minister for it again and again.

In spite of his fatigue after his day's journey, and his delicate and frail constitution, Berchmans begged to be allowed to assist at the midnight service, which is solemnized with great pomp in the basilica. He remained the whole time on his knees, fixed in prayer, like a statue, never raising his eyes, or making the slightest movement. The crowd who thronged the church gazed with wonder at the sight of his marvellous recollection. Many indeed were so struck by the beauty and uncommon look of the young religious, that they were persuaded he was the son of some Prince, who had come, unknown and in disguise, on pilgrimage there: no rare occurrence in the days of faith.

John Berchmans had the happiness to receive holy communion, to his unspeakable consolation, in the Holy House. The travellers stayed for two days at Loreto, and it seemed as though they could never have been long enough within the dark and time-stained walls of the cottage of Nazareth. At last they started again on their way, and in five days more the dome of St. Peter's came up before them as they passed the little chapel of La Storta, on the Flaminian Way. That night, the last of the year 1618, the weary pilgrims entered, with beating hearts, the House of the Gesù—the home of St. Ignatius and St. Francis Borgia, and in a few moments were receiving a fatherly welcome from Mutius Vitelleschi, the sixth General of the Society of Jesus. If likeness of character is a bond of affection, that Father, who was called by Urban VIII. the 'angel,' must have felt specially drawn towards one, the fame of

H

whose sweetness and modesty had already gone before him. All the Fathers of the Professed House joined their Superior in greeting the new comers; and the Circumcision being the great festa of the church, they were made to stay out the following day to join in the celebration.

A few days after, they went across to their new home, the Roman College. The novices, who were taking their turn, as was the custom, to serve in the Professed House, were so struck, during his short stay, by John's rare modesty at table and elsewhere, that when they went back to the Novitiate on the Quirinal, they told Father Tesauri they could not help calling each other's attention to him as to a living miracle. The greatest care is ordered by the Constitutions of the Society to be given to those who are just beginning to practise in religious life what they have learned in the noviceship. Berchmans was accordingly placed with the juniors, as these young men are called, in a part of the house separated from the other scholastics, until the two years of this sort of additional probation were ended. He then joined his companions of the third year of the course of philosophy, with whom he lived for the nine months that then remained of his short life.

The rector of the College was his future biographer, Father Virgilio Cepari, whose exquisite memoir will be left, almost entirely, for the rest of the Life, to tell the story as he best could tell it to whom holiness had become familiar, and whose *Life of St. Aloysius* has been cited by Father Faber as perfect in its way. His professor of logic, natural and moral philosophy, was Father Francis Piccolomini,[3] of the great patrician house

---

[3] Father Piccolomini was of a younger branch of the family, which has given so many statesmen and enemies to Europe, and which the name of Pius II. (Æneas Sylvius) alone would make illustrious. He had a brother Jerome, also in the Society. His niece Frances married Augustin Chigi, brother to Pope Alexander VII.

of Siena. **His humility,** patience, and learning, ennobled him, more than his illustrious birth, and several years later he was the next General of the **Society.** John owned to a **special** fondness **for this** professor, because, as **he** said, he seemed not less anxious to make his scholars **advance in** holiness than in **learning.**

Father Horace Grassi, a man of some position in the scientific world, taught him higher mathematics. Father Tarquin **Galluzzi, a man** of eminent talents and great **literary merit, was his** professor of ethics. He was chosen, on Cardinal Bellarmine's death, to preach the **funeral** oration, and in 1615 and in 1619, delivered the Passion sermon before the Pope, in the Sixtine Chapel. Though two months of the course had gone by before John's arrival, such was his diligence, **that in a very short** time he got up with his class, without ever sacrificing **his** usual practices of piety. And this diligence he maintained the whole time **of his** studies, never allowing their difficulty and obscurity to damp a zeal which drew all its strength **from motives** of the highest virtue.

His favourite professor, Father Piccolomini, gives the following **testimonial to his** diligence — 'Berchmans, besides **excellent talents,** which were peculiarly capable of taking in a number of different subjects at once, possessed an ardour and application for work, such as no one, in my opinion, ever surpassed, and few are able to **equal.** He was anxious, **as much as in him** lay, to become skilled in all subjects, even though they would never be of any use to him, from a conviction, as he used **to tell me, that** a child of **the Society** should have a heart **large** enough to hold half the world. And so he spared **himself no toil or fatigue thoroughly** to learn various languages **and** sciences, and everything that goes to make a **learned and erudite man.'** We see the same motive recurring which made him take such pains to

H 2

acquire French at Mechlin, for among his other hopes, he looked forward to the possibility of ministering, as several of the Fathers were then doing, to the soldiers in the Catholic armies, whose ranks were recruited from so many nations that they needed a polyglot chaplain. The very last time he went out to the villa, as was the custom on recreation days, Thursday, the 5th of August, 1622, he was speaking of his plans for gaining facility in foreign languages to his companion, Philip Alegambe. Philip must have been himself a good linguist. A Belgian by birth, he had been an *attaché* to the Duke of Ossone, on his embassy to the Court of St. James, had been with him to Madrid, and had accompanied him when made Viceroy of Sicily, to Palermo. Even in the Society, he was travelling tutor for five years to Count Eggenberg. This familiarity with so many parts of Europe fitted him, no doubt, for his future great work as the successor of Ribadeneira, as historian of the writers of his Order. He wrote also *Mortes Illustres Societatis Jesu*, and *Heroes et Victimæ Societatis Jesu*, which two works have been frequently of use in writing these pages. John's scheme, under his Superior's approval, was to spend a year in the English, and another in the German College. 'I have fixed on the coming vacations to renew my acquaintance with Greek and French. I have already begun to read St. Luke.' 'But,' said Alegambe, 'would you not do better to take an author with a greater variety of expressions, and who would for that reason be more useful to you?' John did not at first seem inclined to take his advice, till he assured him that there were numbers of Fathers who had written perfectly in Greek upon spiritual subjects, and from whose works he could derive great profit. 'Very well, brother, I will take your advice, but you must not find fault with me if I first finish St. Luke. It will not do to change one's book too often.' He felt so strongly that his great duty was to study, that in prayer, in his retreats, in his monthly recollection, he constantly renewed his resolution to apply himself most earnestly to his work, and to excite himself to this, he kept in writing the following reasons, 'I am come into religion to work and not to be idle. Heretics are so ardent in acquiring knowledge which they will afterwards use against Jesus Christ, and will you be content with only ordinary application when you have to defend our Saviour? Men in the world go in for study with such zeal, because they hope for the empty reward of honour, and will you be less jealous of God's glory than they are of their own? I must apply myself thoroughly to my studies, not allowing the smallest moment to be lost, and never failing to note down anything that is worth noting in the scholastic discussions.'

We have seen how, when but a child, John was most careful not to waste any time, and he never lost that habit, having always about him a book, either on spiritual matters or on his studies, which he read at any spare moment. He tried even to multiply his store by a carefully composed order, wherein all his occupations were arranged beforehand. During the three days of retirement, which twice a year precede the renewal of the vows, he went over his day, assigning to each portion of it its particular employment. This order once made, he never changed; but observed, with the greatest fidelity for the next half year. If he found, at the following renovation, that change of studies or other motives enjoined any alteration, he made a new order, and to this he adhered with the same strictness as he had done to its predecessors.

Not content with thus turning to account every moment of his day, he forecast the best way of doing his various duties with pleasure and profit. He committed to writing what has frequently been reprinted, *Bonus Scholasticus Societatis Jesu*—'The good Scholastic of the Society,' a sketch of what a young religious engaged in study ought to be, with regard to God, to his studies, and to others.

The Good Scholastic of the Society of Jesus.

I.—*With regard to God.*

1. Have no object in study but the glory of God and the gain of souls.

2. Be fervent, and given to prayer, and frequently pray for the grace of making progress in it.

3. Have a great love for solid virtue and for the religious profession.

4. Practise diligently both the particular and general examination of conscience, hear Mass daily with the greatest devotion, and receive holy communion devoutly once every week. Maffei[4] tells us that our holy Founder, during his studies at Paris, attached the greatest importance to these three points.

II.—*With regard to study.*

1. Be persuaded that it is exceedingly meritorious to study according to the true spirit of the Society.

2. Be indifferent concerning the subjects of study and the professors.

3. Apply yourself to study with earnestness and perseverance.

4. Be careful to observe the division of time which is prescribed.

5. Use no books except those whose use is enjoined by the professor.

6. Pay careful attention to the lectures, be diligent in preparing and repeating what ought to be prepared or repeated, and give an example of modesty and learning in circles and repetitions, whether confined to ours or before externs.

7. Everywhere be mindful of modesty and of religious gravity.

[4] *Vita S. Ign.*, l. i., cap. xix.

8. What has been written during lectures should be read over privately, its sense mastered, and sifted by means of objections put to oneself and answered. If one is unable to answer any of these objections, it should be noted down.

9. Whatever is noteworthy in the lecture should be written down, to be afterwards copied out at leisure in another book.

10. Do not continue reading or writing for more than two hours without some brief interruption.

11. Commit to memory whatever has been dictated by the master, and diligently cultivate a good style.

III.— With regard to others.

1. Speak Latin.

2. If it is necessary to speak to scholastics who are externs, ask leave to do so, and speak only on literary or spiritual subjects.

3. Remember, finally, in everything you do, that you are the son of so good a mother, the Society of Jesus.

It may be well to follow John Berchmans in his daily work in the lecture and class rooms. He never omitted a short visit to the Blessed Sacrament before the bell rang for schools, to ask at the source of light and love to make progress in his studies. At the first stroke of the bell, he rose from his knees and went to the door of the lecture-room; and while waiting there till the rest had arrived, he pulled out his book and began to read. One Francis Surdi, a young Roman, who afterwards entered the Society, had often to go to the College on business with the rector, and he chose the time for his visit when the scholastics were assembling for the lecture, so much was he attracted by the sight of such recollectedness. 'I did not know,' he tells us, 'what modesty meant, but I knew right well that I was charmed at that young religious, and that he inclined me instinctively to exercise in my own regard a greater restraint.' John went and returned to class in perfect silence. During the lecture he continued writing, without ever raising his eyes from his paper. He never complained that his professor went too quick in dictation ; but if he missed a word, he supplied it from his neighbour's copy ; or he asked leave, and went to one of his fellow scholars, and having let him know of the permission, requested to see his notes. If any one disturbed the professor by talking or making a noise, John gave evident signs of annoyance. When he heard the bell give the signal for the end of a lecture or discussion, he started to his feet out of a sort of instinctive feeling of obedience, and if the summons was not promptly attended to, as often might happen in the heat of an argument, he twisted just—as Cepari puts it—as though he were on hot coals. Then followed, for another half hour, a repetition of the subject-matter just delivered, which, as is the custom of the Roman College, is made by the students in little separate parties, under the guidance of one of the scholastics. To John had been intrusted some young men of the best families of Rome ; and it was quite marvellous to see how submissively they obeyed, and what reverence they showed him. When the time was up, he led them to the door of the lecture-room, and left them at once, without ever staying to finish his answers to their difficulties. On reaching his room, he went over the matter he had just heard, and if he found in his notes any difficulty he could not master, he knelt down and prayed for light. 'My Lord, Thou knowest I cannot understand this without Thy special aid, so I beg Thee to help me.' 'Give me,' he prayed with Solomon, 'wisdom, that sitteth by Thy throne, that she may be with me, and labour with me.' 'Make me understand this.' And often his prayer was heard. What, however, still remained unsolved, he carefully noted down to lay before his professor. He always studied standing, perfectly quiet, **never** ceasing **his application** during the time allotted for work, **unless** headache, to which **he was** subject, **forced him to seek rest from** mental exertion. This rest he found **in saying his beads,** or reading **some spiritual book.**

When he carried his difficulties to his professor's room, **John waited patiently outside if** he were engaged, and **when free, entered** with **his** eyes modestly cast down, **and made his reverence, cap** in hand, nor did he put it on unless begged **to do so.** Then, at each new question or answer, he raised his cap for a moment, as was his habit, when speaking to any of his Superiors. Although in accordance with the rule, he soon acquired Italian, which he spoke with a correctness and elegance rarely found in those who are not Italian by **birth ; yet, out of** love for the rule which imposes on all those **actually** engaged in study the obligation **of** speaking **Latin out of** times of recreation, **he always used that language when** speaking to his professors. If he did not at once understand the answer which was given **him, he** considered for a moment, and then, with a modest smile, he frankly said, *Vere, Pater, non intellexi*—' Really, Father, **I do** not understand.' When, however, **he perfectly took in** the answer, but **it** did not seem **to him to solve his** difficulty, not to appear to controvert his master's **solution,** he put his objection again in **such a way** that might appear to put the fault on his own want **of** comprehension. Once satisfied, without a useless word, he made a respectful reverence, and went away.

He acted in the same way whenever he was called, with the others, to his professor's room, leaving as **soon** as it **seemed to him** that he was at liberty to do **so ; but** he tempered his **want of any human respect with such a** pleasing **manner, that no one** ever took it **ill. At the** ' circles,' **or private discussions, which** St. Ignatius enjoins as the surest way of making one's own the matter of study, and at the public discussions, Berchmans was all attention. He always came provided with pen and paper, to note down any argument, for or against, which appeared to him solid. When it was his turn to put objections, he did so with great vigour. But he always allowed his opponent time to repeat his argument, to reply to his, and develope the answer at his ease, never once interrupting him.

When his adversary had had his say, John again came to the attack, and pushed his advances firmly, never losing command of himself, or even raising his voice, in the excitement of the debate. Any one who has seen with what warmth such public tourneys are carried on in foreign Universities, will understand the merit of his calm. When he had to be defender of his professor's theses, he seized the objections with marvellous clearness, and repeated them, as is the custom, before giving his answer, almost word for word. His reply, orderly and clear, in strict scholastic form, was given with modest looks and downcast eyes. While on this subject, it may be as well to speak of his examination in philosophy, which extended over the whole matter of his three years' course. It had to come off on the feast of St. Joseph, 1621. We have, preserved by Father Cepari, the notes in which, as was his custom in all circumstances, he had penned down the preparation which he had resolved for so important a trial. 'The patron of this examination shall be St. Joseph ; and the Blessed Virgin shall be my intercessor. But first, for that intention I will take a discipline, some mortification, or a penance in the refectory ; I will say five decades, and ask Father Rector's blessing. If I succeed, I shall say the whole rosary in honour of St. Joseph and others, &c. In the morning I will look over my notes on such and such a question ;

and should our Lady and St. Joseph help me to go over them all, I will do such and such devotions in her honour. During the examination I will be cheerful and answer boldly, always in form—*Nego, concedo, distinguo, explico.* When answering, I shall insist thus—*Nego, et do instantiam.* When explaining, I shall be brief and clear. I shall not make any answer to long speeches before either my professor or myself have reduced them to a few words.'

When the day arrived, he begged Father Gaudt, a Fleming, to say Mass for his intention. On his trial, he adhered most faithfully to his resolutions, and with such care and success did he repeat the arguments of the Fathers who examined him, that they were not ever obliged to prompt him—for he did not once leave out or alter a word of their objections. Father Cepari himself, present, no doubt, as rector, has left us this account. So brilliant was his success, that John was chosen by the votes of all concerned, to hold a public defension. But in time of prayer a thought such as occurred to St. Aloysius came before him, the desire of shame, the fear of applause. He asked his holy old confessor, Father Ceccotti, if he thought it would be to the greater glory of God if he were to do all in his power to get off this defension, or whether he should simply accept it without a word. The good Father was delighted at his humility, but urged him not to make any difficulty, but to undertake the work laid upon him. So he set to his task, with the same care, and using the same helps, as he had employed for his examination.

The issue of the trial will be told in its proper place. But we have forestalled many months of our saint's life that we might at one glance look at Berchmans as a student. His study was not for study's sake. The motive of his study raised it far above its own natural worth.

Charity, the love of his Lord and Master, was the sole end of his application. Obedience, the expression of that love, made him ever sure that his labour was all for God, and urged him to bend all his faculties to his work. So it is a saint rather than a student that we see in Berchmans. His youthful talents only shone out to fade away in death. The lustre of his life, the glory of his name, the lesson he gives us, is that of a saint. A model student, it is true, but because he was a saint. And in this aspect we must now consider him.

It has been said more than once that, in the three youthful saints who have glorified the Society of Jesus, there was rather the absence of sin than the presence of virtue ; or that a naturally good disposition, fostered by the first fervour of religious life, and never exposed to the temptations of manhood, is their sole claim to the distinction which they have received from the Church.

It happens necessarily in biographies of saints like they —comparatively bare of incident, especially when written in a compendious form—that their freedom fromsin and their singular innocence should come out in special relief. But an attentive study of their lives shows that, if great natural and supernatural gifts were given to them, as to so many other saints, great correspondence on their part fully entitles them to their exalted dignity.

This adverse judgment has been most frequently passed on John, who had not, like St. Stanislaus or St. Aloysius, to make any sacrifice of social position or of riches. Nor had he, as they, to conquer such obstacles to his vocation. But the fulness of details we possess of his short life most convincingly prove of him what we have asserted of all the three. God—wonderful in all His saints—has His design in each. A certain type or sanctity has to be produced, and grace does not take the place of nature, but it perfects it, and, upon a natural character, builds up a creation which, though new, takes therefrom much of its shape and colour. So John, being designed as a perfect model of a young religious student, had received natural gifts, and a disposition best suited to take his after form of holiness. But no one can rise from reading his life without profound astonishment at the loving painstaking care and heroic fidelity with which he worked with God.

To give a complete picture of Berchmans, we must join to the witnesses of his daily actions, and to the testimony of those who best knew his inner life, his own notes and resolutions, which fill up and explain much that otherwise would be but half understood. To speak first of his marvellous innocence, we have the positive declaration of his various confessors — from Father Emmerick of Diest, to Father Cepari, who assisted him on his death-bed—that he never lost the first grace of his baptism. The last-named found among John's papers one on which were noted down in short the various favours he had received, as a reminder for thanksgiving : *Fecit Christianum, socium Jesu, amicum; Sponsam conservavit sine peccato mortali*—' He made him a Christian, a companion of Jesus, His friend ; He preserved His spouse from mortal sin.' His humility faintly veils the grace under the third person. Thus it was that, when he went through the Exercises of St. Ignatius on his entry into religion, he could make nothing out of that meditation on sin, which stirs ordinary souls to their lowest depths. ' In the exercise on the sins I committed in the world I was quite dry, hard, and unmoved.' And when he made the same meditation in Rome he noted down—' It has passed without any feelings at all.' And in his last retreat, in the vacation of 1620, he wrote—' It has passed without any feeling, and in the first and second point I suffered great desolation'—the *processus peccatorum*, as it is called, the arraignment of past life, and the consideration of the moral heinousness of sin.   Such was the purity of soul on which John built up his perfection—a perfection so singular and rare, because, as Father Cepari says, 'it extended not merely to one or two virtues, but to all, and to each virtue in particular, as though he had possessed fully and perfectly that and that only.   And this is a thing so unusual as to astound any one who understands what it means to be full of the virtues which are called those of "purified souls," which, as St. Thomas rightly teaches, are not to be found but in the blessed in heaven and a few most perfect souls on earth.   This is what we all admired in him, that in every virtue he showed himself to be perfect; and whatever he did, how different and opposite things they might be, by the aid of God's grace and his own most diligent correspondence and cooperation, he performed them with the utmost perfection, so much so that, whoever observed John's actions, the way in which they were done, and the circumstances which accompanied them, was forced to say, "That could not be better done."   And had those who saw the outside of his actions but have known thoroughly the hidden acts of virtue which accompanied them and gave them all their life, their merit, their supernatural being, I am sure they would have formed a most exalted idea of his signal goodness and holiness.

'And this was just my case, when twice every month he used to come, of his own accord, to give me, as his Superior and Father, an account of his conscience, and open out with perfect frankness the innermost of his heart, his every thought, feeling, and wish.   I remember once while he was telling me what God was doing for him in the secret of his soul, and how he was corresponding with these graces, I was quite overcome with more than usual astonishment, and I said to myself, without giving him any sign of what I felt, "O happy youth, in whose soul God is so well pleased ! O blessed child, to whom God has given a privilege which seems like to that gift of grace and original justice which He infused into Adam, like to the other favours and succour which went with them in the blessed state of innocence !" One does not form such ideas of a person who possesses merely ordinary innocence and goodness. Of course John, in the course of his life, fell into those defects and faults into which everybody ordinarily falls, weighed down by a body inclined to evil. To think or to assert the contrary, would be quite a mistake, for he himself used to accuse himself of them, and confess that he had committed faults in many things. But these defects were so light, that we could not detect them, and it needed that great light from above, which filled his understanding, to be able to find them out. The perfect care he used in all he did, the constant watchfulness, which kept him continually attentive and fully alive to the very smallest action he performed, made him in our eyes so consummately exact and faultless, that no one has been found who could say that he had remarked in John the smallest moral fault, or observed even a little imperfection in what he did. This is a privilege so great, as to be more fit for the blessed in heaven than for poor pilgrims of earth ; more like the happiness of angels than the frailty of man. John was about five years in our order, in which, as all are aware, religious discipline, by God's grace, is in its first fervour and fresh observance.[1]

---

[1] Berchmans' notes.—'Father Coster used to say, with the greatest joy, that he had never seen the Society in such a good state. This was in 1617.' Father Coster was received into the Society by St. Ignatius, and has justly been called the Canisius of Belgium. He died in 1619, at the advanced age of eighty-eight, having lived to say the Mass of his holy Founder.

He studied in the Roman College, so great in numbers, where the eyes of so many Superiors are ever open and watchful to see that the rules and orders are observed by all, and the smallest defect, the lightest transgression, is noted with special care, above all in the young men, who are carefully tended, in order to bring them up in the right way. In spite of all this, never any one, Superior or inferior, Father or brother student who lived in the same room, or went to the lectures with him, nor any one of those in the College who used to see him or talk with him, has ever noticed in him the least imperfection or fault, however small, remarked the first rising of any passion, nor heard from his lips an idle or ill-considered word. No one ever saw him lift his eyes more than modesty permits, make a gesture that was not well regulated, laugh without moderation, nor be wanting in composure in his person, nor speak in times of silence, make use of Italian when bound to speak Latin, lose a moment or remain idle, ever commit a fault through human respect, or from any cause whatever. All this is as easily narrated as it is difficult to practise, unless one is continually the favoured object of God's watchful eye, and blessed with a special aid and unusual share of divine grace. And if one single virtue in a perfect degree is enough to make its possessor worthy of note, an object of admiration and imitation, you can easily conclude the wonder, devotion, and delight caused by the sight of such a cluster of so many and such perfect virtues in this young man. It was a long-drawn harmony most sweet to hear, with never a discord to mar its delights. That all may be convinced I am not exaggerating, and that the perfection of his outward actions was merely the outcomings of inner virtues which replenished that blessed soul, in addition to what I can assert from my own knowledge in the guidance of his interior, I wish to insert in this place the evidence of two other Fathers, who used to hear his confession from l   first arrival in Rome to his death. This they could c   with safety, both because they were attesting to a matter of perfection, and because John always gave leave, o his own accord, both to his confessor and his Superior, to speak freely and publicly about all that concerned himself. He even left this permission behind him in writing—" I give permission to use entirely and freely the knowledge which is gained from confession." One of these Fathers was John Baptist Ceccotti, a man whose purity of life, and skill in direction of religious souls, is known to all. He was a thorough master of the spiritual life, and was confessor and Spiritual Father of the juniors, an office he was to fill[2] for long years. These are his words—" In obedience to my Superiors, who have enjoined this upon me, I can say with truth, as regards the inner life of John, that I have never found a soul of greater purity and spotlessness than his, though in my present office I have had numbers under my direction ; indeed, it seems to me that there was a something in the highest degree privileged about him. His sins were

---

[2] Father Ceccotti held this office for the juniors in the Roman College during more than forty years. John tells us in his notes, that this Father ' at first had been very much troubled by vainglory, but afterwards got so that there was no enemy he feared less, and that he told me once, when we were making the visit to the seven churches, that now he had no friend on earth to whom he was too much attached.' John's openness seems to have merited a like confidence on the part of his confessor. It is worth while noting that Father Ceccotti was most strict in his fidelity to the ' order of the day ' he drew up for his own use. With the exception of one meal a day, he gave up his whole time to spiritual duties. He never would pay attention to conversation which was not about God, or on some subject tending to His glory. We see the impress of the Master in the conduct of the sainted scholar. One trait of resemblance more was, that those who knew his interior tell us he never lost his baptismal innocence, or committed one deliberate sin.

I

never of the kind *de naturâ suâ*, mortal, and which fail
to be grievous merely through want of consent, or small-
ness of matter; but they were only those which are
venial of their own nature, and which, according to the
regular law, cannot be avoided altogether; and these,
very slight sins, and not committed with deliberation,
such as even great saints sometimes fall into through
mere fault of our corrupt nature. Even these were very
rare, owing to the great watchfulness and care he had
over both his interior and exterior, and the even tenour
of his life, which never altered, save by growing more
perfect. He owed this to a special grace and assistance
of the Holy Ghost, Who had that holy soul in His
keeping. He possessed a clear insight into all his
own defects, even the very least. His conscience was
most delicate, but yet never scrupulous or troubled,
modelled exactly on the type of our holy Father
St. Ignatius in the book of Exercises, in the golden
treatise 'On Scruples.'

'"Whatever he was taught regarding perfection, he
not only imprinted it all upon his mind, but put it into
practice. When I was engaged in instructing our
brothers, as my rule obliges me, I strove to give them
the requisite knowledge of our whole spiritual life,
by reducing to a few heads the principal virtues, and
arranging them under the three ways, drawing all the
matter from our own sources, chiefly from the Summary
of the Constitution, and from the Common Rules. When
I see each one separately, as I do every fortnight, they
render an account of those virtues which we are called
on to practise, one after another, quoting the rules which
speak of them. They tell me the result of previous
self-examination, how they understand and how they
practise them. By this means, in our private conversations, we go through, in the two years of the juniorate,

the whole of the Summary and Common Rules, and the way to sanctify their lives as scholastics. John took in my exhortations with all docility and diligence, and practised them to the letter, to such a degree that one could not desire a greater perfection in accordance with our holy Institute. So that the perfection taught in our rule was the perfection to which he attained. And this was plain to all, and all could give undoubted witness to it, as I do more especially, as having enjoyed for so long a time, with more than usual intimacy, his most holy acquaintance; and having seen close the treasures of heavenly grace with which that soul was filled, I can aver that I never noticed in it a single inordinate affection or movement of the will.

'"His brethren loved and revered him as an angel from heaven, and he was endowed with such simplicity and goodness, that he never could notice any defect in others, a thing which gave me great satisfaction. His modesty and external behaviour, which inspired devotion in those who saw him, was an image of his interior, whence, in fact, they sprung; but there was much more within than was seen without. I say no more of this innocent youth, because I cannot find words which express and tell as fully as I should wish the idea I have of the angelic purity and innocence of so blessed a religious. And I piously believe, that on his blessed soul leaving the body, it went forth so cleansed and spotless, that it flew straight up to heaven without touching Purgatory, and laden with much merit through the exact observance of our rules, and that perfection which the Institute requires of us. Neither do I seem ever to have witnessed greater or more exact observance than his.

'"So, as witness to the truth, I sign myself,

'"JOHN BAPTIST CECCOTTI."

Father Ceccotti gave his exhortations three times a week for half an hour, immediately after the night examen, and Father Tesauri, who was prefect of the juniors, tells us that, while most of the young men were unable to keep awake, what with the lateness of the hour and the gloom of the chapel, John never once was seen to be drowsy, but ever followed so closely all that was said that he could turn it to account the following day at recreation.

Father Thomas Massucci,[3] who was the Spiritual Father of the entire community, with the exception of the 'juniors,' and a man, therefore, of no small weight in spiritual matters, and known for his virtue, gives a similar testimony to the holiness of John—

'In compliance with the order of holy obedience to tell what I remember about the extraordinary virtues and holy life of our blessed brother, John Berchmans, I do it all the more willingly because the glory of God and our edification seemed to oblige me to make it known, even without such an order. I was his confessor during the last year of his life, that is, from the beginning of January, 1621, till the August of that year, on the 13th of which month he left us to go from earth to heaven, as we have reason to believe. During that period he came to confession once a week or oftener, and at least once a month gave me an account of his conscience, generally bringing noted down what he had to tell me; nor did he ever allow the day appointed for this to go by—and the same is true of confession— but he always used to be the first to come at the hour fixed.

---

[3] Father Massucci, after teaching philosophy and theology in Poland, returned to Italy, and held in the Roman College for many years the post of Spiritual Father. He wrote a Life of St. Paul and a book, *De cælesti conversatione.*

' I think, with so intimate an acquaintance of him, I can with perfect truth declare—

' 1. After Blessed Aloysius Gonzaga, with whom I lived and whom I knew in the Roman College the last year of his life (1591), I never have been acquainted with a youth of more exemplary life, of purer conscience, or greater perfection than John.

' 2. He had put before himself, as the aim of his religious life, to attain a high degree in every virtue, and to derive the greatest possible benefit from his studies; and this for no other reason than for God's glory and the good of souls, and to correspond fully to the grace and spirit of our vocation.

' 3. The one means to gain his intent was the exact observance of the rules, in which, without any scruples, he was most precise; so much so, that though our rules are many and varied, he never violated one deliberately. This, too, not merely during the time he was under my direction, but during all the previous years passed in religion. Indeed, during his whole life, not only was he not conscious of mortal sin of any sort, but not even of deliberate venial sin. This is a point of great moment, because it proves that he not only preserved his robe of baptismal innocence and his virginity, but besides this he ever, from the beginning to the end, walked with perfection in the spiritual life, a thing granted to but few even amongst the great saints.

' 4. In the keeping of the three religious vows, he was so watchful, that I do not recollect he had to accuse himself of having ever failed in this matter. And above all, as to the vow of chastity, he was so strict and so fortunate, that I think he never had even a sting of the flesh, or imagination, not even in sleep, from what I could gather during the time I had charge of his conscience. Indeed, he was most frank, detailed, and clear in giving an account of himself, as he has written—" I will be most frank, most open, and like the clearest water in dealing with Superiors and my Spiritual Father." No wonder he arrived at so high a grade of purity, for with such a grand foundation of innocence, he kept careful watch over his feelings, was very temperate, and given to continual mortification, and with his mind always —when not engaged in study—fixed on God or spiritual things.

' 5. He derived such fruit from his daily meditations that, when I considered the enlightenment of his understanding, and the fervour with which, from morning to night, he went on in religious observance and the practice of every virtue, I always judged him to be confirmed in grace; that is, so forestalled and aided by actual grace and God's help, that it would have been morally impossible for him to fail in any serious degree in good doing, and in this state he persevered till his most happy passage to another life.'

We shall have occasion to cite the same authority later on.   There are many other witnesses whose testimony is nearly as explicit; while their names, known to history, might add weight to their words. His two school-fellows, Alexander Gottofredi,[4] and Paul Oliva, the grandson and nephew of two Doges of Genoa, and the friend of Condé, both of whom became Generals of the Society, besides Cornelius à Lapide, the great commentator, who has left a splendid eulogy, might be quoted. We will be content,

---

[4] Father Gottofredi met with great obstacles to his entering religious life on the part of his relatives, who were of a great Roman family. He was sent by them to Cardinal Perbenedetti's palace, with the view of testing his vocation. His constancy at last prevailed, and the Cardinal is said to have dismissed him with the prophetic saying—' Go, and God speed you, to the Society of Jesus, whose General you will one day become.' This was verified forty years later. He was in authority little over a month, dying in 1652.

after such long citations, with a concluding extract from the notes of Father Francis Piccolomini. As has been already mentioned, he was the favourite professor of John. So great was the esteem his holy pupil had of him, that, with his Superior's leave, he used to consult him, not only about difficulties in philosophy, but on matters concerning his spiritual progress. The professor in turn conceived the most exalted idea of the young man's holiness. And, after his death, it fell to his lot to make a panegyric of his virtues in the refectory. Father Cepari, the rector, begged him to put in writing what he had delivered. After some preliminary remarks, Father Piccolomini goes on to say—'As to spirirual things, since he himself was pleased to speak to me on these subjects, perhaps for his greater humiliation and better guidance, or to confound me, first, I declare that, during his three years of philosophy, having to do continually with me, and coming generally once or twice a day to my room with perfect freedom, I have never observed in him, either in public or in private, the smallest fault, but, on the contrary, the greatest modesty, and un-changed behaviour, seen both in his countenance and in his actions.

'Secondly, I never saw any one so absorbed in spiritual matters and the presence of God, with such ease and almost naturally, and what is more astonishing, at the same time most self-possessed, and fully alive to what he might have in hand, and scrupulously attentive to others.

'Thirdly, I have never known any one of his age who had such thoughts and such knowledge of God, joined to so ready a practice of religious perfection.

'Fourthly, none have I ever seen who in an ordinary and common life had less that was ordinary and common, and who pictured more to the life the solid virtues and

lofty perfection of our early Fathers, with whose lives
and actions he was more familiar than any I have ever
known.

'Fifthly, not only was he constant in what he had
once undertaken, but he was always adding something
fresh that he had found out, in order to advance the
more. Once when he was narrating to me what he used
to do, beginning with the morning of each day, and how
many new practices he had kept on adding, I was forced
to tell him he certainly could not hold out long if he did
not stick to the principal points merely, and cease taking
account of the smaller details, for it was exacting too
much from a head already over fatigued by studies.
What I then told him was shortly verified.'

So far the perfection of John has been drawn for us in
broad outline by master hands, eminently qualified in
every way for the task. It is now time to fill up the
picture in its minutest details, as far as we can, with the
aid of contemporary authorities, and his own spiritual
notes.

CHAPTER VI.

How John maintained his purity of heart. His fidelity to his rule.

WE are now to study in what John's perfection consisted, to look into its construction, to examine its parts, that it may be to us, not a mere subject of admiration and of loving reverence, but a lesson of great usefulness. How was such a stately building reared? Was it the work of angel hands, the building of a night, where the sound of neither hammer nor axe was heard? Or was it the fruit of painstaking toil and labour, marvellously aided by grace, but, for all that, exertion ever keeping pace with heavenly help?

The answer has been more or less forestalled. A careful insight into the religious life of Berchmans will show that it is but one long commentary on the words of our Lord, 'Well done, good and faithful servant, because thou hast been faithful over a few things, I will place thee over many. Enter thou into the joy of thy Lord.' Fidelity over a few things, in things we call little, and in consequence, great graces and a state of exalted holiness. Yet, these *little things* were nothing less than an exact carrying out of a rule, which is a perfect system of holiness, whose every detail was the fruit of long experience, and thought, and prayer, coming from a mind eminently prudent, and accustomed in all things to seek, with a marvellous singleness of aim, the one end of personal sanctification. Built upon the principles of the Spiritual Exercises, St. Ignatius has carried out in his Constitutions to their highest excellence the conclusions which are found therein. And John's Beatification is as a fresh approval of that rule, for all his holiness was written there, and his life was but its perfect realization.[1] There was no out-door work, no stirring deeds, no external show of extraordinary gifts, no astonishing austerities. It was all—fidelity, for God's sake, to the little things of God.

Such had been his correspondence with grace, that, as we have seen, Berchmans had none of the impediments to clear away which the loss of baptismal innocence leaves behind in the soul. But this happy preservation did not make him the less watchful. Not merely did he guard, by constant examination of conscience, and unabating care against the commission of the smallest deliberate sin, keeping off with special jealousy anything, however remote, that threatened his chastity; but his notes testify the horror he had of the lightest offence against his rules. In these notes we find such passages as these — 'I will make meditations on all the rules, the first three days of each month. If ever I do anything against rule which deserves a penance, I will ask for it humbly the whole course of my life.' 'Rather die than transgress the smallest order or rule. May I utterly lose my health, than for its sake break a single rule.' This was the practice of his life. Father Oliva declares—'I am ready on my oath to declare that, for the three years I was his class-fellow, I do not recollect having noticed him break a rule, or having

---

[1] To the objection that, if Berchmans were beatified, every perfect Jesuit should be declared a saint, the procurator of the cause replied by citing St.Vincent Ferrer and Pius V., who say the same of all who carry out St. Francis' rule.

observed a fault in any of his words or actions.' Father Anthony Sbarra, minister of the Roman College, and charged by his office to see to domestic discipline, writes —'I have never heard nor remarked myself that he ever broke a single rule, nor did I ever see any imperfection in his actions. On the contrary, they all breathed holiness and devotion.' Twenty others deposed to the same. Father Thomas Bisdomini, who was then professor of moral theology, set himself to see if he could notice in him some small failing, any deviation from the highest perfection, either in words and conversations or in discussions, things in which one who is not thoroughly perfect is wont easily to go astray, but he never could see in him the least little defect, even any want of good breeding. A Dalmatian scholastic, Ignatius Tudisio, seems to have been more successful. 'There was no one so ready as Berchmans to go to the Gesù to serve High Mass, and he had almost always the office of acolyte. When at the altar, he used to say his beads with his usual modesty and recollection, so that I was forced once to admonish him to be a little more attentive to be ready to do the ordinary ceremonies. But, from that day I never had to speak to him again; he ever after acquitted himself perfectly of his office.'

'One day,' Cornelius à Lapide tells the story, 'I heard a knock at my door. I said, "Come in," but no one entered. A moment, and then a second and a third rap. I rose and went to look out, and there stood the modest young man. "I beg pardon, Father, for having disturbed you, but I had not asked leave to go into your room."' Shortly after Berchmans' arrival in Rome, a Father whom he had seen at Loreto, met him in one of the corridors of the Roman College, and the first expressions of civility over, he evidently intended to continue talking to him, but our saint frankly said, 'Reverend Father, I cannot have a conversation with you now, for it is time of silence, but, if you wish, I can go and ask Father Minister's permission, and will be back in an instant,' He did so and returned, delighted to rejoin the Father, who was greatly edified by his regularity. During the two years of his juniorate John was an example to all, the ideal of observance, and beloved by every one. He never quitted the portion of the house allotted to the new comers without permission, nor spoke, as the rule forbade, to the students of the third year of philosophy. One recreation day, while coming home from the country house, or vigna, with two other young scholastics, Berchmans met another party of those who had gone up from the juniorate, who invited them to walk back with them; John begged firmly to be excused. Once, after he had left the juniorate, in the House of the Gesù, he came on the Belgian Father, John Brisselius, one of the General's secretaries, who was talking with Berchmans' old fellow-novice, William van Aelst, who had lately arrived, and was therefore a junior. The Father called him, and Berchmans came at once, but when he noticed that one was present with whom he was forbidden to speak, he begged to be excused, saying that he would wait till the junior had gone. In fact, sometime after, when at their country house at Frascati, taking a walk with Father Octavius Lorenzini, the latter asked him how often he had spoken to Van Aelst since he had been at Rome, and if he ever went out a walk with him. 'It is now so many days,' said Berchmans, telling their precise number, 'I have not spoken a word to him.' 'What,' said the Father, in fun, 'have you quarrelled?' 'Oh, no,' said John, 'but we cannot speak to one another, for he is still a junior.' It was one of his sayings in jest, that it would be a good thing when any one committed a fault if his Superior gave him a penance, because then it would show that he had made it up with his Superior.

When the **two years of** special protection and assistance **had come** to an end, he did not say a word, but waited quietly till his Superiors should themselves advert to the fact. And this they did not do for full two months; and it was only in the beginning of November, 1620, that he rejoined his companions of the third year. The day of his change he took to the Father, who acted as minister for the juniors, a paper with a list of mortifications, penances, and prayers which he engaged to offer up for his intention, as a mark of gratitude for the care he had taken of him, and begged the minister in return to give him such advice as he might think he needed.

When first he came to Rome, many of the community, seeing Berchmans so joyful and obliging, and withal so regular in every action, were sure that this fervour which he had brought from the Novitiate could not last. A year passed, and Berchmans was as gay and as exact as before. But still the most obstinate among these prophets would not give in. ' It is all very well in the juniorate; wait till that is over. Once fairly launched in the scholasticate, he will soon begin to grow tired of such faultless precision, and give way somewhat to human frailty.' However, they were at last compelled to own they had been deceived; for, far from changing for the worse, Berchmans only seemed to grow more careful. He used to ask permission for things so trivial, no one else would have thought of. The very last visit he paid to the vigna, he was walking up and down a walk with a hedge of nut trees, the fruit of which had been gathered by the vineyard keeper. Nicholas Radkaï, a young religious from Galicia, with whom John was always able to act with freedom, spied a nut left on the tree, stretched out his hand and plucked it. Berchmans, who knew there was a prohibition against taking anything, said at once, 'Brother, what are you doing?' Nicholas laughed, and said the nuts had already been gathered, and as this one had been left behind, it did not come under the prohibition; but John shrugged his shoulders, saying, '*I* certainly would not do it, neither would I admit such interpretations.' Another time, on the eve of St. Agnes, he was going with the same scholastic to visit the shrine of the virgin martyr. As usual, the road to the Porta Pia was thronged with crowds going to the first vespers in the venerable basilica that covers her relics and her ancient home. An order had been given forbidding the Jesuits to talk in the streets when unusually crowded. Berchmans proposed at once that they should say their beads, as it was forbidden to talk. But Radkaï, who seems to have had a broader way, insisted that was not the intention of Superiors, but merely that they were not to talk too loud. However, faithful to his practice never to soften down rules by private interpretation, Berchmans continued his prayers, and the two together said the rosary three or four times before their journey's end.

After Berchmans' death, Father Cepari found noted down in short, in accordance with a resolution he had made, all the various injunctions and orders that had been given out during his stay in the Roman College, a proof of the value he set upon the least expression of his Superior's wishes. The secret of all this was, as he expresses it almost in the words of his rule, 'I will endeavour to find God in every Superior.' It was because he recognized the voice of the God he loved, that his obedience was so exact and perfect. So much, in fact, did he love subjection, that he never would ask a general permission for anything; his reason being that there was less danger of error, and more merit in going each time to ask leave with humility and submission. During his first year at Rome, by advice of his Superiors, one day each week, he rose an hour later than the community. But instead of getting leave once for all, he preferred to go every time for the required permission; and this he carried out on numbers of similar occasions. He made a rule to hate a dispensation from any rule as he would hate the plague. One day his companion, who lived in the same room with him, told him he thought of asking permission for something or other not permitted by rule. John dissuaded him, saying, 'I would not do so because it does not seem necessary; and besides, I could never bring myself to ask for anything which is forbidden, either by the rule, or by any order of Superior;' and he added that twice his conscience had smitten him because, at the wish of his professor, he had asked leave not to go to the afternoon lecture on Holy Scripture, which was then, and is still, given on Sundays and holidays in the Gesù. His reasons in support of asking the exemption were sufficiently strong; but, said he, 'I will inform myself more exactly, and if the rule which enjoins on all to be present in the church during a sermon refers to the Gesù, I shall never again ask to be dispensed.'

Much less would he allow himself to heed the unauthorized remarks of others—'I will not mind what others say about keeping my rules and resolutions.' The result of this exactitude was that he never gave the slightest trouble to his Superiors. When a junior, he but rarely went to the rector, and often a fortnight passed by without speaking to his Superior, except in time of recreation. He often expressed his edification at the regularity he saw in the Roman College, and he was especially delighted at what he witnessed daily, when the sound of the bell broke in upon an animated conversation in the garden, or the loggia, or the recreation-rooms, and in an instant, all, young and old, ceased, even without finishing the word on their lips, and retired in silence to their cells.

On his way back from the Gesù, one St. Ignatius' day, after assisting at the solemn High Mass, his companion inquired of him what grace he had been asking of his holy Father. 'To die in the Society, without having ever broken a single rule.' His love of obedience found its expression in the love of its symbol, and he used to keep his rule book open before him on his table while studying. At night he put it under his pillow, and when dying he held it in his hands, as the title-deeds of his reward.

CHAPTER VII

His watchfulness over his innocence.

BUT however diligent he was in the observance ot his rule, John was not less watchful to fly the most distant shadow of fault against the angelic virtue. 'If you wish to be a child of Mary and the Society, be a zealot for thy chastity. I will ever detest,' he wrote, 'and execrate the merest imperfections which any way might lead to faults against chastity, such as fondness for eating, carelessness about guard over the eyes whether in or out of doors ; because to be impure is to be worse than the demons of hell.'

It was this strong feeling which gave him such a disgust for the vice of gluttony, which he called 'the enemy of chastity'—the 'hindrance to the delights of prayer ;' and he used to say that, if we except impurity, there is nothing in a religious which so scandalizes seculars as when they see him given up to the pleasures of the table, and hear him talking about eating and drinking. Father Cepari has preserved his remarks on this fault—'The vice of gluttony is an inordinate love of eating. Its acts are—often thinking and speaking about food ; not being content with ordinary diet, but seeking for dainties and special dishes ; eating in an unseemly way, with too great greed and haste.' At his age—just growing into manhood—he felt often, as was natural, the cravings of appetite ; and he used, with his habitual

J

delicacy of conscience, to accuse himself of having now and then yielded to gluttony. He made it a subject of much reflection and frequent examination. But, if there was any fault, he certainly erred rather on the side of abstinence. His constant mortification must in the long run have told most seriously on his frame. He made the resolve—'I must remember to feed Christ as well as my body : his food is mortification, and so I must never leave table without having denied myself in something.' And accordingly, as we saw during his noviceship, he always left something of what was placed before him. He eat without hurry. 'I shall be content with ordinary food ;' and he never would consent, on plea of health, to have special dishes prepared for him. He used to say that he trusted in God's help that what he eat would do him no harm, because he took it in order not to be in any way different from common life. If he got something against which his stomach revolted—as, for example, the strong cheese used in Italian cookery —he simply did not take the dish, but never asked for anything in its place.

He made war upon his body by fasting every Saturday in honour of our Lady, observed the weekly abstinence at the evening meal prescribed by the rule ; and as, with the exception of vacation days, when he had to walk to the vigna, he never took any breakfast, he really might be said to have fasted twice a week. He scourged himself Monday, Wednesday, and Friday every week, for the space of a *De profundis* recited leisurely. Now and then he added an extra penance on the Saturday, and, during Lent, on every day except Sunday. On certain great feasts he wore the hair-shirt. Obedience, the only measure of austerity in the Society, would not allow him more. But he sought self-denial in everything. When seated he never rested his back, when kneeling he never leant upon a support. 'Let what is sweet be bitter to you, what is bitter, sweet;' and the rod that made the bitter waters sweet was his love of the Cross. 'Do you want to know if you love your vocation? See if you love to mortify yourself. Your vocation is to be a companion to Jesus; how can you be so if you are not crucified with Jesus?'

To these victories over the taste and touch, Berchmans joined the strictest watch over his eyes. He had made a covenant with them never to raise them from the ground, except when duty or necessity obliged him. If he met any one he just looked to see to whom he was speaking, and then resumed his habitual position. When he went to the room of his professor, as he knew to whom he was speaking, he never raised his eyes at all. The out-door students, who attended the lecture-room, often made a plot to create a sudden disturbance in class, with the hopes of startling him out of his accustomed reserve; but they never succeeded. So careful was he on this point, especially when outside the College, that several persons told Father Cepari that out of curiosity they had again and again, and for a long time together, watched John, but had never been able to tell the colour of his eyes. And in fact there were many who were constantly with him in the College who could say they had never seen them at all.

The scholastic who lived in the same room with him asked Berchmans, one day, how he managed to keep always so recollected. 'A good guard over the heart,' was his reply; 'and, because this could not exist without bridling the eyes, a continual mortification of my eyes.' So entire was this mortification that he lived for nearly three years in Rome, the city of pageant and splendour, and—with the exception of the procession of Corpus Christi, when the triumph of our Blessed Lord was the attraction—he never witnessed any of its solemnities. On the Good Friday of **1619**, his professor of ethics, Father Galluzzi, preached the Passion sermon before the Holy Father and his Court; and the next year that distinction was conferred on Berchman's favourite professor, Father Piccolomini. But even these inducements do not seem to have made the mortified student break through his self-imposed rule. Up to our very days, the arrival of princes and ambassadors and the state progresses of the Pope, made the streets of Rome the scene of frequent spectacles. In the days of John they were both more frequent and more magnificent; but if he came across them they went by unseen, as they were unsought. The funeral of a Pope, the coronation of his successor in St. Peter's, and his *possesso*, or enthronization at St. John Lateran, are amongst the most striking ceremonies of the Church, and crowds flock in from every country to be spectators. On the *possesso* all the Papal Court in its greatest magnificence, accompanied by the foreign ambassadors, the Cardinals then in Rome, and numbers of princes and nobles, invited for the occasion, go in a splendid cavalcade, with the newly-elected Pope, who is mounted on a white mule, to his Cathedral Church of St. John Lateran—the *Omnium ecclesiarum*, *Orbis et Urbis*, *mater et caput*—and there the Pontiff is enthroned as Bishop of Rome and the Universal Church.

The 9th of February, **1621**, Cardinal Alexander Ludovisi was chosen to succeed Paul V., under the title of Gregory XV. The coronation on the loggia of St. Peter's, but just completed by the deceased Pope, and the accompanying ceremonies within the church, did not seduce Berchmans from his books and work. 'I have seen one procession since I came to Rome, and that is quite enough for me,' was his only

answer, given in the best of good humour, to the
brilliant descriptions which were made to induce him to be
present. On the day of the *possesso*, just three months
later—the 9th of May—he could not so easily escape.
It was the custom of all the Jesuits in Rome to assemble
in the Piazza del Gesù, and receive the blessing of the
new Pope, kneeling on the ample steps that lead up to
the church door. So Berchmans had to be there with
the rest. But he seems[1] to have asked his companion,
Ladislaus Bercka, a Bohemian scholastic, to leave him
behind, or to let him stay out of the way till it was over.
The young Radkaï, whom we find so often with him,
asked him on his return to the College what he thought
of the cavalcade. 'To tell the truth,' he answered, 'I
was so completely blocked out by the crowd I saw
nothing at all, so I took advantage of the time to spend
it in prayer.' A short time before this, Cardinal Maurice
of Savoy, who was afterwards to make such a figure in
the history of Piedmont, made his entry, with almost
regal pomp, into Rome. His Eminence made a state
visit to the Roman College, and while he sat at table he
was welcomed by a round of speeches and sonnets.
The learning and varied nationality of the professors and
students were represented by twenty-seven Fathers or
brothers, each of a different country, who had to develope
in their various tongues the eighth chapter of the Book
of Wisdom. From a list of those who took part in the
entertainment, preserved in the Burgundian Library,[2] we
find that Father Thomas Coleford, then minister at
the English College, represented our language; John
Mambrecht, whose love of the crucifix bore him up
through a life of labour and suffering, through severe
imprisonment in Edinburgh gaol, and the toils of army
chaplain in Flanders, spoke in his native Gaelic; a

---

[1] Testim. P. Joan. Benci., Summ., n. 15.   [2] No. lxxxv.

Richard ——, his surname unknown, represented Ireland in a Celtic speech. It may have been Father Richard Comerford or Father Richard Walshe. In the passage selected, Solomon, inspired by the Holy Ghost, tells in beautiful but simple words how, in his youth, he had chosen Wisdom to be his spouse for ever. The allusion was transparent, for the Cardinal was then only twenty-seven, and had worn the purple for fourteen years. Whether by chance, or by choice of his Superior, there was allotted to John to paraphrase in Flemish a portion of the eleventh verse, *Et in conspectu potentium admira-bilis ero*—'And I shall be admired in the sight of the mighty.' The instant he had finished his little discourse, instead of staying to see the rest of the entertainment, or to hear those that were to follow him, he drew near to the subminister, and asked him if there was some work for him in the kitchen—washing up the dishes, or anything of the kind. Being told there was nothing to be done there, he left the place, and went to pray in the church.

One day the boys of the Roman Seminary performed, in presence of two ambassadors to the Holy See, a Latin play. Its title was *Flavia*, and its author was Father Bernardine Stefonio, S.J., a distinguished professor of the Roman College, who died about that time, while engaged as tutor to Alphonsus, the son of Duke Cæsar of Modena. The drama seems to have been very popular—*Semper placita, sæpius postulata* [3]—and the community of the Roman College had been invited to be present. John was there, but he chose the lowest place, and never once raised his eyes during the performance. One of the gentlemen of the ambassador's suite was

---

[3] Cnobbert, of Antwerp, published it in 1634 at Antwerp, it having been already printed in Rome in 1620. Father Bernardine at his death begged that his MSS. might be destroyed, that no memory of him might be left.

entranced by the indescribable charm of that modest face, and whispered to a scholastic who was sitting behind him, Octavius Falconi, 'That young Father is surely an angel!' Octavius felt at once how true were these words. 'Sir,' he answered, 'virtue makes itself known to all.'

This constant guard of his eyes had nothing repulsive about it, because it was all in harmony with the perfect composure of his whole person. When walking, when sitting down, at table, or over his books, he was a living comment of the rules of modesty written by St. Ignatius; and, as some one said, if these rules were lost you would have had only to look at John to find them again.

The same impression was expressed in another saying, that if an angel were to put on human form, and have a body, he could not have a modesty beyond what one saw in Berchmans. The memory of St. Aloysius, then so fresh in the community, enabled them to draw a comparison, and they were forced to own that the saint's modesty did not surpass that of their new Belgian scholastic, for the simple reason that John's was fault- less. The day students called him Father Modesto, or Modestissimo, and held him in such favour as to send him messages, begging to be remembered in his prayers;[4] and people would stop in the street to gaze after him he passed. As has been mentioned above, he generally attended the afternoon conference on Holy Scripture given in the Gesù on Sundays and holidays. As soon as he entered the church, he knelt down in some retired spot, with his eyes cast down, and there he stayed without stirring, engaged in prayer till the vespers were over. A Genoese gentleman, who had frequently noticed him, said to Father Ignatius Lomellino, his countryman, 'What do you think is the reason why I come here?'

---

[4] Father Horace Grassi's evidence.

'I suppose, sir, to assist at vespers,' answered Father Ignatius. 'My chief reason,' the gentleman explained, 'is to see and watch that young man who is present every holiday. As soon as he has got in, he kneels down there quietly and modestly to say his prayers, never raising his eyes. I am persuaded he is a saint. When I look round the church, some are listening to the music, some staring about them, others talking and amusing themselves. This youth, in the midst of all, is the only one who is praying—motionless and modest. I am sure he is a saint.' Though all this became nearly natural to him, still he took every pains to perfect himself more and more; he watched over himself with the greatest strictness. 'Brother,' he said to Alexander Gottofredi, 'I fear, when walking I bend my head too low; please notice, and tell me if I do so, for I am determined to correct myself.' He wrote a detailed scheme of the virtue of modesty, for his sort of academy in honour of our Blessed Lady.

To this self-restraint he added, as an additional outwork of his purity of heart, the greatest respect for others, never allowing the intimate terms on which he lived with his companions to degenerate into familiarity. He gave one of his brethren, who no doubt had asked it of him, this three-fold advice, 'Never to have a particular friendship with any one, nor get too close a familiarity with another. Secondly, to conquer any inclination to gluttony courageously for some space of time; in course of time he would have made himself so completely its master, as never to be guilty of faults against temperance. Thirdly, to make use of affections, moving ejaculations, to God; so he would feel his heart grow more tender and filled with confidence towards Him.' The only time we find that he threatened to denounce a companion to his Superior is in one of his notes on this subject, 'If

any one breaks the rule by touching me, even in joke,
I will let my Superiors know at once.' And he remarks
that one of the points to which he is instructed to answer
in the manifestation of conscience is, 'Whether he is
more familiar with any one more than another?' As
an additional precaution, he copied out the signs of too
close a friendship, as described by St. Bonaventure in
his *Progressus Religiosorum.* To these he added of his
own, that a friendship is always disordered as soon as
it leads to the violation of a rule, without your having
the courage either to notice it to your friend, or to refuse
to have any share in it. 'As for me,' he told a lay-
brother, Alexander Saraceni, 'I have not a single friend
to whom I am not ready to answer, should he ask anything of me against rule, " I cannot, I must not, do what
you ask me." Besides, all special friendship to one, is a
want of charity to the rest; and if it be true, as St. John
Climacus tells us, that young people in the world who
have an attachment, however holy, break it off rather
than be a scandal to others, how much more should
those consecrated to God avoid private conversations,
when too frequently repeated.'

Such extraordinary care had its reward, even in this
world. The lily bloomed in his soul as if the north
wind had not blown across it, as if it was the inclosed
garden of original innocence. To him was granted what
is given only to those who bear their baptismal robe in
its first whiteness, and only even to few among these.
No unclean temptation ever troubled his soul. This he
assured one of the lay-brothers, when talking of the
purity of our Blessed Lady he declared he owed this
favour to her. 'By God's grace, and favour of the ever
Blessed Virgin, I am not aware of ever having had
thoughts against purity or chastity ; and, indeed, I have
the greatest loathing for anything opposed to that

virtue.' He showed this in the opinion he passed on St. Augustine's *Confessions*. Father Cepari had suggested that he should read them, to profit by the many spiritual lights and affections they contain. But he could not bear the allusions to the early life of the great penitent. *Pater, lectio Confessionum S. Augustini non sapit mihi—* 'I do not relish the *Confessions* of St. Augustine;' and so his rector bade him put them aside. Would that his example were followed by those who run much greater risks; and in these days, when daily papers bring the worst scandals within the reach of all, when art and literature alike cater to corrupted and degraded tastes, that our young men would keep their eyes away from vice, which is none the less dangerous because covered with a varnish of culture or artistic merit! Not only was his soul unclouded by even the approach of evil, but his body showed this angelic privilege, as Father Cepari assures us he learned from John's lips, when he came to him to give the usual account of his conscience in the December of 1620; and this, as was his wont, he said he owed to our Blessed Lady, who had special charge over him by night and by day, especially since he had adopted the practice of saying every evening a Hail Mary in honour of her Immaculate Conception. Again, on the 18th of June, the last year of his life, during the triduum of recollection before the renovation of vows, which was to take place on St. Aloysius' day, he told his rector that during the past half year he had been still more perfectly and absolutely free from anything in body or mind, and as he wrote it down, according to his custom on such occasions, 'With regard to chastity, I have experienced nothing, nor do I seem ever to have been better, thanks to our Blessed Lady.' This is confirmed by the deposition of Father Massucci, who had been his confessor since November, 1620, to

the effect that neither asleep nor awake had the slightest
imagination come across the spotlessness of his mind.
Father Thomas Bisdomini was telling this to the venerable
Cardinal Bellarmine, whose full days were just about to
close, and who was practising in the retirement of the
Novitiate of Sant' Andrea on the Quirinal his *Preparation
for Death*. The holy old man was moved to tears, and
said with astonishment, 'This is a very rare gift in a
young man, so full of spirits and life as he is.'

We cannot pass over in silence another privilege
granted to Berchmans, which is witnessed to by a cloud
of testimonies, and which we find recorded of the Angelic
Doctor, St. Thomas, of St. Stanislaus Kostka, and of other
saints. His face was not only a sermon in praise of
purity, moving to sorrow for the past, on which the most
modest loved to gaze, asking God the while to grant
favours for his sake ; but its sight filled those that looked
upon him with a holy influence, before which temptations
fled abashed. A penitent who concealed his name, but
whose deposition was attested to as genuine by his
confessor, declared that he found such relief in the
grievous assaults to which he was subject, that he used
to come frequently to catch a glimpse of him at the
College. 'When I heard,' the statement continues, 'that
he was dead, I hurried at once to the house, and saw
his body several times, both in the church and the
sacristy. I stayed for a long time looking at it, full of
deep feelings of devotion ; I kissed his holy hands and
angelic brow; I touched his virginal body—lily pure ;
nor could I tear myself away. From that time to this
I have experienced great relief. I often visit his tomb,
ever with the same result. As it is not right in so
delicate a matter to make known my name, and as,
moreover, my confessor has forbidden me to do so,
I authorize the Reverend Father Thomas Bisdomini,

theologian of the Society of Jesus, to whom I have made an attestation under oath of the graces I have received, to confirm in my stead what I have above declared. He has written this at my dictation, that I might not be known by my handwriting. I hold for certain that what I narrate is a great miracle due to the intercession of this young and holy religious.' Many others, solemnly under oath, attested the same favour. Father James Seco, who was during the lifetime of John professor of theology at the Roman College, and who afterwards was consecrated bishop with the right of succession to the Patriarchate of Abyssinia, used to say he had only to look at our saint to be freed from any cloud of melancholy and to be filled with a spiritual gladness. Another of the Roman College declares, 'The modesty of his face could not be likened to anything so well as to a picture of the Virgin Mother which is at the House of the Gesù, *alla Natività.*' When Father Bisdomini told Cardinal Bellarmine that his looks inspired the love of purity, 'Oh!' said the holy old man, in tears, 'this was a privilege granted to the Mother of God, and it must have been granted by her to this her servant and child.' This opinion is confirmed by the fact that Berchmans was accustomed every day to say a rosary of twelve Hail Marys in honour of our Lady, pondering as he repeated it on the stainless purity of his Queen, and begging the grace that he, by his way of acting and dealing with others, might create in their hearts a love of the angelic virtue, and so share with her the power of driving out from them all contrary thoughts and feelings. Here are his words, as he wrote down his intention, 'The Blessed Virgin drove away impure thoughts from those who looked upon her; do you too ask that by your dealings with others you may create in them a love of chastity.'

The favour which the anonymous client of John declared he had received after his death was similarly attested by numbers, who acknowledged that they had been freed by his intercession from the imminent danger which menaced them with the loss of their innocence, either by temptations from within or from without. Many there were who hung up *ex votos* at his tomb as a token of their gratitude.

If we search out some of the means by which John warded off not merely deliberate sin, but the smallest breach of his multiform rule, we may class them under his carefully ordered life, the guard he set over his tongue, the care he took in examining his conscience, and the day which he set apart each month exclusively for the work of looking after the progress of his soul.

When speaking of his studies, we mentioned his practice of arranging at the half-yearly triduum of recollection the employment of his time for the coming six months. This forethought descended to the smallest details, so that, however his day might be taken up, however any public duty might change its usual order, he was never found unprepared; all his duties had their time and place. Not content with this, he used to consider how he could *best* perform each action, however trivial it might seem to be, as going to bed, when in bed, getting up, preparing for meditation, hearing Mass. In a word, every duty, great and small, was written down with its intention, its time, the circumstances in which it was to be done; so that when it had to be done, it was done with the greatest thought and in the most perfect manner. Nay, more, his care extended further than the duties he would have to perform; he tried to imagine contingencies, and to settle how he should act if they occurred. 'If this or that shall happen, I will do so and so; should any one ask me a certain thing, I will answer in this way.' All was carefully written out, as we see in his diary which has been published. This was the secret of his blameless conversation, as he told one of his companions, 'I never speak without first thoroughly thinking what I ought to say, and recommending it to God, so as never to say anything that may displease Him.' The result was, he never said a really idle word, according to St. Ignatius' definition, 'Something which is no good whatever to oneself, or to one's neighbour, or which is not said with an intention to be of any good.'

He thoroughly possessed every rule or custom of the Society on this subject, and as thoroughly observed and practised it. He was a man of few words, every one of which was well weighed and carefully corrected before it was uttered. 'Speak little, do much' was one of his mottoes. Father Cepari remarks, and his Tuscan ear makes him an exacting critic, on the purity of Berchmans' Italian, and the rare correctness of his accent, which he gained in so short a time, though he spoke so little. The silence ordained by the Jesuit rule out of hours of recreation is by no means so absolute as in some of the other religious orders, and it is not violated by a few chance words. Berchmans never was known to avail himself of this saving clause, and kept the rule with the exactness of a Carthusian. Though he knew French, and had countrymen to whom the sound of Flemish would have been sweet, he always spoke Italian at the hours of recreation, as his rule enjoined. For the same reason he used Latin when he required to speak out of recreation time. One of his religious brethren had permission from his Superiors, on account of his and their great opinion of Berchmans, to have recourse to him for advice in all his affairs. He came frequently to him in time of silence. If a word or two sufficed, Berchmans settled the matter at once; if a larger conversation were needed, he deferred it till the next hour of recreation.

The third means used by Berchmans to purify his soul was the examination of conscience. The value he set on the Institute made him esteem most highly a means on which St. Ignatius, as had all saints before him, laid the greatest stress. He told Father Cepari a month before his death, and this declaration in writing was found among his papers—'Among the means which the Society makes use of to gain its end I make great account of prayer, the examen—both general and particular, and openness with my Superiors; nor do I recollect I have ever omitted any of these duties, nor would I omit them for the whole world.' He had made a resolution never to do so, even when ill in bed, for he used to say—'Through them any one can arrive at great purity and perfection.' On his way back from the Gesù, where he had been present at an exhortation of the Father General, he said to his companion—'Let us make our examen in the streets, for the College bell has rung for it by this time.' We find ever the same punctuality. One morning, when he had been assisting at a general communion in the Church of the Trinità dei Pellegrini, another time, while walking in the vineyard before dinner on a vacation day; in fact, he never allowed any human respect to hinder the fulfilment to the moment of so important a duty.

But he set special store on the particular examen. The *Divide et Impera*—the old fable of the bundle of sticks—had in the practical mind of St. Ignatius taken the shape of those rules, so minute and precise, which he has given us in his Book of Exercises, and which he had already tested by his own experience. To take each fault, one at a time, and crush it thoroughly, or each virtue and gain a facility in its practice before going on to fresh successes, had been one of the great secrets of the perfection of the soldier - saint. Berchmans stirred himself up to faithful compliance with its laws by remembering how punctually the founder of his order had adhered to this exercise during the years spent at the University of Paris in engrossing study and labour for souls ; and again, how much all his first children in religion had esteemed this practice. If ever, through forgetfulness or of any other cause, John neglected any of the prescriptions on the subject, not only did he impose on himself a good penance, but he would go of his own accord to tell his fault to his Superior or to the Spiritual Father—as a rein and bit, as he put it, to make him more watchful another time.

The day on which he began some fresh subject as matter for his particular examen — for example, to conquer pride—he started by imposing on himself the practice of two acts of the opposite virtue, as would be, in this case, of humility, one in the morning, the other in the afternoon. Next day he exacted from himself the practice of four acts, the day after six, and so on, till the acts were legion. The wonder is that his head, already so taxed, was not seriously injured by the severe stress such a practice must have entailed.

Not content with the two examinations his rule prescribed, he imposed on himself an additional one—a sort of supplement to his particular examen—which he repeated constantly through the day. Every time he came into his room, no matter how often, he took holy water, and then, making the sign of the Cross, knelt down for a moment or two, renewed his intention, and cast a glance forward over the action he was just going to commence. The result of this three-fold examen, repeated every day with great care and attention, was that he acquired a perfect knowledge of himself, and took notice of the very smallest thought that passed through his mind, each feeling, even though an inde-liberate inclination. And, not content with this, he noted them down in writing.

Still, in spite of such minutiæ, in spite of the exquisite delicacy of conscience thus acquired, there was no disease or exaggerated tenderness, such as is properly called scrupulosity. Not only Father Cepari and his confessors testify to this, but he himself frankly owned to one of his companions that he had never in his life suffered from scruples, which are the plague of pious souls. The way he judged himself was gathered from the chapters of faults he gave in to his Superiors, to extort from them admonitions and public reprehensions in the refectory. The faults were so slight that they proved the great spiritual light in which he ever dwelt, and the spotlessness of his life. All that heard them were profoundly touched and edified, and many kept these chapters as a relic, out of veneration for the holiness they displayed.

To keep these practices in full life, Berchmans devised an additional plan. Each month, with the knowledge and approval of his Superiors, he resolved to choose a day when there were no lectures and to spend it as he would in time of retreat. The only exception from rule he ever asked was to absent himself from recreation the preceding evening. Four hours he employed in medi-tation, the rest of the time was passed in a careful examination of himself. Aided by his notes he compared one week with another, one month with that which went before it, to see whether or no he had made progress. He studied whether he had kept his rules, his reso-lutions, the order of life he had laid down for himself; how he had made his examens, how he had kept guard

K

over his eyes; in a word, as Father Cepari says, whom we are almost entirely quoting, 'if he found a string of his well seasoned instrument at all slackened, he tuned it to its right pitch, so as to delight with sweet harmony the ear of God.'

CHAPTER VIII.

*John's practice of virtue, attachment to his vocation,
obedience, and love of poverty.*

WE have seen how Berchmans laboured at the preservation and increase of his purity of heart. Now we are
to study the beautiful tower of holiness that arose from
foundations so deep and so wide.

Thankfulness to God for His blessings is so often
forgotten, that we may safely give the first place to
Berchmans' gratitude for his vocation to religion. Besides,
this gratitude, which found its expression in the love of
the Society to which God had called him, was but an
acknowledgment that his call to religious life was the
special way Divine Providence had chosen for him, and
therefore the sum of all the other graces—his *via, veritas,*
and *vita.* It was no narrow love, no party feeling,
that made his whole heart cling to the order he had
embraced.

He spoke of other religious orders with a respect that
he had inherited from his teacher and Father, St. Ignatius,
a respect enjoined by the Spiritual Exercises, and which
the very motive that made him love the Society obliged
him to have towards others equally authorized by the
Church, founded by saints, equally the work of God.
He spoke of them all in language their own children
could not have outdone, and which would have delighted
them had they overheard his expressions. He saw in
them the representatives of their sainted founders, and

K 2

so, whenever he met any religious, he always took care
to be the first to raise his hat, and he begged his
companions to do the same, no light labour in the
streets of Rome.

But it was to his beloved Society, as to his mother,
that he gave the largest share of his affection.   His
deep-seated love, so childlike, so tender, made his heart
throb with joy at its successes, filled him with zeal for
its good fame and name, made him ardently desire
its increase and preservation. 'Whenever,' says Father
Carminata, 'he spoke of the Society, he did so with
such ardour, with such profound esteem, that to hear
him talk seemed as if he were Father Jerome Nadal
himself, who has been so justly styled the "Soul of our
Constitutions."' 'I will be as zealous for the honour of
the Society of Jesus as a really ambitious man would
be of his own honour,' is John's own expression in his
notes.   This love made him kiss reverently his habit
before putting it on in the morning. The old Jesuit
dress, the Spanish cassock of St. Ignatius' time, with the
Spanish cloak and hat, worn till lately at Rome, had
become the adopted costume of the order, though, as
it is well known, no peculiar habit is enjoined by the
rule.   Its association with the sainted founder, with all
his great followers, gives it even in our time a special
interest.   In his order of the day, which he wrote while
at Rome, he notes down, 'When you take your cassock
into your hands, before putting it on, kiss it, rejoicing
in your mind that to-day you are still allowed to wear
the livery of Christ.'   It was the same feeling which
prompted him at his death to ask to be allowed to die
clothed in his habit. He considered his rule the way God
had manifested to him by which to arrive at perfection.
'The more you love your rule, the more will you make
progress. Make yourself familiar with it, for the Exercises

show us the mind of St. Ignatius, as do the Constitutions in writing—his life in action.' He had conceived a great love for it while yet a secular, from seeing its results in his masters. The longer he remained in religion, the deeper grew that esteem, and so much the more did he feel that he was unworthy to be a member of the Society. Here is a letter to the point, addressed in 1619 to his old benefactor and master, Canon Froymont.

'Very Reverend Sir,—

'Pax Christi.

'I should fear to incur the reproach of ingratitude if I let slip so favourable an opportunity,[1] without paying my respects to your Excellency, to whom I owe so much. For it is to you, reverend sir, I confess I am indebted for any success I have had in my studies, for whatever has flowed into my mind of the milk of piety and the fear of the Lord. Yes, and even my being in the Society of Jesus; for though so unworthy and wicked—I own it, and I willingly own it—I am, for all that, a companion of Jesus, and that is enough for me; all this I owe to your most religious training. I enjoy very good health at Rome, whither, last year, by my Superior's orders, I came from Mechlin. I have finished my first year's course of philosophy in the Roman College of our Society, in which there are more than two hundred Fathers and brothers, for the most part continually engaged in study. How wonderful it is! Nearly all are of different nationalities. There are Spaniards, Poles, Germans, Portuguese, Dalmatians, Sicilians, Neapolitans, Belgians, Frenchmen, and men of other countries. And yet they are united with such a bond of love and charity, that they might be all sons

---

[1] Probably some Belgian Fathers were returning home at the conclusion of their studies.

of one mother. And amongst such as these am I !
Good God ! [Here follows an inquiry about the precise
date of his birth.] For the rest I only commend myself
to the holy sacrifices of your Excellence, and I will ever
be mindful of you. Given at Rome, in the Roman
College of the Society of Jesus, November 23.

       ' Your Excellency's servant in Christ,

                    ' JOHN BERCHMANS.

' Affectionate regards to M. d'Ittré, Giles and his
people, my brothers and sister, and all at Diest. I
should wish your Excellence to take care that my
brothers and sisters (*sic*) go to confession every week,
and receive holy communion every month. About
anything else, I have no anxieties. That my relations
had to beg their bread from door to door would not
be a trial or a shame to me. That they should offend
God mortally, I could not endure.'

In the December of 1620 he told Father Cepari,
' I live most content in my vocation, and often
experience a great tenderness of feeling towards the
Society.' And again on the last June of his life, ' I
live very content ; never, praise be to God, have I
been tempted ; and this half year I have felt such
affection towards the Society as I never felt before.'
Berchmans had the idea that the Society should not
exceed the limit of sixteen or eighteen thousand members,
for he thought, were that otherwise, its discipline would
fail, and it would be impossible to govern it rightly.
His college companion, Father Oliva, lived to see the
Society extended to what John thought should be its
maximum ; and the verdict of the Catholic world would
hardly justify his apprehensions, when, in 1759, before
the expulsion of the Society from Portugal by Pombal,

it had reached the number of twenty-two thousand five hundred and eighty-nine members. Another of his sayings was, that he had hopes that the Society would last a long time because of two things in its Constitutions —the door was always open for the bad who had to be turned out, and bolted for the good, since they are unable to accept any dignity, neither can the professed Fathers be dismissed. These two statutes were a subject of great satisfaction to him.

The affection and esteem Berchmans entertained for the Society made him value practically, as he had done in the Novitiate, the common life of the Society. He knew that in following this he was not only doing God's will, but that he had, without going a step beyond, or outside it, full scope for the exercise of the most exalted perfection.

'Follow in all things the community; and hate, above all, singularity.' He defines this fault—separating oneself and keeping at a distance from the community, or from duties, or anything else which are common to all, without cause or necessity. Its actions, he notes down, are, wishing to have special food, or extra clothes, or taking them without necessity, keeping things which others do not have, withdrawing from what is done in common, as, for instance, in the Society, from the public recreation, or not doing what others do at the same time as they do it; 'neither,' he goes on to say, 'does permission or approval of a Superior make the action cease in such cases to be singular, but only hinders it from being a fault against obedience.' He adds that singularity is hostile to charity, and that common life, besides being very safe, is a certain way of attaining holiness, and takes away all danger to vainglory.

To these principles Berchmans adhered with the greatest exactness, trying at once to come in to every-

thing just as the rest, and at the same time to do
everything with the greatest perfection, however small it
might be. He loved to render every action he offered
to God in some sort worthy of Him, and the exquisite
finish which he bestowed on each gave a rare beauty to
the simplest thing. We must give an example of John's
practice. He was not fond of games, but preferred to
talk and discuss subjects. Still, on vacation days, when
the scholastics went out to the vigna—to which allusion
has been already made—if any one asked him to play
at *trucco* or *piastrelle*,[2] he joined at once if it was any
convenience to the others. He would take for his
partner it did not matter whom, however unskilled,
though sure, in consequence, of being beaten. He gave
his whole mind to the game, and spoke of nothing else,
paid no attention to anything else ; in fact, played
admirably. Before giving a stroke he made, openly,
the sign of the Cross ; but this was only what he
did before beginning everything, to show that all was
God's. He never shouted, whether he hit, or whether he
missed. If beaten, he knelt down at once and recited
a Hail Mary for the winners ; if he won, he did not
say anything, showed no extraordinary joy, much less
did he crow over those whom he had beaten. This was
but one instance of what made up his whole life : the
smallest actions done most exceedingly well.

If John practised with the minutest perfection every
duty of his religious life, we may be sure the root and
reason of it all was his genuine obedience. St. Ignatius
desired that the true children of his Society should be
distinguished by this mark—that they never considered
the person who gave an order, but only Christ our Lord,
for Whose sake they obeyed. It was not that he thought
this easy, as it often appears to those who have not tried

---

[2] A sort of seventeenth century croquet, still played in Italy.

it, but he hoped that as Simon the Cyrenean had helped Christ to bear His Cross, so Christ would help him to carry His yoke. He aimed straight at the grand principle, 'I will endeavour to find God in my Superiors. Never wish the Superior to give you a reason for his order. Take care not to excuse yourself to your Superiors. I will obey my brother the sacristan humbly and with great promptness whatever he may tell me to do.'

And these resolutions were most faithfully kept. He was set to serve a Father who was very long at Mass, at an hour which was very inconvenient for his studies. He served for many months, but never made a complaint. Another time the Father was a priest whose bad health prevented his saying Mass at a fixed hour. Sometimes he celebrated early, sometimes at a later hour. The sacristan told him one day he pitied him for the inconvenience to which he was put. 'Oh!' said he, sweetly, 'it is never an inconvenience for me to serve Mass.'

One of the scholastics, by order of his Superiors, had distributed among the young men some papers to be copied. He found many of them had written their parts so badly, that he told them they must write them over again. John was of the number. All the rest found reasons to excuse themselves. He alone, whose handwriting was not good of itself, and who, as a foreigner, was not accustomed to the Italian style of writing, took the order as from heaven, and began at once to carry it out. The minister of the Roman College gave Berchmans the charge of the Spiritual Father's room. He took such pains to keep it in order and supplied with all requisites, that the Father in his deposition specially alludes to this willingness to serve, which he had never seen equalled. He was struck with John's thoughtfulness in endeavouring never to be in

his way; how our saint noticed the hours when he was
out; or, at all events, never said a word, or caused
him any distraction when within. The same principle
of faith made him most respectful to his Superiors. He
always addressed them with berretta in hand, and with
all humility and modesty. He defended against all
comers, not only their orders, but their very sayings.
Not only was he always perfectly free from any feeling
of aversion against his Superiors, but he said that not
even a thought against any of them, or against their
commands or opinions, had ever come across his mind.
It mattered not at whose hands he sought a penance,
as he often did either for real faults, or simply to
satisfy his love of humiliations, he always asked it on
his knees. So full was he of this supernatural view of
obedience, that he took every occasion to make others
share it with him. Nicholas Radkaï tells us he was
talking with our saint on the openness religious should
have towards their Superiors. 'He asked me to whom
I generally went to ask for a penance. "To Father
Minister," I said. "And why not to Father Rector?"
"Because I think Father Rector has already enough to
do, without my going to bother him with requests of
this sort." "I myself generally go to Father Rector,"
was John's answer. And he went on to explain at full
the important place this custom held in the Society, and
so successfully, that in the course of the conversation
he succeeded in making me own that I had some feeling
against Father Rector and one of my religious brethren,
and that in consequence I tried to keep out of their
way as much as possible. "Only," I added, "do not
betray me; this is a secret I have confided to you
under the seal of our old standing and close friendship.
Take care not to tell any one." This ran counter to
John's ideas and resolutions. "Listen, my dear Nicholas;

never confide to me **what you do not wish to have told
to your** Superiors, if I think it right to do so." However,
he promised for this **time to keep my secret on condition**
that the **same** day **I** would **go** and make all **straight**
with **my** Superior and with **my** brother, and by **dint of**
reasoning and entreaties, he wrung **from me the** promise
to do so.'

For the same reasons, he confided everything to **his**
Superiors. 'With my Superiors and Spiritual Fathers I
will endeavour to be candid and sincere, and like the
clearest water.' Not content with the frequent occasions
his rule gave him, he went every week **to** give an
account of three things; how he had observed the rule
of silence; how he had spoken on spiritual subjects;
how he had kept **the** resolutions he had made in his
meditation.

He could **not even bear to** see his fellow students
holding different views **from those of** their professors.
With all the **energy of** his soul **he** stuck to their opinions.
His great ability always enabled him either to uphold
these victoriously, or at least to make in their behalf a
plausible defence. This loyalty was so well known, **that**
some at recreation time used to amuse themselves with
attacking the views which the professors adopted, simply
to enjoy the ready and skilful battle which Berchmans
did with great animation **in** their defence.

Amabo cellam—'I **will be fond** of my room,' comes
again and again in his notes. He used to say that a
Jesuit who is engaged **in** the ministry should, **when in**
his room, wish to be **out** helping **his** neighbours, and
when out of doors, should **wish** to be back in his room,
so as not to give **himself** up too much to retirement,
or too much to society. But this was no natural love,
such as **abundance of books or** creature comforts might
create. Poverty **of the** strictest kind was the sole

adornment of his room. During his juniorate, he had not even a crucifix before which to pray, but merely a little cross of common wood, blackened with ink. When he died, he left a common print of our Lady and Child nailed up to the wall at his bedhead, and a similar one at the table where he used to study. One of these came into the hands of Father Oliva, who kept it as a relic. Everything was kept beautifully in order, and he never left his books or papers unarranged, or his table undusted. His love of poverty, sincere and profound as the love of a child for his mother, was seen in all his doings. When he noticed that the girdle he had brought from Belgium was of a finer material than those worn by the community, he gave it to the lay-brother, Biagio Pedretti, who had charge of the wardrobe, and begged to have a common one in its place. He carried at his waist a very poor old rosary of ebony, several beads of which were wanting. Another was offered him, but he refused it, saying that he did not need it as long as his own rosary lasted. He carefully put out his lamp the moment the daylight he caught at his window enabled him to see without it. The shutters served to keep out the keen cold of an Italian winter morning ; but he opened them as soon as he had done his meditation, to save the consumption of oil. Anything satisfied him ; he never showed the slightest sign of discontent at the clothes which were given out to him. On the contrary, he was delighted when they were old and poor. 'A Jesuit,' he said, 'should be like a statue, which never complains, whether it is covered with gold and jewels, or is stripped of its finery and clothed in rags.' If he required anything, he asked very humbly and respectfully for it from the person in charge. He went so far as to economize paper by writing very closely and leaving little or no margin.

He had brought with him several of those pious engravings from Belgium, to the delicate beauty of which we have elsewhere alluded. They were all parting gifts. But as soon as he reached the Roman College, he gave them all up, except a few which bore the names of those who had asked him to pray for them. But he even made a sacrifice of these when asked if he felt equal to it. And after that, whenever he got any sent to him, or pressed upon him by any of his countrymen who might come to see him, he took them straight to Father Rector. If his Superior was not in, he left them at his door, and said no more about them. However, Father Cepari easily guessed from whom they came. Two of these, etchings by Jerome Wiercx, which once had been in John's room, are kept bound up with some of his other writings in the Jesuit College at Louvain. One represents the Baptism of our Lord, the other our Blessed Saviour on His knees, surrounded by the instruments of His Passion. However, these, also, he gave up, and the two found in his room at death were probably placed there by some of his brethren to console him in his last hours ; for one day he told Father Cepari with great glee that, by God's grace, he simply possessed nothing at all, not even a print, and if he found he had anything he would bring it at once to him ; and not only that, but he did not wish to have anything from that time, nor even any affection for anything on earth.

The Greek Father, Andrew Renzi, the first of that nation who was penitentiary in St. Peter's, took him one day on a visit to Cardinal Bellarmine. Some one asked him afterwards if the Cardinal had given him anything. ' No,' he replied, ' and I would not have accepted it had he offered it to me.' This was told to the holy old man, and he said it reminded him of Blessed Aloysius, who, too, always wished to be poor and to possess nothing.

No Superior being at hand, John once made a present of a little pious print without having obtained permission, confident that leave would have been readily granted, and intending to let those over him know what he had done. But his delicate conscience reproached him for what he had done. Not content with accusing himself again and again of what he looked on as a fault, he wrote down his transgression, and the paper was found at his death. He told his companions that this affection for the poverty of Jesus Christ had been taught him in the Flemish Novitiate, where the novices were wont to begin their confessions by stating whether they had offended or not in any way against that virtue and against the silence enjoined by their rule.

CHAPTER IX.

John's humility and charity.

POVERTY is not of itself a virtue. Christ ennobled it by
taking it as His livery. Or as Dante puts it—

While Mary did remain below,
She with her Christ up to the Cross did climb.[1]

Since then, when embraced or borne for His love,
poverty has taken its rank among the great supernatural
virtues. It becomes a vice when it is a bid for esteem ;
or when a sign of contempt for others. Humility, true
Christian humility, as St. Francis of Sales defines it, and
as St. Ignatius had described it—desire of lowliness,
because we are thus more like our Lord—must be the
foundation of this evangelical virtue. Obedience, true
submission, cannot exist at all, or will soon wither away,
if it does not spring from humility. Thoughts like these,
put so plainly before the children of St. Ignatius, at the
very threshold of religious life, recalled to their minds
constantly in their rules, and in the Book of Spiritual
Exercises, of which they are the ultimate conclusions,
could not have failed to be deeply graven on the mind
of John. We do not read that he felt any of the
temptations to vainglory which assaulted St. Aloysius.
But he knew well that the one danger for those who are
raising a lofty structure of perfection, and venturing on
the higher paths of spiritual life, is pride, and he

------

[1] *Paradiso*, canto xi.

evidently felt it necessary to keep the love and practice of humility with all the care and earnestness of a beginner. Amongst his spurs to perfection, under the head of 'Pride,' he wrote—

'"*The beginning of all sin is pride.*"[2]

'Motives for doing away with pride: (1) Christ on the Cross, saying to me, "Learn of Me, you who pretend to be of My Society, because I am meek and humble of Heart." (2) If in your heart you foster pride, you are a liar, for your dress tells that you are a companion of Jesus, when, nevertheless, within you are really a companion of the devil. (3) I must root out pride, if I wish to have for my Mother Mary, the so lowly hand-maid of Christ. Remedies: (1) I will choose for myself a patron, who excelled marvellously in the opposite virtue; it shall be the most Blessed Virgin Mary. (2) I will diligently attend to self-knowledge. What I was —nothing; what I am—the ulcer of the world; what I shall be—a corrupted corpse.'

His third remedy is, frankness with Superiors. At the beginning of 1620, probably during the triduum of recollection before the renovation of vows, he drew up, with his usual diligence, the plan of a campaign against the subtlest and deadliest enemy of all virtue—

'*Resolutions for humility against pride.*

'I resolve the whole of this next year, 1620, with God's grace, to go in for humility. (1) That I may proceed in an orderly way in building up the house of holiness, by beginning with the foundation; (2) because if I am not humble, I am no use to the Society; (3) because "Nothing is difficult unto the humble, and nothing hard unto the meek." I resolve specially to

---

[2] Ecclus. x. 15.

direct to this all my prayers, desires, actions, and particular examens.

' My first particular examen for the next fortnight shall be noticing, that if my eye—*i.e.*, my intention—is pure, my whole body will be lightsome. The matter of the examen must be, to do nothing to be seen by men, and every day to make two acts of humility, one in the morning and another in the evening.

'The second examen: to give up nothing on account of men and human respect ; and every day to make four acts of humility, two in the morning and two in the evening.

'As to the other points here adjoined, they will be seen to when the first two examens are done with, observing in what you chiefly fail, and where you run any danger ; only take notice that you must add on each day two more acts of humility.

'1. To cut down any thoughts which make me feel proud about myself, for thus the axe is laid directly to the root of pride itself, which is self-esteem.

2. To say nothing which could redound to your own praise, unless obedience otherwise requires, for thus you take away the food of vainglory.

'3. Not to do in public what you can do within your room ; for the same reason.

4. When you are praised, be ashamed internally that you are considered by others to be what you are not; for the same reason.

'5. When another is being praised, drive from your mind all displeasure, which has its source in envy, and excite yourself to rejoice ; for in this way you easily will give every one the preference over yourself.

'6. Desire and manage to give the better part to others, and practically to consider all as your Superiors, treating them as such with humble respect, for this is what our

L

holy Father Ignatius commands.   Put yourself above none, and think highly of every one, because, though your brother now seems to you imperfect, how do you know but that he is chosen by God to be a martyr, &c.

'7. Have a dread, as far as you are concerned, of favours *gratis datæ*—such as working miracles, &c., because, oftentimes, man is by them exposed to the danger of eternal damnation.

'8. Accept humiliation, (1) *patiently*, for thus you increase your crown ; (2) *promptly*, for thus you imitate Christ, when He said in the Garden, "Arise ! let us go ;" (3) *joyfully*, for you will have a heaven on earth.

'9. Desire to be held as a vile person, and if this does not happen to you, be heartily sorry, for so you will become precious in God's eyes.'

The principles Berchmans here lays down are repeated again and again in his notes.   These are a few more of his maxims—'Contempt of oneself is a short cut to perfection, and causes great quiet.   Be vile in your own eyes ; desire to be considered so.   If others think you vile, be not sad.'   'You are safe, Peter, in crying out, "Depart from me, O Lord, because I am a sinful man," for Jesus does not go away, unless you first go away from Jesus.'

As we have seen, what he wrote on paper was perfectly copied in his daily actions.   He always made way for others, and gave them the first place, the first choice. He always sought by preference, in the refectory, the place near the reader which was allotted to the lay-brothers, the seat, by the way, of predilection of St. Aloysius, nor would he ever let a brother fill up his glass for him.   And, when he came to ask the refectorian for his breakfast, he always did so cap in hand.   If the scholastic who shared his room were busy or unwell, he was sure to make his bed for him. Wherever he was, his companion had always the place of honour, and he paid to all such reverence as though they were his masters. 'I will always act towards my brethren as their servant and worthless slave.' Naturally enough, the lay-brothers and his companions felt abashed at so much attention, especially as they knew it was not mere ceremony, but through pure devotion and love of humility. Far removed from any affectation, he never gave unusual titles, never saying 'your reverence' to any but to priests, calling his other fellow-students 'brother,' and those who were teaching 'master,' as was the custom in the Collegio Romano. He never congratulated any one after examinations, defensions of theses, sermons, or other actions, for he said—'To do it to some and not to others might be looked upon as partiality, while to do it to all would be to run the risk of flattery.' The same feeling of humility made him always the first to salute those he met, with a simplicity far removed from the ceremonious politeness of Italian manners—'I will act towards my brothers everywhere with great modesty and humility.'

Humiliations are the surest lessons of humility; and, as the saints have always done, he sought them greedily. His idea was that he had been admitted into the Society like a beggar, out of pure charity; and he strove to fancy that whatever was done for him was by simple favour. 'This thought,' he writes, 'moves me—in the Society I ought to be the slave of all, not the master, and this should be my boast; for how can I wish to be master when Christ our Lord came not to be ministered to, but to minister; and the ever Blessed Virgin Mary gloried in being a handmaid? So I will bear myself towards all my brethren, as should a slave and a vile bondsman.'

L 2

One Holy Week he was sent with some scholastics to help at the ceremonies in the Jesuit Church at Frascati. They stayed at the Villa Ruffinella, for a long time the country-house of the Roman College. The villa is situated on the upper slopes of the Tusculan hills, on the site of the ancient city. Many are the memories of that beautiful spot, where, we have good grounds for believing, stood the Villa of Cicero, and where St. Aloysius spent so many holy hours. In later days it passed into the hands of Lucian Bonaparte, and then into those of the royal house of Piedmont, who gave it, under certain conditions, to the Roman College. In 1848 the advisers of Victor Emmanuel claimed it back on the expulsion of the Fathers from Rome, and his property it was until, after the fall of Rome, it passed by sale into more worthy hands. No sooner had John, who was one of the first comers, entered the villa, than he began of his own account to sweep down the stairs. After a time the rest arrived, all splashed with mud. Without a word, he took their shoes on the sly, brushed and cleaned them. He was caught, however, in the act, and asked why he had done so. He parried the question by the graceful silence of a smile.

Though Berchmans had to serve, like the others, two days a week in the refectory, he got leave from the minister to serve two days besides. Whenever a fast-day came, he helped to clear away after supper. But the rector at last noticed his frequent reappearance, and forbad him to serve oftener than the others. He made no opposition, nor allowed himself to be at all put out. It was a pleasure to be waited upon by him, so attentive, so quick was he in forestalling each one's wants; and, although so modest and reserved, none ever had to wait or want for anything. He had a special liking for serving those Fathers and brothers who, from their occupations, were prevented from coming in time to table. Before and after serving he always said some prayers on his knees. He was generally the last of those who had been serving to leave his post and retire from the refectory at the close of the public meal, or the first table as it is called. The few moments that elapsed between the first and second table, or the dinner for those who had not been able to dine with the community, were spent by Berchmans in the church before the Blessed Sacrament. Even strangers noticed his punctuality; for it often happened that, coming in late, he had scarcely knelt down before the bell rang for second table, when at once he got up and went away. None of the scholastics left their places so frequently as he did to perform penances in the refectory. 'I shall not be ashamed of doing penance frequently in the refectory.' Every week he came forward, now with an old and ragged habit, now with other marks of humiliation. And the apparent pettiness of these mortifications did not induce him to give them up. He, by his example, lead others to imitate him. It was an opportunity of strengthening his love of humility; and he told Father Cepari that God gave him a great delight whenever he kissed the feet of the community, which he often did, in his fervour clasping them with both hands, as he reverently imprinted a kiss upon them; for he saw in spirit only his Lord, Whose love had taken captive his heart, as it did that of Mary Magdalene. So, when he used to ask a penance of his rector, he often got for an answer, 'Go and do your favourite penance.' Once a week it was the custom to gather in baskets, and carry to the College gates, the broken victuals. There the religious distributed them to the crowd of beggars who were gathered; and we can well understand why Father Oliva calls this 'a work of labour and great humility.' The destitute poor, like other classes of men, easily become **hard to** please when they know that what is given to them they can claim as a right. And in a Catholic country, **where** Christ's word is law, they do know they have the right to some share in the riches and good things of **their** betters. And **as** everything on this earth has its abuse, many **a** sturdy and lazy man mingled in the crowd **outside the** monastery gates; **and,** because they had neither claim nor right, were **only the** more insolent **and more exacting.** Dirt and the loathsome diseases of the mendicants, added to the repulsive nature of **a** work, always for that very reason dear to the lovers of Christ Crucified. **It** was **a** duty for which **John** eagerly intrigued, and only too glad was he **to** take another's place. Father Carminata narrates—'The Superior, it once happened, named several scholastics, out of whom I was to choose one to help me to make the usual distribution of food to the poor. All, one after another, excused themselves on the plea of being so busy that they could not possibly **come.** I told the Superior, **and** he said at **once,** "Very well! take Brother **Berchmans ;"** and his **tone of voice showed clearly I would not** have to seek further, **and that** the saintly brother was his ordinary refuge whenever he did not **know to** whom to turn to get a disagreeable duty done with **a** good grace. **And, in** fact, I had hardly let Berchmans know the Superior's wish **when he** hastened off at once, leaving **the** work **he was doing.'** Father Cepari confirms by his own testimony the surmise of Father Carminata.

Every Saturday, John went to the scullery, **both** morning and evening, to clean the dishes ; and all the year round he had, as at Mechlin, the charge of the lamps in the various corridors, no light task **in so** vast a house, but specially dear to him because it had been forty years before the office of St. Aloysius. His devotion to the saint added to his diligence, and he performed his unpleasant duty with the greatest exactness. Never a day passed without his inspecting them; and even on recreation days, when he went to the vigna, he used either to do his work before starting, or came back in time to set them in order. He was only afraid lest this duty should be taken from him, and he begged the rector to let him keep it on, spite of what he suffered during winter, when, owing to this work, his hands and fingers became so swollen and chapped that it was quite pitiful to see them. One day a Father noticed that the sharp north wind, which cuts like a knife in the clear sky around Rome—blowing as it does from the snow-covered Apennines—had bitten his ears and taken the skin off his face. He suspected at once that this was the result of some imprudence in corporal austerities. 'Brother John, you are going in for too severe mortification.' 'Oh, no, Father; but if it were so I should not be ashamed of it, because, in religion, one should not be afraid of practising acts of mortification.' He would keep on the old cassock and apron in which he did his work even in time of recreation, proud of the livery of the workshop of Nazareth.

As he cherished every opportunity of minting money and coining gold, so if he chanced to break a lamp glass, or to spill some oil, or in fact injure anything belonging to the house, he went at once to ask on bended knees for a penance; and this, in his resolutions, he put among others, *Non erubescere*—things he must not be ashamed to do, even when a priest, or whatever should be the post he might afterwards fill.

Charity towards one's neighbour, as it finds its greatest obstacle in pride, so it seems almost to come naturally to the humble. To those with whom he lived, John seemed to find no difficulty in the practice of the first of Christian virtues. But we see him giving to its acquirement all those pains which he used to gain the other points of his sanctity. He aimed, indeed, at the very highest perfection of charity, loving God in all, and all in God, and laboured to get that habitual faith which this supernatural practice requires, while he availed himself of every other means to acquire this virtue. He has left us a scheme of a series of particular examens, which he went through for this end.

A Particular Examen on Charity towards my Neighbour.

1. To suffer patiently the defects of my brethren, and perform one act of charity.
2. Never to judge any one, and perform two acts of charity.
3. To think well of all, and perform three acts of charity.
4. To feel for others, and perform four acts of charity.
5. To be glad and be pleased when others succeed, and perform five acts of charity.
6. I shall be kind, and ready to oblige, and do favours for every one, and perform six acts of charity.
7. Always to make excuses for my brethren in my own mind, as well as to others, and perform seven acts of charity.
8. To say good and kind words to others, and perform eight acts of charity.

His love was, first, for those of his beloved Society; while honouring all as his superiors, he gave them outwardly the honour and reverence according as each one's state demanded. It was quite enough for a Father to have been at any time his Superior; he commanded ever after John's affection, reverence, and respect, just as if he were still in authority over him. Towards the close of his life, he handed in, at the beginning of each month, to Father Piccolomini, of whom we have had so often to speak, a list of practices of devotion and penances, which he engaged to offer up as a proof of his gratitude. He did the same to his other Superiors, and even the General used to receive, on the eve of great feasts, this simple tribute of filial affection. It was a positive pain to him when he noticed that any of the community entertained a feeling of distrust towards his Superior. If he was walking with any of the Fathers, he took care, out of respect for their priestly character, to let them slightly precede him—*medio passu*, as he writes in his resolutions —not feeling worthy to walk in line with them, and in their presence he was reserved and respectful. 'Having gone out one day with me,' says Father de Britiis, 'Brother Berchmans kept at a little distance from me, telling me that he had a long time before made the resolution to do so, out of respect for the priestly character with which I was clothed, and that then, at least, he wished to begin seriously to keep his determination.' And we know from others that he adhered faithfully to his resolve. Father à Lapide tells us—'It has frequently happened to me to meet him in the court of the College, whilst he was walking about sharply to warm himself in winter time. The moment he saw me he stopped, and there he stayed, with cap off and downcast eyes, till I had passed.' And this was his ordinary conduct. He paid special respect to the professed Fathers. If, when out, he recognized by their dress any of the Society, he saluted them with a smiling and pleasant face, though he had never seen them before, and when one who was walking with him asked him why he showed such civility to persons he did not know, he replied, 'Because they are my brothers.' In fact, he always was as familiar with any Jesuits who chanced to come to the College, as if they had been his old friends and acquaintances. His notes reveal still more clearly how high was the source of this his conduct. 'When you see any one of the Society belonging to another College, reverence him as an angel.' When any came from foreign countries, he was most careful to give them the **embrace** of peace, which, in accordance with the old monastic customs, **and** the habits **of** southern people, is permitted by the rule of the Society. **If he** happened to be engaged in conversation with any one **at** the **time, he** left his circle for a moment to give the strangers **a** welcome **by this** mark of brotherly love. He was always careful **to do** the same for those who were leaving the College or returning to it, and **to** those **who had just taken** their vows. So fond was he of these **opportunities of** showing his charity, that he told some **one** he would like on **such** occasions the bell **to** ring, to summon all to say welcome or good-bye to any travellers. But, making **all** due allowance for **foreign** etiquette, Berchmans avoided **any** exaggeration **or** singularity in these signs of respect, save that of the singular charity which animated all he did, and he rigidly excluded everything which comes under the name of 'compli-ments.' His speech was to be, *est, est,* and *non, non—* 'Yes, brother; no, brother;' which must have seemed bald **to** Italian ears. If he saluted in the persons of **the** Fathers **the sainted confessors, he honoured in** his **companions and equals the angels. Here** are some of **his resolutions on this head, and we** have seen how **unfailingly they were carried out. He** had to guard **himself against** that weapon of spiritual pride the devil **can so** easily use against one who **is perfect** in the midst of the less perfect. 'Mind your own defects, not those of others, and consider yourself inferior to all. I will mind seriously what I am bound to do, and not what is done by others. I will take care diligently not to judge others, nor to meddle with the affairs of others. If anything comes across me which cannot be excused, I will be compassionate; I will turn my eyes to myself, and will say for the person's amendment a Hail **Mary,** or so.' 'Get into a habit of excusing others in the bowels of charity.' 'Yield to others whatever is most convenient.' 'I will show myself very willing in lending what has been dictated at lectures, and other such things, and I will guard charity as the apple of my eye.'

The Roman College was at the time of Berchmans so full, that a separate room could not be given to each of the scholastics. When John first arrived at Rome he was placed in the room up till then occupied by Paul Oliva, who had to give up his desk and bed to the new comer. 'I think,' he writes, 'there was in that a special arrangement of Providence, for that room was the one where Blessed Aloysius Gonzaga used to live, whom Berchmans deserved so well to succeed, as he took such pains to give us, in his person, the living image of that blessed youth (*beato*).' Another scholastic shared with him the small chamber which served at once for study, private oratory, and sleeping-place. If no one is a hero to his valet, it would require a charity of no ordinary temper not to be severely tested by this constant living together in such close quarters. If there were a flaw it would soon become apparent. Four religious, at different times, lived in the same room with John, Julius Scotti, Alexander Rimbaldesi, Peter Alfaroli, and Marcellus Spinelli. Each of the two last were his companions for a twelvemonth or more. Yet one and all came forward to witness to his uniform and unvarying charity. Marcellus was son of the Neapolitan Prince di Tarsia, and had a hard fight with his father before he could enter the Society. While a boarder at the Roman Seminary, he asked to be admitted, but the Prince carried off his son and locked him up in his palace at Naples. He however contrived to escape, and was received. Furious at the event, his father gained to his side the then Viceroy, the tyrannical Duke of Ossuna, who placed guards round the various houses of the Society and threatened their inmates. However, a severe illness, and the delay of the troop-ships which he expected from Spain, made Ossuna turn to St. Ignatius, whose octave was then being kept; and on his recovery and the arrival of the reinforcements, he at once countermanded his arbitrary measures and made a public reparation by a solemn procession in our Lady's honour.

On his entering the room, as has been already noticed, John made the sign of the Cross, took holy water, and then knelt down for a minute to pray. He stood quietly at his desk, in the place where it had been put, never in any way disturbing his companion.

'As soon as ever we were sent together,' says Brother Scotti, 'he took care to let me know I might do whatever I liked in the room; and it would be his greatest pleasure to suit himself to me, always and in everything.'

'During the time I shared his room with him,' says Brother Rimbaldesi, 'he was ordered by the Superior to sleep an hour longer than the rest. Fearing lest this arrangement should put me to some inconvenience by the care I should have to take not to awake him, he begged me very earnestly not to take any notice of him, for, said he, our Lord always grants me the favour of sleeping through no matter what noise, till it is time to get up. I never came in without his taking off his cap or even rising from his seat to salute me. Once, I informed him that Father Rector had authorized me to talk in our room on anything relating to studies. From that moment he was always accustomed to be the first to propose to have a talk together, with such graceful kindness, that you would have said it was he and not myself who was to benefit by it.

Alfaroli tells nearly the same story. 'His charity in helping others was so great that whenever I asked him a question about my studies, he put his work aside at once, and answered all my difficulties with the greatest kindness. I used on these occasions to be surprised at the clearness of his statements and the breadth of his mind. And yet he had so modest an opinion of himself that he never had the appearance of wishing to get the better of me, in discussing the point on which I had consulted him. As soon as the lecture was over, he hurried to our room, to sweep it out and save me that labour. When I used to complain that he had not waited for me, he answered modestly, "Do not mind, brother, you get very fatigued with this work, but it is capital exercise for me." If he ever noticed that I was not quite as well as usual, he lost no time in letting the Superior know. He made my bed, and showed himself displeased that I had not, as he said, more confidence in his charity.'

John, in spite of his other duties, went over the whole of his course of philosophy with one of his companions, and engaged to assist another in his logic during the vacation.

Father Bargagli, who was for four months Minister for the juniors while Berchmans was amongst them, adds his witness on the same subject. He was very much beloved by our saint, and when his Superior called him elsewhere, the tears of the young religious testified to his merit. 'In his room he was of singular edification to his companion, and it was always looked upon as a real misfortune to be separated from this angel of charity, who never caused one the least inconvenience or the smallest trouble. One day I had determined to put a fresh scholastic in the room, but the poor junior who had up to that time shared with him his cell, all in tears, told me with such eloquence the consolation he gathered from the company of that angelic youth, that I was forced to give up my idea of severing rudely so holy a tie.'

He was specially fond of the lay-brothers, and took great delight in talking with them. Though he never showed partiality in the choice of others for his companions, he made an exception in their favour, and would seek them out in time of recreation. He thought he could deal with them with greater simplicity and openness, and speak with greater freedom on spiritual topics, could tell them what thoughts had come to him in his prayer, what fruit he had gathered from it. And they on their side, from the great opinion they had of him as a saintly and innocent young man, coveted his company. They came to him with great confidence to confer with him on the affairs of their souls, and seek instructions from him. When they could not get with him at recreation, if they chanced to be going out on Sundays or holidays to visit some church, they begged the Superior to be allowed to take Brother John along with them, and, this granted, went to fetch him from his room. He consented at once with cordial and sincere charity, and as they went through the streets, the happy party spoke of nothing but of God.

One summer evening he noticed a lay-brother walking alone in the garden of the inner court of the College. John was engaged in conversation with Fabricius de Britiis. 'Father,' he said at once, 'let us go and take recreation with that good brother, who is all alone.' Even if he saw two left to themselves, he would politely leave his companions and their more intellectual conversation, to cheer by this act of charity his dear lay-brothers. 'Indeed, we must confess,' said those whom he had quitted, touched and edified by his thoughtful kindness, ' he is truly a blessed Giovanino !' If any of the brothers happened to fall sick, there was no sort of care he did not lavish on them, going to see them several times a day, and cheering them with his bright and holy conversation. If it were summer time, he would go down to the fountain that leaps up in the garden below, and fetch a jug of its fresh cold water to wash their feverish hands and cool their parched mouth. The poor sick brothers felt their hearts glow, and their sufferings become lighter, at the very sight of such ardent charity and the brotherly affection which he showed in waiting on them. On Fridays he would go amongst them to repeat, as he did for the other sick, the pith of the spiritual instruction or exhortation which had been given to the community. Every day he came with a fresh story about our Blessed Lady. They looked forward to his coming, and if ever anything prevented him, they begged the minister to send to them their kind young teacher.

But it was not only the lay-brothers whom he visited in times of sickness. He had a general leave to go once a day to the infirmary on this errand of charity, and he never let a day pass without availing himself of the permission, and going right through the various rooms. He stopped the longest with those whom he thought the most needed his consolation, and had the fewest visitors. If he found a room full of people, he went on at once to another where the patient was alone. We must let the brother infirmarian, John Baptist Ballera, tell this tale. ' I affirm, for I saw it myself, that this saintly young man never let a single day pass without visiting all those who were ill, and he made his visit, not at recreation time, as is the custom, but in the middle of the day, when every one is taking their siesta in their rooms. He knew well that hour was of all the day the most painful for the sick, on account of the excessive heat, and because,

while all are taking their siesta, the poor invalids are left
all alone. He went to see them all, as I have said,
without exception, and brought water to those who
needed it, but always after having first asked my leave,
though I had told him, once for all, that at that time of
the day it was an excellent thing to give a glass of water
to the sick, both to refresh and to keep them awake.
To these comforts for the body, he added spiritual consolation by telling them some apposite and edifying story,
or by reading them some pious book.' He was all the
more ready to do them this service, as the weakness of
his chest prevented him from taking his turn of reading
in the refectory. 'Many used to say, when he was gone,
that the presence of this charitable brother did them
more good than the visit of the doctor. If one of the
sick was a little less attended to than the others, that
was quite enough to make Berchmans go and stay with
him. Once during his stay at the College, the infirmary
was so full, that I had reason to fear that the prevalent
sickness was catching. The rector, being alarmed for
our brother, who showed ever the same unchanging
charity and solicitude, withdrew from him his general
permission to visit the infirmary, so as not to expose him
to the risk of his falling sick too.'

The holy young man submitted; and Brother Valeri,
on meeting him two days after this, asked him, 'Please
tell me, brother, how are the sick; you know you visit
them twice a day?' 'I beg your pardon,' answered
Berchmans, 'it is now two days since I put foot in the
infirmary.' 'And why so?' 'Because Father Rector
has told me not to do so for some time, for fear I catch
this illness.' 'But what will you do then, my good
brother?' 'I will have patience.' 'You will have
patience? Now, tell me frankly, have you had no
difficulty to submit your judgment under the circum-

stances?' 'Oh, as for that, not at all; I have not felt the least difficulty.'

This marvellous charity put John at the service not merely of the sick, but of one and all in the community. One could hardly ask a favour, before he answered, 'Father, yes, with great pleasure!' If any one wanted to go out, and the Father Minister had none to send as his companion, John was always his refuge, because Father Sbarra knew he would go directly, without making any answer.

Once when the time was close at hand for his public theses of philosophy, and every moment of study was of great importance, he was sent for to accompany another religious. He felt interiorly a slight rising of repugnance, but he went, notwithstanding, without giving the slightest signs of it. As soon as he got back, he began to reflect on the disturbance he had felt in his mind, and for several days turned his particular examen to the task of entirely subduing himself. He pondered carefully over its rise and its causes. And when next he came to see Father Cepari, he told him that by God's grace he had gained a complete victory over himself, and felt no longer any repugnance whatever.

When he had finished his public act, the minister constantly sent him out as a companion with others. Whether it was that many asked for him, or because there was at hand no one else so ready and so willing as he, he sometimes had hardly returned home with one, than he had to go out again with another. We must remember at that time it was summer, and in Rome! One day when he had already been out three different times, Marcellus Spinelli, who then lived in the same room with him, met him in the corridor. He could not help pitying him, and at the same time was annoyed at what seemed to be carrying his condescension

M

too far. 'Brother John, pray have a little discretion and prudence; otherwise you will make yourself ill with going out so much in this heat.' 'Brother,' he replied, 'I must leave prudence to those who command; *I* am only bound to be obedient.' One of his companions, a Dalmatian, by name Tudisio, and who was afterwards to gain some notoriety as professor of philosophy and theology in his native town of Ragusa, narrates as follows—'John was appointed one day to go out with me in Rome. I had scarcely opened my lips to tell him this, when without even asking where he had to go, without a single idle word, he said, "I will go for my cloak." When we got into the streets, he asked me if we should be back for the Litanies which are said in public every evening. I answered, "Yes; because I have only to stay a few minutes at the House of the Gesù." "It is not that I have anything to do at home," he said, "but this morning, while meditating on the casting out of the devil from the man in the Synagogue,[3] I made a resolution to be with the community as much as I could, because it is on these occasions especially that our good God casts out our faults." And he went on in the same strain, talking during the whole of our walk on spiritual things.'

Our saint's charity was not confined merely to acts of kindness such as we have been describing. He looked forward earnestly to future fishing in deep waters, to labours in the camps of Flanders, or, still better, in the far-off islands of the East. Meantime, every opportunity of working for souls was eagerly turned to account. The young scholastics used to be sent out on Sundays and holidays to preach in the squares to the idlers and passers-by, or to teach the catechism to the poor and uninstructed. Berchmans used to say that the scholastics

[3] St. Luke iv. 33, 34.

of the Society, while engaged in their studies and not as yet allowed to undertake work for their neighbours, are like trusty dogs chained up in their master's house; still on Sundays and holidays they were loosed, and let out into the piazzas to bark for a little time at sinners. He was very fond of taking part in these excursions. It fell out once that he was sent to preach in the street hard by the Church of the Madonna de' Monti, a sanctuary now glorified by the shrine of Blessed Benedict Joseph Labre, the poor one of Jesus Christ. It is in the midst of a thickly populated and poor quarter of the city. The moment was most unfavourable for our young preachers. Several sbirri, guardians of the peace, were engaged in a violent dispute; and when the religious were taking a table to serve as a pulpit, some other men, who were playing at ball, seized hold of it, telling them they would have none of their preaching, they wanted to continue their game. Berchmans did not answer a word, and went at once up the steps into the church. There he threw himself on his knees, and after a short prayer he came out again, resolved to commence his discourse. His companions warned him that there would certainly be some disturbance. 'Do not be afraid,' he answered, 'I have confidence in the ever Blessed Virgin, that the moment I begin they will leave what they are about and come to listen to me.' He got on the table, and while he was saying the Hail Mary as the opening prayer, the sbirri ceased their quarrel, the players left their game, and all gathered round to hear. When the sermon was over, the whole audience escorted the two religious, peaceably and with great respect, back to the Roman College.

John had a little pastoral charge indoors; for his Superiors had given him the spiritual charge of the lay servants who worked in the house. He looked after them with care, diligently instructed them in their religious duties, induced them to go frequently to confession, and he desired them to go to communion at least every month, when he arranged that they all should approach the holy table together and receive the Blessed Sacrament from the hands of the rector.

There yet remains to be told a mission still nearer home, one having still greater claims on the charity of Berchmans. He had no special charge over his brother scholastics, and he knew too well he had no right to exercise such unbidden. But he loved them all too well not to desire that all should grow perfect in their high vocation, and this desire found its expression in every action of his community life. A constant example of the most perfect realization of St. Ignatius' ideal, a word of comfort in times of trouble and discouragement, a word of advice given with a prudence not of this world, and, above all, the practice of a thoroughly spiritual conversation, such as we saw that he introduced and fostered at Mechlin—these were the instruments he used to help on all around him. Berchmans had observed in one of his brethren a negligence in his religious duties which troubled him sorely. We know how free he was from groundless suspicions or rash judgments. The fault must have been serious and glaring to have been noticed by one so accustomed to view all in the best light. After some time waiting for a change for the better, John, faithful to his rule, wrote a note, every word of which had been carefully weighed, stating his convictions and informing the Superior with a charitable reticence that he had observed this fault more than once.

Another time, on a holiday, one Bernardine Victorinus asked permission from the Father Minister to go out. It was in the middle of the day, in the month of July.

Who would like to venture out at such an hour but
the ever charitable John? So to him the scholastic was
sent to seek his companion. Bernardine found him in
his room, saying his beads; he had scarcely time to
ask him, so ready was Berchmans to serve him, and
John was the first down and waiting at the gate. They
mounted under the broiling sun the slope of the Quirinal
hill, and went as far as the Charterhouse, that unique
cloister of Michael Angelo, built amidst the ruins of
Diocletian's baths, and which takes from the vast church
the name of Santa Maria degli Angeli. Our saint
had before noticed that there was some cloud over his
companion's mind, and had warned him in a moment
of conversation to beware of gloomy thoughts. 'Take
great care never to neglect your prayers, or any other
exercise of devotion, when this melancholy comes over
you, because the devil only seeks to disquiet you that
he may bring about his own plans. You should, on
the contrary, trouble him by stirring up your fervour,
and you will soon feel help from on high come back
to you, and with it spiritual joy.'

When they reached the monastery, Bernardine asked
to see the prior, and went with him into a parlour at the
end of a suite of apartments, leaving John in a room,
with another intervening, all three opening out into each
other. The Carthusian and his visitor however sat far
back and quite out of his sight, and out of his ear-shot.
John, notwithstanding, as Bernardine declared in his
deposition, saw and heard all. The visit over and once
outside—'Brother,' said he, 'you think I do not know
what you have been arranging; but I do know. You
have been planning to give up your vocation, but you
will not succeed, for I shall say so many prayers for
you that you will not be able to do so.' Bernardine,
finding he was discovered, was completely astonished.

He had in fact arranged that the prior should go to the College and settle the matter with the **rector.** It would not do, now that all was known, to be there during the Carthusian's visit, **and so he** tried to get **John to go** round by the Gesù and stay for the Scripture lecture, which is given **in** the afternoon **of Sundays and** holidays. Berchmans **was** obstinate. *Non, sed eamus domum, veniamus domum—*'No,' he answered, '**let us go** home, **let us** come home.' **And back** he came, went straight to **Father Rector, and told him** the whole affair. Father **Cepari, who carefully conceals** the name in his **narrative,** sent for the young man, who, he **tells us,** 'was an excellent religious, and I found that it was all a mere temptation of faintheartedness and **melancholy.** He imagined he was of no use for the **duties** of the Society, and that he never would be **fit to** be an operarius (engaged in work for souls), and so had begun to think of retiring to some place where he would have nothing to do but to look to himself. I spoke **words** of comfort to him, and made him see that it was a temptation. **He was** grateful for it. And,' he goes on to say, '**he** is now living as a good religious and **a good** labourer **in religion.' We shall see** how **at** his death-bed the devil tried to make capital **out of** this incident to trouble John's last hours.

Even on his first entry into religion, so full was his heart of God and the things of God that at Mechlin he could not speak of anything else. Though his studies enlarged the field of his thoughts, they were so saturated with a purity of intention which referred them all to God, that they never turned his habitual thoughts from the one object of his love and life. Indeed, as that love grew deeper and wider, so did it more completely absorb his mind, and naturally came to the surface whenever the time of recreation took off the restraint or obligation of silence. There was no preaching, no solemnity, no *gêne* for himself or for others. He was always bright, always winning, always natural, because to speak of holy things was his delight. His face kindled as he went on, and there was something like the light of inspiration resting upon it as he talked. He often said he really could not understand how there could be religious who dislike to speak exclusively on spiritual things. ' It seems to me that can only come from their not practising it enough, so that they understand but little about it, or perhaps from their not attaching sufficient importance to it. It is almost like what happens with scientific subjects—the more advanced we are in them, the more we like to be engaged on them, to make them a subject of conversation, and find in them a useful recreation.'

Berchmans did not fail to observe on arriving at the Roman College that the young religious with whom he was placed regularly fell into two parties during the hours allotted for recreation ; one set always speaking on spiritual subjects, the other amusing themselves with any topic that might arise. He was very sorry to see this sort of defined division ; and took care not to follow his own leaning, and go exclusively with the religious section. He mixed with all, and contrived, with prudence and holy ingenuity, to introduce his favourite topics with such a grace, and with so much interest cast around them, that they were always well received. So deeply had he this at heart that he said, one day, if anything could make him ill it would be not finding any one with whom he could talk about God. And such was the warmth, the power, the charm of his words, that the most venerable Fathers, in a house full of the celebrities of the order, used to say they felt their hearts stirred, softened, and set on fire, and that they gained spiritual help from John's conversation at recreation time such as they did not gather even from meditation and their spiritual duties. Every one enjoyed to hear him so much that they led up to this favourite subject, and let him talk. He was sought for by all, while he himself showed no preference. If he fell in with those who were younger than he, or less advanced in their studies, he exerted with the gentlest hand a sort of authority, broaching the subject at once, and the rest were delighted to follow suit. If his companions were his seniors, simply and frankly he proposed some good subject. So successful was he that he left in his notes, that all the time of his studies in Rome he only twice had any difficulty in introducing religious matters into conversation, and this not through any fault of others, but simply because, as they were all standing together, it was very hard to keep to one subject. This reason made him always try to be with not more than two or three at a time. Father Gottofredi, the future General of the Society, was one of our saint's pupils in this holy art of sanctifying every-day conversation. 'One day that I was walking about with him, tepid as I was, he so inflamed me by his thoughts on the guard a religious should put on his tongue, that I made up my mind henceforward never to speak but on spiritual subjects. I begged him to be so good as to help me to carry out my resolve; because, as I said very rashly, and merely in self-excuse, if I do not speak of God, it is because I can find none who will talk with me about Him. "Brother," he answered, "do you know the way to talk on spiritual matters with every one? It is to make open profession of aiming at interior life." "Yes, yes; that is all very fine," I said. "But it is all in vain to make such a profession when one often finds himself thrown with those who do not like that sort of conversation; and then you run the risk of being looked

on as a bore, and making yourself disliked." "Really,"
he rejoined, "I can assure you, by God's grace, that has
never happened to me ; because I have shown, once for
all, that I do not wish to have to do with anything but
God. And, in fact, what has a religious to say to worldly
matters ? There are only two sorts of conversation
which befit a Jesuit when he is among his own ; it
should be either about the studies on which he is
engaged, or about the perfection to which he is called.
We are forbidden to talk about our studies in time of
ordinary recreation ;[4] nothing then remains for us but
to talk about spiritual things." He then went on putting
before me the way he used to gain his end. "When
they are taking on other subjects, and a Superior is
amongst them, I recollect myself and am silent, because
I have nothing to say to it. If no Superior is there, I
try to turn the subject with prudence to something
better. If I do not succeed, I withdraw quietly to the
infirmary, where I am always sure to find some one to
talk to, or I join the lay-brothers, who are always glad
to talk on whatever subject I like."'

Father Gottofredi owns that he was not very faithful to
the resolution he had made to be with our saint as much
as possible, so as to pass the recreation in a pious way.
'On the contrary, spite of the voice of my conscience,
my great tepidity made me avoid him, that I might not
be forced into conversations unfortunately not to my
taste ; and if now and then I chanced to be with him,
the high idea I had got of him, especially from his
religious conversation, made me feel quite embarrassed
in the presence of one who was always my silent

---

[4] This regulation was no doubt imposed on the juniors at the Roman
College, to prevent the strain of mind being prolonged into the hours
of relaxation. It only held good in the hour after dinner and that
after supper.

reprover. "Well, brother," he would say, "how go the recreations?" And I, poor wretch, stood open-mouthed, not knowing what to answer. Yet I must own in these circumstances, whatever was the number of those who were round me, I was forced, spite of my inclination to the contrary, and without well knowing why, to enter at once on his ground. I was ashamed to let a single idle word pass my lips as long as that pious youth was there. His very look inspired me with a holy reserve!' Father Scotti confirms the fact of the marvellous influence John exercised on his companions. 'When Brother Berchmans joined a group of scholastics who were talking on ordinary topics, in an instant the conversation changed its subject; and more than once, as soon as I saw the saint coming towards us, I would say in an undertone to those who were with me, "John would not like to hear what we are saying," and begin myself to speak on religious subjects.' But it was not his equals only who adapted themselves to his taste. Father Cornelius à Lapide, whose humility and holiness were not less than his marvellous learning, when past fifty years old, and having spent more than half of his life in the Society, found his delight in the company of the young student. 'Oftentimes,' he tells us, 'talking with him after dinner, or after supper, he rejoiced me greatly in the Lord by his holy conversations, of which the history and institute of the Society formed the staple topic. I recollect specially, a little before his death, he talked of nothing else while we were going one day together to St. Paul's of the three fountains.' The road is long from the College to that holy spot where the Apostle of the Gentiles gave up his life for his Lord. If the walk was chosen by John, perhaps his devotion to St. Bernard had no small share in the choice. The venerable Basilica of SS. Vincent and Anastasius, which still exists as when the great Cistercian lived there, and the Scala Cœli, where he had the vision of the mystic ladder, are all grouped about the scene of St. Paul's death triumph. Citeaux, in its first days, could not have been more desolate than the lonely Campagna which is around, hiding out all the world by its swelling surface, as the waves do to a ship at sea. A cross-road full of interest leads from the Basilica of St. Paul, a mile or more nearer to Rome, to the Church of St. Sebastian, with its numberless attractions and memories, its shrines of the soldier martyr, of St. Fabian, the martyr Pope, and its Catacombs, then almost alone in being known to the Christian world, and which had received a fresh lustre by the nightly visits of St. Philip Neri. Father à Lapide wished, on his return homewards, to go round by that holy spot. The incident gives us a good instance of John's unswerving obedience. ' I proposed to the good brother to come with me. But nothing of the kind. As soon as we got outside '—the great Basilica of St. Paul's, which they had entered on their way back, and from which the old Ostian Way goes straight as an arrow, under an avenue of trees, to the city walls—'he stopped like a statue, his hat off, and with downcast eyes, with his face turned towards the Porta San Paolo. There was nothing for it but to retrace our steps. "But why will you not go with me to St. Sebastian's?" "Because, Father," he modestly and humbly replied, "we should get too late for dinner at the country house, unless we go back the same way as we came." After our dinner, thinking that I wanted to return at once to the College, he came and said to me— "Your Reverence can arrange with another companion, for I have not leave to go back as yet."' The good old man preferred to wait the whole afternoon at the country house, rather than forfeit the pleasure of another walk with his saintly companion.

Father Bisdomini, of Arezzo, the professor of moral theology in the Roman College, declared that the presence of John was, even for persons advanced alike in years and the interior life, a sort of check, which preserved them from slight imperfections. 'When he was with me during recreation, it seemed as if I could not speak of anything except literary or pious subjects. If the conversation was not on one or other of these subjects, and the position of his companions at the time did not allow him to change it to something more useful, he had a way of assuming so heavenly an exterior, that he forced, so to speak, those who were talking with him, to follow his bent. I, for my part, have often tried him, but all in vain. I stood firm for some time. I was forced to lay down my arms and come in to his terms, such was the sway the more than human expression of his face exercised over me, and such the delight, beyond all I can describe, I saw that he took in his favourite subjects. The history of the Society, the virtues of his brethren, the story of their varied calls to our Institute, furnished him with exhaustless matter, and he ever had sacks full of these kind of examples, which he told with a rare grace and with still rarer piety.'

Father Bisdomini was not the only one who tested John's fidelity to his purpose. Two Fathers who were professors, were walking about the garden one day after dinner, when they saw him coming towards them to take recreation with them. At once they began to talk about news of the war, no doubt the great struggle between Catholicity and Protestantism, which was for thirty years to deluge Germany and the Low Countries with blood. Berchmans withdrew into his own heart, and with downcast eyes, and hands joined on his breast, walked by their side without saying a word. Amused and edified by the success of their device, they at last owned they had done it for a joke, and resumed the thread of conversation which they had broken off, and which was quite to John's liking. The 'sacks full' of stories of which Father Bisdomini speaks, cost our saint no small labour to keep supplied. The proof of this labour is the note-book preserved at Louvain, of which mention has already been made. The short sayings and anecdotes it contains are gathered from many sources, from Father Sebastian Barradas, the great preacher of Portugal, who died 1615; from Cæsarius; from Father Alvarez de Paz, who was then just dead;[5] from Father Emmanuel de Vega, who, after a life of labours as writer and professor, came to die in Rome, in 1640, over ninety years of age; from Cardinal Bellarmine; from Father Spinello, in his work, *Mary, the Mother of God, the Throne of God*, in which that great client of our Lady pours out the devotion for which he gave up a Neapolitan dukedom, and served her for forty-two years in religion; and from other writers of the Society. Others he gathered from the lips of those with whom he lived. The selection contains many jottings of interest. We are pleased to find two great English martyrs figure therein—St. Thomas of Canterbury and Sir Thomas More. The great Chancellor's sayings are curiously enough placed under the heading—'I.H.S. Some notes about our Society and its members.' He quotes Alvarez de Paz—'St. Edmund of Canterbury used to study before a statue of the Blessed Virgin, and fell so often into ecstasy that his study seemed like to prayer.'

Many anecdotes are in their proper places in our pages. Some few others may be interesting, as their selection shows the bent of the collector's thoughts. Here is one, imitated from St. Augustine,[6] 'Yeast raises the dough,

---

[5] Father de Paz died on June 17, 1620.

[6] St. Augustine, *Quæst. Evang.*, l. i., q. xii.

and makes it light, so does the **Blessed** Sacrament elevate our bodies' (from Father Reina, a then well-known Italian **preacher of** the Society).   **Here** is one of Father Vega, 'Creatures are the mirror wherein the face of **God can** be **seen.   In a** little mirror **God's** face is made small, it becomes large (is "magnified") in **a great** one.   **After** Christ there **was** no mirror greater than the Blessed **Virgin,** and therefore she said, *Magnificat anima mea Dominum.'*

'I have heard it told **of Father** Laynez—I think by Father Coster—that **once at Venice he** had to cross a **piazza full of** buffaloes.   The buffaloes separated right and left, and **threw** themselves on the ground.   None but Father **Laynez knew** the reason, for he was carrying the Blessed Sacrament privately.'   Father Laynez was **the** successor of St. Ignatius in the government of the Society, as he had been one of his first companions. Father Coster knew his sainted founder, when a youth at Rome, and died at Brussels the year after John left Belgium, at the venerable age of eighty-eight.

'Of Father Charles Mastrilli, it is told that when some one **tried to** poignard **him as he was** coming from Mass, **courageously he said,** "Stay, *fermate*, and adore Christ thy God, whom I have now in my breast !"   At that word the assassin dared do no more.   (Told at Rome during recreation.)'   This **Father** Charles was no doubt a **relative of Father Marcellus Mastrilli,** the martyr of Japan.

Here is a **story about Father Laynez, on the authority** of one whose name is well known in the early history of the Belgian **Province of the Society of** Jesus—Master Antony Delrio, the writer of *Disquisitiones Magicæ*, born in Antwerp of noble Spanish parents, who **after** astonishing **the veteran scholar Lipsius** by the brilliancy of his youthful learning, and **studying at Paris, Douay, and**

Louvain, took his full **degrees in law at Salamanca, and was soon advanced from** dignity to dignity till he **was made** Chancellor of Brabant, **and Treasurer to King** Philip. When about **twenty-nine** he turned **his back on** the world, **and buried** himself **in the Novitiate of Pinto;** and, after **his** probation **was over,** passed three years sitting **on the** benches **of a** Jesuit College studying natural philosophy with **the boys that attended the** course, **his** professor being Luis de la **Puente. The rest of his life was** spent, as **soon as** he **had completed** his theological studies, **in** 1589, as professor **of philosophy, moral** theology, and Scripture, in Belgium, **Styria,** and Spain. He won his old admirer, Lipsius, **back to** the faith of his fathers, and died, worn out **with work and** sickness, at sixty-eight years **of age.** But we have let **our** pen run away with **us ; we must turn back to John's** note-book.

'Father Mark van **Doorne heard it from Father Martin** Delrio ; **he was present at a sermon of a Dominican who** had been **at the Council of Trent, and who held, with us, the Immaculate Conception of the** Blessed Virgin. **He** narrated **to** his audience that Father Laynez was suffering from fever when he mounted the tribune to speak **on the** Immaculate Conception. **After** his discourse **he was** cured. A Dominican Father, who **was to** speak **against it, followed him.** He went up **well, and came down in fever.'**

'Father Mutius (Vitelleschi) once was reproving **Blessed Aloysius for asking too often to visit** the hospitals. When he had finished, the saint answered "**Father, what am I to do?** God is ever urging me **on, and I never do anything without obedience."** A Father saw Blessed Aloysius one morning running along the passage of the Roman College which leads to the church. He was astonished at this want of modesty in so modest a youth. He followed him to see where he was going, and found he was going to communion.'

'Father Romæus, rector of the Roman Seminary, used to tell of himself that when Blessed Ignatius had severely scolded him, our holy Father, having to go out immediately after, took him as his companion. (From Father Ceccotti, who had it from Father Romæus.)' 'Father Cepari entered the Society lest in the world he should be forced to have charge of others, and when he was, as an old man, rector of the Roman College, he used to say that he begged the Lord every day always to live as a subject, and to die in the Society.' 'Father Henry Sommalius once rushed down the stairs by Blessed Ignatius' room ; the saint came out, and reproved him sharply. Ever after, when he had to pass, he carried his shoes in his hand.' This Father was a Belgian, whom St. Ignatius received into the Society, and who was greatly beloved by him on account of his innocence. He afterwards became first rector of the College of the Society at Douay, and falling into the hands of the ferocious murderer of the martyrs of Gorcum, was grossly outraged, and narrowly escaped with his life. He died at Valenciennes in the March of 1619.

'A thought came into the head of our Father Gregory of Valentia, while at Rome, that he would like to be Bishop of Cartagena. He asked a penance, and wore a paper mitre in the refectory.' Father Gregory is the well-known theologian, who, after a life of labour in Germany, was recalled to Rome, where he continued lecturing till a short time before his death, which occurred at Naples in 1603. 'Father Cepari, who had been confessor for three years to Sister Magdalene de' Pazzi, told us of her saying, "All the ruin of religious comes from self-love, which has two eyes—self-esteem and self-convenience."'

'Frederick Borromeo, nephew of St. Charles, while making the Exercises, when he came to the third point of the Three Classes, got to such a degree of indifference as to be willing to resign even his Cardinal's hat.' 'A Father of the Society, by name John Baptist Alexandri, noticing that a scholastic was melancholy, asked to have him as his companion on the way to the villa. He took him a walk in an out of the way place, and wanted him to take a run; and, to induce him to do so, said, "I need a little exercise; if you like, run along with me." They both set off, and it quite cheered up the scholastic. This was told by Father Cepari.' 'Some one said to Father Ledesma when he was dying, "Father, you are still needed here." He looked crossly at the speaker, and replied, "Peter and Paul are dead, and God's Church has suffered no hurt." (From Father Andrew, the Greek.)' Father Andrew Renzi, native of Scio, who had been admitted into the Society at Rome, when he completed his studies, returned to his native island. He was, later on, the first to occupy the position of Greek Penitentiary at St. Peter's, and spent the close of his life in missionary labours in the Ægean Islands and on the mainland. He probably knew John when he was confessor at St. Peter's. Ledesma [7] was a Spaniard, who, after brilliant studies at Louvain and Paris, entered the Society at Rome when thirty-six years old. He died during the Jubilee of 1575, worn out with the labour of solving the various cases of conscience brought to him from all sides by the confessors. As more than a month yet remained of Jubilee time, that may suggest the meaning of his friend's words.

Another plan which Berchmans adopted to further the use of religious conversation was the founding what was

---

[7] See Rose's *Ignatius and the Early Jesuits*, p. 500.

N

called in Italian an *Academia Spirituale*, **a word so**
difficult to **render** into English, unless we take the word
as it stands, and to many of our readers an 'academy' will
convey the precise meaning. We quote a description **of**
it from Father Cepari. ' With permission of his Superiors,
while in the juniorate John formed among his young **com-**
panions a **sort** of *Academuccia Spirituale,*' an academy on
a **small scale,** ' to come **off** on the recreation days, when
they **went** to the vigna. **He did not,** however, himself
call it an academy, but " *Spiritual conversation for the*
vigna days." They met during the **day for** an hour on **a**
loggia,' a corridor open to the air, 'and proposed each
time some special virtue to be the subject of their next
meeting. The **choice** was made by a majority **of** votes.
In their first meetings they treated of fraternal charity,
modesty, humility, guard of the heart, self-abnegation,
prayer, patience, spiritual gladness—and I found these
subjects in his handwriting, in the order I have given
them. Then the duty of giving the definition of the
virtue selected fell to one of them ; he had to **say if**
there **was** any **rule or** order **of** Superiors any **way**
enjoining **it, or** alluding **to it.** Another laid **before**
them how it could be **practised** both by interior and
by exterior actions. A **third had to** bring forward the
motives which attract us to embrace that virtue, or which
force us to do so. A **fourth was** required to tell by
what ways and means one could arrive at its attainment.
And **last of all,** another narrated different examples **of**
holy men who had practised that virtue. Each **of** them,
during the week, got **ready his** task ; and on the recreation day, assembled in **the** vigna, at their trysting place,
simply but seriously **they** unfolded what has been explained above. When all had finished, any one of
them could propose **any** question about the virtue
under discussion. **According to** the **same** order they

began to go through **the vices we are to avoid.** And this
institution has lasted after his death, and as I learn is still
in existence (1626). They had no other pretence **or aim**
than to encourage one another in acquiring virtue and
avoiding vice, and getting matter about moral subjects,
so as to be able to assist others in conversation. I find
the pious young man has left written in short all that
was said in these meetings during **his time.'** To insure
its continuance, John wrote **out a** brief sketch of the
form to be followed, and this, with what seems **to have**
been what Father Cepari refers to as a summary of the
meetings, he gave on quitting the juniorate to one Brother
Jerome Longino, who succeeded him as president, and
of this **an** authentic copy, sealed and signed, still exists in
the Royal Library of Brussels.

One might be inclined to think, after Father Gottofredi's very humble accusation **of his** own want **of interest**
in Berchmans' conversation, that however pious it might
have been, **it was** dry and **repulsive.** All the depositions,
however, give a distinct contradiction to **this, and** assert,
as has been already said, that it was exceedingly enter-
taining and exceedingly sought after. We cannot call
a better witness than the future General himself.
'Oftentimes in the conversations I **had** with John he
communicated to me the great lights with which our
Lord had favoured him in time of prayer. He knew
thoroughly the greater part of the history **of our** order,
and he turned his knowledge **largely to account** during
our ordinary recreations in order **not to** make his conversation at all wearisome to any one. **In fact,** when
once he began to talk he threw **such a** pleasant **charm**
around what he said, that **gladness** shone **out on the**
faces of all about him and never ceased **to beam during**
the rest **of the** recreation. He had a special **collection**
of laughable **anecdotes, as,** for instance, certain stories

N 2

about the devil, wherein the enemy of the human race always cuts a very bad figure. He had others which excited us to perfection; others which spoke of the joys of the blessed; in a word, stories of every kind his audience could possibly have desired.' His manuscript epitome of Rodriguez' *Christian Perfection* was in great part written for this end. What has been left makes us regret—what it is to be feared has been utterly lost—a collection and list of all the martyrs and members of noted sanctity of the Society of Jesus, classified according to the day of their death: so that when the day came round he might not fail to speak about them sometime during recreation, with all his usual grace and richness of facts.

Father Sacchini, the learned continuator of Orlandini, the chronicler of the Society, was then living at the Gesù, as secretary to the General, and there must have been many other Fathers at that time in Rome, not ignorant of the records of the first century of their history, a period which had yet some years to run. Yet Father Cepari tells us that John's knowledge of the origin, progress, and condition of his order was as great as if he had been its historian, and that many Fathers of standing, after hearing our saint constantly speak on this subject, assured him they had never met any one so fond of talking about such matters, or even so thoroughly well informed about them. We have the motive of all this in the advice he gave a Polish brother, 'If you want to introduce spiritual conversation both pleasantly and easily, read the histories and annals of the Society, because these, as they are all our own, give pleasure to all, and I, for my part, have made such a collection of facts that you could not bring forward any subject that I could not illustrate by examples of some one connected with the Society.'

The Brother Lætus, *alias* Hilarius, was always true to his name, and this joyousness, which had become so natural to him, as Father Gottofredi has told us, possessed a constant attraction, and was as sunshine to the whole community. The fruit of his constant watchfulness, the unruffled calm of his spotless soul, the glad and unbroken peace which reigned in his well governed heart, shone through his beautiful face, and made him beloved by all. A modest smile was ever on his lips. . Always equable, without ever suffering himself to be affected by weather or contradictions, he was never put out, never out of humour.

Once, the scholastic who shared his room with him asked him if ever he felt any coming cloud of melancholy? His answer was he did not know what the word meant, or what it was to be in that state, for he did not remember ever having experienced it. He had heard the rector, in one of his exhortations to the community, speak of the harm done by sadness, calling it the mother and the nurse of every sort of temptation in a religious. This left such an impression on his mind that he often repeated the denunciation, and spoke with horror of so great an evil, but he was forced to own—'I say all this because Father Rector has said so; as for the rest, by God's grace, I have never known myself what it is.'

He was grave without any affectation, joyful without levity, and, even when in his most merry moods, his laugh was always subdued, the expression of his face was ever humble, modest, and edifying. He always acted towards others with a sweet affability and pleasant manner. Even when he was serious and grave in conversation, he never became in any sense heavy or tiresome. No words of banter or ridicule ever passed his lips, even in joke. He never laughed at what others did. If one of the community fell into any fault, and had received a public

reprimand or penance, Berchmans took **the** first opportunity to say something in his favour, **to tell** some good
deed he had seen done by the 'worthy' brother. He
never **had any** dispute with any one, never complained **or**
showed himself hurt whatever might **be** done to him.
Though his character was quick and full of fire, **he was
never seen** out of temper, **nor** excited even to such a
degree as to raise his voice above its ordinary tone. **If**
he was praised, **far from being elated**, his face mantled
with confusion. No **blame or** reproof ever made him
sad ; he only humbled himself, and far from being put
out, gave signs of pleasure and satisfaction. When things
went wrong he never lost heart. **His** courage never
failed him in what he undertook for God's service, but
trusting in the divine assistance, he was always even a
support to others. What he had to **do** he did promptly
and quickly, yet never was over anxious for success. He
neither forestalled the right moment by over haste, **nor**
let it slip through laziness, or through over confidence.

Such, almost in his own words, is the finished portrait
Father Cepari gives **us of John.**

We cannot complete it better, or bring this subject to a
better conclusion, than by the words of the saint—

'Take **care** not **to do** what displeases you in others—
even in natural actions—*e.g.*, by spitting, *verbi gratia.*

'**Slowness and** sluggishness in moving about—displeases me.

'Freedom in speech, even about spiritual matters—
displeases me.

'Frequent contradictions—displease me.

'Being too dainty—displeases me.

'**Freedom** in conversation—displeases me.

'An ironical way of talking—displeases me.

'Keeping one's hands **behind** one's back—displeases
me.

' Looking back carelessly in the street—displeases me.

' Moving one's head about without cause—displeases me.

' Bursting **out laughing,** shouting, laughing immoderately—displeases **me.**

' Talking **in the** refectory, in the church, in the sanctuary, at times when it is forbidden—displeases **me.**

' **Notice** what pleases you in others, and imitate them **in that.'**

And here follows the catalogue, in which no doubt the names were written in full; but in the copy, which alone is known to exist, Father Cepari has suppressed them. **A** few we are able to supply from the office which the Fathers held, and which is marked down—

' I like in our Father General (Vitelleschi) his modesty, affability, cordiality, **and** joyful face ; and **his following in all things the order of the** community. In Father Provincial (Anthony Marchese), his love of literature ; in Father Rector (Cepari), and the Spiritual Father (Masucci), **their being always** the **same; in Father Prefect of Studies** (Father del Bufalo), **his** respect for all ; in **my** professor (Father Piccolomini), his affection and his delight **at** his scholars' progress in their studies ; in Father ——, his patience in sickness ; in Father ——, his silence ; in Father ——, his modesty and bashfulness and love of solitude ; in Father ——, his **zeal for souls,** which never grows weary ; **in Father** ——, his love of his room and simplicity ; in Father ——, his love of the Institute ' in Father ——, his amiability and affableness ; in Father ——, his joyousness **with all** his spirituality; in Father ——, his being the servant of all, cheerful and hardworking ; in Father ——, offering himself to **be the** companion of all ; in Brother ——, his avoiding idleness ; in Brother ——, his supplying for any one ; in

——, his liveliness ; in ——, his meekness and tractability ; in ——, his cleanliness, kindness to guests ; in ——, his sincerity ; in ——, his giving to all things their own time ; in ——, his visiting the sick ; in ——, his devotion.

'I like exterior gladness with great regularity.

'I like visiting the Blessed Sacrament before and after schools.

'I like saluting the Blessed Virgin, and visiting the venerable Chapel of St. Ignatius at the vigna.

'I like not plucking even a blade of grass when there.

'I like giving leave to the companion who shares your room to do what he pleases without minding you.

'I like letting myself be ruled like a baby a day old.

'I like doing heartily, and with thorough application whatever you do.

'I like the hands being kept joined on your breast, and not hanging down.'

CHAPTER X.

Berchmans' spirit of piety.

THE beauty of a tropical country, the rich hues of its vegetation, the teeming abundance of its produce, turn the traveller's thoughts to the power of that sun which gives all the brilliant colour to its flowers, all the ripeness to its fruit, and throws a glory over the whole scene.

God is the sun of the soul; and as the soul is brought nearer to the source of all its life and light and heat, so does it bring forth a more and more abundant harvest, and so too does it become more beautiful, more like to Him in Whose likeness is all perfection.

We have gone together with a loving detail over the spiritual fruits of Berchmans' virtue. In this, almost the last chapter of his life, we turn our entire attention to the cause of all this extraordinary holiness—his close union with God by prayer; and what is a necessary accompaniment of his love of God—his devotion to Mary, His Blessed Mother, and to the angels and saints of His heavenly court.

We have seen much of this already. In an order in which Mary and Martha join to promote the greater glory of God, it is from Mary's prayer at the feet of her Lord that all the activity of the outer life gathers its force.

John's interior life is all told by his biographer in a few epigrammatic words—he performed *well*, and at their allotted times, all the spiritual duties which are done by all in the Society. For St. Ignatius had taken care that the daily food of the soul should be of such a kind, and so much, as would support his children in the busiest and most engrossing of external occupations.

The value Berchmans set on all he heard, read, or saw which could further his spiritual growth, is gathered from his idea that natural gifts and learning, without holiness, are like a drawn sword in the hands of a madman ; and that men with more virtue, though with less talent, are the most useful in religion. Accordingly, he was fully persuaded that to be a true religious, he must be a man of prayer. 'If I do not have an easy habit of prayer, I shall not live in peace in the Society. Have a care about God, and God will have care of you. One who does not value prayer, cannot last out in the spiritual life. I will always be specially attached to spiritual things, above all to meditation, examen, and spiritual reading. Prayer is so displeasing to the devil, that he strives to put every hindrance in its way. Every case of apostacy has had its beginning in some careless-ness about spiritual duties.'

We can easily follow him through his daily round of devotions. His copious notes, supported and developed by the declarations of those who saw him at all times of the day, of those to whom he disclosed every secret of his soul, give us a clearer view of him than many enjoyed who lived under the same roof with him.

At four in the morning the bell sounded the hour of rising. John heard it with the reverence of Samuel, when the holy child recognized at the fourth call the voice of the Lord. He made the sign of the Cross, saying as he arose, 'Lord, what wouldst Thou have me to do? My heart is ready, O God, my heart is ready !' The moment he got up he prostrated himself before his crucifix, or the little **cross of wood** he had in the juniorate, and which, **before** going to sleep, he used to place at the foot of his bed. With deep sighs he kissed it again **and** again. When the caller came round to the rooms with his salutation *Deo gratias*, John answered from his heart, 'Yes, always *Deo gratias.*' He was **so** convinced that meditation depends, perhaps chiefly, **on** the way one gets up in the morning, that he used every means to spend with profit the half hour that elapsed between his being called and the beginning of his prayer. While he was dressing, he blew the coals for the morning sacrifice, kindling the fire in his heart with loving aspirations. Shutting out resolutely every other thought, he ran over the points of the meditation, and created before and around him an imaginary scene, whose influence would—as St. Ignatius teaches—put **the** mind and heart in tune for the thoughts and affections he had intended **to aim at in** his prayer. **One** general idea which **he could apply to** any meditation **was to** think that his Blessed **Lord** was seated **on a throne**, with all his saintly patrons standing round Him, just as he had seen in St. Peter's the Holy Father surrounded by his Court during the Papal High Mass. And in that presence he would entertain thoughts kindred to the subject he had chosen. Sometimes he would recite, and even chant **in an** under-tone, so as not **to** distract his companion, verses of the sixty-second Psalm. 'O God, my God, to Thee **do I watch** at break of day.' Before putting on his habit, as he had always been accustomed, he kissed it affectionately as the livery **of his** Lord. As soon as he was dressed he covered his bed, **and** kneeling down, poured out his soul with such ardour that one would have thought that it was the closing colloquy of a night-long prayer. He thanked his angel guardian, **and the patron of** the preceding day, for their protection through the day and night; he begged them to be with him all the rest of his life, and especially at the hour of his death. Then he selected a new patron; and while he begged him to do for him what his other patrons had deigned to do, he offered through his hands the following prayers, as first-fruits of the morning—the Creed, as a profession of faith, protesting that he wished ever to be a true child of the Holy Catholic Apostolic Roman Church; then the prayer of the sodality, renewing the declaration it contains, and protesting that he wished to be a true child of our Blessed Lady; and, lastly, the formula of his vows, protesting that he wished to be a true child of the Society. To these three declarations of love he joined a four-fold resolution—

1. That every thought, word, or deed that day should be purely for God's glory; in thanksgiving for the favour of communion; or, if it was the latter half of the week, to get the grace to make a good communion; to obtain a true devotion to the Blessed Virgin, and true internal humility; and that his thoughts, words, and deeds might be united with those of Christ His Lord.

2. He determined to look to the virtue or vice on which he directed his particular examen.

3. By God's grace, not to commit any deliberate venial sin, or break the least rule or command of my Superiors.

4. To live and die in the Society.

All these resolutions he sealed by an act of humiliation, three times kissing the ground.

This took some seven or eight minutes. He then made his bed and finished his simple toilet, all the while setting in order his meditation and putting it into shape in his head; now and then he would exclaim in the inspired words, 'Lord, teach me how to pray.' 'O Lord, in my meditation' let 'a fire flame out.'[1] 'Open my lips, O Lord, and my mouth shall declare Thy praise.' His companion, Alfaroli, narrates, 'Twice, deceived by my silence, and thinking he was all alone in his room, he gave full vent to the ardour of his soul, reciting in a tone which revealed the fire of his love, some psalms and other passages from Holy Writ. After a few minutes, I moved about to let him know I was there. He was silent at once, though his heart continued to speak; and when I turned to him with a smile I saw his face was scarlet with blushes. To have allowed the secret devotions of his soul to be known, evidently caused him acute pain.'

When all his little arrangements were completed, he hurried to the church to adore his Blessed Lord; and he was always one of the first in the audience chamber. If, as sometimes occurred, he was asked to go out early in the morning, it might be to serve Mass at some shrine on a great feast day, he always excused himself by saying he could not meditate so well out walking as at home. The moment the bell rang for meditation he rose up and returned to his room, thinking as he went whither he was going, and what he was going to do. A few moments were spent in looking over the points he had prepared. A second signal—he made the sign of the Cross—and standing, as St. Ignatius directs, a step or two off the little table, which served as praying desk and place for study, he considered his Lord present before him and looking at him. He made Him a lowly reverence, and then, throwing himself on his knees, asked earnestly 'that all his actions and operations might be directed sincerely to God's honour and glory.' As a candle just extinguished leaps at once into flame

---

[1] Psalm xxxviii. 4.

when a light is brought near it, the soul of Berchmans, so habitually and so closely united to God, had little of that labour which imperfect souls feel so painfully in endeavouring to keep their mind and heart fixed upon prayer. Every action of the day, as we have seen, was done by him in God's sight; at every difficulty he turned to Him for light and help. As we might suppose, the saint of common life did not aim at any extraordinary method of prayer, but endeavoured with all his might to saturate himself with the Ignatian method; and for this end he kept, with the most religious exactness, every little rule which is laid down by the saint in his Book of Exercises. He was very fond of a book on the practice of meditating with fruit, which was then in use at the Roman Novitiate, for the very reason that it adhered so faithfully to the teaching of his holy Father. But, like all his other actions, though the kind was ordinary, extraordinary was the recollection and the union at which he arrived. No distraction crossed his mind; he did not feel the flies and the more troublesome fleas of an Italian summer, so absorbed was he in God. He knelt erect, without any support. Even when poorly he would not take another position. One day Father Bargagli, knowing he was not at all well, urged him to sit down, or at least not to kneel so erect. 'Oh, no, Father!' he replied, 'I can make my meditation perfectly on my knees.'

At the beginning of the hour he was motionless and quiet, so that you would not have known he was in the room. But as his prayer went on, his fervour rose and rose, until, unable any longer to restrain it, he burst out into fervent sighs, so loud, so deep as to wake his companion, if, as sometimes happened, he had leave for an extra sleep. His face was lit up like a seraph's. It seemed as if his heart would break, so violently was he overmastered by his devotion ; and as the meditation drew to a close, he kissed, again and again, the little print of our Lady and Child which was on the wall, and which was afterwards kept, as we have said, as a precious relic by Father Oliva. Ten or twelve times he pressed it to his lips, with his face all radiant with spiritual joy and a heavenly smile. He ended his prayer, if time allowed him, with the Our Father, and prostrated himself once more, as if to bid farewell for the time, and close, by this act of reverence, his fervent colloquy.

On the first sound of the bell, which marked the end of the hour, he left God at once, at the voice of God. For a short time, standing before the place where he had been praying, he examined how his prayer had gone off; then, seated at his table, he spent the rest of the time allotted for consideration in noting down briefly, what had been his success, what resolutions he had made, what motives had urged him to make them. Great was the light he used to receive in prayer, many and beautiful the lessons he learned and the knowledge he there received, and so filled was he with the sweetness of consolation, that it was very easy to see how tenderly his Lord fostered and caressed him, and how the Queen of Angels gave him of the milk of her bounty. Oftentimes he looked as if filled with the Spirit of God. Eight months before his death, on the feast of our Lady's Expectation, 1620, he told Father Cepari he was flooded with heavenly delights, or, as he himself noted it down, 'Saturday, December 18th. The Lord sent me a river of peace.' No wonder 'to the odour of his ointments' which he gathered in his prayer, and to hear the precious words by which he made known the abundance of the divine sweetness which inundated his heart, his brothers and Fathers in religion alike 'ran *after him.'* Still, like all the saints, from time to time he suffered most grievously from spiritual dryness. But under the leaden sky he neither lost heart, nor slackened at all in his prayer or spiritual duties, but held on persistently and perseveringly spite of the darkness and coldness around him, crying out with a loving earnestness to his God, ' Restore to me the joy of Thy salvation; send forth Thy light and Thy truth.' But he did not merely pray; every means which his spiritual knowledge taught him he used, to regain the light and gladness that had departed. 'I remember,' says Father Cepari, 'noticing several times, that the good young man felt very keenly his being in dryness and desolation (accustomed as he was continually to taste of the milk of divine consolations), and, in fact, he used to tell me his state in such words of bitter sorrow as really moved me to compassion. Still, in times of the greatest dryness, he ever kept himself in great peace and in interior quiet. His will was perfectly conformed to that of God; and he assured me, "In my desolation I always felt great tranquillity of mind." I concluded from this that God withdrew Himself now and again, lest John's constitution should be destroyed by the wasting power of His love.'

After the examen of his meditation followed Mass; Berchmans went there full of the thought that he was about to take part in the most august worship—the offering of the unbegotten Son to His Eternal Father. His own notes are the best description of how he spent that precious time.

The Sacrifice of the Mass.

'On the way to the chapel consider whither thou art going—namely, to God; and what thou art about to do—namely, to offer up His Son. Having arrived there, ask for grace, renew the intentions of the morning—

namely, to promote God's glory in thanksgiving or preparation for communion, and to obtain this or that favour. Finally, unite this unbloody sacrifice with that bloody one offered up upon the altar of the Cross, and this action of thine with that sacrifice.

'From the commencement until the Oblation attend to the words and to what is being done. From the Oblation I will begin to go over the Passion of Christ, starting from the Prayer in the Garden ; so that, when the *Sanctus* is being said, I shall have arrived at that part where Christ, laying Himself down upon the Cross, is fastened to it with nails by the executioners. Here, raising up my mind to God the Father, I will call upon Him, *Aspice, Domine, in faciem Christi tui*—" Look, O Lord, on the face of Thy Christ ;" and by His adorable Head, crowned with thorns, I will pray first for the Sovereign Pontiff, the Emperor, Kings, and Christian Princes, and I will beg that He will give them grace to govern well their respective States, and to defend the Church ; secondly, by His sacred Head I will pray for our Very Reverend Father General, for the Provincial, Rector, Minister, Spiritual Father, Professors, &c. By the Right Hand, I will pray for my relations and friends in the world, that He may give them the grace to observe the Commandments ; and also for my brethren in religion, recommending, in the first place, all who live with me in the same College ; and for others by name, asking for them these three graces—first, angelical charity; secondly, that they may be good instruments of the Society ; and, thirdly, perseverance in their vocation. By the Left Hand, I will pray for all my enemies, for heretics, infidels, and those in the state of mortal sin. By the Right Foot, for all those who live a tepid and irregular life in the Society, that their imperfections may not hinder the fruit of the

o

Society. By the Left Foot, for all apostates, that God would deign to have mercy upon them.

'At the Elevation I will picture to myself the real elevation of His bleeding Body upon the Cross, and I will say, *Adoro te, Christe, et benedico tibi quia per sanctam crucem tuam redemisti mundum*—" I adore Thee, O Christ, and bless Thee, because by Thy holy Cross Thou hast redeemed the world." Then I will say the *Anima Christi*.

'At the *Nobis quoque peccatoribus* I will think of the Wound in His Side, and I will immediately beg of Christ that He will receive therein His Society, and that He will preserve, defend, and increase the same; secondly, I will recommend my deceased relatives and friends, those of the Society who are dead, and those for whom but few pray, and who are the most in need of prayers; thirdly, I will beg Him to receive me into that Sacred Heart, and to give me true charity, spiritual joy, sanctity, learning, if it be for His greater glory. Also that He will make me a good member of the Society, and will give me perseverance in my vocation, devotion towards the Blessed Virgin, and the virtue of my particular examen—for example, charity or true internal humility.

'I will make a spiritual communion, and the rest of the time I will attend to the words of the priest, and return thanks with him.

'After Mass make acts of contrition and thanksgiving; unite your action with the sacrifice; say the *Magnificat* to get pardon for all defects.'

As the Holy Sacrifice proceeded, in his fervour he gradually forgot all around him; and as he pronounced slowly the words of the sacred rite, his lips moved as though he were feeding upon some invisible banquet, the noise they made being audible to those who were near him.

This was specially noticeable on communion days. No care was too great in his preparation for **this adorable** sacrament. **He never liked to** go to communion **on a** recreation day, even though it might be a feast of some note; **because,** as he said, '**I** cannot have the devotion **and** quiet that it requires, as we are obliged either to go **out walking or to the** vigna.' **Neither** would he ever go to holy communion outside the College. He longed for this sacred banquet so ardently that he used often **to** ask for an extra communion, and he owned that each time he approached he felt an evident increase of spiritual strength. If a week passed without that happiness, he felt as feeble and faint as one would do who had been without his ordinary food. **During the** vacations, when at the villa **at Frascati,** he always **went** once a week **oftener than usual; and** nothing could prevail **upon him to go out** for a walk **on** that morning. If a communion **day** fell on a Sunday, he regretted deeply that he had 'one banquet the less.' Like St. Aloysius, as we have seen, he spent three days in preparation, and then for three days thanked God for the great **grace received.** On the **eve of his** communion **he** made with deep contrition and humility his confession. **He has left** us his method of approaching the sacred tribunal, for which, as for holy communion, he made a lengthy preparation.

Confession.

'Before confession. After **the sign of the holy** Cross, I will turn to the Blessed Virgin, begging her **to** intercede **for me** with her **Son, and** to obtain for **me** the grace to **know** and detest my sins, and to possess an intimate **knowledge and** detestation of them. Then

I will turn to the Son, begging Him to obtain the same
of the Eternal Father. Lastly, I will turn to God the
Father, asking Him in His liberality to grant me the
same. After this I will proceed to the examination,
and then to contrition, endeavouring that this may be
pure, intense, and, by God's help, universal for all my
sins; I will add a purpose of amendment.

'In the confession, I will observe the common method
of the Society.

'After confession—first, I will give thanks; secondly,
I will immediately perform my penance; thirdly, I will
renew my purpose of amendment; fourthly, I will invite
Christ with some aspiration—for instance, "Let my
Beloved come into His garden;" or I will say this
prayer, "Grant, O Lord, by the merits and intercession
of Blessed Mary ever a Virgin, and of all the saints,
that this my confession may be grateful and acceptable
to Thee; and that whatever now or at any time has
been wanting to the purity and integrity of confession
may be supplied by Thy goodness and mercy, and that
I may be thereby more fully and perfectly absolved in
heaven. Who livest and reignest world without end.
Amen."'

And we cannot do better than allow John to tell us
also how he approached holy communion—

Communion.

'In going to the chapel I will reflect what I am about
to do—to wit, to receive the true Body and Blood of
Him Who is the Son of God and the Son of the Blessed
Virgin. I will invite my patrons to prepare my heart for
Him. When there, I will beg grace and renew my morning
intention. Then, reflecting a little upon my miseries,
sins, and imperfections, I will grieve for all the sins

which I have committed, and purpose sincere amendment. From the Oblation to the *Sanctus* I will say some vocal prayers, and go through the whole of the Passion of Christ.

'About the time of the Elevation I will call to mind that the same Christ descends from heaven on to the altar, in order that He may from thence in a few minutes enter into my soul. I will adore Him, reciting, with St. Thomas, *Tu Rex gloriæ Christe* to *Salvum fac*, out of the *Te Deum*. Then I will continue in acts of faith and love until the *Pater noster*. Here I will begin to make aspirations to Christ, saying, "Who will give Thee to me, my Brother, sucking the breasts of my mother?" "As the hart panteth after the fountains of water," &c.; "Let my Beloved come into His garden," &c. I will offer Him these desires through the Blessed Virgin, and I will imagine that He answers me, "I will come and cure him." And I will say with humility, "Lord, I am not worthy," &c.; "Into Thy hands, O Lord, I commend my spirit." "May the Body of our Lord Jesus Christ preserve my soul to life everlasting. Amen."

'As soon as I have received I will make an act of faith that what I have received is truly the Son of God and the Son of the Blessed Virgin. Then with all humility I will ask Him, "Whence is this to me that my Lord should come to me?" By some short vocal prayer I will give Him thanks, and beg of my patrons to do the same; then I will offer Him my body and soul, and some little gift in particular—for instance, of mortification; then my vows, renewing them; lastly, a firm purpose of serving His Mother the Blessed Virgin, and I will recite the prayer of the sodality, *Sancta Maria, Mater Dei, et Virgo,* &c. After which I will turn to God the Father, begging Him to look upon the face of His Christ; and by His sacred Wounds I will make the same petitions as above. I will conclude by giving thanks and begging pardon for having received Him so badly, and I will say the Psalm, *Laudate Dominum omnes gentes.'*

In spite of his pressing duties, John gave all the forenoon of his communion days to reading the Fathers of the Church and spiritual writers, among whom Alvarez de Paz held the chief place. His great work, *De Vitâ Spirituali*, had been published some ten years before, and its sainted author died Provincial of Peru in the January of 1620. John always said his studies never suffered by this sacrifice of his time, for God made it up for him. 'I find that by generously giving the whole morning on communion days, and on feast days a whole hour, and every month one whole day to spiritual exercises, I do not at all interfere with my studies.' He never let a day pass without reading some spiritual work for half an hour. So jealous was he of every opportunity, that being forbidden to read in his turn in the refectory on account of his delicate chest, he asked and obtained leave to do so at the dinner which was served in the infirmary for those who were convalescent. In the evening, although he could have prolonged his recreation when he had been serving, or taking his supper at second table, he withdrew to his room immediately the Litanies which are recited in public were over, all to gain more time for spiritual reading. On days when the young men went to the vigna at Santa Balbina, he always carried with him the *Imitation of Christ*, and would give a whole hour to the study of that precious book, the constant companion of his Father and model, St. Ignatius. So, too, when, during the summer holidays, the students went out to Frascati, he gave a full hour each day to this his favourite study; and, in fact, every moment that he could gain by exact economy of time, was given either to prayer or spiritual **reading**. He made his recreations pay their tribute, for whenever **he** was sent out for a walk **in the city**, its aim was always a visit to one **or more churches**. The usual centre of his devotion there was the altar whereon our Blessed Lord reposed; and so enraptured did he become, that often his companion would get up and go to the door without John noticing that he had left his **side**. And when perforce he went back to make the holy young man aware that it was time to leave, he found Berchmans so absorbed in God, so lost to all around, that he was forced to call him loudly by name to arouse him and bring him back to his senses. We have seen, when speaking of his studies, how frequently he **went to visit** his Blessed Lord during **the day**. 'I **will** diligently foster my love towards the Blessed Sacrament, and will visit it at least five **times a day; and every Thursday**, for this end, I will perform some penance in the refectory.' 'On Sundays I will always say something about the Blessed Sacrament during recreation.' No doubt, his collection of stories and sayings about this adorable mystery were made to help this last resolution.

He was always ready to give his prayers for any one's intention, and he, in his turn, often asked the prayers of others. **There** were three things he specially begged them to obtain for him, great holiness, great learning, and strong and robust health—with this great difference, that while the first of the three he sought absolutely, **he** wished the other two to depend purely on God's good will, and as He might see it to be for His greater glory.

So passed **his day, each** moment giving back, **like** a well tilled field, its fruit to eternal life, for **our saint** was ever walking before God, ever mindful of His presence. When evening came, during the time allotted, he prepared with care the subject of his morning's meditation, and he was especially watchful not to lose an instant of the quarter of an hour his rule prescribed for spiritual reading. Then came his night examen, and we quote his own words—' Immediately after examen, I will offer up all my thoughts, words, and actions, to God, by the hands of my patrons of the day, in union with the thoughts, words, and actions of Christ; secondly, I will say the Creed, the prayer of the sodality, and the formula of my vows, protesting, as in the morning, that I wish to live and to die a true son of the Church, of the Blessed Virgin, and of the Society of Jesus; thirdly, I will sprinkle my bed with holy water. While undressing, I will settle how I am to get up and meditate the next morning; and kneeling either at or upon my bed, say three Hail Marys, first, to our Lady of Loreto, in honour of the moment of her maternity, begging her to free me that night from any bad dreams; secondly, to our Lady of Montaigu, in honour of the moment of her Immaculate Conception, that she may make me fall asleep at once, and get up diligently; thirdly, to our Lady of Hal, in honour of the moment in which, after her death, she was united to her Son, begging that I may succeed in my next day's meditation, and that I may have spiritual joy.'

It may here be noted that ' our Lady of Hal ' is a well known pilgrimage in Belgium, near Brussels. It dates from the beginning of the fourteenth century, when the Countess Alix placed in the church of the town of Hal a little wooden statue of the Blessed Virgin, said to have belonged to St. Elisabeth of Hungary. The riches of its treasury, the beauty of the church, attract many who do not go from any spirit of piety.

' While getting into bed, renew the purity of your intention, and unite your rest with the sleep of Christ. Last of all, think seriously of the hour at which you are

to get up, then run over the points of the meditation,
and repose in the Lord. Put your **rule book under your
pillow.'**

The love **of His God and Redeemer had so taken**
hold of Berchmans' heart, **that we look** naturally **for a**
deep affection towards her, who was and **is** nearest and
dearest to our common Lord and Master, that Virginal
Mother from whom He received **His** sacred Body.
And indeed, few saints have ever served and honoured
her as did John. Many have been the proofs we have
already had of his devotion to Mary. We gather up here
what has as yet remained untold. Berchmans seems, as
Father Cepari says, to have been one of the saints raised
up on purpose to glorify her name. He liked people to
know that he was specially devout to **her,** that **so he**
might be privileged **on every occasion to speak about her**
without reserve. He had **taken as his device, ' Thou my
Mother, Mary, ever Virgin, art the patroness of my holiness, of my health, and my studies.'** This devotion **he**
looked on as the bulwark of his **vocation, ' I am** not safe
unless I have a true and childlike affection towards the
Blessed Virgin." The very day before he died, William
van Aelst, who was pressing him with many questions,
asked him **what was the** great foundation of holiness. The
young man had a special claim on John's friendship, for
they had been fellow novices at Mechlin. In that hour
when men's deepest thoughts are shown forth, our saint
gave this answer to his young countryman—' The most
powerful and chiefest means that **I have** used in seeking
to gain religious perfection has been love and devotion
towards the ever Blessed Virgin, and be you, in like
manner, always a true child of Mary.' William was
reserved for the toils of missionary life, first in the service
of the troops, becoming head military chaplain, or Superior of the Jesuit missionaries in the Catholic army, and

then on the mission in Holland, from which he tried, but ineffectually, to push his apostolic labours into Denmark. 'I wish to love Mary,' John used often **to say**: 'I never shall rest till I have got a tender love for **my sweetest** Mother, Mary.' 'I shall devote myself heart and soul **to** her service.' **Again and** again in his notes he returns to the **same subject**—'**Every** Saturday I must say **some-**thing about the Blessed Virgin during recreation.' 'On **Saturdays** I will wash **the** dishes **in** the kitchen in **honour** of Mary.' **Our Lady seems** to have made that **day one of mark, both in his life** and death. He was **born on a** Saturday, he entered the Society on **a** Saturday, he was buried on a Saturday. 'Write on a piece of paper what **you** want, and fasten it to **a** picture of our Lady, with some offering to her.' **This was** the way he got many favours from his Blessed Mother, bribing her with some promise of prayers, or penance, or other good works. One of his sayings was—'That every one needs some settled and safe place as "a city of refuge" in sudden need, and such were the Wounds of Christ, and the bosom and mantle of the Queen of Heaven.' He was asked **once, What were** the remedies he used against **desolation?** 'Prayer, work, **patience,** the bosom and lap of Mary.'

He set **great store** upon the rosary. **He** said it with extraordinary devotion, sometimes on his knees, some-**times** standing up, other times sitting, often walking about in a large room at the top of the College. There he was to be seen, at a regular time, walking backwards and forwards in the furthest and darkest extremity of the room, so intent on his prayer, that—with a marked exception to his ordinary conduct—he did not salute any one who chanced to pass by. He put together a number of thoughts which those prayers suggested, and they served to excite his fervour as he dwelt on the different mysteries. Other times he would spend the whole prayer in stirring up in himself the desire, as he was wont to do so often—'I wish to love Mary.' He would not be without his rosary, even at night ; he used at first to sleep with it twisted round his arm, as the badge of a soldier of our Lady ; but towards the close of his life, before going to bed, he put it round his neck. We owe to him the special devotion of the Rosary of the Immaculate Conception, which consists of three Our Fathers in honour of the Blessed Trinity, each followed by four Hail Marys in honour of twelve virtues of our Lady. He called it the chaplet of the twelve stars, wherewith to crown our Lady. He took the pains to compose short and pithy meditations for each prayer, in all fifteen, which show fully the scope and fruit of this his much loved devotion.

Nine times a day on bended knee he saluted Mary with the Church's exclamation—*Beata viscera quæ portaverunt Æterni Patris Filium,* to honour thus the nine months that she bore her Maker in her chaste womb. After the example of the devotion of the Seven Churches of Rome, he loved to make his holiday walk a pilgrimage to some seven churches dedicated to Mary.

From his well stocked note-book, full of stories and sayings of Fathers about his Blessed Mother, and saints' praises of her, he was ever ready to bring forward his favourite topic. A lay-brother, Cerutti, gives us an anecdote that comes in to the purpose. 'I recollect that one day he was telling me the story of a child of Mary, who, after having received a signal favour from the Mother of God, carried his ingratitude so far, as to need to be admonished very seriously by his heavenly benefactress that he should show more respect for her in his language. This severity frightened me, and I begged him to tell me rather of our Blessed Lady's mercy, than of her justice. "What," he answered, with energy, "is it then so slight a mark of her mercy to have brought you to the Society of her Son?"' Berchmans certainly did not forget what he owed to her. Among his papers was found a list of the favours which his order considered they owed to Mary's intercession. Not content with exciting his gratitude by their perusal, he had determined, if God had spared him, to publish this catalogue, to hand on to others the fire of his devotion.

He was very fond, when he found himself with another during recreation who shared his love of Mary, to engage with him in a sort of spiritual tourney. Each tried to outmatch the other in his praises of our Lady. He engaged joyously in the struggle, and beautiful were the thoughts which his well-stored mind and loving heart brought forth. And if his rival stopped for want of anything to say, John went on, pouring forth her praises with such rich abundance, that the hour ended before he was done.

But the time of the year when his devotion to Mary came out most prominently, was when, after a hard ten months of close application, books and lectures, disputations and dictates, were for a short time put on one side, and the students exchanged the stifling and unwholesome air of Rome for the fresh breezes and broad horizon of the Tusculan hills.

John seemed to have dedicated that pleasant time wholly to Mary. The students used to go to their villa on foot, and their way lay across the broad and parched Campagna. No sooner had they got outside the Lateran Gate, so near at once to St. John's Basilica and to the beloved Apostle's place of torture at the Porta Latina, than Berchmans commenced aloud the *Itinerarium*, or the prayers in the Church's Liturgy for those who are on a journey. And then, as they went on, and the green hills grew nearer, and the giant white city faded behind them, he opened the vacation by reciting our Lady's Office. The long, straight, hot road became as a choir in her honour ; for all the way he would do nothing else but alternate between meditations, and litanies, and praises, and stories in her honour. Close to the Alban hills there is a well-known sanctuary, which became for John the Montaigu and Loreto of his holiday time. A picture of our Lady in a cavern, not far from Frascati, and which was protected by a grating of iron, had been a place of pilgrimage, under the name of Grotta Ferrata, long before the stately abbey of Basilian monks, about the beginning of the eleventh century, rose around the holy place. The gateway and strong walls with which the warlike Julius II. surrounded it, give it the look more of a feudal castle than a place of peace. The miraculous picture is enthroned over the high altar. In a side chapel lie the bodies of the two sainted founders, St. Nilus and St. Bartholomew, and the walls tell in pictured story the history of their lives.

An artist would envy Berchmans' good lot in having seen these frescoes, the first that ever Domenichino painted, then in their first freshness and beauty, and before they had passed through the dubious process of restoration. But it was not these, nor its other art treasures, that attracted our saint to make constant visits to this hallowed spot. And whenever he went down by the borders of Regillus, or along the heights of Tusculum, or through the long ilex alleys, or cypress avenues of the Borghese Villa, recitation of the rosary, prayers to our Lady, were always intertwined with his graceful and attractive conversations. He liked to have as one of his companions in these walks, some Father, skilled as well in learning as in spiritual things, to be at once, as he said, a model to the young men, and a means of helping the conversation from his store. And Berchmans would lead on to the conversation by asking the meaning of some psalm he had met with in our Lady's Office, or of something of the kind, which would bring them at once to speak of Mary. 'Last year' (1621), says Father John Baptist Canaceli, 'I made acquaintance, while we were together at Frascati, with John Berchmans. Each day, during our walk, we used to say together, according to agreement, the Office of the Blessed Virgin, to which we added a little rosary of three *Paters* and twelve *Aves*, for John was very fond of that devotion. He took care to tell me, before we commenced, that the three *Paters* were in honour of the most Blessed Trinity, and then at each Hail Mary he mentioned some virtue of our Blessed Lady, which we were to ask of her. After that, we generally read some psalm or other, and at each verse we told each other the pious thoughts the reading brought to our minds. He always had the most sublime ideas, far beyond what I could bring. We used also to say the rosary, or talk on spiritual matters, sometimes reading a sentence of the *Psychagogy* (a compilation, by Lewis of Blois, from the works of St. Augustine and St. Gregory) to help our conversation, or, at all events, we spoke on some philosophical subject.'

Naturally enough, with so great a love for our Blessed Mother, he shared with all the doctors and writers of the Society in his zeal for Mary's Immaculate Conception. He made a vow that the first book he should write should be on that her great privilege. He had already planned in his mind the order and arrangement of the work ; and whenever he read the Fathers, or other ecclesiastical writers, he noted down anything that bore on the subject. The first part was to have contained all the comparisons and analogies by which this mystery may be illustrated. The second part would have given the proofs by which it is established. A third part would have added the various miraculous interpositions by which God had manifested His mind on its behalf. We see in his notes on our Lady a foreshadowing of the work he never lived to write. Sometimes it chanced that our saint, as yet unskilled in theological science, would bring forward some of his arguments in recreation. Love of opposition, or desire to add to the interest of the conversation, would suggest to a bystander some flaw in the proof, or even that it was altogether without force. Berchmans became at once unusually excited, and brought all his logic to support his thesis, and rebut the opposing objections. But it was the reasoning of his heart, more even than the proofs of sacred science, that convinced him of this truth. He offered up his communions to God to obtain from Him the spread of devotion to this crowning glory of Mary ; 'for,' said he, 'it is fitting that we, children of so august a Mother, should defend her in that very point on which her enemies assault her with such vigour.' At meal time, before he touched anything at table, he always said a Hail Mary in honour of her Immaculate Conception. Among his effects, after his death, was found a small paper, which ran thus—

'I, John Berchmans, most unworthy child of the Society of Jesus, protest to thee and to thy Son, Whom I believe and confess is here present in the most august Sacrament of the Eucharist, that always and for ever, unless the Church judgeth otherwise, will I be the supporter and defender of thy Immaculate Conception. In faith of which I have subscribed this with my blood, and signed it with the seal of the Society of Jesus. A.D. 1621.

I.H.S.   'JOHN BERCHMANS.'

This relic was sent to Belgium, but was returned to Rome, with his other writings, for the cause of his Beatification, and is now to be seen, with so many other precious memorials of the saints and great men of the Society of Jesus, in the rooms of St. Ignatius at the Gesù. When Father Bisdomini, the professor of moral theology, told Cardinal Bellarmine of this vow, the holy old man, who was just on the eve of death, said—with the authority his holiness and prudence give his words—'Oh ! what a beautiful idea, to write such a declaration to our Lady ! Oh ! what a wonderful thought ! I believe that it was our Lady herself that inspired him with it ; for the Mother of God has wished to have this child as her own.'

As the love of Mary comes naturally to a heart filled with the love of her Divine Son, so the devotion to the daughter of Anne led John naturally to a special reverence for that venerable saint, and for all those near and dear to our Blessed Lady ; and therefore, above all, to her glorious spouse, St. Joseph. He gathered up from various sources the favours and miracles the holy patriarch had obtained for his clients ; and, like St. Teresa, he used to declare that never had he found a prayer unheard, a grace asked and not given, since he had chosen him for his advocate.

Among his other intercessors his Angel Guardian, the Beloved Disciple, St. Ignatius and St. Xavier, St. Aloysius and St. Stanislaus, held the first place, though these last four had not then been canonized. He distributed the days of the week among these his patrons ; and, as we have seen, on that assigned to each, offered all his actions to God through their hands, and performed other practices of devotion in their honour. He never passed the pictures of these saints, which in his day hung in the common room of the College, without reverently saluting them. But amongst all these he had a special affection for St. Aloysius, and paid to him a worship of loving service. He said he had a particular trust in him, as he was his brother in Christ. He never mentioned his name without raising his cap. Whenever he paid his frequently repeated visits to the adorable Sacrament in the old church of the Roman College, he used to go to the chapel beneath whose altar St. Aloysius then lay buried. He made a summary of his life, with the virtues and miracles approved by the Congregation of Rites. Perhaps it was to serve as frontispiece to this little work that he copied in pen and ink a portrait of the saint, the same which is engraved by the Bollandists after a medal or coin of the Duchy of Mantua, which had been struck in his honour. The last letter of John which is extant deserves to be quoted here; only the rough copy exists, and is kept at Rome, nor is there any sign to whom it was addressed. But it would seem to have been written to his old confessor, Father Anthony de Greeff, then engaged in the mission of Holland—it was perhaps the one whose loss he lamented ;[2] and we may readily believe that the rekindling of the war between Spain and the Dutch Republic would have prevented it reaching its destination, or account at all events for its being lost.

'There is very little hope, or none at all, that our Blessed Father Ignatius' Canonization, so much desired by the whole Society, will take place under the present Pope [Gregory XV.]; for it is already settled that Blessed Isidore the Spaniard, for whom the King of the two Spains has worked so zealously, is to be enrolled in the catalogue of the saints, and the preparations for this are being made for next Easter [1622]. I own that here we are very grieved; but the hope that this delay will turn to the greater glory of our most blessed Father is a

[2] See p. 28.

P

consolation in our sorrow.' John's forebodings were fortunately not verified; for on the 12th of March, 1622, the then reigning Pontiff canonized St. Ignatius and St. Francis Xavier, along with St. Isidore. 'There is a remarkable devotion to Blessed Francis Xavier. A special altar is now dedicated to him in the church of the Professed House. All are astounded, even the very auditors of the Rota, at the number and greatness of his miracles. I myself heard our Very Reverend Father Mutius Vitelleschi say distinctly, in presence of sixteen Cardinals, that among the miracles attributed to Blessed Francis are twenty-four or twenty-five cases of dead raised to life; and that as to seventeen of these they are so certain, and so attested to by witnesses, that they cannot in any way be called into question.

'On his last feast, his right arm, enshrined in a silver bust, was exposed to veneration. It is entire, but dry, and without its juices. It was placed on the right hand of the altar, while a silver bust of St. Ignatius was on the left. Doubtless he venerates the right arm of the noblest of his sons, and receives that arm which baptized one hundred and twenty thousand. I repeat it again, lest you think I have made a mistake, ten (*sic*) hundred thousand. So he who preached the panegyric of Blessed Francis in our refectory asserted, and this number is given in the compendium of his life published in Italian.

'As Blessed Francis Xavier has brought into the Society the title of Apostle, so Blessed Aloysius has with exceeding glory brought into it that of Angelic, for his process is entitled by the Auditors of the Rota, "On the Life and Miracles of the Angelic Aloysius Gonzaga, of the Society of Jesus." He has been chosen the patron of the Roman College; and our Very Reverend Father General has allowed the renovation of vows, which used other years to be on St. Mary Magdalene's day, to take place on his feast. On that occasion, a Latin speech, a Greek oration, and a poem, are recited, by three youths of the first families, in the presence of the Cardinals in the church of the Roman College in the chapel of the saint, which is constructed of most precious marble. There are very many living in the Roman College, and at the Professed House, who were quite intimate with him, and among others, our Very Reverend Father Mutius Vitelleschi, and Father Virgil Cepari, who wrote his Life, and was the Promoter of his Beatification. Both, too, declare they used to leave a recreation spent with Blessed Aloysius with their hearts more inflamed than by a meditation. Once, when Father Mutius was taking recreation with our blessed brother, the conversation turned on the excellence and dignity of our Society; Blessed Aloysius said that the excellence and beauty of the Society seemed to him such, that he would have been content to pass even through hell to look at it, though but for once. Father General told us this himself in his exhortation in the Roman College, and I heard it from his own lips. For your Reverence's satisfaction, I subjoin here the title of the process of the Blessed Aloysius presented by the Auditors of the Rota to the Sovereign Pontiff.' This, and a long list of princes and people petitioning for the Canonization, need not find place here.

Berchmans did not confine his devotion to his brother saint to words of prayer or praise, but offered up in his honour many little acts of penance; and Father Cepari found in his handwriting that, on May 25th, 1621, he offered to God the homage of a hundred acts of self-humiliation to be done in honour of St. Aloysius. But more than all this, he honoured him by imitating most closely his life and virtues. Even to any one who reads the Life of the ex-Marquis of Castiglione in the pages

P 2

of Father Cepari, or in the beautiful memoir by Healy Thompson, side by side with the Life of the Flemish scholastic, the resemblance is most striking. We cannot be surprised, then, to find that all who had known St. Aloysius, whether ecclesiastics or religious, saw in John a perfect likeness of his patron and model.

On the 15th of June, 1620, there was a solemn ceremony in the College church of the Annunziata, for the relics of St. Aloysius were to be translated from the chapel of the Madonna to the other, which Berchmans has described in his letter, dedicated to the blessed saint.[3] At the head of the long procession of Fathers and brothers walked John, in his familiar office of acolyte. The venerable old Father Croce, Assistant for Italy, who had seen St. Ignatius when a child, and had known St. Aloysius at Rome and Milan, could not help, as he noticed the modest youth, saying to his companion, Father Theodore Busée, the Assistant for Germany—'This youth seems to me another Aloysius.' And this expression, which gathers its force from the circumstance in which it was uttered, the gravity of him who said it, and the warning St. Ignatius has left, to be chary of such comparisons, was the common judgment of all who had known the two. So near in likeness on earth, they were, in another year, to be joined together by death.

[3] See p. 276.

CHAPTER XL.

John Berchmans' last sickness.

AT the beginning of 1620, Berchmans had chosen, as the virtue for which he was to labour during that twelve-months—humility.

At the beginning of 1621, he wrote on the frontispiece of the little book he had prepared for the spiritual notes of that year, the words of the seventy-sixth Psalm, 'I said, now have I begun.' And the subject of the particular examen he chose for this, the last year of his life, was the queen and perfection of all virtues, charity, and with it, spiritual gladness. Again and again recurred in those pages the words, 'Charity, charity'—*est vivere in dies et horas*—'is to live from day to day, from hour to hour.' For that love of God had so set his heart on fire, that he thought no more of this life; he was an exile, sighing for his home, longing for his only Good, and he lived on from day to day, resigned to God's good will, but ever hoping to be dissolved, and to be with His Love. He had paid, about this time, a visit to St. Mary Major's, dear to him for so many titles, and where St. Ignatius had offered his first Mass. His companion was Father Famian Strada, the professor of rhetoric, whose *History of the Wars in the Netherlands* has gained him so great a name. On the way home, they began to talk of the great sense of security in which religious generally die. Twenty-nine years of experience in the Society, spent for the most part in the Roman College, enabled the Father to cite many an example of the simple courage with which he had seen his brethren meet that solemn hour. He instanced, among the rest, the peaceful and calm death of a Father Denis Silla. 'Brother John,' he went on to say, 'God grant my soul may die the death of the just.' Our saint turned sharply to him, and gravely, but respectfully, rejoined—'Father, we ought to say, may our soul live the life of the just; so that afterwards we may say, may my soul die the death of the just.'

'I must confess,' says Father Strada, 'that in these his words, and especially in the firmness, or rather, the sort of authority, with which they were spoken by this young man, who always showed such respect to me and to all our Fathers, I saw clearly the cowardice of my conduct in hoping for the reward of the saints, without troubling myself to share in their labours.' He must have seen a further meaning in them when, some short time after, his gentle monitor added another bright example to his list.

On the 23rd of June, 1621, there passed away Father Cæsar Laurentius, who had been master of rhetoric and professor of Greek at the College. The year before, he had been the one selected to deliver the annual panegyric on its illustrious founder, Gregory XIII. John tells us, 'He died a most holy death. Before Extreme Unction, he asked to tell his fault—"By order of holy obedience, that is, of the most Holy Trinity, the Blessed Virgin, and my angel guardian, as a little penance, I am commanded to die."'

The last note Berchmans has left us is on a similar subject, showing the current of his thoughts, was that about the death of Father Ledesma, which has already been quoted.[1]

The feast of Blessed Aloysius had gone by, and Berchmans remarked that the place of honour at dinner

---

[1] See p. 193.

that day had been prepared for Cardinal Bellarmine by the simple adornment of a green cloth thrown over the seat left vacant for him. His Eminence was not however able to come, and the Father General, who took his place, put aside with his own hands the signs of dignity.

Through the heat of a Roman summer, the young man was kept close to his work, preparing for the severe ordeal of holding his ground, on the whole field of philosophical matters, against all comers, in a public defension. The day at length arrived, and on the 8th of July he made a brilliant display, its lustre heightened by the retiring modesty of the young disputant. A group of lay students were gathered together in the open gallery just outside the door of the large hall, usually devoted to theological lectures, where the defension was to come off. The moment they saw John in the pulpit, the post of honour and danger, 'Come in,' said they, to the other loiterers, 'come, it is Father Modestus who is going to defend. We shall be able, for two full hours, to enjoy the sight of him at our ease.'

All were delighted. Father John Brisellius, of Louvain, secretary to the Father General, bears witness that John's defension was made most excellently, most readily, and in a way most fitting a religious man. And the Father Assistant of Spain, Alphonsus Carillo, said of it to some of the community who gathered round him at its close, 'If an angel, in the habit of the Society, had to defend in philosophy, he could not have shown more modesty or gravity than our John.'

With that day's success, Berchmans' philosophical studies were brought to a close, and he was at the service of his Superiors for some new occupation. Different rectors in the Roman province tried to obtain him for their College as a master. His own provincial, Father

Anthony Sucquet, urgently requested that he might be sent back to Belgium.

But what **was not known to** others, seemed to have been breaking more and more clearly upon John, **for just** at this time, talking at recreation time with a Father, he owned, **that** if God were pleased **to call** him **to another** life, he would not feel any repugnance in obeying the call. But **he went further** in what **he** said, some **four days** later, to **Jerome Savignano,** then one of the **masters, and who was afterwards to** fill, for several **years,** chairs of philosophy and theology in the Roman College. **He** was very fond of our saint, and was always glad to **talk with** him, **on** account of the spiritual profit **he** derived from his conversation and holy example. John told him that he felt inflamed **with an ardent desire to** die, in order to be perfectly united with God. Jerome asked him, if he had his house in such order that he did not fear the passage of death? 'If,' replied he, 'it were granted to me to make my own conditions, I would willingly choose to make the Spiritual Exercises first for a **few** days; **but even were I unable to** do so, I would willingly die, in any **case.'** **It was noticed that all this time he** lived absorbed, like **one whose thoughts are** elsewhere— **his body on earth, but his mind in heaven.** As God had **determined to take him to Himself,** He was sweetly disposing **him for his passage by** these loving affections and burning **desires.** Often **those inspired** words were on John's lips—'I desire to be dissolved; I languish with love.' Yet he never dared to ask absolutely to **go, for as yet, God's** will was unknown to him; **his only rule was, as it had ever been, the greater** glory of His divine Majesty.

However, those holy desires were heard by his good Master; warning was given clearly of what was so **soon** to come to pass.

It was a day of great devotion, the feast of his holy Father, St. Ignatius, 1621; and, being the last day of July, the tickets for the patron saints for the following month were given out. Berchmans read upon his paper the words of St. Mark, 'Take ye heed! Watch and pray; for ye know not when the time is.'

The whole truth flashed upon him. He had no longer any doubt but that the words were meant for him; and, full of joy, he went to tell the news, for such he held it to be, first to his professor, Father Piccolomini, and then to others also. Had not our Lady obtained for him on her Saturday the welcome message? The Thursday after, August 5th, the feast of our Lady *ad Nives*, he had a slight attack of diarrhœa—no uncommon thing in the great heat—so he paid no attention to it, and it did not prevent him going with the rest to the vigna, being a holiday. It was hardly out of the direct road to go by St. Mary Major's, where the beautiful festa of the dedication was being celebrated in the new and superb Borghese chapel. The Roman devotion to the Madonna, the music, the shower of white petals that rains down from the dome during the solemnity, attracted crowds, among whom as usual the devout sex prevailed. Nothing would persuade John to go into the throng. When dinner was over he made up to Father Octavius Lorenzini, of the Gesù, whom he knew to be well acquainted with the authorities for the story. He drew him a little aside, and spent more than two hours talking with him, and asking question about the history of the Society and its first Fathers. During the whole time our saint showed the most lively interest in everything relating to it, and a strong desire to walk in the footprints of its great and holy sons. He seemed never to be satisfied with hearing about them, asking over and over again first how they had practised one

virtue, and then how they had practised another. He
told the way that he followed to imitate them as closely
as possible. Among other things, he spoke of the great
help he found in reading their lives, whether printed or
in manuscript; and how much he wished that every
Jesuit would explore the same rich mine. 'For,' he
added, 'the road these blessed souls have traversed
we too have to tread. Whatever acts of virtue I meet
with in their lives I note down with great care, as
well as any information I get in the ordinary exhortations, especially when Father General makes one; and
I enter there any answers that Father Rector or Father
Provincial is kind enough to give me to any difficulties
I put to them. You should see, Father, this little note-
book, for perhaps you would be able to add something
to my collection. I made it,' he repeated this several
times, 'for my spiritual consolation; but in time it may
turn to some use.' We should be glad to know if the
notes he has left us are the ones he spoke of. At last
they separated to go to the Litanies; and John spent
the rest of the afternoon with the scholastics, talking
exclusively on spiritual subjects.

On the following day, as he had said nothing about
his indisposition, Father del Bufalo, the prefect of studies,
sent him to object in a philosophical defension at the
Greek College, then under the care of the Dominican
Fathers. That same year it was placed under a Cypriote
nobleman, who, on October 31, 1622, handed it over to
the Society of Jesus, which had formerly governed it in
the time of Gregory XIII.

Spite of feeling unwell, Berchmans obeyed without
a word. An unlooked for homage awaited him; for a
doctor of the faculty, who had been invited to open the
contest, not having come, our humble saint, who always
chose the last place, was forced to take the vacant chair

of honour, and to begin the discussion—a distinction which he owed no doubt in part to his late and brilliant public act. With such address, with such proofs of genius and learning did he put his arguments, and yet withal with such exquisite modesty, that, for the mere pleasure of listening to his powerful words, he was allowed to continue his discourse for an entire hour.

The distance between the Via del Babuino, where the Greek College stands, and the Roman College, is not slight when traversed under a burning sun, the heat reflected back from the pavement and the palaces. The walk, and the exertion of disputing, no doubt aggravated John's malady; and that night an attack of fever, with a return of diarrhœa, prevented his taking any rest.

He waited all Saturday morning to see if the fever was going to abate; but finding it only increased upon him, and feeling his strength failing him, he felt he would not be faithful to his rule unless, in obedience to it, he let his Superior know of his illness. About two in the afternoon he set out accordingly for the rector's room. Father Cepari met him on the way, and noticing how ill he looked, asked him how he was. He told his Superior frankly what was the matter, and the rector ordered him off to the infirmary. John made a low reverence, and then, without going back to his room, went at once to where he had been sent. The infirmarian showed him to one of the rooms, and bade him lie upon the bed and rest himself. The fever was then raging. About five o'clock the rector came to see him; and finding that the fever, which, like the Roman fevers, was intermittent, had left him, ordered him to be put to bed. It was near half-past five when these orders were executed. 'Well, Brother John,' said the lay-brother to him, when he was at last in bed, 'what will be done?' 'Oh!' he answered joyously, 'whatever pleases God; we are in His hands.' Just then **Father Piccolomini** came in, and our saint, full of delight, **reminded him of** the message he had received, with **the name of his** monthly **patron,** saying **that he hoped** 'the time' had **now come.**

Another night passed by without any sleep.

Next morning, August 8, being Sunday, according **to** custom, the Blessed Sacrament was brought at an early **hour to the** infirmary. **John** wanted to get up, and **prostrate** himself on the ground at the entry of his Lord. **But** he was only allowed to throw himself upon **his bed.** He received his Divine Guest with great feelings of devotion. After his thanksgiving he rested **quiet** till the doctor's visit, who **found** him somewhat better. All that day the patient was tranquil as usual. To those who came to see him he spoke of nothing **but** of God. There was some contagious disease hanging about at the time, and an order had accordingly been published in the College that care must be taken **when** visiting the sick **not to go too near to them.** John himself reminded each **one of the necessary precaution.**

That **evening he evidently grew worse, and a third** night passed as sleepless **as the last two.**

Monday morning, August **9,** the doctor accordingly prescribed **a dose;** and in those days science had **not** succeeded in cloaking the noisome compositions of the dispensary. John not only took it at once, but when he had swallowed it, turning to a Flemish Father **who** was there, asked him to say the long grace after meals, which is said in communities after dinner and supper. He suffered much all day, and the fever returned at the usual time. In the evening he asked the infirmarian whether next morning, August **10,** being the feast **of** St. Laurence, they would bring him holy communion.

The brother told him **that it was not** usual **to do so** except on Sundays, **but** if he wished **it he** should have it. 'No, brother,' **said John,** 'it is not right **you** should mind what *I* **wish for,** but only what is the custom with others.' So he **did** not **go to** holy communion. **He noticed that the room** was **close,** and, with his delicate **refinement of charity,** he prayed the infirmarian to keep the room well aired, even though he himself should suffer **a little, so** that those who came **so** kindly to visit him might not be put to inconvenience.

So far the doctor had not considered the illness to be dangerous, though some symptoms of inflammation of the lungs had begun to show themselves.

But on Monday night John's strength failed him ; **and** on St. Laurence's day he became so feeble that restoratives had to be administered every four hours. **Yet** he received all his visitors with **his usual calm, as though** there was nothing **the matter. On Tuesday, the** 10th, after the night **examen,** Aloysius Spinola happened **to** go **to the rector's room** to ask leave for something. 'I am just going to see Brother Berchmans,' said Father Cepari ; 'I very much fear we are going to lose that good young man.' 'Oh, please Father,' said **the** young scholastic, 'let me go with you.' 'I shall **be very glad.** Come.' So they went together to the **infirmary.**

There they found, waiting outside the door, several of the community, who availed themselves of the presence **of the** Superior to go into the sick-room. John welcomed them all with a graceful salutation, and began, as one of them tells us, to speak **of** death and the joys of Paradise with all the satisfaction and pride with which a victorious general tells of his well-earned triumph.

Some one suggested that he would have plenty of suffering and hard **work yet to** go through for God's glory. 'When I was still a novice in Belgium,' said Berchmans, 'Father Coster told me I should bring back to the Catholic faith a great number who were out of the fold.' And then, after a pause, he went on. 'I do not know whether he did not mean I should do so from my place in heaven.'

The conversation lasted for some time longer, and then all withdrew, very sad and depressed. It was decided that if that night brought no evident change for the better, the last sacraments must be administered. When all the rest had gone to their rooms, with the promise of the rector that they should be called, if it were found necessary to anoint him during the night, Father Cepari re-entered the room, to break the news to John, little thinking he would be prepared for it. He tells us himself what passed. 'If our Lord God should want you in heaven, would there be anything that would trouble you?' 'No, Father, unless it be some slight fear lest the charity that exists between our two provinces should be somewhat cooled by my death. For, perchance, when they learn in Belgium that both my companion and myself are dead, they may make up their minds not to send any more subjects here, and so would take away the communication that exists, and which is so beautiful, and so according to the spirit of the Society, between one province and another.' John here alluded to the death of Bartholomew Penneman, who had been sent with him from Belgium, and who had died of consumption and hemorrhage at Naples. 'But,' he continued, 'if it pleases God that I should die, He knows well what He is doing. As for myself, I am quite resigned to the divine will; yet my desire and choice would be to go, rather than to stay.'

Delighted as the rector was to find John so resigned, and in such good dispositions for heaven, still he could not wish to see his College deprived of such a rare model of virtue. He charged Brother Ballera, the infirmarian, not to allow the patient to be left alone during the night, and ordered that either himself or his assistant should remain by the bedside.

Towards eleven o'clock, John, finding he could not sleep, began to talk to the brother about God. Ballera felt his pulse, and perceiving it grew fainter and fainter, 'Brother John,' he asked, 'did Father Rector say nothing to you? Because I think to-morrow morning you ought to receive holy communion.' 'As Viaticum?' rejoined the holy youth. 'Yes, brother ; for it seems to me there is but little hope of life left for you.' At these words, as at a piece of most welcome news, John seemed all of a sudden to gather strength, and full of joy, he threw his arms round the infirmarian's neck and clasped him in a long embrace, as if he could not tell in words the profound joy that he felt. But the poor brother, deeply moved, sobbed and cried so bitterly, that he was unable to say a word. Our saint tried to comfort him. 'Come, brother, let us be glad, let us make ready. This is the best of news, the greatest joy that I could have.' Then he asked him to give him a crucifix, and taking it in his hands, 'My Lord,' he cried out, 'Thou knowest that Thou art all I ever had, all I have in this life. Do not Thou, then, my Lord Jesus, abandon me.' As he went on pouring out his soul to his crucified Love, the infirmarian, more and more deeply affected, took courage, between his tears, to beg that his saintly patient would not forget him when in heaven, and would obtain for him certain favours he had at heart. John promised he would do so. Ballera told him that such prolonged transports would exhaust the little strength there was left. 'I assure you, brother,' was the answer, 'that my soul feels quite refreshed with these prayers.'

Shortly after midnight (August 11th), he begged the brother to write down the following words—'I beg pardon of my very dear (*dolcissimo*) Father General, and I am very sorry to have been such an unworthy child of the Society. I likewise thank my sweetest mother, the Society of Jesus, for the great favours she has bestowed on me, though most unworthy. I thank Father Rector and my professors, Father Francis Piccolomini, Father Tarquin Galuzzi, Father Horace Grassi, for all the trouble they have taken about me. I thank the Father Minister, and the lay-brother infirmarians, for their great kindness towards me. I thank all those who have visited me during this my short illness. I wish my mattrass to be laid on the floor when I receive holy communion, and that the new scholastics may be present, whether close to me or at some distance. As I am not able to give the parting embrace to my dear Fathers and brothers, I pray Father Rector to allow it to be given, according to the custom in the Society, by a substitute. I wish to die in the habit of the Society.' He then begged that this paper should be given into Father Rector's hands, and began again to pray.

About one or two in the morning, he begged to see Father Rector. They sent at once to call him, and on his coming, Father Cepari tells us, he found John with his whole heart fixed on God, and ready to set out for heaven. We must again remind our readers that Berchmans had given all his confessors the most complete freedom from the obligation of silence as regarded his confessions. John spoke at length with him about his conscience, and then asked if he thought it would be well to make a general confession from the time he entered religion. Father Cepari, however, who knew so thoroughly how angelic was his purity, how watchful a guard he ever kept over himself, and his perfect observance of the rules, said he had better not; and he submitted at once. He made simply an ordinary confession in the following words—'I accuse myself of having sometimes prayed with want of fervour and with distractions, and I promise to amend. I accuse myself also of not having been sufficiently grateful to God for the benefits I have received, and of not having taken care to excite in myself an ardent desire to suffer for Jesus Christ.' Such were the only faults, if they could be called faults, which this chosen soul could discover, when on the point of appearing before his Eternal Judge.

As soon as the confession was finished, the infirmarian came back, and gave the rector the paper which had been dictated to him by John. Father Cepari consented to all that was asked therein, and promised that the juniors should be present when he administered the Viaticum. He went himself, before the hour of rising, to order the caller to tell them that, as soon as they got up, they were to go to the church, to accompany the Blessed Sacrament.

Meantime Berchmans, with the forethought which was habitual to him, begged the brother to wash his feet, out of reverence to the holy oil which was so soon to flow upon them. Four o'clock came, and the callers went round to each room, telling the sad news that the Viaticum was going to be given to Brother John. The unexpected news went like a barbed arrow into every heart, and all exclaimed with one voice, 'Oh, what a loss we are going to suffer! Oh, what a saintly brother we are going to lose!' It seemed like some awful visitation of God's justice, as though for some unknown fault He was going to deprive the College of its greatest treasure. Short time was spent in dressing, and all hurried to be present at the heartrending rite. Aloysius Spinola was the first who got to the room, and John, with a sweet smile, welcomed him with the words.

Q

'Good day, brother, good day to you. We are off to
heaven !'   The poor scholastic's heart felt as if it would
break, he faltered out a word or two in reply, and then,
to hide the tears which began to flow, burst out from the
room, and went to the sacristy to await the rest of his
brothers.   Father Cornelius à Lapide came in soon after,
and going up to the sick youth's bed, asked him, with
a freedom that their intimacy permitted, if there was any
scruple, or anything that at all troubled his soul at that
moment.   *Nihil omnino*—'Nothing at all,' he answered
calmly and sweetly, as he opened wide his feeble arms.
A mattrass was then laid on the floor, and he was
stretched upon it, in the habit he loved so well.   The
room began rapidly to fill, and none could restrain their
tears when they saw the wasted frame of him they loved
so well on that lowly bed, and heard the burning words
of love which, as if unconscious of their presence, he
addressed, now to Jesus, and now to Mary.   Towards
half-past four, a number of the community and all the
juniors issued from the church, walking two and two,
reverently and sadly.   Father Rector closed the procession with the adorable Body of our Lord.   As
they entered, and the blessing of the room and the
Confiteor was gone through, Berchmans lay motionless,
absorbed in prayer ; but the moment the Father drew
near to place the Sacred Host on his tongue, then, quick
as thought, he bounded up and threw himself on his
knees, but his love was greater than his strength, and he
would have fallen had not two who were at his side supported him under each arm.   And kneeling thus, in
face of his Sacramental Lord, he broke forth into a
magnificent Latin act of faith, unstudied and unprepared,
his voice vibrating with love, which gave it a power and
clearness far beyond its natural strength.   'I declare
that there is here really present the Son of God the

Father Almighty, and of the most Blessed Mary, ever a Virgin. I protest that I wish to live and die a true son of our holy Mother the Catholic, Apostolic, Roman Church. I protest that I wish to live and die a true son of the Blessed Virgin Mary. I protest that I wish to live and to die a son of the Society.' We recognize the same thought that he had been in the habit of expressing in his first and last prayer each day. This sudden act, so touching in itself, and so touching from the way in which he did it, went to the heart of every one there, and when the words, 'Receive, brother, the Viaticum of the Body of our Lord Jesus Christ,' were pronounced, so solemn a warning that any hope of keeping him amongst them was over, all were so completely overcome that, as Father Cepari tells us, none but those who heard it could form any idea of the loud cry of grief that burst from their lips. As soon as John had received his Lord, he bowed down his head, placed his arms crosswise on his breast, and remained completely taken up with the fervent reception he offered his Heavenly Guest.

When they had laid him down again he asked for Extreme Unction, and the Father Assistant of Germany, Theodore Busée, who had just come in from the Gesù, sent to ask the rector to administer it in his presence. The room was then so crowded that it was impossible for those present to kneel down. As soon as ever he began the usual prayers, the storm of grief which had been lulled for a time, began again to rise, and Father Cepari himself could scarcely pronounce the words, so broken was his voice with poignant sorrow. In the midst of all this, John alone remained calm and tranquil, his hands joined together, his eyes raised towards heaven, all intent on the sacrament he was receiving, and all diligence to receive it with fervour. He was the only one who was able to **answer** the prayers of the priest, and answer them too in a firm and loud voice. Then he recited the *Confiteor*, and asked leave to tell his fault. He got permission, and performed this act of humiliation in the **ordinary** way in use **in** the Society, but with unusual **and** extraordinary humility.

The **rector drew near to** him, and asked him if there was anything he would like to say for his own consolation or for that of his brethren. He answered by beckoning **to Father** Cepari to come **close** to him, and whispered **in his ear,** 'If your Reverence thinks fit, you may tell **my** Fathers and brothers that the greatest consolation I feel is, that **since I** have been in the **Society,** I do not recollect having committed a deliberate **venial sin,** nor am I aware **that I have** voluntarily broken a single one of our rules, or disobeyed any regulation of my Superiors. But I leave all to your judgment.' He made this avowal with great humility and submission, the only motive that prompted it being the strong passion **he** had that scrupulous observance of rule should be appreciated and loved **by them all.** Father Cepari, whose experience and **prudence were** alike **beyond doubt, deemed it** well **for** his community they **should** know this marvellous fact, **and told them aloud what he had just** learned. This announcement **left** one conviction on their minds—it **was the clearest proof of** the saint's approaching death, **for they knew his modesty and** humility never would have allowed him to speak of himself in that way, **if he** was not certain **that** he was soon to die. **At** this fresh intimation of his speedy departure the wail of grief **rose** again from the weeping crowd. Before **his** starting **on** his last journey, spite of his weakness, **John** prayed to be allowed to embrace each member of the College. The rector, not wishing to expose him to so great a fatigue, said **he would embrace** him in the name of **all.**

He begged at least to be permitted to embrace those who were present. This could not be refused him, and one by one they clasped him for the last time in their arms, and gave and received the kiss of peace. Some there were whom he kept by him, as they gave him their messages and commissions for heaven, and he, with a like simplicity, offered them some word to be a reminder of him for ever.

The last to draw near to him was his professor of mathematics, Father Horace Grassi, who had concealed himself behind the bed of the dying youth, to hide the violence of his emotion. 'Father,' exclaimed his saintly scholar, 'I did not forget last night your Reverence's charity. The memorial I dictated will witness to that. I thank you for all the trouble you took when teaching me.' The Father could bear it no longer, and weeping bitterly, he threw himself on his knees beside the pallet, begging his pardon for not having shown towards him the charity and love he should have done, and for not having profited by his good example, and he implored him, when he got to heaven, to obtain for him from God the gift of prayer. This was too much for the deep humility of Berchmans. It was to him most painful to see a priest and one of his professors on his knees before him. He most earnestly begged him to rise, promising to do him this service when with God. While this touching scene was going on, Father Rector had gone to say Mass for his beloved child. All of a sudden, John turned towards Father Piccolomini, who had stayed with him, and exclaimed, *Pater Rector luctatur pro me, ut Jacob—* 'Father Rector is wrestling for me, as Jacob wrestled.' A little later, Father Cepari himself came in, and without knowing what the sick man had uttered, 'Brother John,' he said, 'I have been complaining somewhat to our Lord, for His wanting to take you away so soon.' John

cast down his eyes and smiled, but he said nothing—he
knew that already.   And twice the same day he told his
professor, 'Father Rector is fighting against me, but he
will not win.   I am afraid Father Rector is opposing the
will of God.'   And Father Cepari owned that again and
again that day, he had earnestly implored God to grant
health and life to Berchmans, though he could not tell
how the young man was aware he had done so.

Another physician was called in to a consultation, one
Angelo Bagnarea.   Accustomed as he was to death in
many shapes, on his very first visit he was so struck with
the resignation, the joy and peace with which John was
waiting for his end, that he could not restrain his tears.
'My good father,' he asked, 'do you feel any pain?'
'None,' was the reply, 'only it seems to me as though I
were going little by little.'   'Have you ever been ill?'
'No, never.'

As he left, he said to the minister who accompanied
him, 'This is another Aloysius.   Happy are religious
who are so cheerful, so ready for death !   One does not
meet with such happiness everywhere.'

The doctors had prescribed as restoratives some
remedies and perfumes, which the saint thought rather
contrary to holy poverty.   Among other things, Doctor
Bagnarea had ordered that his wrists and temples were
to be bathed with old wine of Belvedere.   Gaudt, a
fellow scholastic and countryman of his, was charged
with this duty.   *Meus hic morbus pretiosus est*—'My
illness is a very costly one.   It is a good thing it will
not last long.'   'Yes,' said his friend, 'if we were in
Belgium, but here this wine has no value except from its
age, and this is only three years old.'   'In that case,'
John said merrily, 'pour it out a little more plentifully.
Go on, for so the Society wills and orders you.'   Being
a day of class, at every spare time a number of his

companions came in, and strove to render him any service they could. In the afternoon he was a little better. All testified their delight, and showed that there were hopes still of his being saved. He, however, without allowing himself to be carried away by their sanguine expectations, simply said, 'Yes, yes, I know very well Extreme Unction can cure me.'

That day the Father General came to see him. 'Well, brother,' he said as he entered the room, 'did you want then to run away without saying a word to us about it?' John bowed his head and smiled, assuring his Paternity that he had very earnestly desired to see him before he died, and to thank him for the care he had had of him, and to beg his pardon. Father Vitelleschi answered that there was nothing to pardon in him, and taking some holy water, made the sign of the Cross on his forehead, and sprinkled some upon him, and went his way.

Father van Doorne shortly after came in with some pebbles, gathered at the foot of an oak which had held the miraculous statue of our Lady of Foye, near Hui, in Belgium. He pressed Berchmans to vow a pilgrimage to the shrine, if it were granted him to return to his native country. He told him of a person who had been cured by some of these very pebbles when at death's door. Our saint, who no doubt knew the decree of God, showed no anxiety to recover his health. He did not even take the proposal seriously. The poor Father was not pleased ; so to satisfy him, no doubt, he acceded to his request, as we shall have to tell in its proper place.

Late that evening, Wednesday, the doctor repeated his visit. He saw nothing could be done, and so merely spoke a few words of encouragement to the dying saint, which won him such grateful thanks, that he withdrew delighted at his visit. Every one begged for the privilege of staying out the night by John's bedside, for they feared to miss the sight of so holy a death. A few only were selected, but the rector promised that all should be called if the danger became imminent. Unable to rest his body, the sick man sought repose for his soul by close conversation with heaven. His favourite and most fervent ejaculations were addressed to his Blessed Mother. 'O Mary,' he would exclaim, 'do not disappoint me; I am your child. You know I have sworn to be your child.' Once he broke the silence by a sigh: they asked the reason—'I am thanking God for the favour of my vocation.' Later on, Father Gaudt asked him, as he saw John could not sleep, whether he would like to hear something read to him, and proposed either the Passion of our Blessed Lord, or a chapter from St. Aloysius' Life. 'Yes, the chapter about the saint's death.' There was one who was privileged to enjoy the preference of John; for from the first day of his illness, he had asked the minister, on whom especially falls the care of the sick, to send a Polish scholastic, Nicholas Grodrenski, to read to him some pious book or to talk with him; for our saint said, and happy was one who could merit a eulogium from his lips, 'I feel myself very much incited to virtue by the conversation of this good brother.' However, that night Brother Bruno fulfilled that office of charity. When he came to the passage where it is stated that the saint never showed through all his long illness the slightest sign of impatience, John turned to his crucifix and exclaimed, 'Lord, if I have sinned in this respect, though I do not know that I have, oh! pardon me.' When the book went on to say that St. Aloysius, on hearing that he was near death, intoned the *Te Deum*, his faithful imitator made those around recite with him that hymn of grateful praise. When the reading was done, John's mind went back to Father Mark van Doorne's request, for he found he had been hurt by his refusal. 'Father,' said he to Father Gaudt, 'do you know what has been done with the little pebbles that were brought me to-day?' 'Yes, here they are.' And he gave them to the dying youth. 'I am thinking,' he went on to say, 'of making a conditional vow to visit that chapel, if ever I return to my province. I will tell you later on, *when* I propose to make this vow.' Shortly after, Father van Doorne himself came in, and this was the opportunity for which John was waiting.

We can imagine with what pleasure and hope Father Mark placed the stones in the hands of his dear brother, while John, making the sign of the Cross, began as follows: 'In the name of the most Holy Trinity, and in honour of the Holy Virgin Mary, I promise—' and there he stopped. Father Gaudt suggested—'If I return safe and sound to my country.' 'No,' he broke in upon him, 'that "to my country" wont do.' And then, continuing in his own fashion—'If I return to Flanders, to visit that chapel.' And as soon as he said that, he was in as great a hurry to get the pebbles out of his hands as though they burnt his fingers.

A slight sleep then settled on him, and all left the room to go to rest, except Aloysius Spinola, who remained with him, only stealing out now and again to breathe a little fresh air, for the night was exceedingly hot.

CHAPTER XII.

Last days of John Berchmans.

ON returning to the sick-room after a stroll in the corridor—it was then about one o'clock on Thursday morning—Aloysius found John awake, with his arms outside the coverlet, and chilled through and through. He did not, however, pay much attention to this, fancying that the cold would be very agreeable to him. Berchmans owned, later on, that it had caused him great pain. He was too weak to change his position, and he did not like to awaken the poor lay-brother, who was fast asleep close at hand.

About four o'clock, the hour when the community got up, he told the infirmarian—'Father Rector is doing all he can that our Lord may leave me on earth, for the sake of my province, but I think he will not obtain his prayer.' Very shortly after the rector came in, and bade him pray for his recovery, if it were for God's glory.

Father Cepari had no doubt been watching before the twilight, in earnest pleading for so precious a life. Coming in again, he quoted to his sick child the responsory of the second lesson of the day within the octave of St. Laurence, which was said on that day, the feast of St. Clare being then merely a simple. The words, borrowed from Daniel, Isaias, and Jeremias, so applicable to the martyr deacon, had fallen in with the one thought and the one desire of Father Cepari.

'Brother John, in saying my office, I remarked a responsory, which I think just suits you. It runs thus—" My
son, fear not, for I am with thee, saith the Lord, if thou
shalt go through the fire, the flames shall not harm thee,
and the swell of fire shall not be on thee. I will deliver
thee out of the hands of the wicked, and redeem thee
out of the hands of the mighty." I trust all this will turn
out true as regards yourself.' 'I hope so,' answered
John, 'but through the merits of the ever Blessed
Virgin.' And then he went on several times repeating
to himself, and turning over in his mind, the quotation.

Whenever the room was empty, or there were only a
few present, he burst out into short and ardent collo-
quies, in which Mary's name especially recurred. Again
and again he said—'Do not abandon me, Mary; do not
deceive me, for I am thy child. Thou knowest it; for
I have sworn it.' The young Paul Oliva—the future
General of the Society—was alone with him in the room,
when he happened once to repeat this fervent prayer.
'Do not doubt,' he said to John, 'the Blessed Virgin,
the Mother of Mercy will never abandon you—she who
could never abandon any one.' These words, intended
to comfort him, seemed to imply some doubt of his love
and confidence in Mary, and he answered, in almost an
angry tone—'Oh, I do not doubt, Oliva. No, no, I do
not doubt.'

With the break of day, those members of the community who had only left on the preceding evening
at the bidding of their Superior, returned to the sick
man's room, and others with them, so that the place
was fuller than on the previous evening. Among
them was one whose name is famous in the Church,
Francis de Lugo, who, twenty-three years after, was
unwillingly to wear the purple. He had but lately
arrived from Spain to fill the chair of theology at the

Roman College, and had an affair of great importance in hand, which he took the opportunity of recommending to the prayers of the dying saint.

The news had gone abroad in Rome, that Berchmans had spoken distinctly of his approaching death. He had made no acquaintances in the city, but the lustre of his modesty had drawn many eyes upon him, and he was widely known as a religious of rare innocence and sanctity. Persons of the highest station called at the College, and requested to be allowed to see him. He was asked whether they were to be shown in. 'Oh, the rector knows best; I leave it to his decision.' He begged the lay-brother to arrange his bed—'For,' he said, 'in the Society, tidiness should go hand in hand with perfect poverty.'

At first the rector, out of fear lest the sick man should be fatigued, refused to admit any visitors. He even ordered a notice to be put up at the infirmary door, by which no one was allowed to go to John's room without special leave. However, he found it was impossible to resist the numerous applications, or refuse persons whose position gave them a title to his respect. He therefore consented that they should be allowed to spend a short time at least with the dying saint. Among those who were so favoured was Mgr. Angelo Cesi, son of the Duke of Acquasparta, and whose uncle was in the Sacred College. He had been a great admirer of the saint, and had even come to the garden of the College during recreation time, on purpose to watch him as he was talking with his companions, and to see the punctuality with which, at the first sound of the bell, he broke off his conversation, and betook himself to his habitual recollection. He was not less rejoiced to see the calm face, telling of so deep a peace within, as though the hand of death were far from him, and hear him talk so freely of that awful passage, and the future that lies beyond. On leaving, the Monsignore promised he would pray for him, and take the discipline that very day for his intention. It seemed to him as though he had seen the vision of an angel lying on that bed. He kept his promise that very evening, at the meeting of a confraternity of which he was one of the most illustrious members. Next came Signor Jerome Martelli, who was a great benefactor of the Society. The rector brought him to the room, and asked John if he recognized him! 'I know him? Oh, yes, very well indeed; it is Signor Jerome Martelli, who has done so much for us. If I live, I will say the three rosaries, to which he has a right as founder of the College of Spoleto ; and if I die, I shall not forget him in heaven.'

During the day, Father Cepari brought to his bedside Francis Gavotta, who had just completed his rhetoric at the Roman College. 'Here, brother,' said the rector, ' is a young man who is going to enter the Novitiate of St. Andrea on the vigil of the Assumption.' John took his hand in the warmest manner. 'How glad I am,' he said, 'to have one brother more. Well, Reverend Father, here is one in my place.' Gavotta reverently kissed the wasted hand, and recommended himself to his prayers, and then went away, astonished, as every one was, at our saint's calm and self-possession.

After dinner Nicholas Radkaï, of whom we have spoken so often, entered with Alexander Roche.[1]

---

[1] Father Cepari speaks of this Father as a German, without giving his name. Father Vanderspeeten gives the name from the processes, with the detailed conversation here reproduced. Rocca is certainly no German name, and the words spoken square more with Ireland than with any portion of Germany. Father Alexander Roche was certainly with John at the Roman College ; and perhaps his having been brought up at some College in Germany, or having made his noviceship there, may account for Father Cepari's mistake, if mistake it is. The Irish Fathers always experienced a special hospitality from the various provinces of the Society of Jesus in the days of persecution.

'Come, come here, my very dear Brother Roche,' was
the welcome of John. 'Come, and let me say good-bye,
for it is likely I shall leave to-morrow. Take good care
always to prove a true child of the Society, and a stout
defender of the Holy Roman Church against the
heretics of your countries of the North.' 'I wish for
nothing more,' answered the scholastic, 'only you, on
your part, must obtain for me from heaven the virtues
and qualities which are wanted for a missioner in those
lands. And do not forget the immense wants of my
poor country; you know well enough how great they
are!' 'Yes, yes, very well,' said John; 'I shall
remember it all in heaven.' Just then the two medical
men arrived, and they found that Berchmans was
rapidly growing weaker. John thanked them very
politely for their attention, and said, with a smile, to
Signor Bagnarea, 'We are going, sir, we are going!'
'Where to?' 'To heaven!' 'I am sure you will not
forget me when you get there.' 'Oh, no; I shall pray
for you.' One of them, Signor Filandro, on leaving,
said that the illness of the young man was not in itself
so serious as to reduce him so low; he could only say,
in a quotation from Hippocrates, '*Moritur divinitùs*—
"He is dying in a superhuman way," and our art will
not reach so far.' The doctors would have wished the
patient to be left quiet; but as they opened the door
when leaving, John saw that there were a crowd of the
Fathers and brothers standing outside, who were prevented by the rector's orders from coming in. He
begged that they might be allowed to enter one by one,
as it would be his last chance of seeing or speaking
to them. Such a request could not be denied. So, in
succession, they approached his bedside to receive his
last adieux and embrace, which each one prefaced by
an ardent recommendation to his prayers, and a request

for some parting word of advice. To nearly all he recommended three things—first to have a great devotion to our Lady; secondly, to display great zeal for prayer, because, he said, it was an efficacious way to keep up union with God; and thirdly, to observe scrupulously all the rules of the Society. John, though so worn out in body, kept his mind as strong and clear as ever.

On this the last evening of his life there was one thing which struck every one that approached him, that this young man, who always considered himself so thoroughly the last and lowest of all, now spoke with a confident tone of authority—'as one having power.' He told many of them what could have been known only to God; and gave advice which, as some of them afterwards told their Superiors or their Spiritual Father, proved of the greatest advantage to them. To his well-loved professor, Father Piccolomini, he engaged to ask for all his scholars—devotion to our Lady.

Father Andrew Eudemon Joannes, of Candia, was at that time professor of philosophy. In his veins ran the blood of the Paleologi, but he was still more distinguished for his varied learning, which gained him the appointment from Urban VIII. as theologian to his nephew Cardinal Barberini, when legate to the Court of France. The parting words of the saint to Father Andrew, who was then engaged in controversial works against French and English heretics, were to urge him to continue to write against the errors of Calvinism. To Father Joseph Copponi, who was a preacher of some note, John gave a pressing entreaty ever to defend the Immaculate Conception, unless the Church should order otherwise. He charged Father Ferrari, the learned Hebrew scholar and botanist, to endeavour to promote the glory of the saints of the Society. 'I thought,' this Father tells us, 'that by these words he recommended to

me the imitation of their virtue; but three of ours to
whom I told them said that, without doubt, our good
brother wanted to persuade me to write something in
their honour. In fact, I then remembered that, some
years before, I had had the idea of writing a panegyric
on each of our *beati*, but am not aware that I ever spoke
of it to any one.' When Aloysius Spinola came to John,
'Brother,' said the dying saint, 'may God make you a
child of prayer—a child of the Blessed Virgin, and give
you the double spirit of St. Ignatius—the love of God
and your neighbour.' Aloysius asked him to obtain for
him a special favour. 'Very well,' was the answer;
'I will see to it.' 'Yes, but do not forget it; for I will
not leave you any rest till I get this grace. I will remind
you every day of your promise.' 'No, no, be at your
ease; I will be as good as my word.' The one that
followed Spinola was a scholastic bearing a name
rendered so glorious in our day—that of Ferretti. With
the familiarity of an old friend, John exclaimed,
'Oh, Brother Angelo! Brother Angelo! Well! Good
evening. Come, sit down near me.' 'Brother John,'
said the young man, 'so you want to go to heaven, and
leave us here below? Oh, how fortunate you are to go
so young into the joys of our Lord! How I envy your
lot. Oh, if I could go with you, what a pleasure would
it be to me to be quit of the miseries of this life! How
willingly would I receive this favour of our Lord should
He deign to let me share it with you!' The sick man
smiled. 'Well, Brother Angelo, you will follow me
soon, be sure of it.' 'Would to God He would do
me such a favour. With what joy should I accept it.
I do hope for it; but I beg of you help me with your
prayers, and ask our good Jesus to deign to grant me
this great grace.' 'I will do so very, very willingly.'
'And, brother,' said Ferretti, 'do you wish me to do

anything for you?' 'Oh, yes; when I am dead offer for my intention a communion and a discipline.' 'And now,' said Ferretti, 'give me, brother, I beg of you, some good piece of advice to further me in perfection.' 'Oh, good brother, there are so many.' 'Well, but point out for me one in particular, I beseech you.' 'Well, always have recourse to your Superiors; but you see, my Brother Angelo, I cannot talk any more, I really cannot.' Ferretti hurried from the room to tell the good news to the rector; he even put down in writing John's promise to him. But two years later, on the very same bed as that on which his forerunner had died, and just at the same age that John was at his death—being the very next, too, to follow him from the Roman College—Angelo turned towards Father Cepari, and reminded him in his dying breath of the prophecy of Berchmans.

Up to this time our saint had spoken in terms more or less vague of the time of his departure. On that evening, a Father remarked that as he had fallen ill on the same day of the month as that on which St. Stanislaus took sick, so perhaps he would die on the anniversary of the saint's death. He answered at once, 'If it be so, I shall die sooner than he did, for I took to my bed sooner than he.' But he spoke much more clearly to his countryman, William van Aelst. As he was going away, he told him to take great care 'that to-morrow all my brother-juniors are present at my death.' 'And are you to die to-morrow?' 'Yes, to-morrow.' Van Aelst and Van Doorne pressed him to tell them still more precisely. 'It will be about the time when the bell rings for school, or after that.' And this was said when there seemed little chance of his getting through the night.

The last to come near was his dear friend, Nicholas Radkaï, who had looked on John rather in the light of

R

his director and the guide of his conscience, than as his companion and equal. He had been one of the first to come to the bedside to make his last farewell, but as John wished to talk to him perfectly at his ease, he begged Nicholas to wait outside till all had gone. We must leave the young man to tell the interview in his own words. 'When, with Father Rector's consent, we were left by ourselves, our *beato* looked towards me with a sweet expression of countenance and said, " Now, brother, I give you my last embrace ; I shall never more speak to you in this life. You know I have loved you on earth. I shall love you, too, in heaven."' Father Cepari tells us that at these words, full of emotion, his eyes brimming over with tears, Nicholas threw himself on his knees before his dying friend. 'I asked him,' he goes on, 'under promise of secrecy, to help me, by obtaining for me from our Lady—first, the gift of chastity, and deliverance from long and cruel temptations of the flesh ; and then, the grace to prove myself the true and lawful child of the Society, and that she, my good Mother, might recognize me as such. John seemed to consider for a moment or two. At last, raising his eyes to heaven, and then fixing them upon me, he answered me in precisely the following words— " My dear Nicholas, I will obtain for you the gift of prayer, the spirit of chastity, and the spirit of mortification." Then he embraced me twice, and said his last good-bye. But I had no intention of leaving him so soon, but went on to beg him not to forget my public act in philosophy, as he had promised me several times on the day previous. He renewed the promise he had made me, in a very special manner, adding that he had great hopes that the act would come off well. In fact, when I consider what I am, when I think of the state I was in at the time of the fearful ordeal of that public **defension of my theses, I am** quite convinced **that** it was he who helped me from **on high** ; for immediately **after I had got** through **my** act, my **head** was out **of order** beyond **all expression,** from over-work, prolonged **through several days,** and through two nights in succession. **Thanks be to** God, to our Lady, and to John Berchmans. At the close of our interview I begged him **to tell** me frankly and sincerely if he really thought **he** would not die before the **morrow.** He paused for some moments, then looking fixedly at me and raising his voice, he answered—"Yes, my dear Nicholas ; it is certain **I** shall **die to-morrow** morning." I asked him if **I should be able to be** present. "**Try to** be," was his reply. After that, he said good-bye, and embraced **me once more,** and **then bid** me go. Before leaving, **I cast myself** on **my knees, and begged** him to **give me** his blessing. This he absolutely refused to do. I pressed him **very hard, both for the love he had always shown me, and for the sake of the** mutual **confidence we had** ever had in one **another ;** till at **last he let** himself be persuaded **by my entreaties, and** raising **his** hand, with a beaming **face and great signs of** affection, **he** blessed me twice.' **He then** raised Nicholas up, and thanking him for **a reliquary** which he had **lent** him during his illness, **he begged to be allowed to keep it to the end as** a protection and a comfort to him.[2]

Father Cepari had noticed what a crowd had pressed around **the bed of Berchmans, and how priests had** knelt at **his feet to seek his counsels and even his** blessing. **He dreaded lest the devil should profit by this to** suggest **temptations of vainglory.** He made **all leave** the room, and **turning to John, he said—'Brother, the devil may** attack **you now** with two **temptations :** one, that against faith, **the other of** vainglory. **So you** must arm yourself

---

[2] **See Appendix.**

against both.' 'Father, thanks be to God, I think I am well armed against any attacks upon my faith. Against the assaults of vainglory, the Spiritual Father has strengthened me thoroughly, should any come up against me.' In fact, it was only a moment before that the holy youth had begged to be left alone with his confessor, as he wished to tell him something. Father Massucci had taken that opportunity to ask him if he was not afraid that the devil would tempt him at that his last hour. 'No, Father,' was his answer, 'unless perhaps by suggesting some useless thoughts.' And it was then that he had given John the advice to which he alluded.

Though so spent with the fever, he never lost his old love for virginal modesty, and noticing his chest was a little uncovered, he at once drew up the clothes, and begged Father Gaudt to see to that when he had himself lost all strength to move. 'Please, Father,' he added, 'do me this favour, even when my speech has failed me, and I seem to strive to prevent you.' He was not accustomed to wear a nightcap. The infirmarian, according to the Italian notion, thought it would do him harm to be without one, and put one on his head, saying at the same time, that a sick man ought to wear one.

John made no reply; it occurred to him that he might have committed a fault against his darling virtue. 'Father,' he said to à Lapide, when the brother had gone, 'is it against rule to be in bed without a night-cap?' 'Not at all,' said the professor, 'it is neither against rule nor the most strict modesty.' This answer put him completely at rest.

As the evening however advanced, John learned more and more clearly the fight that was awaiting him that night. At the hour of the *Ave Maria*, according to our time half-past seven, he called for Father Gaudt, who had stayed up with him the previous night, and begged him to be with him that night as well. 'Oh, why so, brother?' 'Because on to-night the whole thing is to be decided.' 'What, brother, are you to die to-night?' 'No, I shall die to-morrow, but there will be a struggle to-night.' He had told the same to Father Piccolomini —'Father, I shall have to fight to-night.' And three times during the day he had begged the infirmarian to pray for him, giving the same reason in almost the same words.

Towards nine, the hour when the community retired to rest, the corridors and the different rooms of the infirmary were filled with Fathers and brothers, all anxious to be witnesses of a saint's death. Again Father Rector had to dismiss them, with the promise that they should be called were any unforseen accident to occur, though he gave the assurance of Berchmans himself that he would not depart that night. Father Piccolomini said as he was leaving, 'Come now, Brother John, wait for me. Do not go away without me.' 'Your Reverence may be sure of that, you will be present at my departure.' Some were saying that with his illness he might easily die whilst speaking. John overheard them and said, 'So it will be, because I have asked of God one of two graces; either to die on the field, assisting the troops who are fighting against the heretics in Flanders, or to go off in full possession of my faculties, and while speaking. I have no doubt that God will grant me this second grace.'

When the rest had gone to bed, there remained with the dying youth four of his countrymen, Fathers Gaudt, Van Doorne, à Lapide, and Alegambe, besides Aloysius Spinola, and perhaps another scholastic.

Several others, however, spent the night in the adjoining room. Shortly after nine, a spoonful of sirup was offered to John.   He took it cheerfully, and asked Father à Lapide to be good enough to say grace, he answering with attention and recollection.   The Father suggested to him, '**My Jesus, my love, and my all,**' and all trembling with joy, John exclaimed, 'Yes, yes ! Jesus the centre of **my heart,** God of my lot, and my **God for all eternity.**'   And then **he repeated, as he** had done so often, the antiphon of St. Laurence's office, which begins, ' **My son,** fear **not,** for I am with you, saith the **Lord.**' About half-past **nine, the infirmarian** brought **him** a little **broth, but he only sipped it.**   'Thank you, brother, that is enough.   **There** is no longer time for **eating, but only for prayer.**   '**Father,**' said he, turning to à Lapide, 'pray God that I **may not** grow disgusted **at** all the good things with which I am overwhelmed.'   '**Is there** nothing else you want from me?'   '**Oh,** yes ! please say Mass to-morrow morning for my intention.'   'I did so,' Father à Lapide tells us, 'and I got, not his cure, as I so much desired, but his deliverance and his return to God ; **for** he died **at the close of my Mass.**'

At ten or a little after, Berchmans asked **Father van** Doorne to begin the recommendation of a departing soul, 'for perhaps,' he said, 'we shall **not** have a more favourable opportunity.'   When **they** came in the Litany to the **confessors, he begged them to** insert the names **of the Beatified Fathers of the Society,** as well as those **of** St. Francis Borgia, Blessed Alphonsus Rodriguez, **and** Venerable Father Joseph Anchieta.[3]   The prayers being finished, the **sick man tried to sleep.**   However, it was **of no avail, so he** turned round in his bed, **and began** with loud and cheerful **voice to sing** the *Ave Maris stella,* and then skipped all **of a** sudden to the verse, *Monstra te*

---

[3] St. Francis Borgia **was** beatified in 1624, and canonized **by** Clement X.   Blessed Alphonsus Rodriguez was beatified in 1825. The cause of Fathe Anchieta was introduced many years back.

esse Matrem. The infirmarian told him he must not tire himself. 'We must be joyful,' was John's rejoinder, for a dark storm was near, and again he implored all to pray for him, because he feared temptation was at hand. They tried to encourage him. Brother Borella seeing he was growing faint, asked him if he would take something to eat. 'I have no appetite,' he replied, 'but if Father Rector orders it, I am ready to take whatever you wish.' The brother accordingly felt his pulse. 'Well,' said John, 'what do you think?' 'We are near the end,' was his answer. With a thoughtfulness which never left him, Berchmans from that moment would not allow the priests to do him any of the little services which, up till then, he had accepted from them by preference. He had got somehow the false idea that by so doing they might incur suspension, if they accidentally hastened his death. It was about midnight. 'We are going, Father,' he said with a smile to Father Gaudt, 'we are going.' Alegambe on hearing this, began to suggest pious thoughts and devout acts to the dying saint. 'Now you must love Christ and the Blessed Virgin, she whom you loved on earth and whom you will love in death.' 'Whom I have tried to love in life, and she will love me in death,' was John's reply. 'And you will both love one another for ever.' 'So indeed I trust.' Then, a short time after, Alegambe again said, 'John, if you had a thousand hearts, would you not love Mary with them all?' Faintly, he could not say more, he answered, 'I would love her with them all.'

Wearied with talking, John turned his face towards the wall, as if he wanted to rest. A moment of quiet followed, and then he threw himself back into the middle of the bed, his eyes open and fixed on heaven, his whole countenance showing signs of trouble and consternation. From his pale and trembling lips, words full of terror went forth with a piercing cry, which reached even into the neighbouring rooms, and brought their inmates around the sufferer. 'I will not do it, and offend Thee, my Lord! Mary, I will never offend thy Son. Far be it from me. I will not do it; I would rather die a thousand times, ten thousand times, one hundred thousand times, a million times!' And again and again he repeated—'a million times.' And as he poured out these heartrending words, he battled with his arms, all worn and weakly though he was. 'Away, Satan!' he added, turning fiercely, as though he saw the hideous spirit; 'I am not frightened at you.' All the lookers on threw themselves on their knees, and while they gazed and prayed, sprinkled the sufferer, his bed, and the room, with holy water. John asked for a rule-book, and Spinola handed him one. He looked through it rapidly; the copy did not contain the special rules of the scholastics of the Society. He asked for one that did. When one was brought him, he took his rosary from his neck, and placing the rule-book on his crucifix, wound the beads round them, and pressing the three to his heart, together with the reliquary, he exclaimed—'These are my arms. Oh, how brilliant is my crucifix, it is all gold! How my rosary sparkles! Good God, good God!' And looking at the one side of medal attached to it— 'O St. Charles Borromeo!' and then at its reverse —'O Angelic Salutation!' Then taking up the Rosary of the Five Wounds—'O chaplet of the Five Wounds, how brilliant it is! O Wounds, O precious pearls! My rosary is all gold!' And as he replaced his beads round his neck, he repeated the same exclamation—'My rosary is all gold! But, my God, what am I going to do? Where am I? Everything shines, everything sparkles!' Then he opened his rule-book, and ran rapidly over the different headings till he reached the formula of his vows. When he found the place, he began to repeat it, with deep emotion, and aloud, as is the custom at the half-yearly renovation. One change he made, or rather, one omission, leaving out the clause by which he bound himself 'to spend his life for ever' in the Society. It had no further meaning now; his life was so nearly done. Among those who were present was the Father Peter Gravita, or, as we know him better, Caravita, whose oratory and its confraternity near to the Roman College, and the City Missions which he founded, have lasted through all the shocks of political changes down to our time. The storm of temptation was over; complete tranquillity had come once more over the heart of the dying saint; and Father Peter began to intone the Litanies in a sort of half chant, as he was wont to do in the squares of Rome. John, who had no doubt often accompanied the zealous missioner in his work for souls, answered in the same strain, and suiting the action to the word, took hold of the crucifix, and lifting it up, turned it, as though preaching in the streets, first towards himself, and then towards the standers-by. When he got to the *Parce ei Domine,* he made them stop, and fixing his eyes on the figure of his crucified Lord, he said, over and over, and over again, with great devotion, perhaps some thirty times, *Parce Domine, parce Domine, parce Domine.*

The infirmarian just then felt his pulse. He found that it was sensibly growing more feeble, and was sure that the end was drawing near. He went straight to the rector, and was by him sent to summon the other Fathers, who had been promised the privilege of assisting at the death of the saint. It was about half-past one on the morning of the 13th of August, when they gathered round the bed of Mary's child. He was to die on the day of her death. Father Cepari suggested to him some short acts of faith, hope, and charity—'I am sorry, my Lord! I believe, my Lord! I hope, my Lord! I love, my Lord!' And he made him repeat again and again, *Paratum cor meum Deus, paratum cor meum*—'My heart is ready, O God, my heart is ready.'

Anxious to give him the last absolution, the rector asked all to retire for a few moments ; and then in his turn made way for Father Massucci, who was the ordinary confessor of John. As they were waiting in the passage, the rector learned for the first time the fierce fight which had taken place for the sick man's soul during the early part of the night, and he went in at once to ask him about it, when, to his sorrow, he found he had lost the power of speech. The room was full in an instant, and kneeling round his bed, the Fathers began the recommendation of a departing soul. Berchmans was lying on his back, in full possession of his senses, holding with both hands his little crucifix and his rule-book, with the rosary twined round them. To keep them ever in sight, he had raised his knees, and leant against them his clasped hands, and the treasure they contained. He was motionless, save now and again the eyelids rose and fell. Thus he stayed for more than three hours, those around him repeating over and over again the beautiful prayers of the Church's ritual, varied every now and then by other devotions and pious aspirations ; and they could read in his eyes what pleased him best. He was specially delighted when they sprinkled him with holy water. Several times he made an effort to raise his crucifix to his lips, and when, by others' help, he succeeded, he kissed it with earnest devotion.

Some of those who were there were much disturbed at his protracted silence. They knew he had foretold he would die while speaking, and they felt grieved that at last one of his predictions seemed likely to prove false. About five o'clock, Father Piccolomini noticed a slight movement of his lips. 'John,' he asked, 'do you want anything?' With a great effort at length he contrived to articulate, *Vellem posse loqui*—'I would like to be able to speak.' His professor told him to repeat the Holy Name with his heart, if he could not do so with his lips; and, with a violent struggle, he managed to repeat it once, and then again, and again, each time more distinctly, till at last he completely regained his speech. About six, Father Cepari, seeing he was now able to speak without difficulty, left him in charge of those around him, saying, as he went, 'Brother John, it is time for me to go and say Mass; you must wait, and not die till I come back.' 'Yes, Father,' he answered, evidently pleased at the opportunity of practising obedience. During the time of the rector's Mass, the clouds of temptation gathered once more over the calm of the departing soul. All at once John began to grow disquiet. Full of terror, he tossed himself about on his bed, and broke out suddenly, 'I did not do it willingly; I did not wish it. Come home! come home!' Father Piccolomini saw at once the drift of his thoughts. 'John,' he said, 'listen to me. Say nothing but what I shall say—I believe, my Lord, I hope, my Lord, I love, my Lord.' John repeated these words after him, but he did not seem to heed their meaning; his thoughts were elsewhere. But a few moments after, raising up one of his hands, with a piercing tone of anguish and trouble, he began again—'Let us come home. I did not do it willingly. Let us go home.' 'John,' urged Father Piccolomini, raising his voice, and speaking with still greater earnestness, 'John, you have always been obedient to me, be so now; mind nothing except what I say; say nothing but that.' Once more he obeyed; in a moment the storm lulled; calm shone again in his

face. The words of sorrow died away, and he began
again to follow the aspirations and prayers suggested to
him. There can be little doubt it was the visit to the
Charterhouse with poor Brother Victorinus that the
devil had brought up again to trouble the innocent soul
of the saint.[4] About half-past six John gave signs that
he wanted some one. 'Who is it you want?' asked
Father Francis. 'Reverend Father Rector,' was his
reply. He was sent for at once. He had but just left
the altar. The dying youth, now calm and resigned,
showed by his glad looks that his act of obedience in
waiting the rector's return had been a great joy to him.
He bade the litany of his monthly patrons to be recited,
a wish Father Piccolomini was delighted to fulfil.[5] The
holy youth repeated each name with great devotion, and
when, owing to the enlargement of his tongue, he was
sometimes unable to pronounce them accurately, he
strove until he had succeeded. Another Father then
began the Litany of our Lady, and not merely did John
repeat each petition, but even if a word was forgotten
or changed because the Father who was reciting the
prayer looked, as he did from time to time, at John,
he himself corrected the mistake. It was noticed that,

[4] See p. 180.

[5] It would seem as if the professor learned well the lesson taught him
by his holy pupil. Thirty years later Father Piccolomini, then General
of the Society, was on his death-bed, tortured with the most exquisite
agony, yet with a bright face he said to a Father who was by him, 'I
am dying, and still I am merry.' When some water was given him to
cool his parched tongue, he poured it all on the ground, with the words,
'*Libamus Deo*—I make a libation to God; otherwise I should be
seeking luxuries upon the cross on which God has placed me. Keep,'
he prayed, 'a corner for me on Thy Cross. My crucified Jesus, here
behold me, ready to suffer more, still more, and through all eternity, if
such be Thy will, O God.' When Holy Viaticum was brought, he
threw himself on his knees to receive it, and there made a solemn protest, that he never had wished for anything but God's glory and what
was His holy will. Nadasi, in his *Pretios. Occupat. Morientium, S.J.*,
gives many other beautiful anecdotes of his last illness, pp. 212—216.

though he followed the whole with great devotion, yet, when the priest pronounced the words, ' Holy Virgin of Virgins,' 'Mother most chaste,' 'Queen of Virgins,' he made signs of more than usual affection, raising his head from his pillow, and making a reverence to the picture of his Blessed Mother, with a look full of tenderness and love.

'With this religious preparation, with these continual acts of devotion, wasting away more and more, on the morning of August the 13th, 1621, at eight o'clock, being a Friday, with his eyes fixed on his crucifix, clasping in his hands his beads and rule-book, and pronouncing the most sacred names of Jesus and Mary, his pilgrimage came to a happy close, and he gave back in peace his blessed soul into the hands of his Creator, leaving us all edified by his innocent and holy life, and consoled by so precious a death.'[6]

[6] Father Cepari.

CHAPTER XIII.

The Funeral.

HE was dead. The body had been laid out with the simplicity and poverty befitting a religious, when the cold features got back again the softness of life, and to have seen him you would have thought he was not dead but sleeping. But this strange change did not last long, the pallor, the hardness came again, the beauty of the form passed, never to be seen again till it shall bloom once more in Paradise.

Father Cepari paints his portrait for us in a few precise lines—' John was of a fair height, of a ruddy complexion, and excellent temperament, by no means thin. His face was really angelic, pink and white, his forehead broad, his eyebrows so thick that they seemed to be black, and the same might be said of his eyelashes. His eyes were bright and lively, but bashful, and full of goodness and sweetness, and ever downcast. His nose was regular and slightly aquiline, his lips small and ruddy. There was always a modest smile playing about them. His hair was light, and his upper lip and cheeks were just beginning to be slightly covered with an auburn down.

' His hands were always quiet and composed upon his breast. His walk was neither slow nor hurried, but moderate and grave. His whole carriage was so modest, as to strike all who met him, and make them strive to imitate him. People would stand still to gaze at him and enjoy the spectacle of so rare a model of modesty. To sum up all, we may say that to a pure and beautiful soul God gave a body beautiful to match, and that his outward look was an image of his mind, a form of justice, as St. Ambrose wrote of Mary ever a Virgin.'

The passing-bell sent the sad news through the class-rooms and lecture-rooms of the Roman College, which had just been filled with the numerous crowd of students, great and small, for the day's work. The few whom duty had not called to class, hastened to the infirmary. They kissed with reverence the cold hands of the deceased, and recommended themselves to his prayers. Their next thought was to secure some memorial of him, to treasure up as a relic. But they were almost too late. The prints before which John used to pray, his discipline, and little objects of devotion, had been already carried off some three days previously. Nothing was left but his clothes, and these soon disappeared—his shirts, habit, shoes, everything was seized. The most venerable Fathers, the first in authority, the most learned, begged like the youngest junior of the house, one for his beads, another for his little book containing his monthly patrons, or even for a piece of his shoes, or anything at all that he had used, or even touched.

The toll of the bell made a hush of sorrow in every class. Professors and masters faltered, and broke off their lesson, and tears came to the eyes of many, for the angel of their College was gone ; they had not had the sad consolation of witnessing the death of a saint. Their thoughts were on him alone, and each and all burst out into an improvised panegyric of John, whose sweet face was familiar to so many among their hearers. In the great hall, Father Diego Seco, a Portuguese, was lecturing on theology to a numerous audience. At the warning bell he burst out crying, and he told the reason of his grief, and the greatness of his departed brother's holiness, in words which had their weight from the learning and reputation of their speaker. The next year, November 17, 1622, as Coadjutor Bishop of Abyssinia, he sailed to that post of danger with the Patriarch Mendez, but died on board ship during the long journey. We have his praises of John preserved in a document which he left behind, one of the last he ever penned, before setting out from Rome.

'I, Diego Seco, priest and Professed Father of the Society of Jesus, declare that I have been intimately acquainted, while in the Collegio Romano, with Brother John Berchmans, by birth a Fleming, a scholastic of singular innocence of life, purity of mind, and sweetness of manners. I often said these gifts showed him to be a true servant and child of the most Blessed Virgin, whom he loved and served with most ardent devotion. Often, too, during the closing days of his life, when he was serving my Mass, I was troubled at the thought how unworthily, and with what little devotion, I treated the Blessed Sacrament, knowing, as I did, how dear John was to God for the purity and the other virtues of his soul. When at last he fell ill, close on the feast of the Assumption, though the sickness was trifling at the outset, nevertheless, because of the idea I had of his sanctity, I said clearly to Father Mark van Doorne,[1] now the rector of Ghent, who was then, like myself, censor of books at the Roman College, that John would in all likelihood die, not on account of his illness, but because God must wish to have with Him in heaven so pure and so dear a

---

[1] Father Mark was then at Rome for the second time ; he had been rector of Ghent from 1605 to 1611, when he began the old church of the Society of Jesus in that town, which he completed during his second period of government. The State University has taken the place of the College buildings.

servant of His Mother. After his happy death I offered up the three Masses which the priests of the Society are obliged to say for any one of theirs who dies in the house in which they are then living. But instead of saying my Masses for the dead, I said three of our ever Blessed Lady in thanksgiving to God, Who had granted one so innocent and such a servant to His Mother in heaven. I could not persuade myself that I might, without outraging God's promises, offer up either Mass or prayers to Him for the soul of one in whose spotless life, closed with so blessed a death, there had never been seen aught which was not according to the divine law and the rules of our holy Institute. And in my judgment, I am not less certain that he has received a great glory from God in heaven, than if I had beheld him there enthroned with my own eyes. Were I to speak of all his virtues, I could bear witness to many things concerning him, for I consider him to have been most specially remarkable in all. To these four things, however, for God's glory, for the honour of our so holy and innocent brother and child of the Society, as an example to us all, on the oath of a priest, it has seemed to me good to bear witness.'

The words spoken by the various professors made all present most anxious to see and honour the servant of God, and no sooner were schools over than the students, both young men and boys, tried to go to the infirmary. As they were nearly two thousand in number, this could not of course be allowed. They dispersed and went home, and soon spread the news over Rome that a young Belgian Jesuit of marvellous sanctity had died at the Roman College. Many were the regrets among the nobles of the city that they had not learnt the news of his illness in time to have the privilege of visiting the saint during

S

his life.   Among these was the venerable Cardinal
Bellarmine.   On the 16th of that very month in which
John had died, he had at last obtained what he had so
earnestly desired, permission to leave the Vatican, and,
free from every care and anxiety, to prepare for death
amongst the novices of the Society in their Novitiate on
the Quirinal.   The place was familiar to him, for every
year he had been accustomed to spend the month of
September there in retreat, making himself again a
novice in his exact observance of every little rule and
custom.   One affair alone he had refused to give up,
the active promotion of the cause of St. Philip Neri's
canonization, both for the love he had borne that great
saint, and out of a close friendship towards his great disciple, Cardinal Baronius.   Two days after his retirement,
Father Bisdomini, professor of moral theology at the
Roman College, went with Father Fabius Bellarmine,
a relative of the venerable Cardinal, to pay him a visit,
on which occasion he expressed the deepest regret that
he had never known Berchmans personally,[2] and had
never heard of his illness.   The crowd of affairs
which naturally required his attention before quitting
the Court, and the deafness under which he was
labouring, explain naturally enough his ignorance.   As
he heard the story of John's virtues, tears flowed fast
from his aged eyes, and when the two Fathers were
forced to leave he accompanied them far beyond the
humble apartments which he himself had chosen.   Spite
of his feeble health he went down a long corridor
to the head of the stairs, talking all the time of the
departed saint, and, on bidding them good-bye, he
again repeated his expressions of sorrow at not having

---

[2] Father Camillas Gori, however, deposed that John had paid a
visit to the Cardinal.   He no doubt had forgotten the circumstance.
See p. 157.

had the privilege of visiting him. It was no childish admiration on the part of one who had been the intimate friend and confessor of St. Aloysius, and what happened a few days previous only strengthens the force of his testimony.

Father Thomas Fitzherbert, of Swinnerton, ancestor to the present family of that name and place, who after a life of much suffering for the faith, and seven years after the death of his noble wife, entered the Society of Jesus, at the advanced age of sixty-two, was at that time, and had been from the December of 1618, rector of the venerable English College in the holy City. He it was who told Cardinal Bellarmine, while yet at the Vatican, of the death of a holy Belgian scholastic at the Roman College, of the number of miracles attributed to his intercession, of the wonderful graces which God had given him in life, and, above all, that of coming to the age of manhood without committing a deliberate venial sin. Bellarmine paused for a moment, and then measuring others by himself, said in all simplicity, ‘I honour the young man; but what do you see wonderful in that? Who would ever think of committing such a sin?’

When Father Cepari heard what had taken place in the various class-rooms, and the rush that had been made to get to see the body of John, he summoned not only his ordinary consultors, but others also of the Fathers of the greatest standing among his subjects, to take advice on what was best to be done. All agreed on the following measures—(1) A painter was to be called to paint Berchman’s portrait; (2) contrary to the usual custom, his body was to be inclosed in a coffin, so that should God be pleased afterwards to glorify the name of His servant, his remains might be kept separate from those who lay in the common vault; and lastly, four Fathers were to be continually stationed around the bier during the Service for the Dead, to prevent the crowd approaching too near.

The first resolution was not, unhappily, carried out. What was the success of the last we shall see.

A word must be said here to explain the position of the rooms once occupied by our saint, the place where he died, and where he was buried. John, on his first entry into the Roman College lived, as we have seen, in the room of St. Aloysius, very probably the one now turned into a chapel, at the top story of the building. The room, now called Blessed Berchmans', must have been one he occupied at a later period, either on leaving the juniorate or when the room of St. Aloysius was made a chapel. The constant tradition at the Roman College is, that John died in the same infirmary in which St. Aloysius departed, and that it faced to the street which separates the College from the Dominican Convent of Santa Maria sopra Minerva. It was destroyed in 1626, to make way for the Church of St. Ignazio, built by the princely liberality of Cardinal Ludovico Ludovisi. The particular room in the infirmary where St. Aloysius died was, at Cardinal Bellarmine's expense, converted into an oratory after his Beatification in 1605, and the present chapel of St. Joseph occupies its site, doubly hallowed, for there St. Aloysius' body lay from its translation in 1649 till its final enshrining in 1699 within the glorious altar-tomb of silver and lapis-lazuli, where it now reposes.

The Church of the Annunciation, which existed in Berchmans' time, was evidently much humbler than its magnificent successor. It was in this that the funeral we are now to describe took place.

The body of John was carried thither and laid out upon the bier, the doors being kept closed until the hour of service. Before the dirge began, Fathers and brothers from the Gesù, St. Andrea, and other houses of the Society flocked in to touch the holy remains with their beads, and imprint on them a reverent kiss. It is no stretch of fancy to imagine that the English Fathers in Rome were of the number, Father Fitzherbert and Father Edward Coffin, venerable confessors for the faith —Father Edward being then Spiritual Father and confessor at the English College; Father Coleford, minister at the same, and Father Edward Bentley, English Penitentiary at St. Peter's, whose missionary life in England was yet to come, and who were both to labour and die there, and Father Edward Webbe, the Procurator of the English Province at head-quarters, who a year later, full of merits, was to be laid near Father Parsons in the old Church of St. Thomas of the English; and a novice from St. Andrea, an old fellow-student of John's, would have been there, who, under the assumed name of Salvin, concealed his good Yorkshire birth and real name of Robert Constable. His time of probation was nearly run, for he was to take his vows at St. Andrea the next month, and on the very day on which Cardinal Bellarmine's soul left that holy spot for heaven. As Father Constable he was to be for fourteen years a faithful labourer amidst the dangers of the English mission,[3] and then, in spite of a painful illness, for thirty years professor of Scripture and controversy in the English College at Liége.

Many of the scholars got admission at the same time. The fellow-students of the deceased from the English College surely were there—the learned Edward

---

[3] Father Constable was for some time with the Royalist army, and we find him in Yorkshire in 1642. He was noted for his diligence in early rising, and was an example of humility and self-denial. He was for three years a convictor in the English College at Rome. See Appendix.

Courtenay, who, a fortnight after, was to enter the Novitiate of the Society, and had just held a public defension, *De Universâ Philosophiâ*, before the Cardinal Bentivoglio, with Henry Morse, one of the forty-four martyrs who have rendered glorious that venerable Seminary, who was to make his novitiate for the Society in York Castle, also John Dormer, and Ralph Salvin of Durham, and last, not least, Nathaniel Bacon, who became a distinguished author under the assumed name of Southwell (Sotvellus).[4]

A boy of the Roman Seminary, much esteemed for his good sense, innocence, and excellence, got close up to the body of John, and was riveted by what he saw. Again and again he came back while the office was going on, and now standing, now kneeling, he seemed as though he could not tear himself from the sight of that face. On his return home he asked the prefect of his camerata why the Fathers had put those diamonds on the forehead of John. 'There were no diamonds,' was the answer ; but the boy insisted that he had seen two lights like diamonds over the eyebrows of our saint, and besides that, a very bright glory all around his head. The prefect urged him to tell all this to Father Francis Piccolomini ; however, when he saw what importance was attached to his story, he did not do so. The prefect, however, next morning told Father Cepari, assuring him that the boy was very intimate with a certain Father of the College, to whom he believed he had told what he had seen. The rector accordingly charged that religious to interrogate him carefully on the subject, and though

---

[4] After being Secretary to five Generals of the Society of Jesus, he was relieved of his office to publish his Dictionary of the Writers of the Society of Jesus. His *Journal of Meditations*, written in Latin by N. B., are well known in many of our Colleges and religious houses. See Appendix.

the student blushed as he repeated his story, he could not
be shaken in his account, that he had seen what looked
like magnificent jewels on the forehead of Berchmans,
and round the body an aureola of such bright light as
dazzled him when it met his eyes.[5]

Many secular persons meanwhile continued to enter
the church, and the flowers which had been scattered,
as the ritual requires, over the body, were all carried
off. Then his crucifix disappeared ; his cap, his shoes
went too, and over and over again the rosary which he
held in his hands was exchanged for another.

At last the Office for the Dead commenced. Father
Theodore Busée of Nieumagen, Assistant for Germany,
the representative of the Flemish province with the
General, who had grown grey in offices of authority, in
cotta and stole, brought up the close of a long line
of acolytes, cross-bearer, thurifer, and ministers, young
fellow religious once of him, the centre of all this sad
ceremony. The church doors were thrown open ; a great
crowd surged in, and it was with difficulty that the procession could advance to the high altar. At first all
went on quietly, until almost half the office was recited,
when one or two of the crowd contrived to get up to the
body, touch it with their beads, and kiss its hands. Don
Ferdinand Ughelli, a Cistercian monk, who had attended
the course of philosophy with John, and who suffered
from dreadful head-aches, was among these. He placed
the hand of the deceased on his forehead, and was
instantly cured. At once every one tried to draw near.
Not ten priests would have sufficed to withstand the
crush ; the four who were stationed there were powerless.
The cries of ' a miracle ! a miracle !' only added to the
desire of the crowd to draw near to the sacred remains.
The tumult rose and rose, till by its din it drowned the

---

[5] MSS. of Father Cepari, quoted by Father Boero.

voices of those who were reciting the office, just as the mourning of the faithful Irish people has been known to silence the chanting at the funeral of their priest.   Each one strove to secure a portion of John's habit, and in the confusion the body was almost pulled down from the bier.   Six of the Fathers hastened to put a stop to the disorder.   A pall was thrown hastily over the corpse, now almost stripped of its clothes.   But of this, before the service was concluded, only a few remnants could be found.   Then a determined effort was made to rescue the body from the intemperate devotion of the crowd. It was resolved to carry it within the rails of our Lady's altar, hoping that they would serve as a barrier and protection.   The moment the intention of the bearers was evident, the people rushed forward and filled all the space around the altar.   By a happy presence of mind, the opportunity was taken to retreat into the sacristy, and there, with doors bolted and barred, the body was re-clothed.   Then it was found that not satisfied with spoiling it of all that belonged to it, the people had severed a toe from one of the feet.   During the strange scene just described, many there were who though they showed their devotion took no part in the violence of the crowd.   Religious of various orders mingling with the crowd, kissed reverently the hands of the departed, touched his remains with their beads, and struck with the look of sanctity, which the hand of death had not altogether effaced, asked earnestly, but modestly, for something that might serve as a relic. One loves to bring saints together, and would like to think that the humble and much-suffering St. Joseph Calasanzio, who had just founded his order of Scuole-Pie, or 'Scolopi,' had been more fortunate than Cardinal Bellarmine, and had come with some of his brethren that morning to the Church of the Annunciation.   Or may be he, like many others who could **not** satisfy their devotion in the church, came later on, and was allowed to enter the sacristy.

A Belgian religious of the Society during **all the** morning **was** carefully noting down in that place **the** various supernatural cures and graces which were reported to him as having been obtained. Zeal for his fellow-countryman's honour made him adopt **this** precaution, **with a** view hereafter to more **detailed** investigations, when, as **he felt sure**, a formal **inquiry would** take place. These facts, when known, only added to **the** fervour of **the** select few who were admitted within the sacristy. **And though they were** for the most part people of high **position, they were not** much more reserved **than** their poorer brethren had been. **Not content** with applying **their** handkerchiefs **to his face and hands,** touching him with **whole bunches of rosaries, placing** their jewelled **rings for an instant on his fingers,** before long **they had stripped the body, and it had to** be clothed during **the** afternoon **in a** fresh **habit. As** night drew near the number of applicants only increased, and to satisfy the devotion of **a** number of ladies come for that purpose into **the church,** the sacred remains had more than once **to** be carried thither.

It **was** feared that the Fathers would profit **by** the **darkness to** complete the burial, **and some** persons of noble family, whom **Father Cepari does** not name, sent **to beg as a** favour that it **might** be delayed till next morning, **because** they **most** earnestly desired **to** see the body. The ecclesiastical law supported their request, as John had only died twelve hours before. It was accordingly granted. When all the faithful were retired, Father Horace Grassi, as prefect of the church, super-intended the post mortem examination, which was undertaken just as much to satisfy the pious greed for relics, as to discover the cause of death. He first had a cast taken of the face. The lungs and spleen showed signs of inflammation. When he left Flanders, John had been stout and strong, but what with his austerities, his close application to spiritual things and to study, and his unrelaxing and minutely exact keeping of rule, he had gradually worn himself away, his frame was reduced to a very shadow of what it had been; the very peritoneum, which rarely is without some signs of fat, was in his case entirely destitute of it, and the medical men all agreed it would have been impossible for him to have lived much longer. His heart, full of blood, showed how naturally ardent was his temperament, and that grace alone had saved him from the consequences of his character. We shall speak in another chapter of the later history of that relic. Father Horace, who had known John very intimately as his scholar, and knew his sweetness of temper, wished to see how far that was based on physical causes. No vestige of bile was found in the region of the liver. The operation over, the body was again dressed and exposed to the veneration of the public on the following day, Saturday, the eve of the Assumption. Such was the crowd of bishops and prelates, of princes and nobles, that once more the burial was obliged to be deferred until evening. The crowd, though not less numerous than on the preceding day, was more orderly, and yet many were the relics carried off—the hair, the nails, the habit, were all found to have been docked when the remains were removed.

The great event of that day was the instantaneous cure of a lady, one Catharine de Recanati. This miracle forms the subject of one of the beautiful paintings that now adorn the chapel dedicated to our saint in the old Church of St. Sulpice, Diest. For three months this lady, then sixty-eight years old, had been blind in one eye, and had almost lost the use of the other. Hearing of the death of John, and the wonders that had followed it, she came to the church during the Office of the Dead, hoping, by the touch of his hands, or at least of his habit, to regain her sight. But the enormous crowd rendered it impossible for her to approach, and she returned home discouraged and sad.

'The goodness of God our Lord was pleased for the benefit of this poor afflicted lady, and the glory of His worthy servant, that she should, on the 14th of August, be at the house of the Lady Victoria Altieri, who, moved by the renown of his sanctity, was anxious to come and see,' we are quoting Father Spinola's deposition, 'the body of the youth, which, to please many ladies of the highest rank, her Excellency the Duchess Sforza amongst the rest, had not as yet been interred. At this, the desire the poor blind lady had conceived of accomplishing what she had been unable to do the previous day, came back again. "Oh, would that I could go too!" she exclaimed. "If I could but visit the body of that saintly youth, I should have hopes of receiving a *grazia* for my eyes." The Lady Victoria made her get into her carriage with her, and took her to the church. She caused Catharine to be conducted at once to the bier where the body was lying; and, on the poor sufferer being anxious to apply to her eyes something belonging to the servant of God, one of the Society,' it was Father Aloysius Spinola himself who was there, 'told her to take one of the fingers of John, and with it to touch her eyes. She did so, and immediately cried out, "I am cured—I can see." Again she applied the finger, and recovered her sight completely.'

As a proof she gave the names of the ladies around her, described the rings they wore on their fingers, and the stones with which they were garnished. All were anxious to ask her questions; among these were the Bishop of Pavia, Mgr. Landriani (a benefactor of the Society of Jesus), and Mgr. Archinto of Como. They were persuaded of the truth of the miracle. Signor Lorenzo Altieri and his wife, with others, were witnesses to the instantaneous cure; and Father Spinola drew up a *procès verbal*, from which we have largely quoted. Catharine brought, as *ex votos*, to the tomb of her benefactor two eyes wrought in silver.

On a Saturday, as we have said, Berchmans had been born; on a Saturday he was buried. Father Grassi had the precious remains, together with an inscription on a leaden plate, placed in a wooden coffin; and with his own hands he assisted to lay it in a new vault in the recently adorned chapel of St. Aloysius, where as yet no one had been laid.

CHAPTER XIV.

Glorification of John Berchmans.

THE Feast of the Assumption, in 1621, saw an unusual
crowd in the church of the Roman College. The fame
of John's holiness, the rumour of his miracles, had
brought numbers thither with the hope of gazing upon
the body of one whom all spoke of as a saint. They
came too late. They tried to make up for their disap-
pointment by kneeling at his tomb, covering it with
flowers, and kissing it with reverence. Among other
nobles who mixed in that crowd was one whose name is
now well known ; the Marquis Pallavicino was there with
his children, the eldest of whom, Sforza, was then a
youth of fourteen. As a student at the Roman College,
the boy must have known John by sight. Four years
after he defended a public thesis, *De Universâ Philosophiâ*, in its halls, and, later on, stood all comers in
theology ; and just when the highest places and pre-
ferment in the ecclesiastical state, to which he had
devoted himself, were open to him, he entered the
novitiate of the Society of Jesus, on St. Aloysius' day,
at the age of thirty. The world knows him now as
Cardinal Pallavicino, the historian of the Council of
Trent. Forty-six years later, a familiar friend of our
saint, Paul Oliva, then General of the Society, knelt
with many of his brethren around the death-bed of the

illustrious Prince of the Church, once a novice under his charge. The Marquis and his family begged some relics of the departed scholastic, and stayed to hear Mass, which was said at the altar nearest his tomb.

The veneration paid to his tomb grew to such an extent that the General, Father Mutius Vitelleschi, feared lest fault might be found with a cultus that forestalled the judgment of the Church. On the very day of which we are speaking, the 15th of August, 1621, he addressed the following letter, in Italian, to Father Cepari—

'Very Reverend Father in Christ,—

'Though we ought to set on the virtues and special graces conferred by our good God (*Dio benedetto*) all that value they deserve, yet I desire by this letter to remind your Reverence, on the occasion of the happy death of Brother John, to let all in the College and our other houses be careful to bear in mind, both in their words and their outward actions, what was the first spirit of the Society which guided it on the occasion even of the death of our Blessed Father Ignatius, as well as at that of Father le Fevre, Father Borgia, and of so many other reverend servants of God. Moreover, let them remember not to give to seculars anything that has belonged to this same brother, or any relics of him whatever. For it is not fitting in such matters to forestall the dispositions of Providence ; but rather we should await humbly and with great reserve the times by It determined.

'In conclusion, I beg His Divine Majesty to multiply His blessings upon the whole College, so that the modesty, observance, and every other virtue of this brother, may shine forth in each one, and they may be his portraits and living relics. I commend myself to the prayers and Holy Sacrifices of your Reverence and of all.

'Your Reverence's servant in Christ,

' MUZIO VITELLESCHI.

'Di Casa. From the House of the Gesù.
     '15th of August, 1621.'

A fresh measure was adopted. By the Father General's orders the remains of John were transported to the chapel of the Crucifix, the common burial-place of the community, where the body of St. Aloysius had reposed for eleven years. But this change made no difference. Father Grassi, at the close of his narrative of Berchmans' death, writing a month and a half after the translation, says that the new tomb was still covered with fresh flowers, as from the beginning, and *ex votos* of every kind continued to pour in. ' It was all very well,' he says, ' to order them to be removed, as my office obliged me to do ; there were fresh ones the next day.' Not only strangers, but Fathers and brothers of the community, were constantly, late and early, praying at his tomb. Two years later, on the 16th of August, the people decked it out with flowers and sweet smelling herbs, as is the custom in Italy on solemn feast days. Six candles were lighted on the altar hard by, and another of a pound weight was placed over the vault where John reposed. Nor was the devotion confined to Rome. In Belgium it naturally found its home. But a few months after the death of Berchmans, the faithful champion of the Church's cause, Philip, the Duke d'Aerschot, asked and obtained of Gregory XV. that the usual preliminary inquiries should be set on foot for his canonization. This formal sanction gave an impetus to the devotion of those who were proud to call themselves the fellow-countrymen of our saint. Twelve of the first engravers of the time produced various portraits of Berchmans, and between 1622 and 1624, without calculating numbers of inferior works, over thirty thousand of these were sold. We cannot help regretting that, living as John did at the time of Rubens and Vandyck, his beautiful countenance has not won an immortal place in one of their pictures, just as Vandyck has left us the well known portrait of the Provincial, Father Scribani. An old portrait, said to have been sent from Rome to his relatives at the béguinage of Diest, bears intrinsic marks of being a merely ideal picture, while its merit as a work of art is none.[1]   But artistic or not, the rapid spread of his devotion was at once the cause and effect of the multitude of likenesses, which penetrated into every part of Europe.   An account of his death was first printed in Spain, three years before Father Cepari's Life appeared. He was invoked in Catholic Germany ; the news of his virtues penetrated into poor suffering England.   Perhaps the greatest incentive to the devotion of John was that work, which has formed the groundwork of this book, as it will always, in fact, serve for the foundation of any attempt to make his memory live again.   Father Cepari, already so well known as the biographer of St. Aloysius, was ordered by his Superior to undertake the Life of Berchmans.   Completed in 1623, it was not published till 1627, and was at once translated into the great European languages.   Father Mutius Vitelleschi, who had known St. Aloysius so well, and had been present at his vows, placed at the head of this work an eulogium of our saint, which may well be compared to

---

[1] The portrait which finds favour among the art world is an engraving by P. de Malley, prefixed to the first Flemish translation, by Father James Susius, S.J., of Father Cepari's Life, published at Antwerp, in 1629.

that which his predecessor, **Father Aquaviva, had** written for Father Cepari's Life **of St. Aloysius.**

'Our Brother **John Berchmans, of** happy memory, was a youth **of a truly** remarkable innocence and purity, of angelic life **and admirable piety.** Endowed with solid and perfect **virtue, the faithful** observer of the rules of his Institute, **he was ever, in all** times, and in all places, and **on all** occasions, to every **one who** lived with him, such an example, that we have never **found any** one who ever remarked in **him the** smallest defect **or** imperfection. Let us hope then that this Life, which I have read with the greatest care from beginning to end, and which is full of the **acts of virtue** most fitting a singularly exact and **perfect son of** the Society, will be for all who read it, but especially for our Fathers and **brothers, a** great spiritual aid, **and a spur for the acquirement of religious** perfection.

'And all **may rest certain of the truth of everything** that is **narrated in this Life, as to the virtues of this** brother, and **the heavenly favours** bestowed upon **him.** For I have **seen** with my own eyes a **very long** list of God-fearing men **of** weight, learning, and wisdom, who have borne witness to everything of their own certain knowledge. And these attestations **I** myself have read. **May it** please God to grant us the grace to be able to imitate Berchmans in this life—this indeed is my object **in causing this** book to be written—and so may **He** give us to **enjoy one** day those heavenly goods, which we piously believe are now the lot of this holy brother.

'MUZIO VITELLESCHI.

'*18th of July,* 1625.'

Father Cepari, in his evidence before the Commission, declared, 'I depose as true, *on my oath,* whatever I have written **in his Life.'**

T

And the devotion spread.   Kings and Queens loved to honour the humble religious.   The Queen of Louis XV., poor Mary of Poland, in her sorrow and abandonment, kept his portrait, set in precious stones, upon her *prie-dieu;* and crowned heads, as we shall tell elsewhere, were pleaders for his beatification.

But God had chosen other ways by which to set upon a mountain the light which had shone beneath a bushel.

We must go back again to the August of 1621.   At the time of Berchmans' sickness and death there was in the infirmary of the Roman College, a lay-brother, by name Thomas di Simoni, from Perugia, who was just recovering from illness.   His great humility and contempt of self, his marvellous simplicity, rendered him very dear to God.   Every moment that he could call his own, whether by day or by night, he was used to spend in prayer; and several times God gave him light from on high, and our Blessed Lady herself had more than once appeared to him.   This, as other similar facts, we tell on the authority of Father Cepari, who however in obedience to the laws of the Church, could not then publish them, and we owe the knowledge of them to the zeal of Father Boero, S.J., who discovered the manuscripts and printed them in his new edition of the Life.[2]   On the 14th of August, about four o'clock in the morning, being, as he was accustomed at that hour, at prayer, Thomas saw heaven on a sudden open before him, and from a high-seated throne of clouds all full of light, he beheld descending towards him the glorious Mother of God, Queen of the Angels, her face beaming with exceeding joy and more than ordinary gladness.   Two of the princes of heaven bore her on a royal throne.   One of the two wore a cotta, but as he could not see his face because our Lady was between

---

[2] Edit. Roman., 1865.

them as she passed, Thomas was unable to recognize
him, but it came across his mind that it was St. Aloysius.
The other, who was on his side the throne, he saw
distinctly and knew him perfectly—it was Brother John
Berchmans in his Jesuit habit, all joyful and happy.
They passed swiftly on, so it seemed to him, and came
into a widespreading plain, where there were many
glorious and blessed spirits, and to them with great
delight and joy our Lady brought this new gain she
had made, in the glory of heaven, of this her well-loved
servant and child; she called on all to rejoice at it
and celebrate the festival of his coming. The vision,
when it had gone, left the good brother full of comfort
and quite certain that John was enjoying great glory in
heaven, as the favourite child of the Mother of God.
And so he told it all to his Superior, the rector, for
God's glory and the honour of His servant.[3]

There was living at that time in Mantua a Florentine
lady, named Margaret Rossi, maid of honour to the
Duchess Leonora Medici. She had consecrated her
virginity to God at a very early age, and was then
some sixty years old, and leading such a religious
and holy life at the ducal court as to be held in
great esteem for her sanctity. On the morning of the
16th of August, 1621, she came to the Jesuit church of
the city, and sent for her confessor, Father Alexander
Caprara. 'One of your young men is dead in some place
at a distance,' such was the news she brought, 'he is
a saint; there has been a great concourse at his funeral,
and God is working many miracles through his relics.'
The Father declared he knew nothing about it. 'You
will see,' she added, 'that some one will write to you
on the subject.' A few days after he received a letter
from Lucca, written by Father Paul Bombino, giving him

---

[3] This also is painted by Du Jardin in the chapel at Diest.

T 2

the news of John's death and the circumstances that attended his funeral. In those times, the news could not have reached Mantua over two days, and Father Alexander determined to inquire further into the mysterious announcement of the pious lady. Her account was as follows—Between three and four, on the morning of the sixteenth, having finished her meditation, just as she was going, as was her wont, to begin matins of the office of our Lady, which she always said before daybreak, she was rapt in ecstasy, and a youth led her to a place afar off, and into a church, where an immense crowd had gathered round the dead body of a young religious of the Society of Jesus. He was stretched on a bier, his dress was white, and he was receiving the honours of a saint. She did not herself see any miracles being wrought, but she saw clearly a Father who was engaged in writing in the sacristy, and from time to time a young scholastic, who stood guard at the bier, went as though to tell him various things that were happening. It struck her that he was recording miracles. It was near six before this rapture ceased, and at its close she felt all the fatigue she would have suffered coming off a long journey. During the recital of our Lady's office, her soul was filled with spiritual joy at the thought that one of the Society of Jesus was so honoured by God. When she had told her story, her confessor read her the letter that he had got from Lucca. The holy lady thanked heaven earnestly for the favour she had received. She begged the Father to obtain for her a portion of John's habit. A short time after, Father Cepari complied with her request, assuring her at the same time by letter that many miracles had been wrought by that very relic.[4]

---

[4] From manuscripts of Father Cepari and a letter of Father Alexander Caprara, published by Father **Boero.**

CHAPTER XV.

Miracles.

WHEN God desires to manifest the glory of His special friends and servants, miracles are the means He chiefly employs. The Church, jealous of the truth, submits such manifestations to a most severe and searching investigation. To any one who does not disbelieve *à priori* in the existence of miracles, the official acts of the tribunals acting under the Sacred Congregation of Rites must be conclusive proof of the truth of those which it accepts.

But besides the three miraculous cures which were so accepted, as the necessary conditions of John's beatification, numbers are recorded which have all the authenticity the attestation on oath of most credible witnesses can give to them. To a Catholic, to all the human evidence on which the judgment of the Church reposes, there is superadded the final approval of the Sovereign Pontiff, given after much prayer ; an approval which sets a stamp of perfect certainty on the truth of the accepted miracles. Though naturally those cases were selected which were supported by the strongest evidence, it does not at all follow that the others are of themselves less credible.

We can only pretend to give the slightest sketch in our narrow limits of some of these, with a notice of the three approved in the Brief of Beatification. A Father,

John Baptist de Ruschi, and a scholastic, Julius Retta-
bene, were both at death's door, in the infirmary, when
Berchmans died, and both were cured by the application
of some of his relics, the Father rising up well and
strong from the saint's mattrass, on which he had been
laid.

Much the same happened, in the same place and at
the same time, to the lay-brother, Laurence Mori, who
was in acute fever, and delirious.

Father van Aelst, the old friend of Berchmans, tells
Father Bauters, in a letter, that among many cases
reported from Mantua, there was one of a young man
dying of hemorrhage, who was cured instantaneously by
a relic of our saint, which the Lady Margaret Rossi had
brought to him.[1]   In another letter, he tells how Father
Bisdomini, John's professor of ethics, was cured of an
attack of cholera by a relic of his pupil's heart.   In
the July of 1622, William Stanihurst[2] was dying in the
infirmary of the Professed House of the Society at
Antwerp.   'O blessed Brother John Berchmans,' he
cried out, 'obtain for me a cure in my mortal sickness.'
And his old fellow novice heard his prayer.   He was up
and out of the sick ward next day.

Brother Renier Hautmans was dying, in 1622, at
Easter time, in the old College of the Society at Louvain,
whose venerable walls time and troubles have spared
to our days as a boys' orphanage.[3]   He heard the
celebrated Father Leonard Leys (Lessius) reading at
his bedside a letter from Rome, full of the miracles
wrought by Berchmans, which had never ceased since
his death.   The hope of cure, and the prayer for help,
were suggested to the dying youth.   On the Monday
before Ascension Day, he was at his old place in the
lecture-room.   In the often-quoted letter of Father Greeff,[4]

See p. 291.   [2] See p. 48.   [3] Rue des Orphelins.   [4] See p. 28.

the Father speaks of himself in the third person. 'I know a friend who, on the 18th of November, 1623, about ten at night, when crossing the principal square [of Nimeguen], amidst snow and gloom, was assaulted by a soldier, who seized his arm with one hand, while with the other, he aimed a blow with his drawn sword at the Father's head. He invoked the aid of his old acquaintance, Berchmans. To his surprise, he saw at his side a young man of distinguished bearing, wrapped in a cloak, in height, age, and features, like John. "Let him go," said the new comer to the soldier, "he is a burgher, well known to me and to many." The prisoner was instantly freed, and went to his home, which was at some distance off. But he never could discover his deliverer, spite of inquiries about various young men who resembled him. This story he confirmed on oath before the Bishops of Ruremonde and Antwerp.'[5]

Our saint had for God's sake forgotten his father and his father's house, and so we are not surprised to find that God did not forget his family when he was with Him in heaven. His brother Charles, while yet a novice of the Society, was cured instantaneously of a quartan ague by the touch of one of his relics.

The béguine, Mary Berchmans, John's aunt, attributes the very wonderful cure of a long-standing hemorrhage from which she suffered, to an apparition of her nephew.

Jerome van Suerck, brother to two fellow novices of Berchmans, wrote to his rector, Father Bauters, then in Brussels, and absent from his College at Louvain, a long account of another interposition of the saint on behalf of his family. He had it from the lips of one of John's uncles, Paul vanden Hove, chaplain, or curé, of the Barony of

---

[5] See, too, the beautiful story of the cure of the scholastic, Joseph Spinelli, in Healy Thompson's *Life of St. Aloysius.*

Wesemael, a monk of the Abbey of Averbode.[6] A large family party, consisting of John's brothers, Charles and Bartholomew, their uncles, Francis Berchmans, with his wife, 'Aunty van Olmen,' Adrian vanden Hove, and his brother, with their brother-in-law, and our old friend, Canon Froymont, was sailing down the Scheldt. They had been present, the day before, at Mechlin, at the religious profession of Adrian Berchmans in the Augustinian convent, and were going on to Antwerp. The boat sprang a leak in the middle of the river; the waters were chill, and the stream swift, for it was autumn time, the day after Michaelmas. Not a soul on the bank ventured out to save them. And when, without hardly knowing how they got there, all landed safely, can we be surprised that they attributed their escape to the protection of their holy relative.

One more event. It was 1697. The good town of Diest, which had suffered so severely during the long wars, was making merry for the peace of Ryswick. A party of young men, under the direction of Peter Papen, organist to the great church of Louvain, was told off to fire *feux de joie.* A spark fell on a barrel of powder, and in an instant everything was a wreck in the house where it had stood, and the building itself was in flames. But not a soul was hurt, and from the begrimed walls looked out, unseared, untouched, a portrait of our saint, though the picture was immediately over the keg which had exploded. Forty-five years after, when the case was

---

[6] This splendid abbey, which still makes such a conspicuous figure in the view from Montaigu, is in the valley of the Demer, or rather, in the sandy plain through which that river flows, and is the seat of a mitred abbot of the Premonstratensian Order. Matthias Berchmans, cousin to John's father, was also a religious of this house. He was uncle to Paul vanden Hove, the founder of the Convent of the Twelve Apostles in the Diest Béguinage, which was so much bound up with the family of our saint.

resumed in Rome, a **burgher of Diest, and** the daughter of the innkeeper **in** whose hostel **the accident** had happened, testified on oath to the truth of the story.

The **three** officially approved miracles were **all in** favour **of religious.**

Sister Mary Angelica, daughter **of** one of **the** principal **men of** business in the stirring little town of Ronciglione, a place of some importance for its iron works, was a novice there in the Franciscan convent of **St. Anne.** A deadly gastritis and an internal tumour, aggravated by a blunder **of the** infirmarian, who gave **her** a dose of raw **vitriol, had brought her** to death's **door.** A violent hiccup **prevented her** approaching holy communion. **The young** novice **was a** great favourite, and a novena was determined **on to** Berchmans, consisting **of** his rosary of the Immaculate **Conception.** A print of **the** saint was put into **her hands.** Her **confidence was** rewarded **by an internal voice which assured her she** would be **able to receive holy** viaticum, **and would be** cured when **anointed.** Her hopes **were fulfilled, and** the doctor, who **on** passing by inquired what hour she died, found to his amazement Sister Angelica dressed and down-stairs. He examined her and found **all** trace **of her** illness had passed. But **it** was the **old** story of **the nine lepers. An** *ex voto* **heart had** been promised **for John's tomb :** difficulties stood **in the way,** and it was **never sent.** A little more than a month later, the tumour, the deadly symptoms, all returned. The doctor was so convinced that it was entirely owing to the nuns' ingratitude, that he refused **to do** anything **for her,** and bade them recommence their prayers. An offering of candles were sent at once **to Rome** to burn on the altar before which Berchmans was buried, and again the community gathered round **the** bed of their dying sister ; again they recited the rosary of the Immaculate

Conception, **and again,** after Extreme **Unction,** she left
her bed entirely and perfectly cured. Seventeen years
later she made her solemn deposition, **and she was**
able then to **declare** that she had never since her **cure**
suffered **from ill** health.

A poor orphan, another **Mary** Angelica, entered
with broken health **into the Cistercian** convent in the
picturesque Etruscan **town of** Nepi. A body so feeble,
sunk rapidly beneath a **violent** attack of rheumatism.
Fearful convulsions distorted **her** frame, and her case
became hopeless. The Bishop of Nepi had heard of the
cure of Sister Mary Angelica of Ronciglione, and told the
confessor to urge her namesake to seek for help where
it had been sought and found. A **novena** was begun,
and an offering **to** the tomb of the saint **was** promised.
Next morning, as the nuns left the choir, Mary Angelica
came to meet them. She had been up and well from
morning, and now, after a long thanksgiving in private,
had come to show to her sisters the effect of their
prayers. There was **plenty of** work that day, for it was
the eve of their great founder, St. Bernard, and no one
worked **harder than the resuscitated sister, carrying wood,**
sweeping **out the kitchen, and pulling the bells** to ring
in the festa in **the evening.** The **cure was as** lasting
as it was sudden.

Sister **Mary Crocifissa Ancaini** entered the Convent
of **the Visitation** at Rome in **1718.** Frail in health
from her entry into religion, after **some twelve years**
she fell **into a decline, and the** doctors declared her
past recovery. A polypus began to form in **the** region
of the heart, she lost the use of one **side, and was**
subject to fearful convulsions, which **shook the bed on**
which **she** lay. Lock-jaw ensued. **The end** seemed
very **near. The** Reverend Mother **brought her** a print
of John, and **earnestly** begged **her to** have confidence

in his intercession. The portrait was laid on her bed, but she had little consciousness or power to appreciate her danger, or to ask for health and life. A gleam of intelligence came to her the next day at early morning. She pressed the image to her head and chest. That moment she was cured; and when the infirmarian came in, she found her seated on her bed telling the story of the miracle to the sister who had been watching by her that night. She stood erect in her place in the choir the whole time her sisters chanted the *Te Deum*, and then heard three Masses in succession on her knees. The doctor heard on inquiry that she was not only alive, but awaiting him in the parlour. He frankly owned that her recovery was miraculous, and signed a solemn attestation of his belief. A few months later Sister Mary was made portress, an office entailing much fatigue, as every message from the gate had to be taken to the Superioress. Yet she held this office for two years and a half without any extraordinary inconvenience to herself. At the end of that time, mental troubles about her family, joined to spiritual difficulties, came upon her. A perfectly new disease began to show itself—a cancerous tumour on the breast. Unwilling to disclose it to a doctor, she accepted with pleasure the prescription of a friar who professed to be able, without examining the wound, to cure it in a fortnight. He sent her a strong mercurial preparation, which aggravated fearfully her state. The poor self-instructed doctor thought to repair the harm by an ointment which only drove the evil inwards, and Sister Crocifissa's state was soon beyond all medical aids. Her confessor urged her again to have recourse to John, and a novena was begun by the community in his honour, to close on his feast. But little came of it. The priest encouraged her to continue her prayers through the octave. On the 19th of August a sudden feeling

of confidence came over the dying religious. Half uncon-
sciously she left her bed, and, prostrate at the *prie-dieu*
beside it, recommended herself to Berchmans' prayers.
Up till then she had been powerless. When she came
fairly to herself, she felt as if she had been awakened
from sleep and found herself perfectly well. When the
Reverend Mother was told of this she was incredulous;
and though afterwards she could not doubt the evidence
of her senses, wished the fact to be kept more or less
private. The story, however, reached the ears of Father
Senapa, the procurator of the cause, and he insisted on
a formal examination by the medical men, who, with the
sisters, all bore witness to the purely supernatural nature
of the second case. Poor Mary Sobieski, wife of the
exiled son of James II., who was known in Rome as the
King of England, was a friend of Sister Crocifissa, and
learned from her to have a devotion to our saint.

CHAPTER XVI.

The Beatification—its history and celebration.

THE story of John's Beatification, its disheartening delays, its protracted suspensions, is like the story of most undertakings which God intends to bless in the end with success. It furnishes us with a strong proof of the care with which the Church proceeds before solemnly declaring the sanctity of her children, a declaration which no mere personal zeal or undue enthusiasm can bring about or precipitate. Father van Doorne wrote from Rome very soon after John's death, asking for details about his early life. To show how promptly the call was responded to, Father Emmerick, then parish priest of Tilbourg in Holland, before the close of September—in the very year of John's death—had received letters, urging him to give all the information he possessed, from Van Hulst, the then dean of Diest; from Father Otho Zylius, a near neighbour of Father Emmerick, rector of the Jesuit College of Bois-le-Duc; and from a young scholastic, Frederic Beyens, a former fellow novice of Berchmans, and a relative of the good Premonstratensian. Father Bauters, rector of the Jesuit College at Louvain—as Superior of so many who had known our saint, and himself once his novice-master—used every effort to collect materials, which he threw into the form of an interesting memoir, and which he put at the disposal of Father Cepari.[1] Two Belgian

[1] See p. 90.

scholastics of the Collegio Romano—Herman Horst and William van Aelst, old fellow novices of John—kept up an active correspondence with Father Bauters; while other Fathers kept Father Sucquet, the Belgian Provincial, *au courant* of any new facts. A petition for the introduction of the cause from some body corporate, or some personage of rank, is a necessary preliminary in a Beatification. The first petitioner, as we have already seen, was Philip de Ligne—Prince d'Aremberg of the Holy Roman Empire—so well known among the Catholic leaders of the time, who had, by his marriage with Anne de Croy, joined to his many titles and possessions the Dukedom of Aerschot. Aerschot is so near to Diest that he had a more than national pride in promoting the glory of his countryman. The first inquiry lasted for two years.

Meantime, Father Walter Clercq, rector of the Jesuit College at Antwerp, obtained from the bishop of that city leave to have a local inquiry; and before the Episcopal Commission some thirty-six witnesses deposed to John's heroic virtues. Among these, all his personal acquaintances, may be mentioned Father Adrian van der Cruyce (Crucius), who had been with him at Mechlin as socius to the master of novices, and master of the young Jesuit rhetoricians. His life of severe penance prepared him for the foreign missions which he constantly ambitioned, and the accounts of which, in the *Annual Letters* of 1619, he translated for the benefit of others. His prayer was refused, and he volunteered to serve the plague stricken. Nights spent in the sick ward never hindered his allotted hours of prayer. So God gave him the crown, in 1629, of a martyr of charity. Another was Father Cathens (or Cathij), who had won the degree of M.D. at Padua; and, after entering the Society, had laboured many years in his native Holland as a missionary priest, till he was recalled to lecture on Holy Scripture at Louvain, and then, while our saint was at Antwerp, on controversial theology in the College of that city. Adrian bargained with his brother, the parish priest of Ruremonde, not to be long separated from him by death, and, after a most holy and mortified life, followed him to the grave three months after his departure.

In 1625, Father General Vitelleschi appointed Father Cepari postulator of the cause. No one more fitted for the task could have been chosen, both by his intimate knowledge of Berchmans and by his experience in such matters. He was for twenty-five years engaged on the causes of St. Ignatius, St. Francis Borgia, St. Mary Magdalene of Pazzi, St. Aloysius, and St. Stanislaus, and on those of the Venerable Cardinal Bellarmine, Father Anchieta, and the Martyrs of Salsette. He had written a handbook for canonizations, and is cited by Benedict XIV. most approvingly in his great work on the subject. So overworked was he, that a Cardinal used to call him *il facchino*—porter—of canonizations; and Pope Urban VIII., who had forbidden religious in Rome to make use of carriages, made a special exception in his favour.

But that very Pontiff, though personally so indulgent to Father Cepari, rendered vain all his skill and knowledge by a decree of March 13, 1625, forbidding the Congregation of Rites to deal with the cause of any one until fifty years after death. Then Innocent XI., by a decree of October 15, 1678, threatened to put an end to the whole process, by ruling that the depositions of witnesses obtained apart from a juridical inquiry were simply of no legal value. This retrospective legislation was fatal to evidence obtained under a less severe *regime*, and the cause slumbered on the shelves of the archives till Benedict **XIV.** moderated the severity of the **Innocentian** decree, by giving to such informal evidence, provided it **bore clear** marks of authenticity, a subsidiary value in the discussion of the merits of a servant **of God.** Among the **signers of the** twenty-seven petitions **for the** resumption **of the** cause are great **and** historic names. Frederick Augustus of Saxony, **King of** Poland, and **claimant to** the Imperial crown, heads **the** list. There was **John V.** of **Portugal,** whose son, at the dictation of Pombal, was to **be so** fierce a persecutor of the Society of Jesus ; there was the heroic Maria Theresa, then, in **1743,** battling bravely in **face** of terrible odds, **to** place her husband, Francis I., on the Imperial **throne** ; and her **sister,** Mary Anne of Austria, Governess of the Low **Countries in** troublous times, whose husband was the renowned **but ill** starred general, Charles **of** Lorraine. The Cardinal Archbishop of Mechlin, his kinsman, petitioned with four of his suffragans, and supported the prayer of **the** University of Louvain and the town **of** Diest. **The cause** was re-opened, but **a** fresh difficulty arose. **The Congregation of** Rites required that **every scrap of writing of Berchmans should be sent to Rome. The regalist doctrines of the Court of Vienna made it practically impossible to publish the** necessary notifi-**cations, in** order to obtain prompt possession of these documents. **They had to be** got by private means, and **had** not the Pope at last, spite **of** the delay, authorized **the** introduction of the cause, the witnesses **of the** miracles, many of whom were **now of** great age, must have passed away, and their evidence would have been lost for ever. **By a** decree **of** September 11th, 1745, Benedict XIV. signed **a** commission for the introduction of the cause, and John henceforth bore the title of Venerable. A still more serious blow was soon to fall. The Suppression of the Society, the disturbances and wars of the French Revolution, made a long and dreary interlude. Peace once more restored, and with it the Society of Jesus, the cause was resumed. Again fresh delays, for three Cardinals to whom it had been intrusted died in succession, one after the other. At last, the great and good Cardinal Reisach, in 1861, was named procurator of the cause. Another name deserves mention with his, that of Father Boero, S.J., to whose zeal we chiefly owe the glorification of so many of his brethren, whom Pius IX. has raised on the altars of the Church. On the 3rd of May, 1865, our Holy Father went to the Greek College, to honour at the church dedicated to his name, the feast of the great doctor, St. Athanasius. It will occur to our readers that it was in that very College that John received the first stroke of his fatal illness.[2] Then the final decree was published, that 'it was safe to proceed to the solemn Beatification of the servant of God.'

Eight days later, His Holiness signed the Decree of the Beatification.[3]

On the 28th of the same month of May, a month so bright in southern countries, a month so well suited for the glorification of Mary's client, St. Peter's was astir. A great banner over the central entrance represented the triumph of him whose name was to be registered that day in the golden book of the Church's nobility. Within, palely shining in the sunlight which streamed in, spite of half-veiled windows, were nine stars—clusters of burning candles, forming the crown of a veiled picture placed in the apse of the vast Basilica. From the dome a gigantic monogram, I.H.S., written in lines of light, was suspended in mid air. Round the choir were five paintings, the subjects of which were taken from the life and miracles of John.

[2] See p. 234.   [3] See Appendix.

U

By ten o'clock, an august audience was gathered within its walls. The members of the Congregation of Rites, the chapter and clergy of St. Peter's, and bishops, priests, nobles, and religious of Catholic Belgium were there. Three names deserve special mention. The venerable Cardinal Primate, Mgr. Sterckx, the Archbishop of Mechlin ; Mgr. Merode, whose family is so nearly connected with the d'Arembergs, whose ancestor, Philip Duke d'Aerschot, did so much for the Beatification ; and a young Jesuit scholastic who bore the name and was of the family of John's mother, Brother vanden Hove. Another countryman of our saint, a native of Sichem, the nearest village to Diest, Father Beckx, the venerable Father General of the Society of Jesus, stepped forward, and in the name of the order of which he is the head, implored the Cardinal Patrizi, as Prefect of the Congregation of Rites, to proceed to the solemn Beatification. He alluded specially to the help that such an act would give to Catholic youth, exposed as it is now-a-days on every side to the attacks of irreligion and immorality.

The prayer was granted; the decree was solemnly promulgated. The Church had another protector, Belgium a modern saint, and the Society had completed the angelic triad of Stanislaus, Aloysius, and John. The veil fell from the picture, and the humble religious appeared in the centre of Christendom, wearing his new honours, the aureole of saintliness. The *Te Deum* rose from the multitude around, and the boom of the artillery of St. Angelo told the news to those outside. To Mgr. Merode, as deacon, was reserved the privilege of being the first to intone the versicle of the saint, and then Mgr. Vitelleschi—the name of one of whose family has occurred so frequently in these pages—recited the prayer. 'O God, Who didst make the marvellous holiness of Blessed John, Thy confessor, to consist in perfect keeping of regular discipline and in innocence of life, grant, through his merits and prayers, that we may attain purity of mind and body by faithfully carrying out the commandments of Thy law. Through our Lord Jesus Christ.' Then followed the celebration of the Holy Sacrifice, the first offered in honour of Blessed Berchmans.

The illumination shone out again in the subdued light of evening to welcome the Sovereign Pontiff, who came to pay his homage to the newly crowned saint. Thrice and most reverently did he imprint a kiss on the relics of Berchmans, which Father Beckx brought to the *prie-dieu* at which he was kneeling. The treasure was then presented to him, and he stayed for some time in lengthened prayer to him whom he had glorified.

CHAPTER XVII.

John Berchmans' relics.

A SHORT chapter must be written on what the storms
and troubles of two centuries have left us of the relics of
our saint. We do not pretend to a full and complete
catalogue. Rather, after speaking of his blessed body,
we shall allude to some of those best known in Rome
and in Belgium.

Berchmans' remains were not allowed long to remain
in their place of honour. Father Vitelleschi, unable
to put a stop to the indiscreet cultus of which it was
the object, had the remains transported, not many
days after burial, to the common vaults of the Roman
College.

When Cardinal Ludovisi's new church was begun, it
was again necessary that they should be removed. The
wooden coffin had all fallen to pieces. The bones, the
dust, the fragments of the dress, even what remained
of the coffin, were most carefully collected, and placed,
with the inscription which had been left with the body,
within a leaden coffin.

It was laid in the old chapel of the Three Kings,
where now is the chapel of St. Joseph, for a long time the
resting-place of St. Aloysius, and there it stayed until
finally deposited in the common vault of the new church,
where it was put apart under the picture of the Madonna
della Pieta.

In 1639, Father Francis Piccolomini, being the rector of the College, in consequence of the many miracles wrought at John's intercession, determined to verify what the stringent efforts to keep his relics in oblivion must have made to be forgotten, whether his body really was laid where report stated. On opening the leaden coffin, the inscription dispelled all doubt. The skeleton was complete, with the exception of some teeth, fingers, and toes, and a few smaller bones. The relics, wrapped in a shroud, were deposited again in the coffin, which had been thoroughly repaired, and the rector affixed his official seal, while a *procès verbal* was drawn up on the subject. Amongst its other signatures was that of Father Galluzzi, our saint's professor of ethics.

Father Casotti, the successor of Father Piccolomini as rector of the Roman College, fearing lest the extraneous matter left in the coffin should affect the bones, caused it to be separated from them by a medical man, assisted by the sacristan, and placed in glass vessels, with a careful description of their contents. The bones were put into a wooden case, covered with copper.

Father Giovagnoli, then professor of controversy at the German College, describes it, in 1750, as inclosed in a sarcophagus of travertine, and raised upon a pedestal, and says that whenever the vault was reopened for a burial, members of the community crowded down to kiss the sacred tomb. The spot was marked, in the pavement above, in front of the high altar, by a slab of porphyry, bearing the inscription, *Ossa Venerabilis Joannis Berchmans, Societatis Jesu.*

And thus was it found in 1865. It was the 11th of May, two days after the Brief of Beatification had been signed. Members of various Colleges, persons of position, were there. In the afternoon, the coffin, placed

on a richly adorned bier, was brought up from the vault.
The scholastics of the Society, engaged in the study of
philosophy, had their place, by right, as the *cortège* of the
precious relics, clad in cottas, with lights in their hands,
while the remains were carried by four of the professors.
Cardinal Reisach, the Bishop of Montreal, the **Father
General of the Society, and a** large **number** followed.
The path was strewn with flowers.

The chapel of St. Rosalia, belonging to the **confraternity of the students in philosophy,** was the place **of**
verification. Mgr. Minetti, the Promoter of the Faith,
forbade, under pain of censures, that any portion of
the remains should be removed ; **and then the** copper
covering was torn off, and the coffin opened, and the
bones exposed to view. They were laid **out on a** table
by two medical men, who examined them, dictating all
the while an accurate account of them to the notary
who was present.

The skull was well preserved. It presented a facial
angle above the average, the face seemed to have been
long and oval. The saint was tall, rather than short, and
of a delicate, but not a feeble frame. The *procès verbal*
was drawn up and signed, and the doors were locked
and sealed. The next day, Mgr. Minetti placed the
larger relics in one chest, and the smaller ones in
another, sealing them up with care.

On the occasion of the Beatification, severel bones
were taken out to be sent to Belgium. When Canon
Froymont heard that John's heart had been brought
from Rome, he wrote at once to beg Father General
to make him a present of some relic of his venerated
pupil. We can readily understand, as Father Vitelleschi
wrote back, in a letter full of sincere regrets, that such a
request could not possibly be then complied with. ‘ But
if any time, as I well hope,’ he goes on to say, ‘ it shall

please Divine Providence to prove the virtue of the holy youth by such clear signs that the Holy See will allow him openly to be honoured as Blessed, I will most willingly do what now, with such pain, I am forced to deny to your Reverence.' The promise was at length fulfilled by Father Vitelleschi's successor. Father Beckx sent one of the arm-bones to his old professor, the Cardinal Archbishop of Mechlin; and its reception in that metropolitan town was the occasion of splendid *fêtes*, and lengthened processions, which went round the streets so often trod by John when a boy and a novice. Finally, the precious relic was laid in the altar in the northern aisle of the choir of the Cathedral, within the sound of whose bells he had dwelt for part of four years.

A vertebra of the saint was given to the church of the Society in Brussels. The General sent another to the faithful town of Diest. And there it rests in an exquisite shrine, in the old parish church of St. Sulpice, in a chapel where John loved to pray, for it was the Lady altar, and where he used to serve at Mass. And the piety of the dean, and the zeal of his townsmen, have made its old walls and graceful windows glow with the best inspirations of Flemish art.

But there is another relic more touching than these. With permission, no doubt fully satisfying to himself, Father van Doorne brought back from Rome the heart of his young countryman, whom he had loved and venerated during his stay at Rome. There was with him, as companion of his journey, a Flemish Father ordained more than a year before, Andrew Hellin. Such was the fame of John's sanctity that the relic was venerated by the Fathers at the different houses, on bended knees, as though it were of a saint already beatified. On their way home they passed through

Roanne.   As they talked to the rector of the College of the Society there about the death and funeral of the saint, he recognized by their description what he had heard from a holy lady in that place.   Like Margaret Rossi, of Modena,[1] she had supernaturally seen the figure of a cleric, in cotta and biretta, laid out before the altar of a church unknown to her, and had learnt that the soul of the youth was enjoying in heaven the same reward that St. Aloysius had obtained, for their merits had been equal on earth.   At first she had thought the vision referred to a lay-brother whom she had known in that College; but the rector, to whom she told all, assured her the brother was still living. Just while the strangers were wondering at the coincidence, an earnest message arrived from that very lady requiring the immediate attendance of the rector, who was her confessor.   He found her overwhelmed with spiritual trouble; he told her the news, and what a precious treasure the Belgian Fathers had brought.   She begged to be allowed to venerate the relic, and the moment she reverently pressed it to her lips the clouds lifted from her soul, and she was filled with the deepest peace. She repeated to Father van Doorne the story she had told the rector.   She hastened to the church to thank God for this new favour, and a voice told her clearly, 'This is the heart of the young man whom you saw.' She wished to tell the rector of this new intimation, but feared he would laugh at her importunity, and the evening was drawing on.   However, she felt unable to take a step towards her house.   Just then the rector happened to pass, and when her story was told she found no further difficulty, and hastened home.   There she again began to pray, and received from heaven a still more distinct knowledge of the saint's glory; and

____

[1] See p. 291.

had a proof of his power in a grace which she at that moment obtained through his intercession, but which till then she had sought in vain. The letter written from Roanne with this strange history is still in the archives of the Society at Rome.

Towards the close of November, 1621, the two travellers reached the Theologate of Louvain. The rector was Father William Bauters, the old novice-master of John ; and among the students were many who had been his fellow novices. One can easily imagine that, as the news of all that had passed at Rome had gone before, the utmost enthusiasm prevailed at the sight of the relic ; and we are not surprised, in days when the regulations of the Congregation of Rites were not as severe as they have since become, that public honour was paid to it. Father van Doorne, pleased at this reception, decided to make it over to the College, and left it with the following document which is still preserved in the archives.

'I, the undersigned, declare that I received the heart of John Berchmans, of pious and blessed memory, from the Reverend Father Virgil Cepari, rector of the Roman College, and that I have given the same to the College of the Society at Louvain, as a mark of my esteem, and as a motive to excite the piety of the students, both of theology and philosophy. And I beg our Lord Jesus, by the merits of His servant, to deign to regard favourably that College.

'MARK VAN DOORNE.

'*Louvain, November* 29, 1621.'

It must have been somewhere about this time, that the venerable Father Lessius, lying in the College under the most excruciating tortures of his last illness, refused to seek miraculous alleviation from the relic of his departed brother in religion. And yet he asked a public penance from the minister for his impatience under suffering.

Father Sucquet, the first novice-master of John, was then Provincial. He considered Mechlin had the first claim to this relic. At the same time he disapproved of this premature cultus, and wished to put a stop to it. Father Bauters very naturally urged the claims of possession, and the Provincial, unwilling to act hastily, referred the matter to the General. The Fathers and community at Mechlin supported his letter by promises of prayers and penances, to be offered up if Father Vitelleschi would confirm the decision of the Provincial. Father Bauters did not write, he felt sure of the justice of his Superiors, and though urged to do so, awaited his award in silence.

The General did not long delay. This was his answer—

'Reverend Father in Christ,—Your Reverence will understand, from what I am going to say, how displeased I have been at Father Van Doorne's taking the heart of Brother John Berchmans without my knowledge to Belgium, and at its being received at Louvain with such pomp and rejoicing, as could hardly have been exceeded if he had been already beatified by the Apostolic See. Time will not allow me to answer the other points of your letter, but to this I desire to reply, putting off all the others, though they too demand an answer. I wish then that you look to it with all promptitude and zeal, that henceforth no external honour be paid to the heart or relics of this brother, either by ours or by externs, until you hear different from me. When, then, you receive this, please to see that the heart of John be put out of sight, whether at Louvain or elsewhere, in such a way that it may neither be seen or touched by ours or by others, nay, you must take pains that no one may know where it has been put, until I shall have given express permission to the contrary. To let you see how exact I wish your Reverence to be in this affair, I assure you, unless I was confident that on receipt of my wishes you will carry out all most precisely, I should have ordered you to do so under holy obedience. Your Reverence must take care also that none of your subjects send any account about this brother, whether to Rome or elsewhere, except to myself only. See to what the intemperate fervour of ours has driven me! For I consider it must be checked in the way I have just written, unless we wish to damage ourselves and the good name of the Society. And that this may not be I again earnestly urge your Reverence.

'Muzio Vitelleschi.

'*Rome, January 15th, 1622.*

The prohibition of the General against the publication of any writings about Berchmans was made known by Father Sucquet to his province, in a letter addressed March 27th, 1622. At the same time the relic was withdrawn from sight, and probably removed to Mechlin. The scholastics of Louvain kept the first anniversary of his death in a sort of family way, and one of their number pronounced his panegyric in the refectory.

In 1623, by a letter to Father Bauters, dated the 21st of February, the General relaxed his severity after a careful investigation of the case, and allowed the precious charge to be restored to Louvain, on condition that it be kept in a private chapel, and never be taken out to any one not a member of the Society.

In a letter of Father Bauters, addressed probably to Father de Montmorency,[2] the new Provincial, after reciting the permission of the General, he goes on to say, 'I do not permit the heart to be taken to externs, and I even conceal it by closing a wooden door when strangers come to the chapel. All the while it receives honour from Christ with very great profit and a fruit to souls, sometimes quite miraculous.' He then tells the story of what had passed with Father Sucquet, and trusts his conduct will meet the Provincial's approval. An exception seems to have been made in favour of a niece of Berchmans, Jane de Roecke, then a béguine at Mechlin, who went to Louvain expressly to honour the relic of her uncle. She was the daughter of the ill-fated Mary, sister of our saint.[3]

In 1747, on the 11th of July, the Cardinal of Alsace paid a visit to the heart. It was then surrounded with rays of copper and silver gilt. Though a petitioner for John's Beatification, he not only ordered these signs of honour to be removed, but insisted on the relic being again hidden away in conformity with the severe prescriptions of the Congregation of Rites. When the sad day of the suppression came, Father Cornelius Geerts, an ex-Jesuit, obtained possession of it and kept it sacredly with many other things, in the sure hope that the Society would rise again. In 1818 he hastened to

---

[2] Father Florence, who besides being Provincial of Flanders, was twice Superior of the French-Belgian province, was the third son of Louis Montmorency, the head of the Belgian branch of the French Constable's family. The unfortunate Count Horn was a Montmorency, but Father Florence's family were faithful to the Spanish cause. Louis was killed after storming the lower town of Ostende, during the memorable siege of 1602—1604. He left four sons, Francis and Florence, who became Jesuits, and Anthony, who entered the Order of St. Benedict, while John, who was created Prince of Robecque by the Spanish King, succeeded to the fortune and honours of his line.

[3] See p. 9.

give it back to Father le Blanc, the rector of the only house of the Jesuits then in Flanders, the old convent of Oost-Eecloo at Ghent. In due time on the removal of the Scholasticate to Louvain, the sacred relic came once more to the town, though not to the old College, where it had remained so long.[4] Subjected to a fresh examination in 1865, it was placed in a massive silver reliquary. It is now preserved in the sacristy, and on certain days is exposed in the new church of the College of the Society.

The College of Antwerp possesses a sleeve of John's cassock, brought from Rome by Father James de la Roo,[5] who had been cured of stone by putting it on while on his way home. Father James left this portion of it at the Novitiate of Mechlin in 1624. In the Church of Notre Dame in Antwerp, enshrined over an altar dedicated to our saint, is a shirt, which is in all probability the one in which he died, and of which an account is left in a copy existing in the Brussels archives. Father Philip Alegambe, the historiographer of the Society and fellow student of John had received it in 1621 from Father van Doorne, on condition that if on completing his studies he should be sent elsewhere than to Belgium, he should make it over to some College of that province. After studying theology under Father Lugo, he was sent to Austria, where he was for many years professor at Gratz, only returning to Rome in 1638 as confessor to

---

[4] The second College of the Society had been pulled down after the suppression, and nothing of it left but the church and a gable end of the house. Its site is now occupied by the College Marie Thérèse. The house of studies was first established after the restoration of the Society, at the old Dutch College, once the home of Jansenius, and then in its present place, the ancient refuge of the College of Vlierbeke, opposite to what once was the Franciscan house, in the Rue des Recollets.

[5] There were two of Berchmans' fellow novices of the same name, one called Giles, the other Remigius.

his former pupil, Prince Eggenberg, Imperial Ambassador to the Pope, where he spent the remaining fourteen years of his life.[6] Before starting for Styria he destined the relic he held so precious for the College of the Society at Brussels.

The Gesù at Rome keeps among its many treasures John's vow to defend the doctrine of the Immaculate Conception, signed by his blood, some of his letters, and a Latin elegy, perhaps one of those spoken of above. There is besides a little sermonette, preached by him when a child, before a Christmas crib. At St. Andrea, in the rooms leading to that wherein St. Stanislaus expired, is his note-book on the lectures of philosophy, and a draft of his letter from Rome to one of his *confreres* in Belgium.[7] The Bollandists' library at Brussels has his letter announcing his near departure from Antwerp for Rome.[8]

But of all, the most interesting collection is that preserved at the College of Louvain. In a close and neat hand, we have the notes on Rodriguez, the stories about the Blessed Sacrament and our Lady, and about Persons and Things of the Society. These have all been published by Father Vanderspeeten.[9] The love of poverty which prompted the writer to emulate Father Sacchini, one of the historians of the Society, in using his pens to the last, has made the ink so abundant as to eat into and threaten destruction to the frail pages. One page is headed *Ex tomis Alvarez de Paz*, as though he had once intended to jot down sayings and thoughts from his favourite author. In addition to this collection, the two prints already described[10] are also inserted. The little book is bound in red morocco, and bears the blazon of the Society of Jesus.

[6] See p. 84.   [7] See p. 225.   [8] See p. 87.

[9] *B. J. Berchmans, S.J., Spicilegium Asceticum.* Lovanii, 1868.

[10] See p. 157.

This relic had fallen to the lot of Father Horace Grassi, the former professor of our saint, and who had the direction of his interment.

Nothing remains now but to speak of the last translation of John's sacred remains.

The simple cell which tradition records at one time to have been occupied by him was in the same corridor as that which was once the room, and is now the cappelletta, of St. Aloysius. There is but one cell between them, which now serves as a sacristy for both. The little room, so poor and bare when John lived in it, is now bright with rich silken hangings which cover its walls, with gilding and with carving. Over the altar is a copy of a portrait in the Benedictine convent of Campo Marzo, not far from the Corso. There is a tradition that the saint, when in heaven, had retouched this painting, in answer to the simple prayer of a nun, who had asked him whether it were like him or no.

Beneath the altar is an urn containing the coffin in which his sacred remains had so long reposed, and within that again is a vase filled with the ashes of the saint. Other valuable relics, such as his hat, part of one of his habits, fragments found in his coffin, the notes of St. Aloysius on the lectures of Father Vasquez on Penance, the crown of thorns worn by the Venerable Father Baldinucci, and other memorials of holy members of the Society, are stored in that sacred place.

The first feast of the Blessed was drawing near, and the students and community of the Roman College determined to celebrate with all pomp at once the translation and the first festival of him who added a new glory to that great Seminary of learning and sanctity. The urn of lapis-lazuli was not completed, but a temporary shrine was made ready under the altar of the Annunciation, where the body was to rest. There

is a sad contrast springs up before us between what was
then and is now, when the halls of the Alma Mater are
profaned by the shallow and irreligious teaching of the
Government masters of new Italy, and are made a
schola erroris, where youth is taught to mock at and
detest all that before was held in veneration. On the
10th of August, 1865, the Church of St. Ignatius was
most gloriously decked out, its fair proportions not concealed, but heightened by hangings of crimson velvet,
scarlet stuffs, gold and silver cloth. More than three
thousand tapers, defining arch and cornice, were placed
round the building in a triple line of lustres, all converg-
ing to the great apse, where, in a painting, John appeared
rising heavenward on a lightly floating cloud, as though he
were hastening to the embraces of his Father, St. Ignatius,
who, in Father Pozzi's fresco, is looking down from
the heavenly choirs in the vaulting above. The grave
quadrangle of the College, too, was draped and adorned,
and its severe and brick-paved cloisters made bright with
storied tapestries from the Barberini Palace and with lights
and flowers. In the *aula massima*, the great hall where
John held his thesis, the ceremonies began. The shrine
that held his remains was there, and round about it
were gathered the students, taper or torch in hand.

The *Te Deum* was intoned ; and nearly a thousand
persons, between scholastics and religious, set out in
procession towards the church, Mgr. Vitelleschi being
the celebrant. The shrine was borne by four professors
of philosophy, in dalmatics, eight other professors supported the tasselled cords, while eight parish priests
of Rome, formerly students in the College, walked on
either side. So the body, or what remained of it, was
carried through the passages it had so often trod in life,
down to the church, and through the aisles and up
the nave, to the high altar, and thence to its final

resting-place in the **north** transept, **as we may** best describe the lateral **chapel**; and there, **under the Lady altar,** facing **the altar tomb** of St. Aloysius, **his brother and imitator** reposes.   **The tomb, which has just been** completed, **is like that of** St. Aloysius **in form and** material—an **urn of lapis-lazuli,** wreathed **with silver lilies and roses, and bearing on its** front **a** silver **medallion** representing John **in the** act of receiving **holy** Viaticum; **a** boy-angel, **in** Parian marble, kneels **on either** side, one with the book of rules, and **a** crucifix with **a rosary entwined;** while the other recalls the vow **of the saint in honour of** the Immaculate Conception. **And round about the altar are** gathered many **votive offerings, telling of the love** and veneration that the **lowly virtues of the perfect youth attract.**

A second translation took place **on Saturday, the 16th of** August, **1873, after the completion of the tomb, with a pomp not unlike that which we have** described, **contrasting strangely with the 'sad look of** things **without.'**

There, **then, henceforth,** unless sacrilege disturbs them—**near to each other, and that** most fittingly— lie the sacred remains **of the two** sainted brothers **in** religious life.   The model and the faithful imitator, the **patron and** his most worthy client, **are presented** together **to the veneration of** the faithful, **and as special** teachers **and guides of** youth—presented together, **because God has so willed it ; and it needs no divided love to honour** them **both.**

The devotion to St. Aloysius **is only increased by** the glory which **is reflected back** upon him by his blessed counterpart.   **Nor is the life of** John wanting in lessons which tend to give solidity and meaning **to that devotion.** Aloysius **first attracts and rivets by the supernatural** lustre **of his virtue ;**—Berchmans **shows the best and**

Y

safest way to aim at its imitation. The imaginative
are guarded by his example against illusion ; they are
taught the price they must pay to build up so high a
tower of perfection. The timid, who are scared by the
very height of St. Aloysius' sanctity, are roused and
encouraged to follow in the footsteps of John ; for he
teaches us that heroic virtue may be attained even in
the ways of ordinary life.

And all may learn from him that the secret of
success in God's service, as in everyday labour, is
magni facere minima—' to make great account of small
things.'

APPENDIX.

*I.—List of students **at the** English College, Rome, contemporaries of **John** Berchmans, with dates of their entrance.*

1613.

Armstrong, John (alias Strange). **On April 29,** 1620, he received **at Rome all the minor orders.**

1614.

Ward, William (*alias* Ingilby), born in Yorkshire, 1590 ; entered College **Oct.** 4 ; was ordained priest April 29, 1618 ; died in Ireland about 1645.

1615.

Castleton, William **(*alias* Ward, *alias* John Compton), born** in Norfolk 1595 ; studied **logic** at Valladolid. He entered College June 8, was ordained priest Sept. 29, 1618, and **was** sent to England April 29, 1620.

Ann, George (*alias* Anger), born in Yorkshire 1595 ; a. m. ões ord:=d.[1] May 6, 1621.

Vavasour, Henry (*alias* Mannarey), born in Yorkshire **1597 ;** entered College as a convictor Oct. **25, and took the** College oath May **1, 1619.** He left for England on account of health July **12, 1620.**

Green, John (*alias* White, **alias** Wakeman), born in Staffordshire, 1597 ; entered College **Oct. 27 ;** was ordained priest Dec. **19, 1620.** He made great progress in learning and virtue, and left for England April 14, **1622.**

1616.

Constable, Michael (*alias* Rostell, Russell ?), born in Yorkshire 1598 ; entered College **Oct. 8 as** a convictor. Being recalled by his father he left Rome July 12, 1620.

---

[1] **These** letters and abbreviations **are** copied **from Father** Thorpe's catalogue. We leave the discovery of their meaning to **the curious.**

Pole, Henry (*alias* Francis Layton), born in Derbyshire 1595; entered College Oct. 13; received minor orders June 4, 1617, and, owing to weakness of the head, left Rome on May 6, 1621, to escape the great heats.

Harvey, Giles (*alias* Mico), was ordained priest, and left in 1620 to enter the Society. In 1623 he returned to Rome to be English penitentiary at St. Peter's, and was then made minister at the English College, whose library was begun by him. He succeeded Father Risdon as procurator and agent for the Society, and died at Rome Oct. 22, 1647.

Strange, Thomas, defended a thesis, *De Sacramento Pœnitentiæ*, at the Roman College in 1619, a copy of which is in the library of Mount St. Mary's College, near Chesterfield.

1617.

Sulyard, Rodolph (*alias* Sutton), born in Suffolk on Feb. 2, 1598; entered the College as a convictor Sept. 29. He left on account of his health April 1, 1620, having won great esteem on account of his kindliness.

Huddleston, John (*alias* Bornet), born 1596; entered as a convictor Sept. 29. Feb. 14, 1620, he left for England on family business, but returned on May 22 the following year. He was ordained priest August 10, 1621 (just three days before John's death), and was sent to England on Sept. 12, 1624. He entered the Society in 1627 at Watten.

Bacon, Nathaniel (*alias* Southwell),[2] born in Norfolk April 14, 1598; entered College on Oct. 8. He was ordained priest on Dec. 21, 1622, and left Rome for the English mission with John Dormer *circ.* 1623. He was received into the Society *circ.* 1624, and, returning to Rome, he succeeded Father Coleford[3] as minister at the English College in 1627, where he began the diary from which this list is copied.

Walpole, Christopher (*alias* Warner), born in Norfolk April 30, 1598; entered College as an alumnus on Oct. 11; was ordained priest May 16, 1622, and sent to England June 19, 1624.

Dormer, John, was born in London 1598. He entered the Society in 1625, and died in England, after many years of missionary life, in 1661.

[2] See p. 278.   [3] See p. 133.

1618.

Morse, Henry, the illustrious martyr, born in Norfolk 1596. After being ordained priest he left for the mission in June, 1624. During his six years of philosophy and theology he made great progress in virtue and learning, and was specially noted for his modesty. He made his noviceship for the Society in York Castle, under his fellow-prisoner, Father Robinson, who was also an old student of the English College, having entered in 1616, and who was thirteen years in chains for the faith, and once condemned to death, but afterwards reprieved. Father Morse was executed on Feb. 1, 1645.

Neville, Thomas (*alias* Appleton), born in Kent, 1598, Entered the College as a convictor. He defended a thesis in philosophy before Cardinal Alexander Orsini in 1620. After receiving minor orders he left for England. He returned later on, was ordained priest, and entered the Society.

Courtenay, Edward, born in Sussex. He defended a thesis, *De Universâ Philosophiâ*, before the great Cardinal Bentivoglio, the very year, 1621, that John went through the same ordeal ; and, on August 28, entered the Society at Rome. He was famed as a classical scholar, and was in after life rector at Liège, St. Omers, and of the English College at Rome. He died in 1677.

1618.

Clark, William, d.
Haughton, William, d.
Cater, Francis, convictor ; entered the Society of Jesus.
Wild, George, d.
Persy, William, died in the College.
Leeds, Edward, entered the Society.
Forster, John, d.
Gifford, Edward, entered the Society.
Bamford, Thomas, d.
Evans, Humphrey, m.
Foyle, Francis, convictor ; d.

1619.

Bedingfield, Henry.
Harris, Francis, d.

Alan, George, m.
Shelley, Anthony, d.
Taylor, Thomas, a.
Pulton, Thomas, entered the Society.
Taylor, John, d.
Harper, Thomas, d.
Travers, Edward, d.
Fitten, Peter (*alias* Biddulph), d.
Fortescue, William (*alias* Talbot), from Bucks ; entered as a convictor Nov. 23 ; left for England Sept. 21, 1620, but fell ill at Loreto, and returned to Rome in November of the same year, leaving finally on April 16, 1521.
Petre, Robert, c. d.
Owen, Thomas, d.

1620.

Wilson, Simon, entered the Society.
Taylor, Henry, d.
Stephenson, Cyprian (*alias* Ringby), born in London Dec. 26, 1600 ; ordained deacon at St. Onofrio Dec. 15, 1614, and priest at St. John Lateran's Dec. 21 the same year. He died as calmly as he had always lived, in the College, Sept. 13, 1626.
Salvin, Ralph (*alias* Smyth), from Durham county ; born 1600 ; entered the English College as alumnus, ordained priest Dec. 21, 1624, and entered the Society on April 25, 1625, at St. Andrea, but left for Watten, the English Novitiate in West Flanders, on May 4, where he finished his noviceship. He appears to be the son of Gerard Salvin, Esq., of Croxdale, whose will was signed at Paris Aug. 8, 1625.
Harris, Edward.
Rookwood, Robert (*alias* Rowley), m., born in Suffolk 1588, was ordained priest Dec. 28, 1621, and left for England Sept. 21, 1626.
Hoskins, Anthony (*alias* Perkins), d.
Scoble, John, S. Born in Devonshire, 1601 ; ordained priest Dec. 21, 1624 ; and died on his way home at Reggio, in 1626.
Downes, Edmund, entered the Society.

II.—*Brief of Beatification of John Berchmans.*

PIUS IX. POPE.

FOR A PERPETUAL MEMORIAL.

As youth is a kind of foundation for manhood, and as men do not without great difficulty in after life turn themselves from the path upon which they have travelled from their earliest years, therefore that there might be no excuse on the score of age or strength for swerving from the path of virtue it has been arranged by the all-wise providence of God that there should flourish from time to time in the Church some one youth eminent for sanctity, on whom that high eulogium might be passed—'Made perfect in a short space, he fulfilled a long time'—who abundantly compensated for the short span of his life by the greatness of his merits, and excited others to the imitation of his virtues. Among such may be rightly numbered the Venerable John Berchmans, scholastic of the Society of Jesus, who strove so vigorously to guard his baptismal innocence unsullied, and adorned his soul with such an abundance of virtues, that he seems to have shone forth as a new star to illumine the whole Church, and more especially the religious order of which he was a member. He was born in the town of Diest in Brabant, of parents not distinguished by rank or fortune, but conspicuous for religious zeal, and was by them trained to every virtue. The child, being blessed with an excellent disposition, amply repaid them for their solicitude. For to a degree quite beyond his years he became distinguished for the gravity of his manners; never did he give any trouble, nor seek amusement in the sports common to children; but it was his delight to be constantly in the church, and to withdraw himself from intercourse with his companions, in order to betake himself to solitude, and there turn his soul to the contemplation of divine things. He had attained his eleventh year when he was admitted for the first time to the Holy Table, and so great was the ardour of his love when he approached to receive the most sacred Body of Christ that the whole countenance of this most chaste youth glowed with the divine fire. Being sent to college to study the rudiments of literature, piety no less than letters became the object of his endeavours, so that as often as his fellow-students cast their eyes upon him, they were excited as by some silent monitor to the love of purity, modesty, and every kind of virtue. To bind himself more closely to the service of God, he asked and obtained his father's consent to enrol himself among the number of the clergy. Three years afterwards, however, he heard that his father, on account of his narrow fortune, had determined to apply him to some trade in order to have his help in obtaining the means of subsistence. News such as this was sad and afflicting for John ; he began to implore his father not to withdraw him from the ecclesiastical profession which he had so eagerly embraced. He declared that he had cast aside all anxiety for temporal interests, and rested all his hopes upon Divine Providence. Having obtained his wish, he proceeded to put the finish to his literary studies, and to press on with alacrity in the path of virtue upon which he had entered ; and therefore, as he saw his innocence surrounded by very many dangers, in order to place it in safety, in imitation of St. Aloysius Gonzaga, whose life he had long and deeply pondered, having weighed the matter well and implored the assistance of heaven, he determined to give himself to the Society of Jesus. And indeed the particular form of life followed by that religious order was above all others pleasing to this innocent youth, who was all on fire with love for his neighbour, because he felt certain that by embracing it an opportunity would be given him of passing to the remotest parts of the earth to pour the light of faith upon barbarous nations. Long and earnestly had John to struggle to gain the consent of his parents, who placed their hopes and those of their family on their son, and that all the more, as they saw him endowed with such great virtue.

At length, having obtained the desired leave, he was received into the Society at Mechlin, in the seventeenth year of his age. He entered it as a haven of security and rest, and gave himself forthwith to that more perfect course of life, which all can esteem and admire, but very few take up and follow. Indeed, he shone as a most perfect model of every virtue, not only for novices, but even for the more advanced among his brethren. Beginning with humility, which is as the root of all other virtues, full of a mean opinion of himself, he performed the lowliest offices with alacrity. Meek and gentle towards others, but stern and severe towards himself, he often scourged his tender body, and he used to take so little food, that it scarce seemed sufficient to sustain and recruit his strength. The very slightest rules of religious discipline he observed and guarded with the greatest care ; he did not allow the smallest particle of time to pass in idleness, but spent all usefully either in reading, or praying, or conversing upon spiritual things. Nothing delighted him more than to turn his heart and soul to God as to a most loving Father. In meditating upon Him and paying his homage to Him, so great was the ardour of love with which he burned, that his heart was too narrow to contain its noble flame. The most Blessed Virgin Mother of God he honoured with every mark of devotion—even from his earliest years he chose her for his heavenly Patroness to guard for him the flower of his virginity. The two years of his novitiate being completed, he was admitted to the simple vows, which he pronounced all the more fervently because he knew that by these vows he was to consecrate himself irrevocably to God. He was then sent to Antwerp, and afterwards to Rome, to give himself to the study of philosophy. Nor indeed could anything have been more to his liking than to live in the city which is the chief seat and the bulwark of the Catholic religion, where he could pay his homage to the sacred remains of the Princes of the Apostles, as also to the tombs of his Father St. Ignatius and St. Aloysius Gonzaga, in whose footsteps he was walking. And so he came to the Roman College to study philosophy, and led such a life there that the heavenly youth Aloysius, by whose virtues that house had been ennobled, almost seemed to have returned again to life. At length, ripe for heaven, he was attacked by a sickness, which, though trifling at first, grew worse and worse, until it caused his death on the 13th of August, in the year 1621, before he had completed his twenty-third year.

Virtue so eminent and so constant as his, could not fail to draw the attention of all, so that his reputation for sanctity which had been gaining ground during his life-time, increased and spread all the more after the chaste youth had exchanged this mortal life for a more blessed one. Wherefore, according to custom, an account of his life and virtues was drawn up at Antwerp and at Rome, to the end that an inquiry into the heroic degree of his virtues might afterwards be instituted by authority of the Holy See. But his cause was interrupted for a long time, until it was called to life again by the report of the miracles by which God seemed to have proclaimed the sanctity of His servant. Therefore, under Pope Gregory XVI., our predecessor, after the arrangement of such preliminaries as were necessary in a case of this kind, in the Congregation of Cardinals charged with the care of Sacred Rites, an inquiry was set on foot into the virtues for which the Venerable John had been eminent, and these our predecessor, the same Pope Gregory XVI., with the assent of the said Congregation, on the 5th of June, in the year 1843, declared to have reached an heroic height. Next followed an examination of the miracles which were said to have been wrought by God through the intercession of His venerable servant, John Berchmans. All the circumstances being weighed and considered with the greatest care by the judges, three were found to be true and indubitable miracles ; and We, after imploring the help of heaven, at length on the 27th of February of the present year 1865, published a decree concerning the truth of the said three miracles ; and We allowed further measures to be taken without the necessity of an examination of any other miracles.

This alone remained ; to ask the Cardinals of the aforesaid Congregation whether in their opinion it were safe to decree the honours of the Blessed to the Venerable John. Wherefore on the 8th of April of the present year, the same Congregation of Cardinals assembled before Us, after taking the votes of the Consultors, were unanimous in their opinion that the Venerable John might be declared Blessed, with all the usual privileges, until the solemn ceremony of his Canonization should be performed. We then, having implored assistance from the heavenly Father of Lights, published a decree on the matter on the 2nd of May of the current year.

Now in order that in this degenerate age We may propose to the young, surrounded as they are by so many snares laid by perfidious men, a perfect model for their imitation, and that We may find for them in heaven a patron, by whose aid and under whose protection they may come forth from these snares unscathed; moved moreover thereunto by the prayers of the whole Society of Jesus, by the advice and with the consent of the aforesaid Congregation, of Our Apostolic authority, by virtue of these letters, We grant permission that the venerable servant of God, John Berchmans, be called hereafter by the name of Blessed, and that his relics be exposed for the public veneration of the faithful (though they are not to be carried in public processions), and that his picture be surrounded with rays of glory. Moreover, by Our authority We allow a yearly Office to be said in his honour, and a Mass of the Common of Confessors to be celebrated with proper prayers approved of by Us, according to the Rubrics of the Roman Missal and Breviary. The recital of this Office, and the celebration of the Mass, We allow only at Rome and within its district, in the diocese of Mechlin, and in all churches and religious houses of the Society of Jesus, by all the faithful who are under obligation to recite the canonical hours; and as for the Masses, We allow them to be celebrated by all priests, secular as well as regular, frequenting churches in which the feast is kept. Finally, We allow the solemnity of the Beatification of the Venerable John Berchmans to be celebrated within one year from the date of this letter, in the above-mentioned churches, with the Office and Mass of a Greater Double; which indeed We direct to be done on a day to be fixed by the Ordinary, and after the same solemnity shall have been celebrated in the Vatican Basilica, notwithstanding all Constitutions and Apostolic Ordinations, and all decrees issued *de non cultu*, and all others whatsoever to the contrary. And We desire that the same credit which would be given to the signification of Our will in this letter be also given in judicial decisions to printed copies of this, provided they be signed by the hand of the Secretary of the above-mentioned Congregation, and bear the seal of its Prefect. Given at Rome, at St. Peter's, under the seal of the Fisherman, on the 9th day of the month of May, in the year of our Lord 1865, and the nineteenth of Our Pontificate.　　　　N. CARD. PARACCIANI CLARELLI.

III.—*Notice of Nicholas* Radkaï *or* Rátkay.

What was the after-history of Berchmans' closest friend is not clear. There was a Nicholas Rattkai, native of Turócz, in the north of Hungary, who, after entering the Society, laboured for ten years in " Dacia," which might mean Transylvania, the Danubian Principalities, or Croatia. He had the fame of a zealous hard-working missioner and careful observer of religious discipline, and ended a life of great fatigue at Txencsin in Hungary, on Sept. 15, 1689.

A little controversial work in Slavonic gives him a place in Father Stöger's *Scriptores Prov. Austriac., S.J.*

Father Stockleïn, in a collection of letters of Jesuit missionaries published by him, speaking of a John Rátkay who died as a missioner in America, says that he died, like his cousin Nicholas, in the odour of sanctity. This Nicholas was of a noble family—the Barons Rátkay of Croatia. He appears to have been a missioner in the West Indies, and to have died there about 1690.

The great age which they would have reached appears to present a difficulty in identifying either of them with the Radkai of the Roman College.

The Life of St. Jane Frances Fremyot de Chantal.

By EMILY BOWLES. With Preface by the Rev. H. J. COLE-
RIDGE, S.J. Second Edition. Price 5s. 6d.

Ierne of Armorica: A Tale of the Time of Chlovis.

By J. C. BATEMAN. Price 6s. 6d.

The Life of Doña Luisa de Carvajal.

By Lady GEORGIANA FULLERTON. Price 6s.

The Life of Blessed John Berchmans.

By the Rev. F. GOLDIE, S.J. Price 6s.

The Life of Blessed Peter Favre,

First Companion of St. Ignatius Loyola. From the Italian
of Father BOERO. With Preface by the Rev. H. J. COLERIDGE,
S.J. Price 6s. 6d.

The Dialogues of St. Gregory the Great.

An Old English version. Edited by the Rev. H. J. COLERIDGE,
S.J. Price 6s.

———————

BURNS AND OATES, PORTMAN STREET AND PATERNOSTER ROW.

THE LIFE OF OUR LIFE.

*The Harmony of the Gospels arranged with Introductory
and Explanatory Chapters, Notes, and Indices.*

By the Rev. H. J. COLERIDGE, S.J.

[This work is the English version of the *Vita Vitæ Nostræ
meditantibus proposita*, and is the foundation of the volumes of
commentary of which three are already published (on *The Public
Life of our Lord*). Each part of the seven parts of the *Vita Vitæ*
is given according to the arrangement of that work, in parallel
columns, and to each are prefixed a Chapter on the general
history and another on the part borne by each Evangelist in the
formation of that history. Notes are added at the end of each
part shortly explaining the Harmonistic questions.]

Two vols, 15s.

————

THE PUBLIC LIFE OF OUR LORD JESUS CHRIST.

By the Rev. H. J. COLERIDGE, S.J.

Vol. I. "THE MINISTRY OF ST. JOHN BAPTIST."

Second Edition.   Price 6s. 6d.

Vol. II. "THE PREACHING OF THE
BEATITUDES."

Second Edition.   Price 6s. 6d.

Vol. III. "THE SERMON ON THE MOUNT."

Price 6s. 6d.

————